IN THE
PAW

IN 2012 - A CHANCE DISCOVERY, A
KIDNAPPING AND ARMAGEDDON. CAN THIS BE
THE END OF THE WORLD?

A Novel by Ninian G Boyle

First published in Great Britain in November 2011 by AKH
Publishing

Ninian Boyle was born in London in 1959. He is a dedicated amateur astronomer and likes nothing more than writing, teaching and lecturing about the subject of the stars. He has written for the BBC Sky at Night Magazine, Astronomy Now magazine and other publications on astronomy and has made several appearances on the BBC Sky at Night television programme with Sir Patrick Moore and has contributed to Sir Patrick's 'Yearbook of Astronomy 2012'. He has had his own television programme called 'Stargazer' on Sky Television. Ninian is a Guinness World Record Holder having been a part of the team who took the largest ground based image of the Moon ever accomplished. He is also a consultant to the Griffon Educational Observatory based in Southern Spain.

He runs a small business called Astronomy Know How, dedicated to bringing the subject to a wider audience, based largely on a website of the same name

http://www.astronomyknowhow.com

You can keep up with the latest information on this book by visiting the website http://www.inthtelionspaw.com

Ninian lives on the south coast of England with his wife and two sons. He says there are other books 'in the pipeline'.

Dedication

For Sue, my wife - Without your ceaseless support
encouragement and ideas and above all love, this book would
never have been written.

Contents

Disclaimer

This is a work of fiction. Characters, institutions or organisations in this novel are the work of the author's imagination and any similarity to actual characters, institutions or organisations is purely coincidental and there is no intent to describe their current or even possible conduct.

Time Zones

The book changes time zones frequently. To help you keep track UTC (Universal Time Constant – effectively the same as GMT) is used alongside local times.

In the Lion's Paw

Day 7

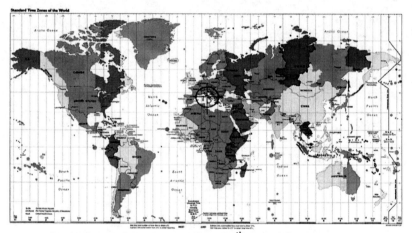

21:48 Central European Time 24th December 2012 (UTC 20:48)

As Father Giovanni Casparo drove towards the Vatican Observatory, he could never have imagined how his life was about to change. The discovery he would soon make would lead to international celebrity status and his very life being threatened. If he had even the slightest inkling of this he probably would have turned the car around.

His old Fiat spluttered its way to the Swiss Guard's lodge at the gate of the Observatory. As Giovanni pulled to a stop the Swiss Guard, as always dressed in his colourful medieval costume, instantly recognised him and greeted the priest with his usual cheery respect.

1

"Good evening Father and what brings you up here on this of all nights?"

The priest acknowledged Antonio giving him a friendly smile as he explained, "I've come to collect a paper I've been working on. Lucky for me I've been given a few days off and I thought I'd make good use of the time. I meant to take it away with me earlier, but like a fool I forgot to pick it up when I left this afternoon." He smirked, "Put it down to my age."

"Okay," said Antonio, "but I'm sure some would call you a workaholic Father," he added with a wry smile. Father Giovanni thanked him and drove on to the car park. He switched off the engine and got out of his vehicle. He buttoned his coat against the cool night air and passed through the courtyard, taking the time as he always did to admire the beautiful renaissance buildings which surrounded him. This was, after all, the summer palace of his Holiness the Pope.

Giovanni knew he was scheduled to say Mass in his local village at 9:00am the following morning but after this, as he'd told the Swiss Guard, he had been given five days off and was looking forward to spending them on his own. He had turned down an offer to go and visit his brother in the United States during his short break, one of the reasons being, until that morning he didn't actually know how much time he would have to himself, if any at all. Being a Vatican astronomer had its privileges *and* its responsibilities. He was, as was often pointed out to him, a priest first and a scientist second. It would have been great to just take off, having been given some relatively unexpected leave, but booking air tickets at such short notice would have been a nightmare. Additionally he thought it would be an imposition this year; at least that's what he told himself. There was though, a part of him that really would have liked to have seen his brother...

He had been working on a paper on x-ray binary stars, two stars in close orbit which emit huge amounts of x-rays, and found this area of research really interesting. In fact he realised he was becoming a little obsessive about it; a few uninterrupted days to work on it would be very satisfying. He was notified of

2

his 'time off' rather at the last minute, or so he felt, as he thought he would be carrying out several priestly duties over the next few days. He was delighted when he received the notice that he would not be needed other than to say Mass in the village in the morning. He drove home and in his excitement forgot the paper he wanted to take with him, so later that evening headed back to the Observatory to collect it. He got the usual friendly greeting from the Guard and headed on into the heart of the palace to his office.

The place was in darkness of course; the Observatory staff were all on holiday or had gone back to their respective parishes to celebrate the festival of Christmas and so he found himself alone as he unlocked the doors, switched on the lights and walked the short distance to his office. He opened the office door and went directly to the filing cabinet where he kept his paper. He pulled out the document and selected a couple of books he needed for reference from the shelf and piled them on his desk. At this point he suddenly felt a strong desire for a cigarette. It was a habit he wished he could kick, but he found himself surprisingly weak willed when it came to it. Giovanni wasn't what could be called a heavy smoker, but he averaged around six cigarettes a day. He never smoked in the office in deference to his colleagues and often went up to the walkway around the Observatory dome to indulge. He was not in a hurry this evening and he'd noticed it was a clear night as he drove to the Observatory, so he decided to have a leisurely cigarette and go and do what he always enjoyed – just admire the starry night sky.

He climbed the familiar steps to the Observatory and let himself out on to the narrow walkway which ran around the outside of the dome. He loved looking through the telescopes of course, but also just liked drinking in the thousands of stars which could be seen with the naked eye from this wonderful hill top site. He took the packet of cigarettes and lighter from his pocket and drew deeply on the filter as the paper ignited in the flame. The tip of the cigarette glowed bright red for an instant, then grew dim as Giovanni removed it from his lips and exhaled the thin smoke. He looked up and smiled to himself as his eyes

3

steadily adapted to the dark and the handful of stars he could see on his drive up to the Observatory, now became a myriad.

Giovanni slowly walked around the circle of the dome picking out the constellations, which was surprisingly difficult, as there were now so many stars to choose from. He never tired of this sight and enjoyed the challenge of seeing how many of these remote points of light he could name or identify as the seasons went by. This evening was no different. He knew the stars well and prided himself on his knowledge of the constellations. Many of his colleagues seemed to be incapable of identifying even the brightest and most obvious of these celestial groupings.

As Giovanni circled the dome for a third time he glanced at his watch and pressed the small button to backlight the figures. Had he really been out here that long? The display showed 22:59. Ah well; he'd better head back down or he would be celebrating Christmas alone out here on the Observatory walkway. The thought almost appealed to him. As he approached the door he took one last glance up at the sky...

23:00 Central European Time December 24th 2012 (UTC 22:00)

The priest stopped in his tracks. He was looking due east and couldn't fail to notice a bright star which he was sure was not visible on his previous circuits. He stood staring at it for several moments and tried to figure out if he was mistaken. It must be an aircraft, he thought. However, he knew that there was no flight corridor in that direction. Perhaps it was a military aircraft; a helicopter? He could detect no movement even after many tens of seconds. He stubbed out his cigarette. Surely he had never seen a bright star in this location before? He made a careful mental note of its exact position and he headed straight for the door. His mind was now racing. Was it a planet? He did a mental inventory of the possible solar system objects he knew might be rising in the east. Jupiter? No, not Jupiter. Saturn then? No, not Saturn either, nor Mars. It was too bright and star-like to be a comet. What the hell could it be?

His heart was thumping. He didn't really know why. There was something about the star which disturbed him. It was like somebody was playing tricks on him, and he didn't like it. His eyes hurt as he blundered into what seemed to be a brightly lit stair well. In fact it wasn't really that bright, but Giovanni had been out in the dark so long his eyes were now very sensitive to light. He clattered down the stairs into his office and lunged for the star atlas. He nervously flicked through the pages as his mind raced to try and identify this seeming anomaly. He found the page showing the area of sky he had been looking at. The starry scene was still fresh in his mind. There was the constellation of Leo and he looked carefully all around the region where he was sure the bright star was. Nothing. Or rather, nothing of any significance. His heart now beat faster. He would have to go back out with the chart to be sure...

Giovanni found himself almost running up the stairs, clutching the book as he hurtled to the door which led out onto the walkway. He turned the handle and was back out into the cool night air. He had lost his adaption to the darkness, but nonetheless, he could still make out enough stars to easily identify the constellation of Leo. And yet it looked disturbingly different. He was now certain that it couldn't be an aircraft as this would have moved in the intervening time it had taken him to go and look up the atlas. He reached into his pocket and pulled out a torch, which gave a dim red light. Old astronomers' habits die hard.

He swiftly turned to the page showing the stars for the part of the sky which he was looking at and by the light of the torch, began to identify the stars in the constellation one by one. Regulus, Denebola, Gamma Leonis. The list went on. The bright star hung there, taunting him. His hands were shaking now. He began to realise what had only be the merest inkling down in his office, might now be a reality. Giovanni was witnessing a bright nova, or even a supernova, a stellar explosion of colossal proportions. A star literally blowing itself to pieces and releasing as much energy in a few hours as a star like our sun would in its entire lifetime!

Maybe, just maybe, he was the first to witness this truly cataclysmic event. If it really was as bright as it seemed, surely someone else must have noticed it? He noted its position as precisely as he could and estimated its brightness by using stars around it for which he had magnitude information. He knew many stars in the heavens were of fixed brightness and these had been carefully measured by astronomers, but some could vary in brightness, so it was necessary to be careful when choosing comparison stars. He also made a note of the time he first spotted this bright interloper. That was easy; it was 23:00 Central European Time, as he had looked at his watch just moments before he noticed the star. He knew his watch to be accurate because he had set it to the Observatory clock just that morning.

Giovanni now debated with himself about turning the telescope on this object. He needed to be sure before he went shooting his mouth off. Too many enthusiastic astronomers, amateur and even professional, had fallen into the trap of announcing to the world that they had made a 'discovery' only to find it had been a mistake. The ignominy of such an error would be difficult to live with, especially for a man in his position. He had to be sure!

He opened the door into the Observatory dome and started the procedure to set up the telescope. He opened the dome shutter and rotated the slit to line up with the object. As the dome slowly revolved, grinding on its rollers, he fired up the electrical systems to start the drive which would slew the telescope around and lock on and track his quarry. It all seemed to be taking a painfully long time. Giovanni was aware he was trembling. He told himself it was the cold but knew this not to be true. As the telescope started to move to the co-ordinates, which he hastily punched into the keypad, he booted up the computer that would control the camera and take the pictures he so desperately needed to back up his intended claim. The telescope came to rest and the whirring of the drive gears grew quiet. Struggling to keep calm and be professional, he quickly moved to the imaging computer and began to take a sequence of images of the field. The star was bright; the exposures need not be very long. After a few seconds the image started to appear on the screen. The merest hint of processing brought up the stars in the field of view of the camera's detector. There was the intruder shining defiantly, almost exactly in the middle of the frame. He saved the image with as many details on the header as he could think to log and began the sequence again, just to be sure. He made a note of the exact co-ordinates of the object according to the telescope's positioning computer. This would be needed to be given to anyone who could confirm his find. Once he was certain he had two good images committed to the computer's hard disc, it occurred to him to carry out some further checks.

Giovanni once again headed back down the stairs to his office. He needed to be really sure before he announced his discovery to the world. Perhaps this was an asteroid or some other wandering body he had maybe forgotten about? He fired up the computer on his desk. The machine was quite old and took a while to boot up. Someone to corroborate this discovery was needed. He knew he should contact the 'Central Bureau', but who would be there on Christmas Eve?

The computer finally grumbled into life and Giovanni wasted no time in opening his Internet browser and doing some final checks on a couple of familiar websites to make sure he wasn't about to make a fool of himself. Still nothing. There was no known object which could be as bright as this star in that position.

Giovanni opened his email program and started to type furiously. His hands had not stopped shaking. He hit the 'send' button and breathed out. He hoped someone would see his email and get back to him quickly, but he knew this was a forlorn hope. It was Christmas Eve after all. Everyone in Europe would be either wrapping presents or attending parties or even going to bed for an early start in the morning, as he probably should himself. In the USA, where his email was heading, it was only a few hours behind his local time and the office which would receive his message was also likely to be shut for the holiday. His own boss was out of contact. He knew Father Giuseppe would be saying Mass and would not answer his mobile phone. He left him a hurried text message begging him to call urgently. Who else could he tell?

Rummaging in the drawer in his desk, he pulled out an old address book. Most people who Giovanni knew these days had electronic gadgets to store names and addresses and to keep their diaries in order, but he was rather old fashioned in that he just liked to write things down. He looked up the number but wasn't sure if the man he was about to call still lived at the address he had, or even if he would remember the priest who he had met at the conference in Switzerland, it must be what, over a year ago now? However, he doggedly punched the numbers and waited.

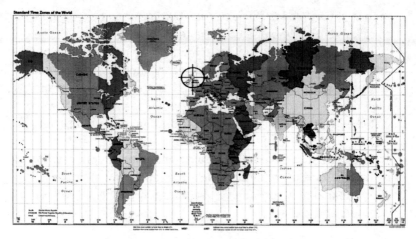

22:23 Greenwich Mean Time 24th December 2012 (UTC 22:23)

The telephone rang at the house of Professor Andrew McVeigh, just as he was sipping his second sherry of the evening while watching the television with his wife, in a comfortable pre-Christmas euphoria. Andy McVeigh worked at the Royal Observatory in Edinburgh and had a teaching post at the University. He lived with his wife Mary in the quiet suburbs of the city.

"Who the devil..?" he muttered darkly, as he made to get up from the sofa. His wife Mary had beaten him to it, explaining that it might be one of the children calling early to wish them a Merry Christmas, in an attempt to lighten her husband's seemingly sudden mood swing.

Almost before she had got out her "Hello," a man with a thick accent, which she thought was either Spanish or Italian, straight away asked to speak to Professor McVeigh. She had to stop herself from saying 'How rude," but reluctantly agreed to the stranger's request.

"It's for you Andy," she said coldly. She covered the mouth piece of the phone and then mouthed quietly, "A foreigner."

Andy McVeigh frowned. Who could be disturbing his most comfortable of evenings? A foreigner, his wife said. He tutted under his breath as he moved towards the telephone, determined to give the caller short shrift.

9

"This is Professor McVeigh," he said into the mouth-piece, in the testiest voice he could muster.

"Professor?" came the hasty response in an accent that Andy vaguely recognised, "I am sorry to disturb you this evening, but I didn't know who else I could turn to."

There was urgency in the voice that took Andy completely off guard and at once intrigued him. "To whom am I speaking and how can I help?" he said more mildly.

"Professor," came the heavily accented voice once again, "I think I've made a discovery, an important discovery."

"But who is this speaking?" insisted the Professor. The apology came instantly from the man, who seemed to be excited and at the same time struggling to recall his English as if he had not spoken the language for a while.

"Forgive me Professor this is Father Giovanni Casparo, you may remember we met at the conference in Zurich a year or so ago, the conference about high output X-Ray sources in the Galaxy."

Andy went back to the conference in his mind and did indeed recall the earnest young priest from the Vatican Observatory. He remembered enjoying a very interesting discussion over a rather too pleasant lunch and that he quite took to this somewhat intense young man.

"How are you Giovanni?" Andy said warmly.

"I am well thank you," replied the priest trying to stay calm and not to sound rude. "Professor, I need your help," Giovanni sounded insistent.

"Aye, so how may I assist?"

"I think I've discovered a nova or even a supernova," Giovanni blurted out.

"Well good for you," said Andy genially, not quite understanding why this young Italian should be telling him about this right at that moment.

"Professor," the priest pressed on, "I need you to confirm my discovery."

The penny dropped with the Professor. "Oh, I see," Andy said deliberately. "But surely there are channels you must go through, other people in a better position to act on your information?"

"It's Christmas Eve," Giovanni responded with a note of exasperation in his voice, "everything is closed." He drew breath and continued, "Professor is the sky clear with you?"

This question immediately struck Andy as odd. Why should he be asking whether the skies over Edinburgh are clear? Over 98 per cent of novae and supernovae are in distant galaxies and are only detectable with moderate or even large telescopes. Surely he can't think I can just look outside and see it? Perhaps he had been drinking? Maybe he was playing a silly joke...

As these thoughts and questions raced through Andy's head, he was aware that Giovanni was becoming increasingly agitated and saying, "Professor, please would you to go outside and take a look, I need you to confirm my discovery."

"Good God man, are you suggesting this is a naked eye object?"

"Yes Professor, that's exactly what I am suggesting!"

There was a stunned silence. Giovanni swallowed hard; he thought for a moment Professor McVeigh was going to put the receiver down on him. He realised that he wouldn't blame him, this really must sound like a 'crank call'.

Andy needed to think. "Just a moment." Now it was the Professor's head that was spinning. He covered the mouth piece of the phone and turned to his wife...

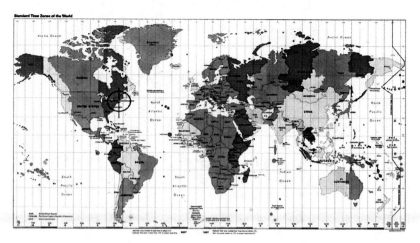

17:26 Eastern Standard Time December 24th 2012 (UTC 22:26)

The 'New Email' alert flashed onto the screen of Dr John Baltar at the Central Bureau for Astronomical Telegrams. John wasn't there to see it. He'd left for home around ten minutes earlier.

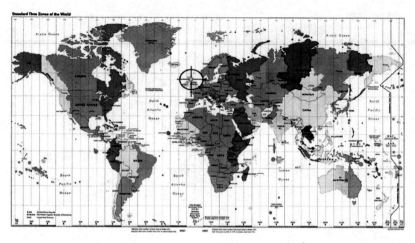

22:27 Greenwich Mean Time December 24th 2012 (UTC 22:27)

Andy McVeigh asked his wife to fetch him a pad and pencil. "Firstly," Andy spoke as calmly as he could to the priest, "let me have your telephone number in case we get cut off."

Andy's wife Mary proffered a pad and pencil as requested and Andy placed it next to the telephone while she awkwardly shifted her weight from foot to foot, trying to drag herself away from this rather interesting conversation.

"...in case we get cut off."

Giovanni immediately understood the sense in this request and replied very slowly and clearly, "Country code 39," then continued, "06-698-862331."

Andy read it back to him. This had given him a moment to think. "Okay. Now, you need to give me the co-ordinates of this star."

The priest stuttered in excitement, "R...right ascension, 9 hours, 47 minutes and 33 seconds," he waited a moment for Andy to finish writing and then continued, "Declination, plus 11 degrees, 25 minutes and 43.6 seconds." Andy repeated this. Once he had confirmed he had taken it down correctly he said, "Okay, give me a few minutes to take a look. I'll call you back."

"Thank you, thank you Professor, I can't tell you how grateful I am."

Andy put the receiver down. Mary looked enquiringly at him. "Do you remember I told you about a young man, a priest from the Vatican Observatory, who I met a year or two back?" Mary nodded, doing her best to recall the conversation. Andy continued, "Well, that was him. He thinks he's discovered a supernova."

"So why's he calling you?"

"A good question my dear," retorted Andy. "He claims he couldn't raise anyone at the Central Bureau and considering the day and the time it wouldn't surprise me. I gave him my phone number when I'd had a glass or two of wine perhaps more than was good for me," Andy admitted. "I guess he must have remembered I was interested in supernova events..."

Andy was already moving towards his computer. He grabbed the mouse and woke up the screen. He clicked on the software which would start the program he needed and waited a few seconds while it loaded. As the star chart flashed onto the computer screen he asked his wife "It's still clear outside isn't it?"

Mary went to the window. She moved the curtain aside and could just make out one or two bright stars twinkling in the blackness. "Aye" she said, "but you're not seriously going out hunting for this so called supernova? It's freezing out there." She emphasised the words 'so called' with a note of cynicism in her voice.

"I said I'd take a look and that's what I'll do," Andy replied bluntly. Mary knew she would not persuade him otherwise. Her husband was a man of principle and he would always keep his word if he gave it.

The program was now showing on Andy's screen. He typed in the co-ordinates of the object which Giovanni had given him. The small circle on the screen highlighted the star. Andy's eyebrows climbed up his forehead in astonishment. "That's 'R-Leonis'," he exclaimed, quite loudly. Mary looked at him quizzically, as she didn't understand the significance of the fact Andy had just stated.

14

Andy checked he had typed in the numbers correctly. The same position was highlighted again. The Professor stood up rapidly and his chair shot backwards.

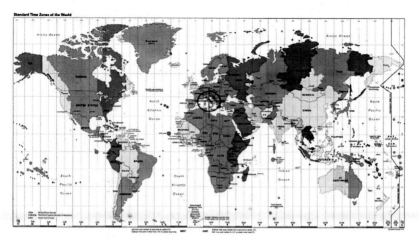

23:28 Central European Time December 24th 2012 (UTC 22:28)

Giovanni replaced the telephone receiver and impatiently drummed his fingers on the desk. He knew he would just have to wait. It was then it occurred to him, having given the Professor the co-ordinates of the star, he hadn't in fact checked what this object was for himself. There were several dim stars in this area of sky. Perhaps this was a known irregular nova, a star that would flare in brightness at different times, which were hard if not impossible to predict. He moved to his computer and clicked the icon which would open the planetarium software he used. In a few seconds the program opened and moments after that the screen filled with the familiar opening display of the constellations looking south from the Observatory. He typed the numbers into the search box and clicked the button. The vista changed from the view to the south to one of the east and as the screen settled, a small circle encompassed the star. The label declared 'R-Leonis'. He frowned; "R Leonis, surely not." He knew this to be a variable star but he didn't recall hearing about it being a supernova candidate.

Giovanni drew breath through clenched teeth. He recognised the position of the star on the screen immediately. To be absolutely sure he pulled up one of the images he'd taken a few minutes earlier, to make the comparison. It was doubtless the very star he saw previously from the walkway of the

16

Observatory dome. R Leonis. The name rang in his head. Could it really be that such a seemingly insignificant star could blow itself apart in a cataclysmic explosion which could outshine every other star in our galaxy and may even be brighter than the entire galaxy itself? He double checked he had typed in the co-ordinates correctly. R Leonis. Giovanni knew it was right, but had to make sure. He had to know more about this star. Opening a browser on the computer, he typed R Leonis into the search box. Various links appeared on the screen and he chose a promising one. Clicking on the link opened the page and the information flashed up in front of him. He skimmed through the text.

It read: *'R Leonis is a red hyper-giant star a Mira-type variable in the constellation of Leo... At maximum brightness it can be detected with the naked eye at magnitude 4.31 but at minimum brightness it falls to magnitude 11.65 needing a telescope of at least 70mm aperture to be seen.'* It then continued with more scientific data, but went on to say, *'It is thought that through this mass loss, this **star will not end its life as a supernova'**.*

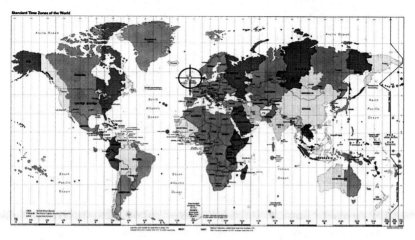

Standard Time Zones of the World

22:29 Greenwich Meantime 24th December 2012 (UTC 22:29)

Andy McVeigh was heading for his porch, followed by a fretting Mary speaking quickly about keeping warm and not staying out too long. He grabbed his jacket and while he changed his shoes his wife proffered his scarf. He dutifully wrapped it around his neck and then eased himself into his overcoat. As Andy headed for the front door he picked up his binoculars which were hanging with the coats. He looped these around his neck as he continued down the hallway.

"I'll no be long," he promised his wife.

He headed into his garden and got his bearings. Immediately he could see the area of sky in which he was interested was obscured by trees. He cursed under his breath and walked to the garden gate. From there he could start to make out the familiar shape of the constellation of Leo. However, the area he needed to view was hidden behind the tree line. He opened the gate and walked up the road a little to higher ground. After a couple of hundred metres he stopped and turned around. His jaw fell open. There was the star shining like a beacon. Andy did a double take. As well as being a teacher and research astronomer, he knew the night sky well. Without a doubt there was a very bright newcomer hanging there in this most familiar of constellations. Had nobody else spotted this? He didn't need his binoculars, but nevertheless couldn't resist the urge to take a

18

look through them. The star was almost painfully bright. He wanted to make sure he wasn't making a mistake and studied the object carefully, checking for movement or any visible shape. It wouldn't be the first time that bright stars in the night sky turned out to be aircraft or satellites. There it hung. Andy was utterly amazed. He started back down the road, breaking into a run as he did so. He hadn't run anywhere in a very long time.

He reached the gate and almost crashed into it in his haste. Storming back up his garden path he fumbled his key in the lock getting increasingly frustrated with his own impatience. Finally the key went home and the lock turned. Andy burst through the door and ran along the corridor almost sending his wife flying as she came out to investigate the commotion. He dived for the telephone as he blurted out to Mary that it was true, the priest had indeed discovered a supernova. Mary had a look of complete astonishment on her face.

The Professor dialled the number he had so carefully taken down...

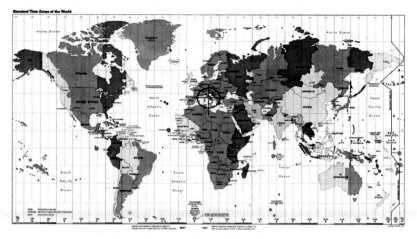

23:37 Central European Time 24th December 2012 (UTC 22:37)

The phone in the Vatican Observatory rang only once as Father Giovanni snatched it from the cradle. He was relieved to hear Andy McVeigh's voice at the other end.

"Giovanni?" asked the Professor with extreme excitement in his voice, "I can confirm your discovery."

The priest tried hard not to cry out in triumph. He took a breath and said as calmly as he could, "Thank you so much Professor, I'm most grateful."

"What are you going to do now?" enquired Andy.

"I have to wait for a response from the Central Bureau and I've left a message with Father Giuseppe the Assistant Director of the Observatory," he paused, "I cannot think what else to do."

"I see your problem," Andy felt genuinely sorry for Giovanni. He understood how excited the young man must feel and at the same time, now so powerless to spread the word of his most important discovery. "Be sure to use m' name as confirmation," he continued. "Good luck w' it and I'll await the full report of this with great interest." Andy pressed the 'end call' button and put down the telephone.

"Well!" He exclaimed to his wife...

Giovanni opened his email program and typed a further short message to the Central Bureau. It read: '*Professor Andrew McVeigh of the Royal Observatory in Edinburgh, Scotland has confirmed my find timed at 22:39UT. Please get back to me as soon as possible.*' He wondered if there was a note of desperation in the message as he clicked the send button.

At this point he decided he had to take another look, so he climbed the stairs again to the Observatory and let himself out of the door to the walkway. He skirted the dome and saw the star shining very brightly. Was he imagining it or did it seem even brighter than when he first saw it about 40 minutes ago? His head was still reeling and he realised that he felt slightly sick with excitement. The full impact of this discovery was starting to impinge upon him. This was the first naked eye supernova to be seen for hundreds of years. If his report reached the Central Bureau first, then he would be credited with it. The kudos for both him and the Observatory would be immense.

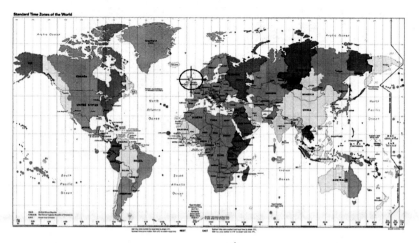

22:42 Greenwich Meantime 24th December 2012 (UTC 22:42)

An email arrived at the news desk of The Scotsman. It said simply that there was a very bright star in the sky and the sender, one John Ramsay wanted to report it as an unidentified flying object. Malcolm Singer who was on duty at the news desk pressed the 'delete' key.

22:43 Greenwich Meantime 24th December 2012 (UTC 22:43)

The telephone rang at the Lothian and Borders Police station in central Edinburgh. A lady was quite agitated as she reported a very bright light in the sky to the 'west'. The officer who took the call reassured the lady that it was almost certainly an aircraft and not to be alarmed. A few moments later a call was received at another desk in the station with a similar report, this time stating more accurately, that there was a very unusual light in the night sky in the east. A call went out to the various patrols around the city to see if any officer could confirm these reports.

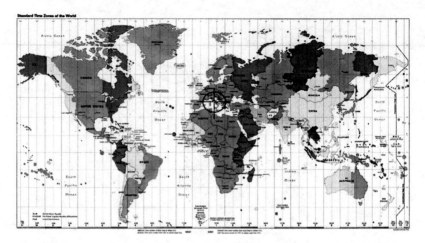

23:48 Central European Time 24th December 2012 (UTC 22:48)

Giovanni decided to walk back to his office to see if he had received any response. It was decidedly cold out in the night air and he was glad to get back into the warmth of the building, although part of him wanted to stay and admire the beautiful new star which shone so fervently from above.

On entering his office he could see the new email icon flashing on his computer screen.

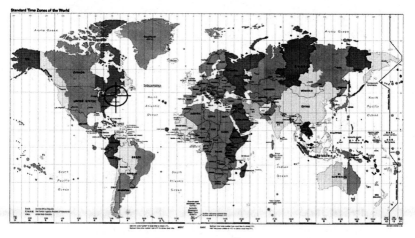

17:42 Eastern Standard Time 24th December 2012 (UTC 22:42)

    John Baltar pulled up outside his house on the outskirts of Cambridge, Massachusetts. The drive home took longer this evening, due to the Christmas traffic. He thought he would just check his email on his smart phone before he left the car.

    There were several 'junk' messages, one from the university about Christmas closures and one, which caught his eye, from the Vatican Observatory. He opened it and read it. He read it twice. As he was deciding what to do a further email arrived from the same source. His decision was made. He hit the reply key and hastily typed that he would log the message as a discovery providing it turned out to be genuine. He then pressed 'send'. John restarted the car, reversed off the drive and headed back to the office...

    At the Vatican Observatory...

    Father Giovanni practically jumped into his chair and opened the message. He read it carefully. He then sat upright in his seat and punched the air. The Central Bureau had logged his claim and he would be credited with it under the usual conditions, but would he be the first?

In the Middle East...

Away from the city lights in the deserts of Israel a few villagers and farmers had noticed the bright star in the sky. Most thought nothing of it, they were used to military aircraft flying above them and a cursory glance would give the impression that this was just another fighter jet coming into land somewhere. A few people though were puzzled as this particular light didn't seem to move. In the large urban areas artificial lights drowned out everything in the night sky with the exception of the Moon. It was such that people didn't even bother to look up any more.

In Scotland...

The phones in police stations in Edinburgh and the surrounding areas were now ringing regularly with reports about strange lights in the sky. The area of cloud which was blanketing most of northern Europe didn't cover central and eastern Scotland. A further email arrived at the news desk of The Scotsman, claiming there was a UFO hovering over the city. This one did catch the attention of Malcolm Singer. He called up one of the journalists and instructed him to go and take a look and see if he could find any eye-witnesses. The journalist dutifully donned his coat, muttering under his breath about being sent on 'wild goose chases' on a freezing cold night and headed off out of the building.

Professor McVeigh persuaded his wife to come with him to see the 'new star'. Mary was now quite intrigued, she knew that her husband was no fool, so she went into the hall and removed her coat from the hook and put her arms into the sleeves while Andy opened the front door for the second time that evening. He felt she was taking too long. Mary was trying to get her hat to sit properly on her head as her husband marched down the path with an air of impatience. "Come on," he insisted as she dithered, then closed the front door behind her. They walked a little too briskly up the road to where Andy first saw the object, and then stopped. As she turned towards where Andy was indicating she let out an exclamation. "Oh my goodness!" she cried.

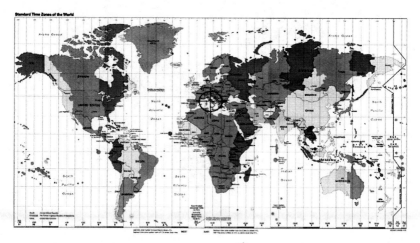

00:00 Central European Time 25th December 2012 (UTC 23:00)

Giovanni heard the Observatory clock chime in the hall way. He was engrossed in the various books he had pulled from the shelves as he read voraciously about the star R Leonis. The sound of the clock brought him back to reality. At that moment he realised it was now Christmas Day. He suddenly felt compelled to say a prayer of thanks to his God for allowing him to make this discovery. A 'Christmas Star'! He hoped that he was the first...

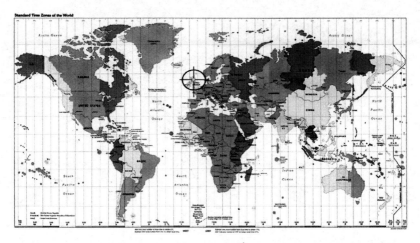

23:01 Greenwich Mean Time 24th December 2012 (UTC 23:01)

Reports were coming thick and fast into various police stations around the east of Scotland and parts of the northeast of England. Police Constable Jamie Stuart was on patrol near the Castle in Edinburgh. He now had a clear view of the eastern sky and sure enough he could see a very bright star shining there. He watched it for several minutes. He radioed in his report to control to confirm there was indeed a bright light in the eastern sky and he thought that there was no evidence of it being any type of aircraft, but sensibly suggested that 'control' check with RAF Lossiemouth to see if they had anything on their radar.

Robert Macleod, the reporter on The Scotsman, had been walking for over 10 minutes. He had stopped one or two people on the street to ask them if they'd seen anything unusual in the sky, only to be met with quizzical looks and negative responses. He got the impression people thought he'd had a little too much Christmas 'spirit'. He'd been heading steadily towards the Castle and higher ground to see if he could get a good look at the sky for himself.

As soon as he thought it practical, he stopped. His breath, steaming in the cold air, was illuminated by the street lights. He scanned the sky slowly, turning around as he did so. As he caught something out of the corner of his eye he spun towards it. The star was now quite obvious even though most other stars

27

in the sky were drowned out by the bright city lights. He gasped in amazement and stood transfixed for several moments. Robert noticed a few other people nearby were looking in the same direction and he headed over to them.

Introducing himself as being from The Scotsman, he asked them what they were looking at. They pointed towards the star informing him they had never seen anything like it before. He asked them to speculate as to what it was. One suggested it was a UFO, chuckling as he did so and another ventured it was a Christmas 'star'. A third man, who believed he was a bit of an amateur astronomer, said it must be the planet Venus as only this particular object could be so bright in the night sky. Robert thought this was a good explanation, and typed a few short lines of copy into his Blackberry for later download into the office computer, for further editing. It read; *'Christmas revellers in Edinburgh were delighted to see a beautifully bright planet Venus shining in the crisp night sky. Venus has often been mistaken for a UFO or other unidentified aerial phenomena. This lovely showing of the planet is due to the exceptionally clear air that we are experiencing at the moment.'* He planned to include a library picture of the planet to illustrate. As he walked back to the office, he had second thoughts about this. The star or planet or whatever it was, seemed to be unusually bright.

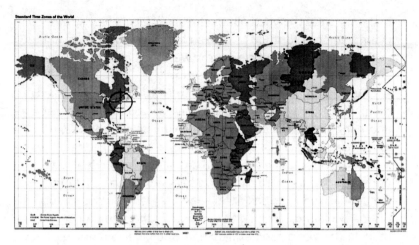

Standard Time Zones of the World

18:04 Eastern Standard Time 24th December 2012 (UTC 23:04)

Dr Baltar's car arrived back at the office for the Central Bureau for Astronomical Telegrams. The return journey had been a little faster than his homeward trip. He headed into the building, threw the light switch and after a short walk down the corridor, turned the handle on the door to his room and went in.

As he sat down he nudged his computer mouse to wake up the screen. It was policy not to turn off the computers even over a vacation due to the time sensitive nature of the alerts that came into and out of the office. The screen woke up and displayed his email alert icon, blinking and demanding attention. 'More junk or more people claiming the discovery?' he asked himself as he clicked his mouse to open his email 'inbox'.

There were now several messages from various parts of southern Europe and the Middle East alerting him to the discovery of a bright supernova in Leo, made by numerous amateur astronomers armed with varying levels of sophisticated equipment. The attached report forms had all been lodged with timings, so that he could easily sift through them in order. It was now obvious something 'big' had happened. Several of the reports gave the co-ordinates of the object and all of them roughly agreed, with only very minor discrepancies on a couple. He hastily typed an email priority alert to go to the major observatories around the globe, giving a very brief outline of the report and the co-ordinates of the object. He pressed 'send' and the message hurtled out through cyber-space to the observatories which were geared up to carry out supernovae research. He next called up a list of the status of these same observatories, and as it flashed up on the screen his mobile phone rang.

He pulled it from his coat pocket and checked the screen to see who was calling, although he already suspected who it might be. He winced. John moved the phone towards his ear and pressed the 'talk' button. "Hi sweetheart," he said distractedly into the air.

"John, where the hell are you?" came the rather irate tone of Sarah his wife.

"I'm sorry darling," John quickly responded, in as much of a placatory voice as he could manage. "I was on the way home when I got an urgent alert and had to head back."

"Well you can 'head back here' just as soon as you like." She snapped, obviously unmoved by John's effort to soothe her. "You know we've got my mother coming, and she'll be arriving any minute and there are dozens of things to prepare before tomorrow. You said you'd be home early to help me!" Sarah now sounded exasperated.

John did not get on particularly well with his mother-in-law. He thought it mildly amusing as it was such a cliché, but he knew the truth was his wife's mother felt her daughter could have married 'better'; a medical doctor or a lawyer with prospects, rather than a scientist who had little hope of promotion or furthering his career, or salary. He liked to try to avoid her if possible. The 'discovery' email had given him the excuse to not be home when his mother-in-law arrived, although John would have hardly admitted this to himself, let alone his wife.

"I'm leaving in just a minute," John lied rather badly.

"Be sure you do!" Sarah put the receiver down, hard.

John knew his wife would forgive him soon enough but he also knew he would face a 'frosty' atmosphere when he got home. He quickly scanned the list now showing on his screen.

Siding Springs in Australia was in daylight. The South Africa Astronomical Observatory was 'clouded out'. Of the two largest scopes at the observatory complex on La Palma in the Canaries, one was down for routine maintenance, and the other was engaged in some imaging of a distant star forming region buried in an obscure nebula. He hoped this one might be able to respond to his request.

As he read through the list, his email notification icon popped up once again. He clicked through and was pleased to see the observatory on Kitt Peak in Arizona had responded already. The message read that the supplied co-ordinates meant the object had yet to rise above the horizon, but they would be on standby as soon as the target had got high enough to produce worthwhile data. John felt a little disappointed. He realised the telescopes on Hawaii would be in a similar position. All now rather depended on La Palma. He decided he would be better off monitoring the event from his smart phone or PC at home. Keeping his wife and mother-in-law waiting any longer would not be conducive to a peaceful Christmas. He stood up; pushing his chair back, he headed for the door.

In Scotland...

Police Central Control in Edinburgh received a call answering their request for information from RAF Lossiemouth, stating that they had no unexpected air traffic in the area either civil or military, and to please let them know if they could be of any further assistance.

Robert Macleod headed back to his office at The Scotsman. He was desperate for a hot cup of tea and he sensed it was going to be a busy night...

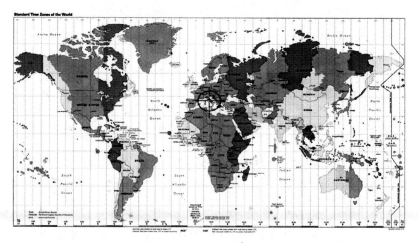

00:15 Central European Time 25th December 2012 (UTC 23:15)

Giovanni was beginning to wonder what to do with himself. He realised the situation was now out of his hands. Events, such as they were, were being handled by others, so rather than being active he had to take a passive role and wait for the 'professionals' to observe and analyse his discovery and confirm the find was definitely his. This did not stop him from being excited still, by the whole occasion. He had enough knowledge to understand that if this star had really gone 'supernova', it would be an almost once in a millennium event and would challenge the current thinking about these kind of stars and their life cycles.

He was itching to inform his superior, Father Giuseppe Carpentiere, but realised he would not get any response from him until after midnight Mass. So, for want of anything else constructive to do, he decided to take another look at this most enigmatic of celestial phenomena.

Once again he climbed the stairs to the Observatory and made to let himself out onto the walkway around the dome. There was the star shining benevolently, for any who cared to look upward. He now was becoming increasingly convinced this star was brighter than when he had first noticed it. He decided he really needed to check this, and went back into the Observatory dome to the telescope, once again setting up the

32

electronic camera to take a further image. While he was waiting for the systems to carry out their digital instructions he opened up the software to analyse the brightness of the stars in the first image he had taken.

The results showed in a window at the corner of the screen. The target star R Leonis, measured magnitude -4.92. Giovanni gasped. "That's even brighter than Venus!" He exclaimed to the empty room.

The second picture confirmed the result. The image he had just acquired was ready for processing, so he carried out the same routine as last time and once again analysed the star's brightness. Magnitude -4.97.

"Magnitude minus four point nine seven!" again vocalizing the result in astonishment. "It's got brighter in just over an hour." Giovanni was utterly amazed. Not only was this star the brightest object in the sky next to the Moon and the Sun, it was apparently getting even brighter. He saved the results with a time stamp, on the computer. He was aware that the large observatories would come up with far more accurate brightness data than he could, but he also knew that the equipment he was working with was set up as well as it could be and so his results would not be far different from the larger scopes.

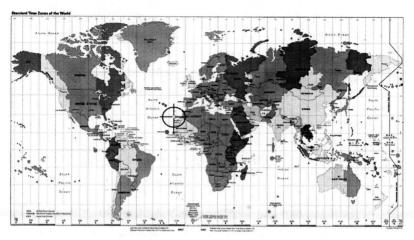

23:16 Greenwich Mean Time December 24th 2012 (UTC 23:16)

The William Herschel Telescope had just finished its imaging duties on a project for the Instituto de Astrofisica de Canarias and the astronomer at the controls of this giant 4.2 meter 'eye on the sky', Dr Elizabeth Price, had just had a 'priority' instruction to turn the telescope onto a supernova suspect in Leo. She duly tapped in the co-ordinates of the object as given and clicked the button to begin the slew of this optical monster to its designated target. Not only did the telescope itself start to slowly rotate on its immense platform, but the enormous dome, its protective housing, also started to steadily move around to bring the open slot to the correct region of sky. The noise of the mechanism was not unpleasantly loud, but it was quite noticeable after the almost deathly hush of the floor area of the Observatory only a few moments before.

Elizabeth, during the 30 or 40 seconds it would take to bring to bear this wonder of modern technology onto the requisite star, checked the likely brightness of the object so that she could set up the exposure length of the detectors. She was annoyed that this rather important piece of information seemed to be missing for some reason and so she adjusted the settings to what she considered to be appropriate.

The telescope slowed as it approached its given destination. The whirring of the great gears died down and the readout on the computer screen in the control room told Elizabeth that the scope had arrived. She set the detector to take a preliminary image of the area to make sure that she was indeed on target. A few moments later an image appeared on the screen. At first she thought that something had gone wrong. The image showed a huge bright disc in the centre of the field that had obviously nearly burnt out the sensitive camera.

"Wow," Elizabeth exclaimed. "What is that?"

She called up the duty technician on the intercom.

"Carlos."

"Si?" came the crackling response.

"Have you had any problems reported with the CCD at prime focus over the last few nights?" Elizabeth questioned as she held the 'call' button down on the intercom.

"No senorita." Carlos stated in broken English, rather coldly she thought. Carlos was very proud of his care of the equipment at the Observatory. He was the team leader and his abilities in keeping the incredibly complex mechanisms operating almost without incident were legendary among the astronomers who regularly used the telescope. If any such reports had been received he would have dealt with it personally, straight away.

"Is there a problem?"

"I'm not sure yet," replied the doctor, her native Australian twang in stark contrast to Carlos' heavy southern European accent. "I'll let you know."

Carlos was irritated by this. Either there was a malfunction or there wasn't. He didn't like not knowing. He was further put out that he was not going to be with his family for midnight Mass at the local church. Being a good hearted soul, he had agreed to do the Christmas shift to let one of his junior engineers have some time with his new baby daughter.

Elizabeth set a much shorter exposure time on the camera and tried again. After the briefest of pauses, a new image appeared on the monitor. This time it looked like a star, a VERY bright star. She continued to take images of the object and brought online the formidable suite of software she had at her command to start analyzing the data.

She thought that she should put Carlos's mind at rest and pressed the call button on the intercom once more.

"Si senorita," Carlos responded a little more congenially.

"All's well Carlos. Sorry to have worried you." The astronomer felt a little awkward at having alerted him over nothing.

"Okay. Thank you. " Carlos, much relieved, went back to studying the sports pages.

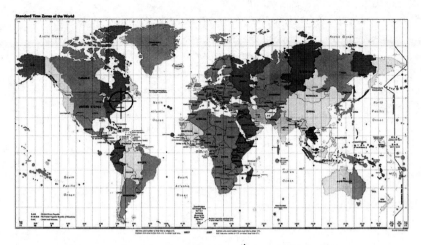

18:47 Eastern Standard Time 24th December 2012 (UTC 23:47)

Dr John Baltar's car pulled up on to the drive outside his house for the second time that evening. This time he determined to go directly in before he checked his email again.

He opened the door and called out to his wife half expecting a tirade from her about his lateness. Instead all he received was a "So what happened?" muffled by the half open kitchen door.

He quickly removed his coat and shoes and went straight to the source of the sound.

"I'm sorry honey," he intoned as contritely as he could.

"So what happened?" Sarah repeated a little more softly.

"I was on my way back here," stated John not entirely truthfully as he had virtually been at the front door, "when I got a very important alert. I'm glad I turned around and headed back, because if what seems to be happening is true, we have got a major astronomical incident going down." He tried to sound dramatic.

"You nearly had a major *domestic* incident going down." His wife tried to look more cross than she actually felt.

This elicited a further apology from John and he put his arms out for a hug of forgiveness. He was relieved when this was forthcoming. The couple kissed briefly and Sarah then said "I need you to sort out the room my mother's going to be sleeping in."

"Is she here yet?" It was a rather pointless question as John was well aware his mother-in-law would have made her presence known long before now, if she had been.

"No, but she will be any minute, and you know what a fuss she'll make if her room isn't ready."

John made for the door and carried on smartly up the stairs, pausing only briefly, as he told himself, at his study to switch on his computer and check his email. While his computer started its 'boot –up', he dutifully went to the guest room to tidy it and get everything in place for the impending visit of their intolerant guest.

On hearing the short music of his computer in the study, he left what he was doing and went straight to his email inbox. There was the message he was hoping to get. He opened it.

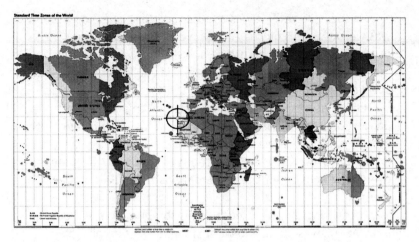

23:52 Greenwich Mean Time 24th December 2012 (UTC 23:52)

Dr Elizabeth Price had introduced another piece of equipment into the light path of the giant telescope. This was a spectroscope, which would break up the light of the star into its constituent rainbow colours. This would enable the software she would call up to analyse the light from the star to tell her what it was made of.

The answer gave her all the information she needed to appreciate this was an unusual event. The star had indeed 'gone supernova', but it was quite a rare type. She would of course be monitoring this very closely over the next few hours to spot any changes to the star's brightness or make up. She knew she was in for a busy night. In the meantime, Elizabeth decided to email Dr Baltar, who had requested the information, with what she had so far.

She began the message: *Can confirm the object at RA 9hrs 47 mins 33secs Dec 11° 25mins and 43.6secs is a Type 1C Supernova. Initial analysis suggests it has yet to achieve maximum brightness. Congratulations to the discoverer.* She then added a personal note saying she thought this one is likely to 'cause quite a stir'.

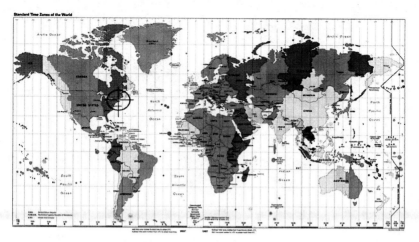

19:23 Eastern Standard Time 24th December 2012 (UTC 00:23)

John read the message with delight. His next move was to send out a bulletin to the astronomical community to credit Fr Giovanni Casparo with the find and to request follow up monitoring of this most rare event. But first he had a bed to make...

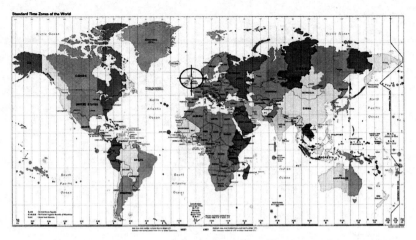

23:24 Greenwich Mean Time 24th December 2012

Robert Macleod decided he should inform a friend of his about the rather amazing phenomena which was going on in the skies above eastern Scotland. Gordon Gregory worked in the newsroom of BBC Scotland, in Glasgow. Robert and Gordon had been at college together and became firm friends. He knew if he sent a story like this to him, Gordon would take it seriously.

Robert sent the email and didn't have long to wait to get a response. It seemed just a few short moments before his mobile phone was ringing and Gordon's number was displayed on the screen.

"Hi Gordon," Robert said cheerily into the device, "I guess you got my message? I wasn't sure if you'd be working tonight?"

"Aye, I'm working right enough," said his friend. "So what's all this about a 'Christmas star' then?"

"We've had a lot of reports coming into the office about a bright star in the sky above Edinburgh, so I went out and checked for m 'self, and sure enough there it was, shining its head off. I've been doing some checking since I got back and it seems a wee bit unusual to say the least. I've even tried calling the Royal Observatory but no-one seems to be there." He continued, "I'm trying to get hold of a number for anyone there who could maybe explain what it is. Someone suggested it was the planet Venus, but I'm beginning to have my doubts. I had a

41

look on the Web and Venus isn't on show at the moment. I was half wondering if you'd heard anything?"

"Not yet a while," replied Gordon, "But if you hear any more be sure to let me know straightaway. I could get a short item on the late broadcast."

"Okay, will do." Robert hung up and continued browsing through the website which was open on his screen. He came across a page that looked helpful; it was a list of the members of staff and their telephone extension numbers and more importantly, their email addresses. Robert hoped someone might be monitoring their email. He hastily rattled off a message to a handful of the most likely people he thought might be able to answer his questions and crossed his fingers someone would get back to him soon.

23:27 Greenwich Mean Time December 24th 2012 (UTC 23:27)

Andy McVeigh was now a little on edge, and for want of some way to keep his mind occupied, decided that he would log into the Observatory intranet and check his email. He found he had perhaps around a dozen messages. Some were from students wishing him a Happy Christmas, there were two from the administrator about Christmas closures and public opening times, and one other that caught his eye. The subject header said *'Bright star in the night sky, can you help?'*

He opened it and read through it carefully. It claimed to be from a journalist on 'The Scotsman', who had been receiving reports about a bright star. He stated that he'd gone to investigate and found the reports to be true. He hoped the Professor could help establish just what it is. Robert included his name and phone number and requested Andy call him urgently.

Andy turned to his wife and said "The news is out Mary. There's a reporter from The Scotsman who wants to talk to me."

Mary McVeigh thought for a moment and said, "Aye, well, it was going to come out sooner or later. You'd better make sure they get their facts right. You know how the papers like to exaggerate."

"That they do," agreed her husband, "that they do."

The Professor picked up the telephone and began to dial the number in the message.

The phone hardly seemed to ring before a voice at the other end said "Robert Macleod, The Scotsman."

"Ah, Mr. Macleod, this is Professor McVeigh from the Royal Observatory. I believe you wanted to speak with me?"

"Oh, Professor," cried Robert, "thank you so much for calling. Now, it's about this very bright star we can see in the sky, can you tell me a little about it?" Robert opened his notebook hurriedly and grabbed a pen as he spoke.

"Well, young man," replied the Professor, "I can indeed."

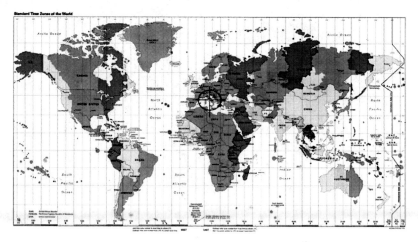

00:34 Central European Time December 25th 2012 (UTC 23:34)

Giovanni was sitting in the office of the Vatican Observatory becoming increasingly fretful. Time seemed to be passing horribly slowly. He kept glancing at his watch wondering when Father Giuseppe would be likely to finish saying midnight Mass and would get his text. He also wondered why it was taking so long to hear anything further from Dr Baltar at the Central Bureau. He began to pace up and down, trying his best to stay calm. He thought perhaps he should go home to bed as he was well aware he had to say Mass in the local parish in just over eight hours time, but he knew it would be pointless even trying to get to sleep as he was so keyed up.

At last the email notification chimed on his computer. Giovanni dived to open it. On the screen was an official circular from the Central Bureau of Astronomical Telegrams requesting follow up observations of a bright supernova in the constellation of Leo. The credit for the discovery was given to one Father Giovanni Casparo of the Vatican Observatory in Italy. The co-ordinates of the star were then given along with the object's type and other useful details for observers, both amateur and professional, to study.

Giovanni was thrilled. Now if only he could share it with somebody. He picked up the telephone and began to dial a number in Chicago.

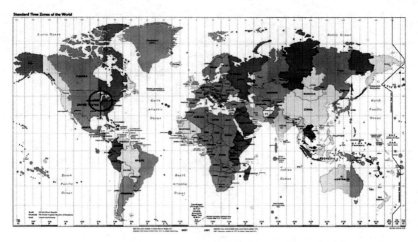

17:35 Central Standard Time 24th December 2012 (UTC 23:35)

Marco Casparo's mobile phone redirected the incoming call to his voicemail as he was busy at that moment.

Giovanni was disappointed as he really wanted to share his amazing news with his brother. He of all people would understand what this discovery meant to the priest. As Marco's voice mail played in Giovanni's ear he was trying to decide what he should say by way of a message for his brother.

"Please leave a message and I'll get back to you when I can. Thank you." Marco's voice ended and then came a brief pause. Next came a short beep and Giovanni drew breath.

"Hi Marco, it's me Giovanni. I've got something I want to tell you about." He was sure he must sound excited. "I've made a discovery, an amazing discovery." There was a slight pause as he gathered his thoughts. "I hope you and Lucy are okay? Make sure you look after her properly. She must be looking forward to the birth now, as we all are. Call me back when you get the chance. Bye for now. Ciao!" Giovanni ended the call trying not to feel disappointed that he wasn't able to share his excitement with his brother. Calling Marco had reminded Giovanni of his impending family status. His delight at the fact he was soon to become an uncle, quickly overshadowed any distress he might have felt at not actually being able to speak to him. He could only guess at how excited Marco and Lucy must be feeling. He

45

put his phone back in his pocket and at that moment felt terribly alone in the silence of the Observatory building.

He also wished he could share his excitement with his parents. The thought caused him a moment's pain.

After the death of their parents some ten years before, the two brothers had become closer. Marco had given Giovanni a standing invitation to visit over the Christmas period; this year he let Marco know that he wouldn't be coming, as at best, he would only have a couple of days away from his work and besides, there was his sister-in-law's condition to consider. He told him that he'd like a quiet holiday on his own this time and he wanted to take the opportunity to continue to work without interruption on his paper.

Giovanni came fairly late to the priesthood, having trained as an astro-physicist and gained a first-class degree from the University of Bologna in Physics with Astro-physics. The stars were always his first love. As a boy he would look up at the night sky from his village in Tuscany and wonder... He was a bright boy who did well at school and excelled in Maths and Physics. It wasn't until the age of 29 that he 'got the calling' as he liked to describe it. At the time he was working at the Jet Propulsion Laboratories in the USA, having secured a good job there with the help of his old tutor at the University. His English improved immensely during his time in the States and although he was a good Catholic and attended Mass regularly, he never considered himself particularly religious. However, he decided to follow his heart, and although he had the chance of studying for the priesthood in America he really wanted to go back to his native Italy to 'take the cloth'. He secured a place in the seminary in Florence, not too far from his old village, and became a theological student. This also gave him the opportunity of keeping an eye on his aging parents. His father was now quite elderly and seemed to be becoming increasingly frail.

It so happened, Giovanni had been back in the old country no more than two months, when his younger brother secured a job in the USA. Marco was a banker and jumped at the chance of furthering his career with the Bank of Italy when they offered him a job with promotion, working abroad. So it was, his brother moved to Chicago and it became a standing joke between them that they travelled around half the globe to avoid each other. There was no ill feeling of course and both Giovanni and their parents wished him luck in his new post.

It was not long after Giovanni entered the seminary, his father became gravely ill. He passed away in the March and his mother took ill herself soon after. Barely 6 months later she too had passed away. Some said it was due to grief.

That was a bad year. Giovanni realised it was nearly 10 years ago now but he still felt the loss of his parents keenly. Even though he and his brother were now thousands of miles apart, they grew closer as they only now had each other left from their family. Marco later married an American girl and also now had a spacious new home. Giovanni knew he was always welcome there, although he had but little desire to return to the USA. Seeing his brother would have been pleasant however and he felt slightly selfish in wanting to stay and work. He did manage to justify his decision to Marco this year as well as to himself though, due to Lucy's pregnancy. With the baby due in early January he felt his presence would only tire her.

It was soon after his parents' death that Giovanni's scientific skills came to the notice of his Bishop. He too was very interested in science, but had little in the way of qualifications. He liked Giovanni, and mentioned to his Cardinal he had a talented scientist working for him.

Some weeks later Giovanni received a telephone call from the Vatican. He was invited for an interview at the Vatican Observatory. He was astounded, but quickly agreed to the meeting and a week later found himself driving up to the Swiss Guard's lodge at the Observatory on the edge of Castel Gandolfo.

The interview went well. It turned out one of the older astronomers had decided to take retirement and so a place became vacant for a junior research astronomer. His priestly duties in the nearby village where he was given charge of a small 'flock' would be light, and he would be doing what he originally trained for. Things were getting decidedly better.

47

That was nearly two years ago now and Giovanni had settled into the routine of being both a working scientist and a parish priest. He never would have thought he would end up discovering a supernova. Giovanni's head swam; he was so deliriously happy.

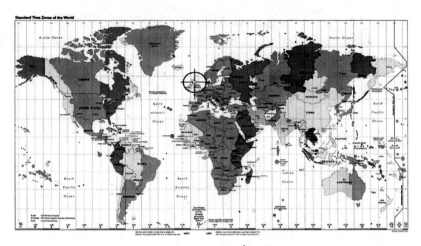

23:35 Greenwich Mean Time 24th December 2012 (UTC 23:35)

Professor McVeigh had been lecturing the poor young journalist on The Scotsman for nearly ten minutes, all about supernovae and the chances of one going off in our galaxy. He also made sure the journalist was aware that the first discoverer of this particular event was an astronomer at the Vatican Observatory and that he, Andy, had merely confirmed the find. Robert Macleod was hastily scribbling notes doing his best to make sense of it all and trying to ask intelligent sounding questions at the same time. As a boy he'd had a slight interest in the stars and was trying to recall some of the terminology he'd learned all those years ago. In fact the Professor's obvious enthusiasm for his subject was quite infectious and Robert increasingly found himself being drawn into the subject again by Andy's increasing excitement. The journalist in him also sensed a lead story. This could be a real fillip to his career.

He was glad that the old astronomer wasn't being too technical; any jargon he used, Robert found the old Professor was quite willing to explain as clearly as he could. Robert now had enough material for a double page spread and he was trying to bring the conversation to a polite close. He felt, given the opportunity, Andy McVeigh would have gone on talking all night.

"Professor, thank you so much for all the information. Would it be okay if I called you again later, if I need to?"

Andy realised that perhaps he had been talking a little too much and quietened down as he said "Oh, oh yes, that'll be alright, as long as it's no too late. I'll be away t' my bed within the hour."

"Well thank you once again sir," Robert said as politely as he could. "Oh and Merry Christmas to you."

"Oh, ah yes, a Merry Christmas to you too." Andy put the phone down. "A nice young man," he said to his wife. "He actually sounded interested in what I was saying. I wish some of my past students would've been so keen."

Mary smiled sympathetically at her husband. "I've a feeling it won't be the last you'll be hearing from him."

Andy made a noise of agreement in his throat and returned to his armchair. He picked up the remote control and switched the television on, once again.

As soon as Robert put the phone down he stabbed at his keyboard and started typing up his story for the front page. He worked frantically trying to make sense of the notes he had taken, while doing his best to remember some of the many interesting words and phrases the Professor had used, such as 'unprecedented' and 'historic' to 'chance in a life time' and 'will rock the astronomical community if not the whole world'. He had only a little time to get his copy into shape if it was going to catch the presses for the morning papers. He swigged the dregs of the cold coffee that sat on his desk. He didn't even have time to get himself another. Probably the most important piece of information the Professor had given him was the name of the discoverer of the star. He was a little taken aback when he was told it was a Catholic priest at the Vatican Observatory but then chuckled to himself at the irony of a priest discovering a 'Christmas Star'.

It took him 25 minutes to get the story into a reasonably readable form and he went straight into his editor's office without even knocking. He then said something that he'd wanted to say ever since the day he had considered being a journalist.

"Hold the front page!"

His editor looked at him coldly. Murray Johnston was not a man to joke with. "What are you talking about?"

"Murray, you've got to hold the front page," Robert said more imploringly this time. Uninvited, he sat down opposite his editor.

"And why should I do that?" Robert, after all, was just a junior hack.

"We've got a big story breaking. There's a new star in the sky and I've just spoken to the astronomer guy at the Edinburgh Observatory who confirmed it, and it's really, really bright." Robert's voice was increasing in pitch and volume.

Murray's eyes narrowed. "Go on," he prompted.

Robert explained about the calls to the 'news desk' and how he went out to investigate and what he had seen for himself, the brief interviews with random people at the Castle, his research on the Internet and the subsequent telephone conversation with the Professor. It all seemed quite breathless. He missed out the part about speaking with his friend at the BBC. He judged this might not go down too well with his editor at this stage.

Murray had been in the job too long not to know this story had real potential. Not only that, it could be a scoop for the paper. His countenance visibly softened.

"Okay," he said. "I need a couple of photographs. Get the duty snapper on to it and you've got the chance to run with this. Get it wrong and I'll demote you to tea boy. Get it right and there could be a pay rise in it for you."

Robert leapt out of the chair with a "yes sir," and flew out of the door. He yelled at Malcolm Singer on the News Desk at the other side of the office, "Which photographer's on duty?"

"I'll check for you." Malcolm could tell by the tone in Robert's voice that something big was going down. "Marion Groom," he called back within a few seconds.

Robert knew Marion to be reliable. He quickly looked up her number and dialled it.

Marion's voice sounded a little annoyed at being disturbed on Christmas Eve. She knew that she was 'on call', but couldn't help hoping for a quiet evening. "Marion Groom," she stated coldly.

"Marion, it's me Robert. I need you to get some pictures of a star."

"Okay, what's his or her name and what theatre?"

"No, not that sort of star; a *real* star."

Before Marion had any chance of replying he blurted out a brief version of the story. "Please Marion; I need you to do this right now."

Marion liked Robert. Of all the hacks she worked with, he was one of the nicest to her and genuinely seemed to appreciate her abilities with a camera. "Okay, okay, you've talked me into it. Where do I find this star?"

"Just go outside and face south east." Robert hoped that she knew her cardinal points. "You can't miss it," he added emphatically.

Marion kissed her husband on the cheek and said "Gotta go." Her husband's shoulders' slumped and he looked dejected. She really hated doing this to him, but he knew the perils of marrying a photo-journalist and it wasn't the first time this had happened. It just made it worse being it was Christmas Eve.

She pulled on her coat and grabbed her camera, checking it over as she walked towards the door. This was a habit which had made sure she never went out with a flat battery, or missing a memory card or lens. "I shouldn't be long," she said as cheerily as she could as she opened the front door. Her husband grunted.

She lived on the outskirts of town, a quiet suburb up a hill. Marion walked to the end of the garden path, opened the gate and turned to close it behind her. She immediately noticed a bright star hovering just over some trees in her neighbour's garden. Her jaw fell open. Could that be it? She did a quick scan around the rest of the sky. It was very cold and clear and the other stars twinkled picturesquely in the darkness above her. Without question, this was the brightest star in the sky. In fact it was incredibly bright. She brought her camera up to her face and started taking a sequence of shots, trying to frame the star with the trees to make it as photogenic as possible. After she had taken twenty or so shots, she went straight back to her front door and called her husband.

"You're back quick," he said with obvious delight.

"Lucien, come and take a look at this," Marion insisted. Her husband looked startled, but moved to get up. His wife seemed very excited about something.

She practically dragged him out of the door and down the path. The cold night air bit into him and he shivered. Marion then pointed into the sky. It took only an instant to follow the direction she was trying to get him to look.

"Wow, that's brrright!" He exclaimed. "What on Earth is it?"

"Nothing on Earth," chuckled the photographer. "It's a star, a new star." She emphasised the last two words. I've got to get these pictures back to the office double quick. As she walked smartly back to the house, Lucien hung back admiring this beautiful bright object. 'That's amazing,' he thought to himself. He shivered once again and made to follow his wife into the warmth and security of their central heating.

23:58 Greenwich Meantime 24th December 2012 (UTC 23:58)

Robert's computer screen flashed a message up to tell him that he had a new email. It was from Marion to make him aware she had uploaded some pictures to the secure area of the newspaper's intra-net, and asked him to take a look. This Robert duly did and was delighted to see a series of superb images of the star in a beautiful setting of silhouetted trees and a couple of distant houses. They looked almost as if they had been taken for a Christmas card.

He quickly emailed Marion back to thank her for a good and quick job and wished her a very Merry Christmas. His next task was to lay out the page ready for printing and to get the approval of his editor. He had taken a little time to flesh out the story while he was waiting for the photographs and was quite pleased with the result. He emailed Murray Johnston to ask him to take a look. Bursting through his editor's door twice in one evening was, he felt, definitely not a good idea.

While he was waiting, Robert decided he should call his friend at the BBC once again. He selected the redial option on his phone and clicked on the name Gordon Gregory. Gordon answered in two rings.

"Robert! What have you got for me?"

The journalist explained what he had been doing since they last spoke and told him they were going to break the story on the front page of The Scotsman, the next day. Robert was rather pre-empting his editor here, but he thought it was worth the risk.

Gordon thanked him for the information, and told him that he could possibly squeeze the story onto a twenty second slot on the news at 1:00am. It didn't seem very long to Robert, but he realised it was the best he was likely to get. At that moment, the editor's office door flew open and Murray roared Robert's name across the floor.

"Gotta go," said Robert to his friend and quickly hung up. He swallowed hard as he stood up and marched towards Murray Johnston. He thought the editor was looking rather stern and his heart sank as he made a cautious approach. He felt a weight lift from him as he drew nearer and realised that Murray was in fact smiling. This was a first. He couldn't recall anyone having reported seeing Murray Johnston smile.

"Good work," nodded Murray. "We'll run with that for the early edition. "Good pictures too."

Robert was now starting to think his editor had his own private stash of whiskey in his office.

Murray continued, "We'll see if any of the other papers or TV channels picks this up. It could be a real boost for the paper."

"Er, actually sir, I've already alerted the BBC." Robert visibly winced at the look Murray now gave him, but is was gone in an instant as Murray realised his junior journalist was just showing some initiative.

"Who did you speak to?" questioned his boss.

"I've a friend who works for the Corporation in Glasgow, in their news office."

"Fine, that's okay then. Only next time, you leave that sort of thing to me."

Robert was relieved by the words 'next time'. "Er, yes sorry sir." Perhaps old Johnston wasn't quite the monster some of the other hacks made him out to be. As he turned to go back to his desk he heard the clock strike the top of the hour. "Merry Christmas," he grinned over his shoulder to Murray. His editor cleared his throat and returned the greeting.

Day 6

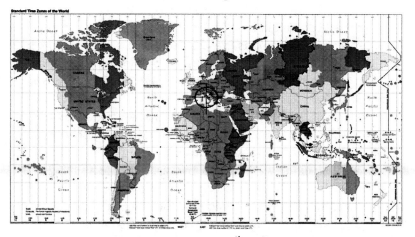

01:02 Central European Time 25th December 2012 (UTC 00:02)

Giovanni looked at his watch for the twentieth time. He knew that Father Giuseppe would be finished saying midnight mass soon and he would no doubt check his mobile phone as soon as he had an opportunity. The astronomer was rather glad he was on his own at that moment as he was becoming aware he was feeling quite tetchy.

He checked his email box. He had done just this less than two minutes ago. In fact he had been doing this very nearly every two minutes for the last twenty. Giovanni knew it was completely pointless as the software would alert him as soon as a new message arrived, but he couldn't help himself. He went back to his mobile phone to see if he had any texts. Not only was he waiting to hear from his superior, but also from his brother. He really was getting quite excited at the thought of being an uncle.

Still nothing. He ran his hands through his thick dark hair.

The phone rang and he snatched it out of the cradle. "Pronto," he said quickly and automatically. He heard a slightly worried voice in English but with a distinct Scottish lilt at the other end.

56

"Is that Father Casparo?" questioned Robert Macleod rather hesitantly.

"Yes," Giovanni now replied in English. "Who is this?"

Robert couldn't believe his luck. Phoning the Vatican Observatory on Christmas Eve was a real shot in the dark and he really never expected to get an answer, let alone the very man he wanted to speak to. "My name is Robert Macleod. I work on The Scotsman, a newspaper here in Scotland. Professor McVeigh kindly gave me your number." Robert spoke slowly and clearly as he didn't know how good the priest's English was and he was a little nervous about speaking to the discoverer of this new star. He didn't want to blow this, as he was in his mind already planning follow up articles for the paper.

"How may I help you?" enquired Giovanni, although he already understood that this journalist would be after a good story. Giovanni aimed to make sure he got one.

"Can you confirm that you are the discoverer of this new star which has appeared in the night sky?"

"I believe I am." Giovanni was doing his best not to sound boastful.

Robert then continued to cross question the priest about the circumstances of his find and how and to whom he had reported it. Giovanni was more than happy to furnish the reporter with the details. As much as anything this was the first human voice, other than the Professor's, who sounded really interested in what Giovanni had found and so he aimed to make the most of this 'captive audience' while he could. He made sure to stress it was pure chance it was he who discovered the star and that it could easily have been any number of astronomers, either professional or even amateur, who could have beaten him to it. He explained about how such discoveries are reported to the Central Bureau of Astronomical Telegrams. It was the second time this evening that Robert was regaled with the fine detail of how astronomical discoveries are made and the reports disseminated. However, he was also aware of the 'human interest' side of the story now he was actually interviewing the discoverer. He then asked a question that was coming to the forefront of his mind.

"Father," he said, "has the co-incidence of this bright new star being discovered on Christmas night by a Catholic priest struck you as eventful or, dare I say it, even romantic if that's the correct word?"

Giovanni was stunned. In his haste to report this as an important scientific discovery, the significance of the timing of the event had completely passed him by.

"Father, are you still there?" Robert thought that the line to Italy had dropped.

"Er, er, yyyes, I'm still here."

Robert could instantly tell that this had never crossed the priest's mind and had come to him like a bolt out of the blue.

"No, I had not," Giovanni said more firmly as he regained control of his thoughts. "I suppose you are right. It is a little um..." Giovanni hunted for the English word.

"Ironic?" suggested Robert.

"Er, yes, ironic," confirmed Giovanni.

The priest's mind was now reeling. How had he not seen this? Was this truly a sign from God? The scientist in him quickly took hold. He knew that supernovae can happen any time almost anywhere in the universe. It was probably about time that one occurred in our own galaxy. He tried to make light of it.

"I suppose it does sound a little strange," he attempted to chuckle, to dismiss it almost out of hand.

Robert sensed his unease and backed off.

"I am sure it's just a co-incidence as you say Father." He continued. "Thank you very much for your time. May I call you again if I need to?"

"Oh, oh yes, I am sure that would be alright." The priest was still a little off his guard.

"Great and thanks again Father; have a good Christmas."

Robert put the phone down. Giovanni leaned back heavily in his chair. He needed to think; to clear his mind. He now picked through the implications of his discovery, in his head and wondered if anyone would draw daft conclusions as this young journalist had pointed out? He found himself glancing at the clock again. 01:15. His brow began to furrow. At that moment his mobile telephone chirruped for attention.

Giovanni looked at the display to see that it was his brother in the States returning his call.

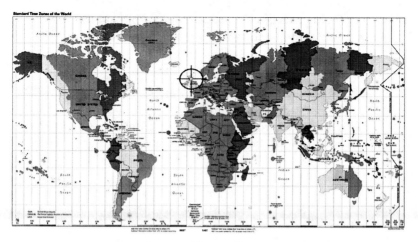

00:15 Greenwich Mean Time 25th December 2012 (UTC 00:15)

Gordon Gregory was busy typing a few short sentences in the Newsroom of the BBC in Glasgow. He had to clear this past his editor so he could put it up on the 'autocue' for the presenter of the 1:00am Christmas Day news. He called to his editor to say that he had some breaking news that was worthy of broadcast.

"Are you sure about this?" Angela Gabriel was very particular about accuracy.

Gordon assured her that the story came with the highest pedigree and explained about his friend Robert doing the 'leg work' on it and how The Scotsman was going to print the story for their first edition.

Angela knew Robert to be a diligent reporter and also young and enthusiastic. She likewise knew that enthusiasm can sometimes cloud judgment.

"Not good enough," stated Angela coldly. "I want you to speak to this astrologer guy yourself and confirm it."

Gordon felt a little hurt at her lack of trust in him. "Okay," he said blankly. As Angela turned to walk away from his desk, he added, "It's 'astronomer' by the way." Angela stopped in her tracks and turned back to face him.

"What did you say?"

"It's 'astronomer', not 'astrologer'."

Angela looked at him quizzically and with slight irritation. She did not like being corrected, especially by a junior.

"The man at the Royal Observatory... he's an astronomer not an astrologer."

Angela raised one eyebrow, clicked her tongue, turned again and continued to walk back to her desk.

With a slight frown, Gordon looked up Roberts' email to get the phone number of Professor Andrew McVeigh and started to dial...

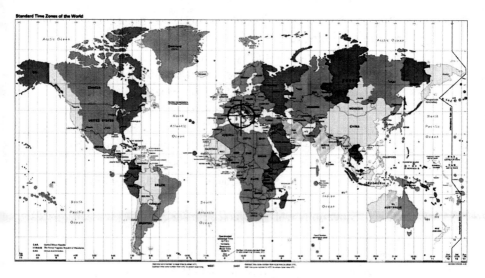

01:15 Central European Time 25th December 2012 (UTC 00:15)

Before Marco left the hospital grounds he remembered he should call his brother to let him know the good news. He switched his mobile phone back on, having made sure it was off during the labour and birth of his son. He thought it wouldn't be a good idea to start taking calls just at that moment! As soon as he had done this, his voicemail alerted him to a message. He called into the service and was pleased to hear Giovanni's message. He wasn't sure quite what he was so excited about, but it must be something good for his brother to sound so animated. He dialled the number and didn't have to wait long for the familiar voice of his brother to answer.

"Giovanni, it's Marco."

"Marco! Good to hear from you. How are you?"

"I'm fine thanks. Giovanni, I have some wonderful news. Lucy's had a baby boy."

"Excellent!" exclaimed the astronomer.

"I didn't have time to call you earlier otherwise I would have let you know he was on the way. Lucy went into labour quite suddenly and I had to get her to the hospital quick. She's absolutely fine now. Just a bit tired."

"Marco, that's wonderful news!" exclaimed the priest. "What are you going to call him?"

We were thinking of naming him after you..."

Giovanni began to make noises of protestation.

"...But," he paused, "we've settled on 'Salvatore'. Marco managed to quell his brother's dissent with this.

"Salvatore," the priest repeated. "Salvatore." He said it again as if he were examining it. "That's a beautiful name," he finally consented. "I'm so happy for you both." Giovanni was choking back his delight. "Give Lucy my love and say 'well done' to her for me."

"I will, Giovanni, I will." Marco promised.

"But brother, you have some news of your own I think?"

"Yes. This has been such a wondrous night Marco. I have discovered a Supernova!" Giovanni said this with a note of triumph in his voice. Marco wasn't too sure exactly what it was but knew it must be important for his brother to sound so excited.

"That's great, Giovanni." Marco did his best to sound pleased through his exhaustion.

The priest quickly realised that his brother might not know exactly what this meant and explained, "It's a star that's exploded Marco. Not just that, it's incredibly bright!"

Marco sounded genuinely pleased for his brother now. "Can I see it?"

Yes, but not yet, it won't be high enough in the sky for you to see it until later. But then I think you may have other things to occupy you." Marco could hear his brother smiling. "Go and get some rest Marco, and be sure to send Lucy my love."

"I will do Giovanni. I'll send you a picture of your nephew soon too."

Giovanni was deliriously happy.

Giovanni's mobile phone rang for the second time in just a few short minutes. He thought perhaps his brother had forgotten to tell him something until he looked at the caller's number on the display. It had almost slipped his mind that he was waiting for this call.

"Father Giuseppe, thank you for phoning back."

"Giovanni, I just got your message. What's going on? It sounds very important?"

"It is Father, it is," exclaimed Giovanni. "I've made an important discovery." The priest then began to explain the evening's events in detail as the Assistant Director of the Observatory listened with increasing amazement to the unfolding tale. At the end of the story Giovanni drew breath and waited for the response. He had to wait longer than he was expecting. Father Giuseppe was almost speechless with astonishment.

"That's... That's incredible!" cried the elderly priest.

"We must inform the Cardinal."

Now it was Giovanni's turn to be astonished. "Inform the Cardinal?"

"Yes, yes," exclaimed Giuseppe. "This is wondrous news. We should be telling everybody. God has smiled on us this evening Giovanni. We have a new star to celebrate the birth of Our Lord. The world should know of this. After all the nonsense talked in recent days about the end of the world, God has given us a sign and is giving us new hope."

Giovanni knew the Assistant Director to be much more pious than he. However, he didn't expect him to go off on a religious rant, supposing Father Giuseppe to be more scientific and level headed. This news had obviously tipped him away from his astronomical curiosity. He hoped his boss would regain his balance quickly. Giovanni was not one for extremism of any sort. He had deeply held convictions about his religion, but also believed that God had given man his intellect to explore His wonders and understand Him better through scientific enquiry.

64

"If you think that is the right thing to do?" asked Giovanni hesitantly.

"I do, I do," replied the Assistant Director. "I'll do it right now." He continued, "Are you still at the Observatory? He may want to speak to you."

"Yes." Giovanni was trying to figure out how best to handle this unwanted attention.

"Good. Stay there," ordered the Assistant Director. Giuseppe hung up.

Giovanni ran his fingers through his hair for the second time, his nervous habit betraying how he felt. The priest tried to formulate in his mind what he was going to say to his Cardinal and how to best calm the situation down. He hadn't bargained on much attention from this discovery, other than from the astronomical community and wished any other interest it might generate would just disappear. He was now beginning to understand the excitement this might cause in the wider world. After all, the star was very bright; you couldn't hide it.

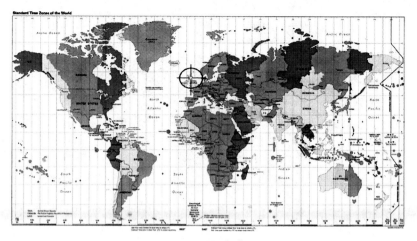

00:17 Greenwich Mean Time 25th December 2012 (UTC 00:17)

The phone rang for the third time in the household of Professor Andy McVeigh. He lifted the receiver and gave a greeting.

"Hello," he said as calmly as possible.

"Is that Professor McVeigh?"

"Aye, this is he."

"I'm sorry to trouble you sir. This is Gordon Gregory from the BBC News in Glasgow. I'm calling to check out a story that has been passed to me by Robert Macleod. You spoke to him earlier I believe."

Yes, I did," admitted Andy.

"I need to know if you can confirm the information that I have about this new star."

Andy sensed the opportunity once again, to hold forth on his favourite subject.

"That I can; that I can," he repeated. "What would you like to know?"

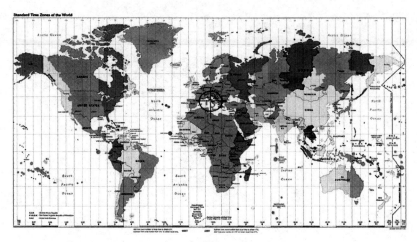

01:23 Central European Time 25th December 2012 (UTC 00:23)

Father Giuseppe Carpentiere ran down the steps of the east door of the church and out into the cold night air. He looked up and there in front of him was the star exactly as Giovanni had described. Reaching into his pocket, he pulled out his mobile phone for the second time. He scrolled through the list of names on the display looking for the Cardinal as he was now almost bursting with excitement to tell of this Earth shattering discovery by one of his own staff. He lighted on the name; 'Leonardo Verdi – Exc'.

Cardinal Verdi was the President of the Pontifical Commission for the Vatican City State. In other words he was the executive authority for the running of the Vatican including Castel Gandolfo where the Observatory was situated. What's more, he was an old friend of Giuseppe's and even better, he knew the Cardinal had direct access to his Hollness the Pope.

Father Carpentiere selected the 'call' dialogue from the instructions on his phone and held the device to his ear. After a few moments the 'ringing' tone sounded and next came the voice of Leonardo.

"Si, pronto."

"Your Eminence?" Giuseppe enquired uncertainly.

"Yes, who is this?" The Cardinal obviously did not recognise the voice of his old friend.

67

"It is Giuseppe Carpentiere, Leonardo. I hope you don't mind me calling you at this late hour?"

Leonardo was in fact rather tired, having just changed out of his vestments after assisting his Holiness at midnight mass in St. Peter's. He did his best to hide his irritation, although he was quite pleased to hear from his old friend.

"Ah, Giuseppe, it's good to hear from you. To what do I owe the honour of this call?" Leonardo sounded slightly more effusive than was really necessary.

"I'm sorry to disturb you so late," the priest reiterated, "it's just that I have something very important to tell you. One of my staff has made an amazing discovery, which you should know about."

This caught the attention of the Cardinal. He knew that his friend would not just call him up on a whim and so started to listen carefully.

"Tell me more."

Giuseppe then went on to explain what Giovanni had described. He then embellished the story with his own take on the situation. "Leonardo, I believe that we are being given a sign from God. You know I am a scientist but I cannot but think that this remarkable discovery has been given to us to help see through the fog of misinformation and delusion that the world has been experiencing in recent days. Please go and take a look for yourself. I've just done so and it's truly wonderful. When you've seen it, please tell his Holiness; I think he really should know about this."

The Cardinal's curiosity got the better of him. "Where do I look?"

"Find a spot that will give you a view to the east."

Leonardo hesitated. "There are so many buildings around here." He sounded frustrated. Almost as soon as he said it, the answer came to him. "I know," he continued, "I can go up to the roof."

The Cardinal started to walk back from the sacristy into the body of the Basilica and headed for the stairs, which would take him up to the base of Michelangelo's magnificent work,

68

probably the most famous and the largest man-made dome in the world.

"Giuseppe, I'll call you back." With that he ended the call and shoved the phone back in his pocket. Now he could concentrate properly on the task in hand. The Cardinal was a fairly fit and healthy sixty years old and thought nothing of the long climb up the stairs. He considered that he could get to the top more quickly than taking the lift, which he considered slow and the 'lazy' way. It took several minutes to ascend the three hundred and twenty steps and he was certainly out of breath when he arrived on the landing. He circulated around the dome checking out of every window as he did. As Leonardo moved around the eastern side of the magnificent building he saw it. He couldn't miss it.

The Cardinal once again reached for his phone and looked up Giuseppe's number. He waited and got his breath back as the call connected.

Before the priest had a chance to speak, Leonardo said triumphantly, "Giuseppe, I see it!"

He ran through the details of the discovery again with the Assistant Director to make sure of the facts, promising he would go straight to his Holiness and announce the news. He hoped that the Holy Father had not gone to bed, as he was uncertain how the Pope would take to being disturbed. Saying his good-byes to Father Giuseppe, he promised to get back in touch as soon as the Pope had been informed.

The Cardinal headed back to the stairs, his footsteps echoing like the report of a machine gun as he scurried ever downwards.

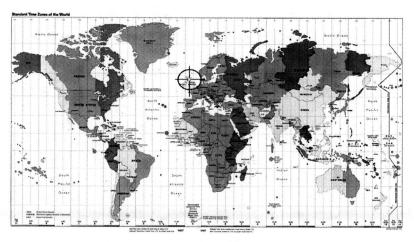

00:48 Greenwich Mean Time 25th December 2012 (UTC 00:48)

Gordon was putting the finishing touches to the short bulletin that was to go out on the 1:00am news on BBC Scotland. He'd spoken at length to Professor McVeigh, not a particularly enjoyable experience, and fired it over to Angela's computer for final approval.

Angela scanned through it and made a couple of unnecessary alterations to the text and sent it back to Gordon with the instruction to 'cue it up' for a twenty second fill in the main headlines. Gordon was pleased and faithfully carried out his orders, so the story was now waiting to break for those who still hadn't gone to bed. He decided to call his friend and let him know.

Robert's phone sang out its tune and he was glad to see it was Gordon calling. He hoped it would be good news.

"Good news Robert," piped Gordon cheerfully as his friend greeted him. "I've got the story a spot in the main headlines with a twenty second filling slot shortly after."

Twenty seconds still did not sound very long to Robert, but Gordon assured him that it would be enough to capture people's attention. If the story grew, they were in a good position to expand on it. "Be sure that you are near a TV at 1:00am and let me know what you think."

Robert thanked his friend and hoped for the best. Out of interest, he decided to check out the weather report to see how much of Scotland or anywhere else for that matter, could actually see this star. He opened the Met Office website... Eastern Scotland-clear; 'that made a change' he thought and the skies were clearing into the west and northern England. The rest of the UK seemed covered in cloud. He looked further afield. Northern France like England was quite cloudy, although it was clearer to the south. Northern Spain had sporadic cloud too. Italy was mostly clear. He carried on surveying the images. Robert began to wonder how many more people had seen this star. He wandered over to the 'news desk' to see what was happening there.

"Hi Malcolm, how's it going?"

Malcolm Singer twirled his pen around his fingers. "I've been getting loads of reports in about this star." A complaining note was in his voice. "I've deleted most of them as I know that you're on to it."

"How many is 'loads'?" questioned Robert.

"Over a hundred I'd say and they're still coming in." Another email announcing the arrival of a Christmas star popped up on the computer screen as he spoke.

"Okay, thanks." Robert wandered back to his desk and opened up the live newsfeed from BBC Scotland on his browser. It was approaching 1:00am and he didn't want to miss the story 'on air'. He decided a visit to his boss to let him know what was going on would be prudent. He walked towards the editor's door and gently knocked. A muffled "Come in," emanated from within. Robert pushed open the door.

"I thought you'd like to know that my story's got a slot on BBC Scotland's main news."

Without responding, Murray Johnston moved his computer mouse and clicked it a couple of times. That done he said, "Well done there Robert. I'll watch the news here. That'll be all."

Robert realised that he was being asked to leave, so he nodded and closing the door behind him went back to his desk. As he sat down, the headlines started and he turned up the volume on the speakers. Various items of interest went by, including the tensions in the middle-east, panic buying in the shops just before Christmas and an item about a celebrity visiting a children's hospital. There was a slight pause and then he instantly recognised the photograph appearing on the screen as the one Marion took, as the presenter intoned, "Reports are coming in of a bright star in the night sky. Could this be a new Christmas star?" As the camera view switched back to the familiar face on the screen, Robert felt that she had what could best be described as a slight mocking smirk on her face.

He tried to suppress his mild irritation at this, as he settled to watch the programme. The news on the Middle-East tensions just depressed him, made only slightly worse by the item on the last minute panic buying in the shops. Consumerism was alive and well and living in Britain. The 3 or 4 minutes spent on the celebrity trying to bring some cheer to the poor kids stuck in hospital over the holiday, he found somewhat nauseating. He blamed this on the way it was presented rather than the act itself, trying not to be cynical about the motives of the so called celebrity, who may have had the best of intentions.

As the presenter then went back to the story of the 'Christmas Star', he moved his face closer to the screen and listened intently.

"Reports have been coming in of a new star in the sky, first seen by an astronomer in Edinburgh."

"God, why can't they report things accurately?" He felt oddly superior. The presenter continued, *"It seems that this star is exceptionally bright and can be seen from most of Scotland. The story was first broken by a reporter on the 'The Scotsman' daily paper based in Edinburgh* (he was going to owe Gordon a pint or two for that one!) *and apparently it is causing quite a stir on the streets of that city. We will let you know as and when we get more information on this. On to the sport now..."*

Robert clicked off the feed as Murray Johnston slung open the door to his office. "Robert!" he roared across the floor. The other 'skeleton' staff that were working late looked up from their stations, "Good job. I'm proud of you my boy. I think you've earned your Christmas bonus."

Robert at first feeling slightly embarrassed, started to preen. "Thank you, sir," he replied, somewhat obsequiously, "I'm glad you liked it." He suddenly felt like a small boy sucking up to the teacher in class and, becoming rather self conscious, ducked his head down towards the desk. He hoped he wouldn't be seeing much more of his boss that night. Murray went back into his office. Robert breathed out heavily.

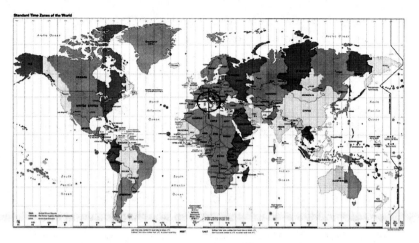

02:03 Central European Time 25th December 2012 (UTC 01:03)

Cardinal Verdi was now heading for the Papal apartments. As he approached the door, the Pope's personal assistant greeted him. "Cardinal! Good evening to you, or should I say, good morning? How may I be of assistance?"

"Monsignor, I need to speak to the Holy Father on a matter of great urgency." Leonardo knew that Monsignor Lopez was the Pope's guard dog and nobody got to his Holiness without going through him first.

"That is not possible Your Eminence, as his Holiness has retired to bed. Can it not wait until the morning?"

"I'm afraid not," replied Leonardo becoming more insistent, "this is a matter that concerns not just the Holy Father but the whole world." If he thought that would be good enough to get him an audience, he was mistaken. The Monsignor was quite used to dealing with pushy priests of any rank.

"But surely," came the rebuttal, "whatever it is can keep for a few short hours?" Monsignor Lopez's tone was decidedly 'oily'; trying to sound pleasant but being quite the opposite. He finished his parrying of Leonardo's pitch with a distinctly sarcastic question. "Has someone declared war on the Vatican?" With this he gave a smarmy smile that made him look a little like a fox licking his lips in a hen house.

74

Leonardo was ready for him. "Monsignor Lopez," he adopted a tone that would have suited an aggrieved parent admonishing an errant child, "if his Holiness does not hear of this event right now, he will thank neither you nor I for keeping it from him." The Cardinal's eyes flashed in such a way that no-one would be left uncertain that he meant business. "This is an event of the utmost importance, otherwise I would not dream of disturbing his Holiness's rest."

The Monsignor visibly deflated. "Very well, I will go and ask if he is willing to see you." He had the air of a whipped dog. As he turned towards the door of the Pope's private rooms, Leonardo nodded a 'thank you', as if to say 'there's a good boy, now run along'. He began to pace in the corridor, wrestling with his conscience about the uncharitable feelings that he held toward the Holy Father's personal assistant, waiting for what seemed like hours, but was in fact just a couple of minutes.

At last the door slid open a crack and the diminutive form of Monsignor Lopez reappeared. "His Holiness has agreed to see you. It seems that he was not yet in bed but at prayer. I waited a few moments before I disturbed him." Leonardo had the distinct feeling that the Monsignor said this as an excuse for taking so long and to make him feel guilty at the disturbance he was causing. Neither worked.

"Thank you," the Cardinal offered once again, this time with a little more sincerity.

"You can go in." Monsignor Lopez pointed limply towards the door.

Leonardo didn't need a further invitation and walked purposefully towards the beautiful varnished wooden entrance and passed into the Pope's private rooms. His footsteps sounded gently on the polished marble floor. As he headed towards the middle of the room, his Holiness the Pope entered from another similarly fine looking wooden door on the opposite wall.

Leonardo genuflected in front of the leader of the Roman Catholic Church and made to kiss the ornate ring on the hand that was now being offered to him.

"Well my son, what is this urgent business that prevents me from retiring to my bed?" The Pope sounded almost congenial.

"Holy Father," Cardinal Leonardo Verdi began as he got back to his feet, "I am truly sorry to have disturbed your sleep but there's something you must know this very hour."

The Pope could see the sincerity in Leonardo's eyes and gave him an encouraging look.

"Holy Father," the Cardinal repeated, "one of your priests, an astronomer at Castel Gandolfo has made a discovery of both astronomical and religious importance."

The Pope was now intrigued and urged Leonardo to continue.

"He has discovered a new star this very night, which shines very brightly in the east." Cardinal Verdi said this with a note of triumph in his voice.

The Pope looked stunned.

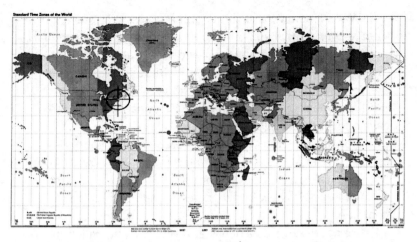

20:18 Eastern Standard Time 24th December 2012 (UTC 01:18)

John Baltar was in a difficult position. He was attempting to be pleasant to his mother in law, be helpful to his wife and fight the very strong urge to disappear upstairs to his study to deal with the unfolding 'situation' regarding this major astronomical discovery. While he gave a part of his mind over to social 'chit-chat', he was desperately hatching an escape plan. After a few moments he said,

"I'm just off to the bathroom." His mother-in-law raised an eyebrow, but said nothing. His wife Sarah on the other hand gave him a sideways look and followed him with her eyes as he disappeared out of the room and headed up the stairs. As soon as he was at the top of the stairs, John dived into his study. He sat down and woke the computer with a nudge of the mouse all in one movement.

He was not surprised to see more email on the subject of the star had arrived, but he was amazed to see the quantity. He estimated that there were at least fifty new reports and some replies to his request for follow up observations, from a few dedicated amateur astronomers. He realised at this moment it was about to become a big issue. He now had to think of a way to explain to his family he was likely to be going to have to absent himself from the Christmas preparations. This was something that he relished on one level and caused grave misgivings on the other. Having already been late back from work, he pictured the level of aggravation that he would likely face if he just vanished into the office for a few hours without explanation. So he thought that the best way of handling the affair would be to try to engage the two ladies and tell them what an important role he was having in the unfolding of this event. He took a deep breath and moved towards the top of the stairs, forgetting to go into the bathroom to flush the toilet.

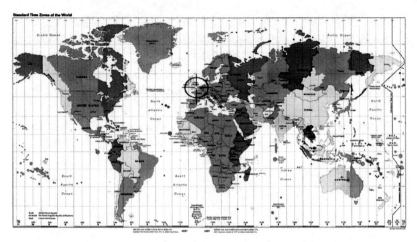

01:35 Greenwich Mean Time December 25th 2012 (UTC 01:35)

Adrika Mistry was checking the regional news stories in her office in the research department of BBC News 24 in London and spotted the short item that her colleagues in BBC Scotland had recently aired. She thought this interesting so called her opposite number in Glasgow.

The person who took the call didn't seem to know much about it, but gave her a couple of numbers to try. The first one rang three times and went to 'voice mail', with the message relating they would be away until December 28th and to 'kindly leave a message and they would call back.' Adrika didn't bother. The second telephone call was answered by an amiable sounding man with a soft urban Scottish accent by the name of Gordon.

Gordon Gregory was delighted to find that someone from 'head office' was interested in his story. He gave Ms Mistry the report as he knew it and thanked her for the call. Adrika said that she would let him know of any developments. In fact she passed it to Edward Thornley, the Environment and Science correspondent who happened to be working the same shift.

Edward was very interested. He'd a personal interest in things astronomical and had helped to promote various documentaries and 'special interest' programmes across several channels in the last few years. He went with it to his producer who gave him the 'green light' to put it out on the network for the 2:00am news broadcast. He checked with his colleague in BBC weather as to the likelihood of being able to see this star from various parts of the UK. The news on that front wasn't good, although the cloud, which seemed to be enveloping most of the British Isles, apart from northern and eastern Scotland and parts of north-east England, was slowly moving away and could possibly clear by the following evening. He prepared the lines for his piece to camera and asked Adrika to obtain copies of the photographs of the star.

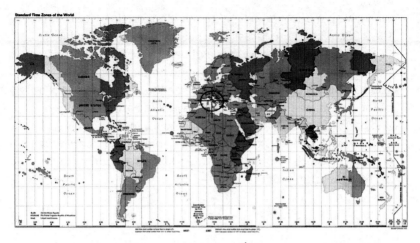

02:36 Central European Time 25th December 2012 (UTC 01:36)

His Holiness stood open mouthed at the story that Cardinal Verdi was relaying to him. Leonardo closed his speech by asking the Pontiff to 'take a look for himself'. It took the Holy Father a few moments to gather his thoughts.

"Where can I see this star?" he now questioned his subordinate. In fact he had many more questions forming in his mind, but thought it was best to begin simply and to try and see this wonder for himself.

"I saw it from the dome of the Basilica your Holiness," began Leonardo. He then questioned, "In which direction do the windows in your office face?"

The Pope looked a little confused by this enquiry and said, "I'm not sure." He thought for a moment and continued, "The Sun comes through them in the morning, so I suppose they face towards the east."

"Splendid," Leonardo clapped his hands together, "that means we should be able to see it from there." He resisted the urge to usher the Pontiff into his office, choosing rather to be led by his spiritual leader into the adjacent room. As they moved through the connecting door, Leonardo suggested that they refrain from putting on the light, in order that they may see out of the windows more easily. They moved towards the first window and almost immediately the head of the world's 1.1

81

billion Roman Catholics let out a startled exclamation as his eyes lighted on the bright star shining through the glass.

"I thought that you'd be amazed," Leonardo could not help sounding like he was lofting a sporting trophy for the delight of the crowd.

"I am indeed," the Pope uttered softly, "I am indeed," his voice almost dying away as he looked on the beautiful celestial lantern, in a state of near reverence. He turned towards Cardinal Verdi with a now determined look on his countenance and said commandingly, "Go and tell the Monsignor that I wish to summon the Curia for an urgent meeting to discuss this remarkable event."

"But your Holiness," Leonardo found himself protesting, "Many of them will be either asleep or have left the Vatican to return to their Sees."

"Then wake all the ones who are here and send for the ones who are not."

"Yes, of course, Your Holiness." Leonardo instantly backed down.

"Now leave me," demanded the Pontiff, "I wish to pray."

"Certainly your Holiness," Cardinal Verdi was bowing as he backed towards the door. When he considered he was at a respectful distance, he all but turned and ran.

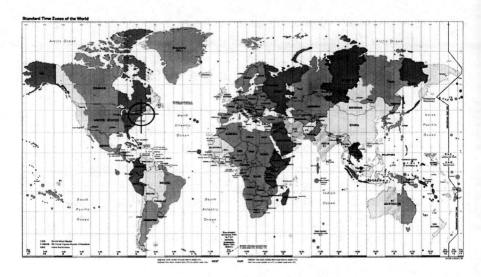

20:55 Eastern Standard Time 24ᵗʰ December 2012 (UTC 01:55)

Dr John Baltar was waiting for his opportunity to tell his wife and mother-in-law about the interesting celestial event that was taking place. All he needed was a lull in the conversation or a way to steer it around to his work. He knew that just jumping in and telling them that he was going to have to spend a lot of the evening in his office would not go down at all well. Talk of present wrapping and neighbours children was beginning to drive him mad, although he dare not show it. At last though, he spotted an opening.

"You know Mummy, John's been so busy at work lately, I was beginning to wonder if he was coming home at all this evening." Sarah still referred to her mother with the childish noun, which she seemed to find endearing, much to John's irritation.

John's mother-in-law looked genuinely surprised, as if she thought that a scientist's life was all about the pretence of working, while they just played with bubbling flasks in a laboratory.

"Ah, on that point," John interjected quickly, "I have something to tell you both." This seemed to do the trick as there was now a sudden expectant silence in the room. John continued, "You know I co-ordinate reports from astronomers around the world about their discoveries?" Sarah's mother for the briefest of moments looked puzzled, but changed her expression to one of knowledgeable boredom. Sarah, on the other hand was familiar with her husband's work, but at this moment obviously failed to see its relevance to the final preparations for their Christmas celebrations. John could see he was now committed and spoke slowly while his mind raced to think of a way of breaking the news, which his audience would find palatable.

"There's been a remarkable discovery in the night sky of a new star." He decided to keep explanations as non-technical as he could and seeing the look of mild puzzlement on the two ladies faces as they were trying to work out where this was going, he decided to play his trump card. "Well I'm pleased to announce that I have been instrumental in bringing the information about it to the world."

Sarah immediately broke into a big smile. Her mother not wishing to have her daughter or son-in-law think that she was being ignorant, joined in. "Well done darling," Sarah sounded pleased. Again her mother contributed, but with significantly subdued praise.

"However..." John now had to inject the poison. Sarah's face changed instantly and her eyes narrowed slightly as he intoned, "...it will mean I have to spend a little time at the computer this evening." There, it was out, now it was time to parry the blows.

"How much time is a little?" Sarah's mouth had turned down at the corners. She was already wondering if this wasn't an excuse to avoid him spending time with her mother.

"Oh, not that long really," John was trying to play down what he thought was likely to be several hours engaged on the project. "In fact it will probably mean that I just have to dart upstairs for a few minutes at a time." This seemed to lighten the mood a fraction.

"Oh, okay." Sarah seemed to acquiesce reasonably quickly. She could tell that what John had told them may in fact be quite important. She knew him well enough to know he was also trying to not hurt her feelings. Besides, a new star, how often does that happen? Her mother remained silent, although her expression had turned to one of deep suspicion.

John could feel the waves of mistrust emanating from her, so in an effort to pour oil on potentially troubled waters he offered, "I hope to be able to show you the star later on, if it's not too cloudy."

"Why can't we see it now?" Sarah's mother queried, thinking that she had found a chink in John's armour and was happy to exploit it.

"Because it isn't up yet," John said simply, struggling to hide the fact he thought this a dumb question.

"That'll be lovely." Sarah did her best to sound interested and turned to go back to the kitchen, bracing herself to face the inevitable barrage of words that she would receive from her mother.

As a further appeasement, John offered to finish off the Christmas cards and drop them around to the neighbours 'in a few minutes'.

"I've done it." His wife stated coldly.

John breathed out heavily and sloped off towards the stairs, trying to convince himself that the conversation had gone quite well.

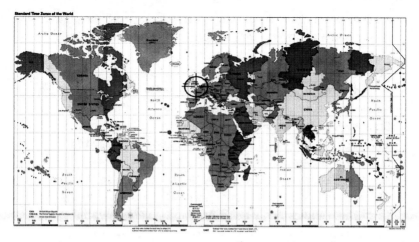

01:56 Greenwich Mean Time 25th December 2012 (UTC 01:56)

Edward Thornley had just finished arranging for his piece to camera with the presenters of the news at the 'top' of the hour. They would introduce him and he would then explain about the new star, what it was and where people could see it in the sky, if there weren't clouds in the way that is. The whole piece would last around 45-seconds. He enjoyed broadcasting and seemed to be on camera quite a lot recently, trying to give a scientific slant on the various hokum stories about the end of the world, which was either supposed to have happened a few days previously on the 21st December or was about to happen on the 31st. Some people were really quite worried and he hoped that he could go some way to help allay their fears. He was well aware of the need for balanced reporting, but it annoyed him personally that so many 'cranks' should be given valuable air-time. He also understood that an event such as a bright new supernova would also be interpreted by the lunatic fringe, as he liked to refer to them, as a portent of calamity. Getting the science in first might help diminish the impact of the nonsense.

Standing in front of the camera, he looked anxiously across the studio towards the presenters as the clock ticked to 2:00am and the music introduced the reading of the headlines. The presenters started their dialogues with their camera. Sophie Campden then announced to the viewers, "We have been

86

receiving reports of a 'new star'," she emphasised these two words heavily, "in the night sky and so we'll hand over to Edward Thornley our science correspondent for more detail about this."

Edward turned to face to camera as the red light came on above it. The autocue started to scroll gently. "Thank you Sophie. We have been receiving reports of a bright new supernova first noticed in the skies above Edinburgh this evening. A supernova is a star that explodes violently and for a short while can be seen as a very bright star. These events normally take place in distant galaxies thousands of light years from Earth and can only be spotted using very powerful telescopes, but just occasionally, once in every few hundred years or so, we have such an event take place in our own galaxy, which can be seen with the naked eye." Edward was doing his best to sound authoritative. He then went on to explain how the viewers could see it and where to look. He went on to stress there was no danger to us and that this was just a wonderful co-incidence to happen on this night of all nights and that everyone who had clear skies should try to see it. Marion Groom's picture made a fitting back drop to Edward's report.

In the next ten minutes, the switchboard at the BBC's headquarters became jammed with enquiries, reports and calls from terrified viewers.

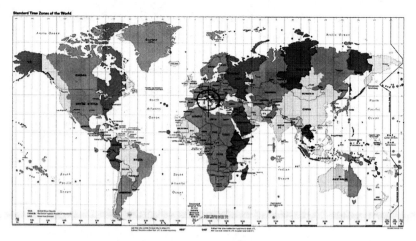

03:10 Central European Time 25th December 2012 (UTC 02:10)

Francesca Comberti was driving out of Rome on her way back home in the suburbs, after a Christmas Eve party that went on a lot longer than she was anticipating. She was a reporter on the RAI Italian State TV News. As she headed along the Via Nomentana she could see a very bright star shining through the windscreen of her car. As she left the city lights behind, this star seemed to become brighter, to the point where she drew off the road by a field and stopped the engine. She stepped out of the car and stared into the sky. Francesca studied the star for several minutes, expecting to see it move or go out, thinking that it must be an aircraft of some kind. The star didn't move. She began to feel a little uncomfortable and decided to phone in to the office to see if they had any reports about unusual sights in the night sky. She knew that her friend Michaela had agreed to work the most unpopular shift of the year and selected her number on her mobile phone and waited for it to ring.

"Hey Michaela, it's Francesca."

"Francesca, what are you doing calling me at this hour? I thought you'd be in bed asleep or with that good looking fella of yours." Michaela giggled slightly.

Francesca ignored the question and went straight to the point. "Michaela, have you guys been getting reports of anything strange in the sky tonight?"

"Well, as you come to mention it, yes we have. Several people from the towns and villages outside the city have phoned in about a bright star. Why do you ask?"

"Because I'm looking at it." There was a slight pause, as this statement startled Francesca's workmate a little.

"You are looking at it?" Michaela repeated questioningly. "I thought these were just crank calls. You haven't been drinking, have you?" She giggled again.

"Yes, I've had a little bit to drink this evening, but not enough to put me over the limit and I know a bright star when I see one." Francesca sounded a little short. Michaela was slightly concerned that she had offended her friend.

"I'm sorry, I didn't mean to suggest you're drunk," she said trying to placate Francesca.

Ms Comberti too realised that perhaps she had sounded a little off hand; she was pretty tired after all. "That's okay. I'm sorry too, if I sounded a bit sharp? I'm a bit weary; it's been a long day. Listen, will you do me a favour and check the news wires, the usual, Reuters, the BBC, CNN you know and see if there's anything going around about a bright new star. I'm coming in."

"Okay, I will. Are you sure you want to, it's very late and it is Christmas Day."

"Yes, yes. I think there's something going on and I want to get to the bottom of it. See you soon." With that Francesca hung up, got back into her car and turning sharp 180-degrees sped off back into the city and her office.

In the Vatican...

The Cardinal and Monsignor were very busy rousing sleeping cardinals, or trying to contact as many as they could on the telephone. The Pontiff was keen to assemble as many of them as he could and at the earliest possible moment. Nobody was going to get much sleep in and around the Vatican this night.

In London...

Calls were now coming into the BBC News office from various news gathering organisations including Reuters and one or two European news broadcasters who had also been receiving reports from the public about the new star. One was from a young lady named Michaela Christofori from the Italian State Television News, who seemed very interested in all that Adrika Mistry could tell her.

Michaela decided to trace the story to its source and put in a call to Gordon Gregory. Gordon admitted that he got the alert from his friend Robert Macleod and kindly gave Michaela his phone number; after all she did sound very sexy on the phone and he thought that it might go some way towards saying thanks to Robert. Passing on a hot European girl to 'coo' down the phone to him, would surely make his day.

Robert was delighted to talk to the young journalist from Italian television. Gordon was quite right; she really did have a very sexy voice. He chuckled when he told her that the story had come full circle and that it was a priest at the Vatican Observatory who first reported the sighting. Michaela chuckled too and gently turned down the invitation to visit Robert in Edinburgh next time she was in the UK. Robert felt a little deflated when she explained that she would be bringing her husband and child next time she visited Britain. As Michaela put the phone down, Francesca strode into the office.

"Hi Francesca," she greeted her friend cheerily, "Happy Christmas!"

"Er, yes uh, Happy Christmas," replied Francesca absently. She looked enquiringly at Michaela.

"You know you asked me to get more information about that star that you've seen?" Francesca looked at her friend with increasing frustration. Was she playing with her, or was she just being stupid? She tried to bury the thought. She nodded expectantly. "Well, have I made an interesting discovery?" She then began to relate her conversations with Gordon Gregory and Robert Macleod. She added that she thought Robert was 'sweet' and that he obviously fancied her even though they had only spoken on the phone.

Francesca completely ignored this and attempted to drag her friend back to the issue.

"So what do we know of this priest?"

"Nothing I'm afraid."

"Well can you try and call him then?" Francesca found herself becoming increasingly irritated. She put it down to tiredness.

"Oh, yes, sorry," Michaela tried to pacify her friend. "I don't know if there will be anyone at the Observatory at this time of night though?"

"He's an astronomer!" Francesca sounded exasperated. "He's BOUND to be up."

Michaela looked a little sheepish and immediately made to look up the number of the Vatican Observatory. Francesca walked over to her desk, sat down and tried to gather her thoughts.

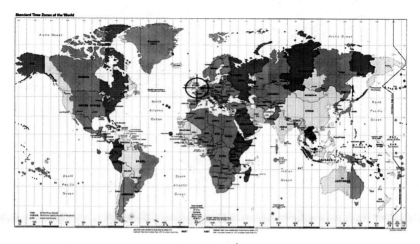

ma

02:30 Greenwich Meantime 25th December 2012 (UTC 02:30)

Since his broadcast Edward Thornley had been busy. He had contacted his colleagues in BBC Scotland and requested a film crew go out and get some footage of the star. He also got the graphics people to rustle up a short animation of a supernova to help explain what was going on with the star. He then considered contacting the usual science presenters for short pieces, but decided he was unlikely to get any sense out of anybody at this time on a Christmas morning.

The piece he had already done would probably go out again on the 3:00am and 4:00am broadcasts, but he wanted to expand it for the 5:00am report and he had his producer's backing for this. The audience should steadily climb from 5:00am as people woke or were woken up by excited children wanting to rip into their presents. Edward also wanted to get ahead of the game, as he now had discovered that Reuters had hold of the story and so various networks around the world would be running it very soon. The thought of the BBC being ahead of these others, particularly appealed to him. Getting the second cup of coffee of the night, he continued working on his script.

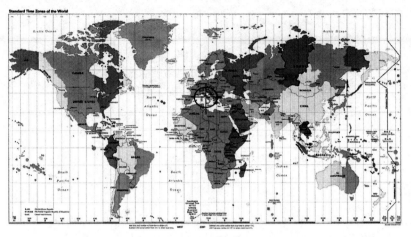

Standard Time Zones of the World

03:34 Central European Time 25th December 2012 (UTC 02:34)

The telephone rang yet again in the office of the Vatican Observatory. Father Giovanni Casparo answered it with some trepidation.

"Pronto." He tried to sound calm and authoritative. The smooth and he had to admit, sexy voice of Michaela Christofori asked if that was the priest who discovered the star.

"Yes, it is. Who is this?"

"My name is Michaela Christofori. I am a journalist and researcher for Italian State Television."

"Italian State Television!" Giovanni repeated in exclamation. This was getting out of control. He fought down his panic and continued, "How can I help you and how did you hear about me?"

Michaela briefly explained with her lilting voice, the events that led to her calling him. Giovanni found, to his consternation, her voice was calming and if he had to admit it, vaguely arousing.

The reporter then asked, "Father, can you confirm that you have discovered a new star this evening?"

"Yes, I can," he replied and went on to qualify his statement. "It is not really a 'new' star you understand, it is an old one that has come to the end of its life and exploded." He hoped that a scientific explanation would help to smother the flames of speculation that were obviously now surrounding this event.

"But you are aware that it is Christmas?" Giovanni thought this question rather fatuous as he was after all, a Catholic priest.

"Of course I am," he uttered with slight indignation in his voice. "That is just a coincidence and nothing more," he insisted.

"Who else knows about your discovery?"

'Probably the whole world by now,' he thought to himself. "I alerted the proper astronomical authorities," he did his best to keep control of this conversation.

Michaela then learned all about the International Astronomical Union, even if she didn't want to know. Next, came the awkward question:

"Did you inform your boss?"

Giovanni hesitated slightly, his mind racing, trying to second guess where this conversation was going. "Er, yes of course I did." Giovanni now wished that he had put the phone down.

"So the Vatican knows of this discovery?"

"Yes, I imagine they do."

Unexpectedly, Michaela terminated the conversation. "Well, thank you very much Father for your information and I wish you a good Christmas."

"Oh, yes, er... have a good Christmas." Giovanni tried to remember his manners. As he put the phone down he had a vague, inexplicable and uncomfortable feeling of dread wash over him. The cat was now well and truly out of the bag!

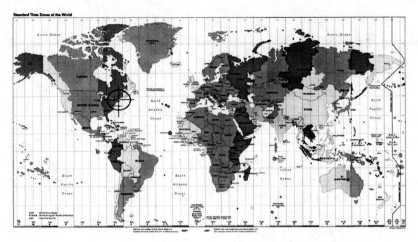

21:35 Eastern Standard Time 24th December 2012 (UTC 02:35)

Dr John Baltar went to check his email for the fifth time. He was still receiving discovery notices, in fact lots of them now, as well as the occasional update from the Canary Islands telescope. One message however caught his eye. It was from someone at the Reuters News Agency requesting confirmation about a story involving a new star that some Europeans were claiming they could see in the night sky. He felt he ought to reply to this as it was a big discovery and sooner or later the world would know about it and he wanted to be sure people had their facts straight.

John confirmed that there was a 'new' star visible and it had indeed been discovered by an astronomer at the Vatican Observatory and went on to explain the nature of supernovae stars and how this one should be visible from most of the United States by around midnight. He sent the email and went back to his wife and mother-in-law with the feeling of a good job done. When he thought about it later, he wondered why Reuters had shown an interest as they had never shown any interest in any other supernovae and there were any number of them in a given month.

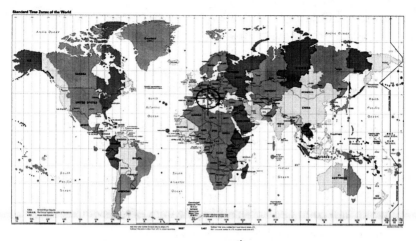

03:50 Central European Time 25th December 2012 (UTC 02:50)

A considerable number of the senior cardinals in the Vatican had now been roused from their beds. Calls had been put out to the others who were not residing within the confines of the Vatican and these too were now preparing to travel back to Rome for this important meeting. There was some grumbling due to the unsocial hour and the fact that the Pontiff had not stated what the nature of this meeting was. The only message was that it was 'urgent'. The meeting had been called for 6:00am and no-one was expected to be late. The cardinals who had to travel a considerable distance were of course given leave to make their way as fast as possible and they would be brought up to speed as soon as they arrived. The meeting was to take place in the Hall of Sixtus V, the Apostolic Library. The meeting was also to take place 'in camera'.

At the studios of Italian State Television things were working up to a fever pitch. Francesca had cleared it with the producer to do a piece about the new star for the 4:00am and the 5:00am news. As soon as he heard that Reuters and the BBC had the story, he was more than happy for them to run it. Michaela and Francesca were deep in conversation about the new information on who in fact discovered the star. A priest at the Vatican Observatory added much needed spice to the story, especially given the Christmas celebrations going on at the moment. They wouldn't go so far as to make any religious claims but the seeming coincidence was obvious and the significance of it would be left to the viewer. Just what was needed to pep up an otherwise dull early Christmas morning newscast?

Giovanni was experiencing a mixture of emotions, he was pleased with himself that he had made the discovery of course and he was thrilled with his brother's news about becoming an uncle for the first time. However, he was worried. This was all getting out of hand. He wanted it all to go away so he could go home and go to bed and have his life back on an even keel. Getting phone calls from television stations was frankly disturbing. The priest now also started to worry about what the cardinal was up to. He was by all accounts planning to tell His Holiness. He was going to tell the Pope! Where was this going to lead? He began to realise that this discovery could easily be turned into some kind of religious 'trophy'. This was not what he wanted, but he was now powerless to do anything about it. He had been told to stay put and so had to obey his superior. He really did want to go to bed...

The telephone rang. It made Giovanni jump as he'd been lost in his thoughts. He picked up the receiver shaking slightly.

"Pronto."

"Is that Father Casparo?" The questioner had a strong Roman accent.

"Yes, this is he."

"I am Monsignor Lopez, the Holy Father's private secretary. I have his Holiness here who wishes to talk to you."

Giovanni swallowed hard. He had met the Pope once or twice before but only briefly. He tried to sound calm.

"Thank you Monsignor, I would be happy to speak with him."

There was a brief pause as the handset was passed over.

"Father Casparo," the Pope sounded congenial even ebullient. "I understand that you made the discovery of this new star?"

Giovanni had to stop himself correcting the Pontiff.

97

"Er, yes Holy Father, that's right." The priest, in spite of his best efforts sounded a little shaky.

"I want to congratulate you," the Pope continued, "this is truly remarkable and a great gift from God."

Giovanni could do nothing but agree. "Yes, indeed Your Holiness."

"You must be tired after all your hard work Giovanni." The Pope used his first name!

Giovanni had to admit that he did indeed feel weary; it had been a long night. He was touched that the head of the Roman Catholic Church should be concerned for him and even used his first name. Then the Pope gave him an instruction.

"You should go home and go to bed Giovanni."

"I would Your Holiness, but I have to say Mass tomorrow morning."

"I think that we can arrange it that you do not have to. Besides, I may need you to come to Rome tomorrow as I am meeting with the Cardinals."

The Cardinals! Why should he be doing that? Giovanni's mind started racing again.

"Th ...thank you Your Holiness, it is most kind of you." Giovanni's tiredness was now causing him to stammer. "Are you saying that I do not need to say Mass in the morning?"

"Yes, quite correct," replied the Pontiff, "you're very tired and you need to rest. As I say, I may need you later."

"Thank you once again Your Holiness, you are most kind."

There was another pause and the Monsignor came back on to the line.

"Thank you for speaking with His Holiness Father Casparo," Giovanni thought that he sounded a little 'oily'. "I suggest that you carry out your instructions and go home to bed."

"I will Monsignor, I will. Goodnight."

"Goodnight to you too Father."

Giovanni's head was reeling. Why should the Pope possibly want him in the morning? Why was Italian State Television so interested in him? Giovanni decided to follow the Pope's direct instructions and pulled the keys from his pocket and went to lock up.

Lorenzo Bonelli began to read the early morning news on Italian State Television. He went through the headlines. The second item was about a newly discovered star in the night sky.

His report stated the star had been found by an astronomer/priest at the Vatican Observatory and that it was easily visible from most of Europe and the Middle East, as well as Africa and even parts of Eurasia. He told the viewers that the discovery had been confirmed by an astronomer in the Royal Greenwich Observatory in England. The broadcaster went on to say that a 'source' in the Vatican had revealed to RAI that several Cardinals were being woken early for a special 'meeting' about the star!

An orderly, who was a lay worker at the Vatican, had happened to be watching the broadcast. He alerted his boss who found Monsignor Lopez and gave him the news.

Monsignor Lopez was not happy. Not one bit. He flew into a rage and quite alarmed several nuns who were walking down the corridor towards him. The Monsignor stormed away muttering darkly to himself as he turned the corner towards the Papal apartments...

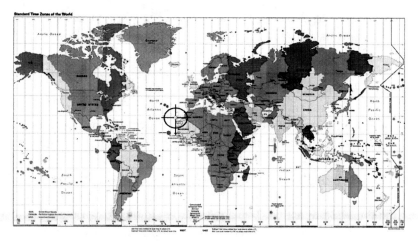

03:25 Greenwich Meantime 25th December 2012 (UTC 03:25)

Elizabeth Price had been monitoring the star for some hours and was gaining a better idea of its nature. The initial tests she'd run had indeed confirmed that it was a Type 1c Supernova. What was unusual was that this star was never earmarked as a supernova candidate. She also thought it was vaguely amusing that of all the stars to go off 'bang', this had not been in the top ten; not even close. It was even more amusing that a while ago some of the newspapers had got hold of the idea that Betelguese, or Beetlejuice as some of the tabloids liked to call it, was going to explode in 2012 and wreak devastation on the Earth. It was true that Betelguese was a more likely candidate for a supernova, which made it even funnier that a rank outsider should in fact do the honours.

There were some astro-physicists who were going to have to have a re-think about this sort of thing.

The star had been steadily brightening, which suggested that it was yet to reach its peak output. This would probably happen in the next day or two, although it was impossible to tell for certain. She emailed Dr. Baltar again with an update which she copied to the observatories on Kitt Peak and Hawaii and went to use the bathroom. On her way back she decided to do something that she seldom did and went outside to take a look at the sky. After all, she had one of the world's largest

100

telescopes to play with; she sometimes thought that looking at the night sky with just the naked eye was a bit of a letdown.

She opened the door of the building and stepped out into the darkness. She shivered in the cold thin air and looked up. She wasn't good on the constellations, she didn't need to be. The skies from up here though were pretty amazing. Stars seemed to literally pepper the sky and the Milky Way ran like a faint river of light across the heavens. It only took her a moment to spot her quarry.

"Jeez, that's really bright!" she found herself saying out loud. She wondered how many other people were now looking in the same direction. This one really was going to cause a stir... She shuddered in the cold once again and turned to head back into the building and her warm little office on the floor of the Observatory.

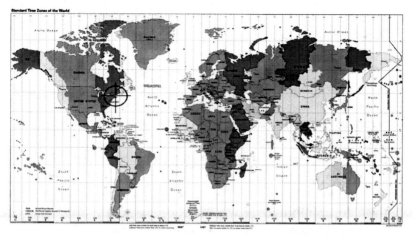

22:35 Eastern Standard Time 24th December 2012 (UTC 03:35)

John Baltar decided to check his email again. He was hoping that his mother-in-law might decide to go to bed, which would make it less awkward to absent himself from the conversation going on in the kitchen. However, she showed no sign of heading to her room, or even of feeling tired. He got a sinking feeling that she wanted to stay up until midnight and see in Christmas Day.

He thought now that the best strategy was to come out and say that he really ought to go and check his messages.

"Sorry to interrupt," he said when a slight pause in the trivia presented itself, "but I really should go and check my messages again. This supernova thing seems to be kicking off. Why, I even had an enquiry from the Reuters News Agency earlier."

These three words did the trick. Both the women turned to him and suddenly seemed much more interested in what he was saying.

"Reuters!" exclaimed Sarah. "You mean THE Reuters?"

"Yup," retorted her husband. "THE Reuters. I said that this might go big."

"Does that mean you might get interviewed?" Sarah's mother interjected. She began to think that her son-in-law wasn't just a useless scientist after all and he might just get famous. Now that would be something to brag about to her friends.

"Well, I don't know about that." John tried to put the brakes on. This he realised instantly was the wrong thing to say. He saw his mother-in-law visibly deflate and obviously go back to thinking that he was useless after all. He tried to rescue the situation and continued as chirpily as he could, "Then again, I might. Maybe even television..."

The effect was magical. Both women in unison said, "Well go on then, go and check your messages."

John turned and walked out of the room allowing himself the merest smirk once he was out of eyesight. He climbed the stairs to his study and once again woke his computer. The window on the screen was flashing a warning about unread email. He opened his reader and downloaded the messages.

There was one from Dr. Price at the William Herschel Telescope, which immediately took his interest. He opened it and read the update about the tests that she had been running. This was turning into a truly fascinating object. He wished he could go out and see it for himself. He had been monitoring the positions of the stars on his PC and realised that the Supernova had now cleared the horizon, but typically, it was cloudy. He cursed the weather. He went back to sifting through his messages and spotted one from the Observatory on Kitt Peak in Arizona. This was one that he definitely wanted to read. It was from the duty astronomer at the Nicholas U Mayall telescope, the largest telescope at the Observatory.

The message stated they had been monitoring the object since it was high enough above the horizon to get sensible readings. John appreciated they would have to let the object climb a bit so they were looking at it through less of the Earth's atmosphere. The message continued that they could confirm the findings of the WHT on the Canaries and this object was indeed a Type 1c supernova approaching maximum brightness and they would continue to monitor this exceptional event over the next few hours. He noted that the European Southern Observatory VLT telescopes in Chile had also picked up on the email traffic and had joined the monitoring the event.

John got excited. 'Wow, this thing really is huge,' he thought to himself. Now two of the world's largest and most important telescopes had confirmed the discovery. He continued to check through his messages and ignored further claims of discovery. His 'mailbox' also contained several 'crank' messages claiming that the end of the world was at hand, which he likewise ignored. He did open another email from Reuters and one from CNN News though. They had obviously picked up on this pretty quickly and were keen to have the 'scoop'.

Dr Baltar emailed back that the discovery had now been confirmed by two major telescopes and a Catholic Priest at the Vatican Observatory was named as the official discoverer. He also supplied his telephone number. As he sent the reply, he wondered if this might have been a mistake. He pushed back his chair and decided to return to the ladies, with the good news.

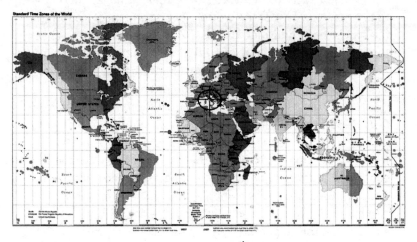

04:35 Central European Time 25th December 2012 (UTC 03:35)

Monsignor Lopez knocked at the door of the Papal apartments hesitantly. He had been debating with himself as to whether it was the right thing to do. He disliked disturbing his Holiness but his horror at what had happened overcame his reticence and he felt he simply must inform the Pontiff of this unwelcome news.

He heard a muffled 'enter' from within. He pushed the door open and stepped inside. The head of the Roman Catholic Church was sitting at his desk. This was a surprise in itself as Monsignor Lopez fully expected his Holiness to have gone to bed. He approached the desk warily, noticing that the Pope was writing speedily.

"Your Holiness," the Monsignor bowed a little as he addressed the Pontiff, "please forgive this interruption, but news of a most distressing nature has come to me."

The Pope stopped writing and looked up. "What is the nature of this 'distressing' news?" he enquired.

"One of the staff was watching a news broadcast from RAI on the television and informs me it claimed that a source from *within* the Vatican has claimed the Cardinals were being called to a special meeting about the new star." There was an unsettling pause that caused the Monsignor to shift from foot to foot.

The Pope's eyes narrowed and he frowned slightly, then his countenance changed and he seemed to shrug. "Ah well," he sighed, "I suppose it was inevitable the news would leak out sooner or later."

"But not this soon!" exclaimed Monsignor Lopez. "I haven't discovered the source of the leak yet," he continued, "but I have my suspicions."

The Pope seemed unconcerned. He disliked the idea of a 'witch hunt' and suggested that the Monsignor forgo any idea of an 'investigation'.

"Sooner or later everyone will see this miracle and the media will no doubt be looking for a reaction from the Holy See. They will have one in good time." There was another slight pause and then the Pope instructed, "Leave me now."

The Monsignor bowed low, turned and marched to the door, still seething.

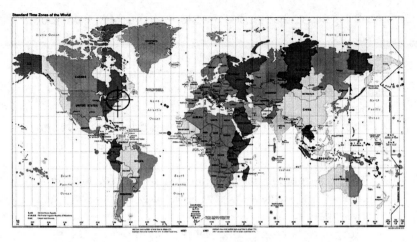

22:44 Eastern Standard Time 24th December 2012 (UTC 03:44)

The phone rang in the house of Dr. John Baltar. Sarah was the nearest to the handset and picked it up. "Hello?" she enquired.

"Oh, hi," a cheerful voice was in Sarah's ear. Is that the residence of Dr. John Baltar?"

"Yes, uh, yes, it is. Who would like to know?"

Uh, yes, sorry, this is Martin Winkleman from CNN News calling from New York City. I wonder could I have a word with Dr. Baltar if he is available, please?" he said very politely.

"Er, yes, yes, just a minute." Sarah looked bemused and covered the mouthpiece of the telephone handset with her free hand. "Did you give our number to CNN News?" she asked with a hint of a frown.

John's heart sank; he thought he was in trouble. He decided to come clean and stammered slightly, "Er, yes, yyyes, I'm afraid I did." He swallowed hard.

"Well, they're asking to speak to you." Sarah's slight frown now turned to a beaming smile and she handed over the phone to her husband, her eyes shining.

John was taken completely aback by this sudden change in his wife's mood. He accepted the handset and said flatly, "This is Dr Baltar."

"Dr. Baltar, this is Martin Winkleman from CNN News. I'm sorry to bother you, but I found your name on a message that was forwarded to me about this new star that's appeared in the sky." John started to draw breath to put him straight about it being a 'new' star, but he didn't get the chance to speak as Martin Winkleman continued, "The message stated that you are responsible for disseminating this kind of information among the astronomical community and the press."

"Uh, yes, that's right," John admitted. He then added a little defensively, "I hadn't been in touch with the press seriously yet, until the discovery had been confirmed."

"Has it been confirmed now?"

"Well yes, it has, just a few minutes ago in fact."

"That's fantastic Dr. Baltar. Would you mind doing a short telephone interview with me about it?

"Alright, when?"

"How about right now?" Martin was keen to give this story some authority.

"Ssshure." John was a little taken aback.

"Okay, I'm recording now, Dr. Baltar." There was a slight pause and then Martin asked, "So Dr. Baltar, you are the person responsible for checking claims about astronomical discoveries?"

"That is correct," John retorted rather formally.

"And can you tell me Dr. Baltar, who actually made the discovery of this new star?"

John had to stop himself correcting his interviewer about the 'new' star in fact being an 'old' star. "It has been credited to an astronomer at the Vatican Observatory in Italy."

"This astronomer is a Catholic priest?"

This question fazed John a little, but he quickly recovered. "Well, yes, I believe he is."

"Can you tell us a little more about this new star, sir?"

"Yes I can." John now felt on surer ground and relished the opportunity to at last correct the interviewer and put the record straight. "It isn't in fact a 'new' star, but an 'old' one that's come to the end of its life and has, to put it simply, exploded."

"Can you tell us how far away this star is?"

"Yes, it's around 370 light years distant from us. This means it exploded around the year 1642 by our reckoning."

"Is there any danger posed by this explosion, Dr. Baltar?"

"None whatsoever." John tried his best to sound reassuring.

"You are quite certain of that? I've heard that these events can emit huge amount of radiation and can sterilise planets?"

John was slightly irritated by this as he had already given his assurance that the Earth was perfectly safe. "Yes, I'm quite sure," John said calmly, "370 light years is a very long way. Although this type of supernova can emit gamma rays, this one doesn't seem to have done this."

"Thank you Dr. Baltar and finally, can you tell us exactly where this star is?"

"Yes, it is in the constellation of Leo and we should be able to see it low down in the eastern sky about now. Unfortunately, it is cloudy where I am and I haven't seen it yet myself." John tried to end on a light note.

"Well, thanks again Dr. Baltar and I hope the clouds lift for you." There was another slight pause and then Martin came back on the line again and once more thanked John for his assistance. He told John that he would 'edit it up' and it would probably be broadcast on the next news bulletin at 11:00 pm. Martin Winkleman hung up.

John put the handset down and looked up at his wife, who was looking very expectantly at him.

"They just interviewed me and he said that it would go out on the next main news broadcast at 11."

Sarah beamed a huge smile. Her husband was going to be famous. She threw her arms around him and hugged him. John felt the warmth of her body against his and it felt good. Sarah's mother was looking quizzically at them. She did her best to smile.

Reports were now flooding into various newspapers, TV and radio stations up and down the eastern sea-board of the United States. Thousands of people were seeing this incredibly bright star in the night sky, at least where it wasn't cloudy. Social media networks on the internet were buzzing with the news and comments from a variety of people. Places as far flung as Lima in Peru to Quebec in Canada had their news agencies dealing with countless calls and enquiries. The police forces of many countries were also inundated with calls from concerned members of the public.

23:00 Eastern Standard Time 24th December 2012 (UTC 04:00)

The Baltar household tuned into the CNN News broadcast. John was stunned to see as the introduction music began to fade, a picture of the Supernova behind the news-reader. "Where did they get that from?" he asked out loud as soon as he saw it. Sarah made a 'shhh' noise. The camera zoomed into the serious looking announcer as the last notes of the music faded.

"The top story this hour is the sightings of a 'new' star in the skies above us tonight." John sucked his teeth.

"Good evening. There is a 'new' star in the heavens this Christmas Eve." John now visibly winced. The newscaster continued, "Members of the public and astronomers alike are being amazed at the presence of a bright star never seen before, rising in the east this evening. We spoke to Dr. John Baltar of the Central Bureau for Astronomical Telegrams based at Harvard in Cambridge Massachusetts, a few minutes ago."

The heavily edited conversation that John had with Martin Winkleman was then broadcast. Sarah was beaming. The recorded conversation was stopped right after the reply to the question, "This astronomer is a Catholic priest?" And John replied, "Well, yes, I believe that he is."

John's jaw dropped.

The Newsman then continued, "Dr. Baltar went on to tell us that he didn't think there was any current danger to the Earth as the exploding star was so far away. No-one should panic. We will bring you more on this story as it develops." A momentary pause followed and the announcer continued, "Children at a major New York City hospital..."

Sarah pressed the 'off' button on the TV remote.

"What about the rest of the conversation?" exclaimed John, "I gave him much more than that; from the way they edited it, you would think the only thing they were interested in is the fact that he is a goddam priest!" John was outraged. Sarah mother's eyes narrowed at John's expletive. She disliked bad language.

Sarah looked a little disappointed, but snuggled up to her husband and said soothingly, "Never mind honey, at least you were on TV, well your voice anyway, so everyone knows who you are now."

John found little comfort in his wife's words. "But they missed the important bits," he complained.

"Well, we could wait for the news at midnight to see if they have a re-think?" Sarah suggested. John nodded sullenly. Sarah's mother was strangely silent. "I'll go and make some coffee," she said more brightly.

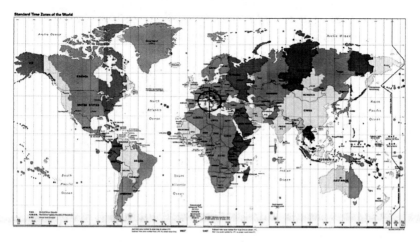

05:15 Central European Time 25th December 2012 (UTC 04:15)

Things were getting busy at the Vatican. Monsignor Lopez was doing his best to prepare things for the meeting the Pope had called for 6:00am and he felt that he had too little time to organise it all.

Cardinal Verdi was fielding telephone calls from his brother cardinals about the impending meeting, trying to find out what it was all about. Some had already turned on their televisions, seen the news and had guessed, but Leonardo Verdi was giving nothing away. He certainly didn't want to steal the Pope's 'thunder'.

Some of the cardinals had already started to assemble near to the Hall and were chatting with each other about the news. Now all of the assembly was aware of the event taking place in the skies above them and as other cardinals from outlying districts arrived they were brought up to speed with the latest news. Some of the more up to date members of the Curia were monitoring the social networking sites on their 'smart phones' and filling in the others with the information, as yet more comments and observations were being made. This entire time Monsignor Lopez seemed to dart around them and then disappear for a few minutes and then reappear again like some kind of small bird chasing insects in a garden.

Father Casparo had made his way home as instructed and was attempting to settle himself down. He knew for certain that he was not going to be able to sleep, even though by now it was his greatest wish. He considered going to bed and then thought better of it. Instead he poured himself a glass of wine and turned on the television, all the while going over in his head, the astonishing events of the previous six hours. As he flicked through the channels he caught the tail end of a report about the 'new' star. There was not enough information for him to glean what they were saying about it, but it made him very aware that the story was well and truly out there and in a few hours the whole of Italy if not Europe, if not the world would be talking about it.

He settled himself in a comfortable chair and within moments his eyes started to close and his head began to nod.

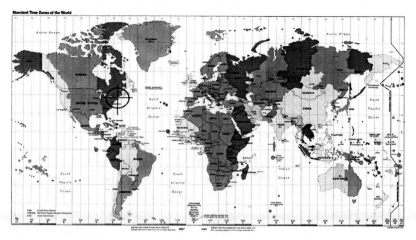

23:35 Eastern Standard Time December 24th 2012 (UTC 03:35)

Several of the major news networks across the United States of America had picked up on the story and were priming their newscasters with the information they wanted their viewing public to have. A bright 'new' star on Christmas Eve was a story too good to miss. Various national and local radio networks were also running the report in an attempt to be 'first' with the latest developments. Television news stations were finding that their website hit rate was rising rapidly.

Many local radio stations had called in astrologers to give their views and opinions as to this remarkable phenomenon. Some TV stations were even attempting to follow suit and were putting calls out to astrologers and anyone that they could think of, who might in some way have a connection to this event. One small television station called up the parish priest at their local Catholic Church for an opinion. He wasn't very happy about being woken at 5:30 in the morning and protested that he knew nothing about any 'star'.

Some more enterprising journalists had attempted to trace the story back to its source and had been calling up the Central Bureau for Astronomical Telegrams, only to get the normal recorded message, that they were closed for the Holiday period. Emails were also now pouring into Dr. John Baltar's mailbox asking for comment and occasionally, explanation.

114

John had been sitting in front of his computer typing out a 'standard' reply that he could send to all of these enquiries; 83 in the last hour. The telephone rang and to avoid it bothering his wife and mother-in-law he quickly snatched the extension phone out of its cradle in his office.

"Is that Dr. Baltar?" A man with a strong southern accent enquired.

"This is he," replied John.

"I'm Lex Newbury a journalist on the Miami Herald," he continued almost without pause, "Would you care to comment on this 'miracle star' that's in the sky? I believe that you discovered it?

"For a start I didn't discover it," snapped John testily, "And it is not a 'miracle star'. Apart from that, what would you like to know?"

"Well you see there, Dr. Baltar," Lex ploughed on unperturbed by John's curt response, "There are a lot of people saying that it's a sign from God and it is marking the 'Second Coming'."

"Nonsense," barked John and hit the button to end the call. He snorted and wondered how many more calls he was going to be getting like that this evening.

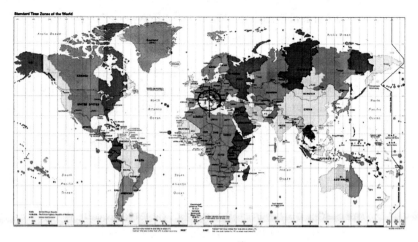

05:45 Central European Time 25th December 2012 (UTC 04:45)

The majority of the cardinals who could get to the Vatican at this unsociable hour, had now arrived. Others were coming from greater distances and would be brought up to speed personally by his Holiness the Pope, later.

The corridor was now buzzing with excitement and speculation. Several of the older members of the consistory were sitting quietly on wooden chairs; some were nodding as they fought sleep. It seemed that the whole of the Vatican was now awake and the sense that something important was about to happen, pervaded more than just the area where some of the most senior members of the Roman Catholic Church were now gathered. Even the auxiliary staff, who dealt with the day to day smooth running of this ancient institution, seemed to be alert, almost on edge.

Monsignor Lopez once again darted into view and stood for a moment looking around the assembly as if doing a 'head count'. He almost as quickly vanished again. A few moments later he reappeared and began ushering the cardinals into the entrance of the room. Slowly in deference to some of the older members, the assembly filed into the Hall. Discussions became immediately subdued and the cardinals began to take their seats.

The cardinals were all seated and looking expectantly from one to the other. The Dean of the College of Cardinals stood up. He asked that his brother cardinals would join him in a moment of prayer. All bowed their heads. He asked God to bless their endeavours on this 'holiest of mornings' as he put it.

This was the cue that Monsignor Lopez used to introduce His Holiness the Pope into the meeting. As the Pontiff stepped towards his seat, all eyes were upon him.

The clock struck 6:00am.

The leader of the world's Catholics began his address.

"My brothers in Christ," he began, "you may now be aware of a most important and miraculous event taking place in the skies above us. This star was discovered by one of our own priests, an astronomer working at our Observatory in Castel Gandolfo. God himself is giving us a sign. This new star that shines in the East as it did for the Magi two thousand years ago, shines again for us. God is showing us that it is time for renewal." The Pope continued, "After the nonsense of the 'end of the world' ideologies being touted in recent days, the Lord God is showing us that we have nothing to fear and that we should redouble our efforts to bring the message of the Christ child to a wider world."

There were murmurings of assent from the gathering. Then one of the cardinals spoke up.

"Holy Father, what should we tell our flocks as to the nature of this wonder?"

"Send the message through our brother bishops and priests to the whole of the world that Christ is asking them for their faith and obedience. This star is the messenger of God and we ignore it at our peril."

The questioner asked for further advice, "And what of the scientific community? They surely will claim that this is nothing more than a natural event and seek to dismiss any other significance."

The Pope paused for a moment before answering. "The Church is not the enemy of science, indeed it was one of our very own scientists who made this discovery known, but science does not have the ultimate answers, it can merely give us inkling into the workings of the Almighty. Science coupled with the understanding of faith enables us to see the truth." Once again the Pope paused and there was an expectant silence in the chapel. His voice now became sharper as he said, "The enemies of the Church will seek to use this event to their own ends, to dismiss our faith and claim that this undermines our beliefs. We must be robust in defence of our faith and of Mother Church. We will support you in whatever way we can if you need to deal with the media and will issue suggested answers to likely questions which you may be asked. It is important that we speak with one voice on this issue."

Another cardinal then cleared his throat and queried, "Holy Father, can we ask the name of the priest who made this event known to the world?"

"His name is Father Giovanni Casparo. After this meeting I will issue instructions for him to be brought to the Vatican to act as a spokesman to some of the press. The fact that he is both a priest and a scientist may help with the acceptance of this event with those of fragile faith. My brothers in Christ, this heavenly wonder is a sign that we need to renew our faith and bring others into our fold. Let us use it as God intended, to spread his Gospel of Good News and to proclaim the Peace of Christ."

With that the Pontiff rose from his seat and marched to the door. The College of Cardinals broke out into spontaneous applause. As the Pope walked through the door of the Hall the room burst into a cacophony of voices. One of the voices was heard to say, "We need to be very careful."

Around the world, news broadcasts at the top of the hour were now headlining the arrival of this 'guest' star. The broadcast from RAI Italian State News now had a reporter stationed outside the Vatican. Francesca Comberti who had persuaded her producer to let her handle the story, began by describing the event and proclaiming that it had indeed been first reported by a priest in the employ of the Vatican Observatory. She then handed over to the reporter in the field, Nicolo Gabertini, for any further updates.

"All I can tell you Francesca," he began, "Is that there is a meeting of the College of Cardinals going on even as I speak about this event. We do not yet know what they are discussing although I would be prepared to have an educated guess. As soon as the meeting is concluded, I'll try to get an interview with one of the cardinals."

"Thank you Nicolo, we will look forward to that." Francesca paused and drew breath. "Now on with the rest of this morning's news..."

Both Francesca's producer and the station's executive producer were delighted. RAI were the first to have the scoop on the meeting at the Vatican.

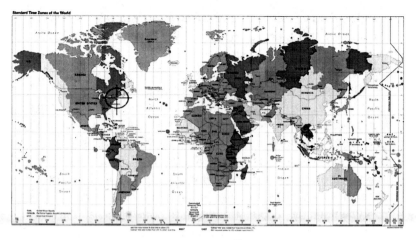

00:17 Eastern Standard Time 25th December 2012 (UTC 05:17)

John Baltar was annoyed. The report that went out on CNN had not changed significantly from the one at 11:00pm and what the entire story seemed to focus on, was the coincidence of the Supernova with Christmas and the religious significance this may have for people. His telephone had not stopped ringing either. The first few times he had answered it, but became so irritated by the questions he was being asked, that he disconnected all the telephones in the house from their wall sockets.

His wife did her best to console him. "Never mind darling," she cooed, "at least you are the one the reporters are asking for. Let's not let it spoil our Christmas."

In reply John made an 'hmm' noise in his throat.

"Well I'm off to bed. Merry Christmas!" John's mother-in-law announced suddenly. This started to make John feel better and he did his best not to show it. Sarah's mother kissed her daughter on the cheek and made to do the same to John. He gritted his teeth as she kissed the air near to his ear. She turned and went upstairs to the guest room.

Sarah turned to John and whispered, "Why don't we go to bed too, honey?" John instantly realised the implication and his mood improved immediately by a very large amount. He moved towards his wife and kissed her deeply on the mouth. His hands

120

wandered down her back. She pulled away and said "Merry Christmas darling. Come on then." They turned and headed for the stairs, John deftly flicking the light switch off as they went past it into the hall.

All across the American continent where the skies were clear, people were outside watching the new bright light in the firmament. Many were transfixed by it. Some found it romantic, others were alarmed, some were frightened and others again believed it to be a sign from the Almighty. All in all, the only people who were not aware of it were asleep in their beds.

Many specialist Travel Agents websites were being overwhelmed by people attempting to book flights and holidays to Israel and Bethlehem in particular. Some of the smaller websites were unable to cope with the traffic and crashed, much to the consternation of their users and owners.

Websites were springing up and blogs were being posted all about the star and its significance. The welter of opinion; some informed but much misinformed, was astonishing. Above all, the most voluminous were connected with 'doomsday'. Many were trying to tie this event in to the 'end of the world' scenario that had been postulated for the 21st December 2012 that had passed relatively uneventfully. Some suggestions were made that the ancient Maya astronomers had got the dates slightly wrong, which was forgivable as they were dealing with events over two thousand years in their future. Others suggested that it was the portent of the new cycle of the Mayan calendar.

There were a lot of postings from places in the southern states of the USA suggesting that this star marked the Second Coming of Christ. Some even went so far as to suggest that there should be a hunt for babies born at midnight, particularly male babies. Other postings more alarmingly, were calling for a war against 'unbelievers', particularly against Jews and Muslims.

There were even one or two postings from orthodox Jews suggesting this was marking the coming of the true Messiah that they had long awaited.

In the White House in Washington DC, the President of the United States of America was being briefed by his Press Secretary on the recent reactions to the event.

"Well Thomas, do we need to go on TV or do anything about this at the moment, do you think?"

Thomas Doubtman the President's Press Secretary was both able and experienced. He knew when and how to use the media to gain the best possible advantage for the President to show him as a great statesman and orator and to help him get his message across to ordinary Americans.

"I don't think so at the moment, sir," he replied. "We are monitoring the situation minute by minute. I have my best people on it."

"I imagine there are reporters who want my opinion though?"

"There are a few, sir, but we are keeping them at bay for the time being. We've issued a statement to the effect that you are and I quote, 'delighted to see this wonderful event happen during your tenure here at the White House and that you wish everyone a very Happy and Peaceful Christmas season.' Suitably non-committal at the moment we thought, sir."

"That'll be fine, Tom. I'll be guided by you on this one. By the way, is there any chance I can see this star myself right now?"

"Not right at the moment I'm afraid, sir, it's kinda cloudy out there but it does seem to be clearing, so maybe later."

"Okay, just let me know. I really would like to see it."

"Absolutely, sir. You have my word that we'll let you know the minute the sky clears."

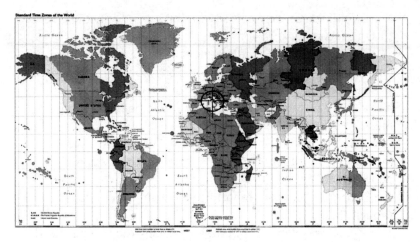

06:33 Central European Time 25ᵗʰ December 2012 (UTC 05:33)

Nicolo Gabertini was waiting, rocking on the balls of his feet, just outside the gate to the Vatican with a microphone clutched firmly in his hand. He saw a cardinal approach and signalled to his cameraman to start 'rolling'. As the unsuspecting clergyman passed through the gate, Nicolo pounced.

"Your Eminence," he almost shouted, "can you tell us the result of your meeting with the Holy Father?"

The Cardinal was taken completely off his guard. "Uh, what do you know about the meeting?" He quickly tried to regain his composure.

"I know that you have been meeting with the Pope to discuss the new star."

The Cardinal, trying not to look surprised, was unsure how much to divulge. He decided to remain non-committal. "We had a very good and informative meeting. His Holiness has declared that the star marks a time for renewal for all peoples of faith."

"Did you discuss the possibility that it also marks the Second Coming of Christ?"

The Cardinal's jaw fell open. He was struck mute. He certainly didn't have a ready answer for this one. He pulled himself together, noticing that the camera was still pointing at him. He cleared his throat and said, "No one has discussed that possibility." As soon as the words left his mouth he realised that

123

what he just said could easily be misinterpreted. Nicolo Gabertini wasted no time in seizing the opportunity and to exploit it to the full.

"So you admit that it is a possibility?"

The Cardinal's head swam. He was tired; he'd had little sleep. "No, I mean yes. Er, I mean no." He drew breath and did his best to recover. "What I'm saying is that it was not discussed in the meeting and that it *might* be a possibility, but highly unlikely don't you think?" The Cardinal thought that he had managed to recover quite well and even turned a question back on the questioner.

"But it is still a possibility?" Nicolo knew that he had the cardinal on the defensive now.

"In God's universe everything is possible. Good morning." The Cardinal sped away as fast as he thought was seemly.

Nicolo turned to the camera and said, "Well there you have it, a senior member of the clergy admitting that the star in the east could be a sign of the Second Coming. With that, I'll hand you back to the studio."

Francesca was fighting the urge to grin. She was seeing in her mind the ratings sky rocket. "Thank you Nicolo." She turned back to her autocue and continued, "And now for the rest of the morning's news..."

The cardinal was still pacing rapidly down the street, wishing that the ground would open up and swallow him. His mind was racing. 'It's possible that this marks the Second Coming of Christ?' He ran through this in his head over again. He hoped that nobody was out of bed yet and watching the news. With luck it was a very small audience.

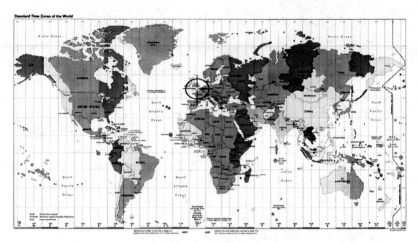

05:45 Greenwich Mean Time 25th December 2012 (UTC 05:45)

Christmas was just starting at No.10 Downing Street. The Prime Minister's Personal Private Secretary was just greeting the staff and went into his office and woke up his computer. He hadn't had much sleep with the Christmas party going on into the small hours but he managed to slip away soon after midnight as he knew that he was on duty for at least part of the day.

He opened his email and scanned through the list. One caught his eye marked 'Urgent: New Star for the attention of the PPS.' It was from one of the media staff at the Home Office. He opened it and read through its contents quickly. It contained reports from various media outlets including the BBC and a link to a report that had gone out on CNN. He picked up the phone and started to dial the Prime Minister's Press Secretary.

The phone rang several times before a rather bleary sounding voice said 'Hello'.

"David? It's Brian. Sorry to wake you and all that but I think you need to come in. Something seems to be brewing that may need your expert attention."

"What is it Brian? Can't it wait? It's bloody Christmas morning."

"I wouldn't have called unless I thought it was urgent now would I? There's a good fellow. Chop, chop."

"You haven't told me what it's all about yet." David's voice was now sounding more firm and decidedly unhappy at being woken so early after the Christmas party.

"No I haven't," stated Brian coldly. "You'll be briefed when you come in." Brian put the phone down. He wasn't very fond of David Cunningham. In fact he thought he was 'jumped up' as he liked to put it but the PM was seemingly enamoured of him, so he had to bite his tongue most of the time. Getting him out of bed at this hour of the morning when he was hung over seemed rather pleasing.

Brian Masterson now spent some time scanning the Internet for more on this story. He found plenty of material. He thought of placing a call to the Royal Greenwich Observatory, but realised that his call was unlikely to be answered. He rather wanted to have it confirmed though. He continued his searches and found a link to a story on the BBC website uploaded by a reporter at BBC Scotland, stating that the discovery had been confirmed by an astronomer at the Royal Observatory Edinburgh. 'At last' he thought, 'somebody with some credentials'. The next call he placed was to the BBC offices in Glasgow. He got through to the switchboard who immediately, on hearing who he was, put him through to Margaret Henson, the Deputy Controller.

"Good morning Mr. Masterson, how may I be of help?"

"Thank you for taking my call," Brian Masterson was nothing if not polite. "I understand that you broke the story about this new star that apparently has popped up in the sky?"

"We did, sir. In fact it was one of my researchers here. Would you like to speak to him?"

"Yes please." Brian had a note of irritated patience in his voice.

"I'll be a few moments if that's okay?" Margaret put the call on hold. She needed to find the extension number of the news desk researcher.

Gordon Gregory practically jumped out of his chair when his phone rang. He was watching the clock and day dreaming, looking forward to when he could go home. He was even more surprised when the Deputy Controller of BBC Scotland came on the line.

"I believe it was you who broke the story about this new star, Gordon?" enquired the soft lilting voice.

"Er, yes, that's right, ma'am" Gordon spoke hesitantly.

"I have the Prime Minister's Private Secretary on the other line. He would like a word with you, if that's alright?"

Gordon swallowed hard. He had never spoken to anyone *really* important before. A few minor celebrities and lowly officials, yes, but not senior government people. "Yes, yes, that'll be fine, thank you."

"I'll put him through just now." The phone line clicked and Gordon realised that he was now connected to the Prime Minister's Private Secretary.

"This is Gordon Gregory. I'm sorry to have kept you waiting, sir. How may I help?"

"Ah! Mister Gregory, thank you for your time. I believe that you broke the story about the new star?"

"Yes, sir, that's correct." Gordon realised that he was shaking slightly.

"Well Gordon," Brian continued more familiarly, "Could you tell me who it was at the Royal Observatory in Edinburgh that you spoke to?"

"I can, sir. His name is Professor Andrew McVeigh."

"And can you give me the Professor's phone number?"

"I can and would you like his email address too?" Gordon was trying not to sound like he was grovelling.

"That would be good." Brian sounded like a parent who was doing his best to be patient with an errant child.

"I'll just put you on hold a moment, sir."

Brian heard the line go quiet and he pursed his lips wondering how long he was going to have to wait this time. Gordon couldn't find his smart phone among his papers. He searched his pockets. In desperation he rummaged around his desk again and found it buried under some other papers he hadn't checked the first time. He started to scroll through the list of names and phone numbers so he wouldn't waste too much time. Brian didn't sound like a man who enjoys to be kept waiting. He pressed the 'un mute' button and reconnected with Brian Masterson.

"Sorry to keep you waiting sir," Gordon sounded slightly out of breath, "I have the details now."

"Carry on." Brian did his best not to sound tetchy.

Gordon quickly gave the Prime Minister's Private Secretary the contact details of Professor McVeigh.

"Thank you Gordon," Brian sounded aloof, "I appreciate your help. Goodbye." And with that Brian hung up.

Gordon mouthed a 'goodbye' as he heard the line click. 'Was that it?' he asked himself, 'A chance to speak to someone really important and all I did was give him someone else's phone number.' He seemed annoyed at himself. The phone rang again; he composed himself and lifted it to his ear. It was the Controller once again.

"So Gordon, what did he ask you?"

"He just wanted the contact details of that Professor at the Observatory in Edinburgh," Gordon admitted.

"Oh, just that?" Margaret too sounded disappointed.

"Yes, ma'am, just that."

"Okay. Thank you Gordon." She then tacked on, "Good work."

"Thank you ma'am." The phone clicked and hung up once again. Gordon felt deflated.

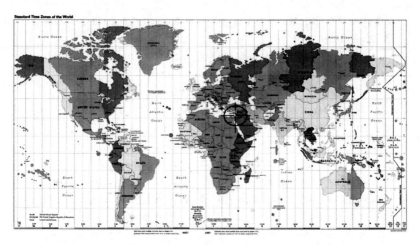

07:58 Israel Standard Time 25th December 2012 (UTC 05:58)

People in Jerusalem and Tel Aviv and most outlying areas in
Israel were waking up and receiving the news of the 'new star'.
Many had gathered in groups and were looking at the sky, which
was now in daylight. The stars had all gone out, bar one. Low
down in the western sky, the Supernova shone like a beacon.

The newspapers were full of it. So were the TV channels.
Social Media sites on the Internet were awash with comments
and speculation. Many people were just simply amazed; they
had never seen anything like it in their lives. Some were
frightened and worried. Last minute bookings for hotels and
lodgings in and around Bethlehem were always high at this time
of year; nobody had seen it like this before though. There was
not a hotel or room to be had anywhere. Thousands of people
were being disappointed. All flights into Israel were now booked
solid. People were attempting to get into the country overland
from Jordan and even Egypt.

The Prime Minister of Israel had called an emergency
meeting of the cabinet to decide how to handle this sudden
influx of humanity. They decided, in the interests of safety, to
close their borders with immediate effect. They were also aware
of pressure from more extremist religious groups to make a
statement about the 'star'. Some were becoming concerned
about the stance of many Christians already in the country and

also abroad. A 'spokesperson' was put on television to explain the reason why the government had closed the country's borders. This gave rise to even more speculation...

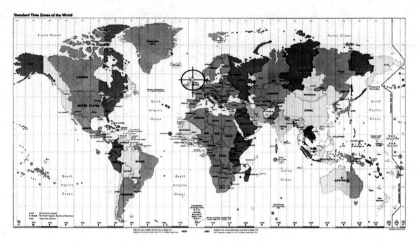

Standard Time Zones of the World

08:02 Greenwich Mean Time 25th December 2012 (UTC 08:02)

The phone rang at the house of Professor and Mrs. McVeigh. Mary picked it up and gave a greeting. Andy who had just come back into the room looked at his wife quizzically as she said into the mouth piece, "He's come back just now. I'll put him on the line for you." As she motioned for Andy to come towards her, she proffered the telephone mouthing almost silently, "It's the Prime Minister's Private Secretary."

Andy didn't quite catch all of what she said and thought that she meant that the Prime Minister was on the line. He looked a little surprised as he took the handset from his wife.

"This is Professor McVeigh. How may I help you sir?" Andy quickly realised his mistake as the caller identified himself to Andy. He was not however, that disappointed.

"I'm sorry to call you so early on Christmas Day," Brian Masterson sounded as cheerful as he could, "but can you assure me that you did indeed confirm the discovery of this new star?"

"I did that, sir." Andy continued to explain that it wasn't a 'new star', but an old one. Brian did his best to interject but Andy was already in full flight. Almost without a pause he carried on to regale the PPS that it was discovered by a young Catholic priest from the Vatican Observatory. Brian was aware of this as he had been reading a lot about it on the Internet. He was pleased to have it confirmed by the slightly irritating old

Scot. As soon as Andy's story lulled, Brian took his chance to stop him before he had to listen to yet another diatribe.

"Well thank you so much Professor. This has been most useful. I'll try not to bother you again but I hope you won't mind if I do need to call you later?"

"Not at all sir, it has been a pleasure to speak to you." Andy felt rather pleased with himself and before he forgot he proffered a 'Merry Christmas to you, sir."

"Oh, yes," Brian had almost forgotten his usually impeccable manners, "And a Merry Christmas to you too."

Andy put down the telephone and turned to his wife saying, "What a nice man." Mary nodded.

As Brian Masterson finished the call, he breathed out heavily. He sincerely hoped that he wouldn't have to deal with any more people like that again today. At that moment there was a faint tap on the door and it swung open a little. One of the household staff put their head around the door and notified Brian that the Prime Minister was awake and breakfasted and would like to see him. Brian nodded his thanks. Collecting his thoughts he headed for the door and then the stairs to the Prime Minister's private apartments.

In the Middle East...

Top level meetings were now being called by various governments in Amman in Jordan, Cairo in Egypt and Damascus in Syria. Heads of state in other countries in the Middle-East were also convening their senior politicians and advisors from Riyadh to Tehran. Two topics were on the agenda; what should be the response of government to this unusual phenomenon and how should they respond to the sudden closure of the Israeli borders.

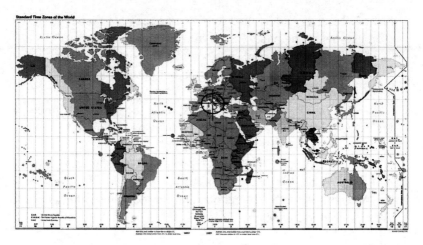

09:15 Central European Time 25th December 2012 (UTC 08:15)

The Italian Prime Minister had been watching the coverage of the Supernova on the television with his family. He decided that he too would call in his senior advisors and more especially his press secretary to discuss how they could use the reports to their advantage. After all, the man who discovered this was an Italian. He kissed his wife and children with promises of coming back as soon as possible and called his driver to take him to the parliament buildings. He was greeted by paparazzi at his front door. There was nothing unusual in this but this time they were not asking him about the economic situation or stories of alleged philandering, it was all about the 'star'. He fobbed them off with the promise of a press briefing later and bundled himself into his waiting car as quickly as was seemly. His driver sped away leaving camera flashes still firing, in his rear view mirror.

The Prime Minister switched on his mobile phone and started to call several members of his cabinet. He wanted to have a pre-meeting briefing with his political advisor and his minister for science in particular. He hoped this meeting would be short and to the point. As his car drew up outside the Palazzo Montecitorio he was greeted by yet more reporters. His driver got out of the car and pushing some of the more determined members of the press out of the way opened the door for the

133

Prime Minister. He handed his charge over to the Prime Minister's bodyguards who were following in another car and who then jostled the reporters and cleared a path to the door of the building. Once inside the Prime Minister headed directly for the meeting room. He was pleased to see that his most senior ministers were already there. Without formality, he sat down and convened the meeting.

He wanted his minister's opinions on how they could get good press for the country, and more importantly the government, out of this whole affair. He particularly wanted to hear from his press secretary.

Vincenzo Palermo had that role and was a smooth and efficient operator. That's why the Prime Minister liked him. He made several suggestions and pointed out it was possible that the Vatican might try to 'steal all the thunder' of this story. The political ramifications of this would be that the government could appear to have been caught on the back foot and this would make them look weak and indecisive. It was agreed that Vincenzo should stage a press briefing to be held by the Prime Minister in one hour. This did not give him long to put together a speech and so he retired from the meeting to draft it. The science minister in the meantime tried to bring his boss up to speed on the factual information so he could sound authoritative on camera. His political advisor let it be known he had just heard that Israel had closed its borders with Egypt and Jordan. No one paid much attention to this.

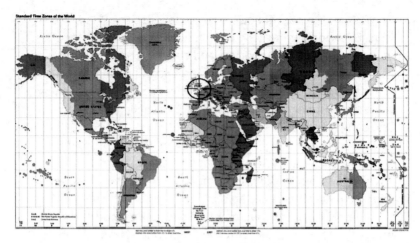

08:35 Greenwich Mean Time 25th December 2012 (UTC 08:35)

The Prime Minister listened carefully as Brian Masterson briefed him on the morning's events. He was gratified to hear it had been a British scientist who had confirmed the discovery of the star. He asked if the Americans were aware of all this and Brian assured him they were. He asked Brian if the President had anything to say about it and was slightly re-assured when his Private Secretary told him that as far as he knew, he was still in bed. He didn't want the Americans trying to somehow take the credit for it. Brian then turned to the matter of the press and stated that David Cunningham was on his way in. The PM looked relieved. Brian wished that he could share his enthusiasm for the man.

"Prime Minister, I thought you should be aware, I've just heard that Israel has shut its borders." The PM looked alarmed; tensions in the Middle East were as usual, running high. "Don't be overly concerned Prime Minister. I believe it's just a precaution, as they're being overwhelmed with visitors." The Prime Minister nodded.

"Has this caused any problems anywhere else?"

"Not that I am aware, sir."

There was a noise at the door and a dishevelled David Cunningham entered the room looking decidedly the worse for wear. Brian 'tutted' under his breath.

"Sorry PM," David did his best to look contrite, "Still recovering from the party." He grinned ineffectually.

Brian urged David to sit down and did his best to bring him up to speed as efficiently as he could.

"Right!" David said emphatically. "I think we should arrange a press conference. The PM should be seen to be 'in the know' on the event. I'll arrange it with the Beeb and the Independents." David jumped to his feet and nearly tumbled over. Brian winced and shook his head.

"I'll request that the Minister for Science come in, shall I Prime Minister?"

"Oh, er, yes, good idea."

Brian too rose from his seat and moved to the door. "I'll keep you briefed, obviously." The PM nodded once again.

Brian followed David down the stairs to his office.

"Jeez, do I have a headache?" David moaned softly.

"For God's sake man, get a grip." Brian hissed back...

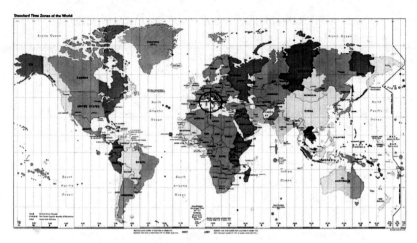

09:45 Central European Time 25th December 2012 (UTC 08:45)

Father Giovanni Casparo jerked awake as his telephone rang. His neck hurt from the position he had been sleeping in, sat in his arm chair. He stumbled over to the phone and uttered a bleary 'Pronto'.

"Giovanni, it's Leonardo Verdi."

"Yes, Your Eminence." Giovanni was doing his best to bring himself back into wakefulness.

"I have a message from his Holiness for you."

Giovanni was now fully awake and was doing his best to rub some warmth into his neck.

"You are instructed to come to the Vatican. The Holy Father wishes you to act as spokesman for this miraculous event." In spite of the fact that the Cardinal himself had little sleep, he sounded remarkably cheerful.

"Okay." Giovanni sounded a little hesitant.

The Cardinal continued, "We are sending a car for you. You need to be ready in an hour. Bring a bag with some clothes; you may be staying a day or two." Before Giovanni had a chance to question his caller, the Cardinal put down the receiver.

Giovanni's heart sank. He was tired and uncomfortable and now he was about to be thrown into the 'limelight', a role he neither sought nor wanted. He just had enough time to have a shower and change. He hoped the hot water would ease his aching neck. Ascending the stairs, he went to start preparing himself for an uncertain day or two.

In the USA...

Maternity hospitals across America were receiving phone calls from journalists asking about the birth of babies, particularly male babies, around midnight. Some hospitals refused to divulge the information saying that it was 'not hospital policy to give out such information'. Others were more co-operative. Of these only a handful could admit to births around midnight and a couple of those were of baby girls. A woman had placed a call with the Chicago General Hospital asking if they had a baby boy born at 4pm on Christmas Eve. The receptionist did not think that there was a problem disclosing this information and told her that they indeed did have such a child. The lady asked if she could confirm the child's name and birth weight. The receptionist told her the child weighed 7lbs 10 ounces and was in good health and his family name was Casparo. The lady thanked the receptionist having explained that it was her neighbour across the street's child and she had been told by a friend the boy had been born at 4pm, but she just couldn't remember their name. This seemed plausible enough to the receptionist and she asked if the lady needed any other information. The lady once again thanked her and said no that would be fine and she would try and get along tomorrow with a present and a bunch of flowers. The phone went down and the call was immediately forgotten by the busy receptionist. Unbeknownst to her, there had been several other calls to maternity units in the region that evening.

One journalist got through to the same hospital and managed to speak to the ward sister where Mrs. Casparo and her new arrival were now settling in. The journalist chatted to the nurse for a few moments in a friendly manner and then asked if they had any baby boys born at or around midnight as they may be in for a 'special treat' from his newspaper.

"Why yes," exclaimed the sister, "we do have one; a little boy born at the stroke of midnight."

The journalist could hardly contain his delight. He asked for the mother's name and the ward number. The ward sister liked the man and told him that the family name was Alvarez and that the mother had told her the child was going to be called Jesus. The ward sister could not see the harm in it, especially if the family were going to be showered with gifts from the newspaper. The journalist was very excited. He thanked the sister and said he would be in touch again soon. As he put the phone down, he burst into laughter, stood up and still chuckling, marched into his editor's office.

In the Middle East...
There had been a few reports of sporadic rioting at a couple of border crossings into Israel. The border guards had made no exception. They had been told to keep people out. This seemed to include not only tourists but also migrant workers from the West Bank and Gaza as well as Israelis themselves who had been out of the country and who now wanted to get back home. The only way into or out of the country was by air. The Jordanian government was in the process of filing an official complaint. Television news crews were at the border crossings filming the unrest.

10:47 Central European Time 25th December 2012 (UTC 09:47)

The Mercedes pulled up outside the house of Father Giovanni Casparo. The driver got out and knocked on the door. Giovanni greeted him and picked up his bag. He closed the door behind himself, climbed into the car and got as comfortable as he could. Giovanni noticed there was a small flag on the front of the car showing the emblem of the Vatican. His neck felt a little better for the hot shower. Somewhat refreshed, although still tired, he didn't feel like chatting to the driver and so they sped along in silence. It was only a fairly short drive into the city and the silence was not uncomfortable. What he was not prepared for though, was the waiting army of paparazzi as they pulled up to the gates of the Vatican. He sank down in his seat with an exclamation of dismay. The driver had taken the precaution of locking the car doors and he did his best to edge his way through the crowd. It didn't take long for the photographers to figure out who was sitting in the car and within a few moments, the astronomer who made the initial discovery of the 'new star' had camera flashes firing strobe-like into his face, albeit through the glass of the car window. Within a matter of hours, his face would be on practically every front page around Europe and on several websites even more quickly.

Giovanni breathed a sigh of relief as the car finally slid past the Guard and the photographers were kept firmly behind the Vatican gate. He thanked the driver for his care which was acknowledged with a simple 'Prego'. As the car pulled to a stop in front of one of the buildings, Cardinal Verdi flew out of a large wooden door, cassocks flapping around him like a demented bird and greeted his astronomer friend as if he were a long lost brother.

"Giovanni!" he cried, "It's so good to see you again; I'm so glad you could come." He opened his arms to give the priest a familial hug.

Giovanni felt like asking if he'd had a choice, but managed to bite his tongue. He also managed to muster a weak smile and had the good sense to take the proffered contact. He even managed to hug the cardinal back.

"Come my friend," beamed Leonardo, "you must be tired after all the excitement of last night. Come and have a glass of wine."

This actually sounded attractive to the priest and he quickly nodded his acceptance. The Cardinal ushered him into the building and then to a small side office. Giovanni sat down in a comfortable chair and began to feel a little more appreciated. Leonardo poured two glasses of Chianti and handed one to the priest.

"Well now," said the Cardinal in a paternalistic tone, "the Holy Father has instructed me to have you act as the Vatican spokesman for all things related to this miracle in the heavens."

Giovanni did his best to keep his expression blank.

"So, I hope you are willing to talk to the press about what you discovered and how you discovered it?"

"If the Holy Father requests this, then of course I will comply."

"Good, good." Leonardo paused and then continued, "Be careful what you say, though. The Church's line on this at the moment is that this is a sign from God encouraging us to renew our faith. There has been speculation in some quarters about this signalling the 'Second Coming'."

Giovanni made a noise in his throat and looked aghast.

The Cardinal ignored him and went on, "This just may be the case, but until we have proof of such an event we cannot be seen to endorse this view."

Giovanni turned white and nodded silently. He wanted to say that there would never be such a proclamation from *his* lips. Somehow though, he felt that he should just say nothing.

"So, are you ready to be thrown to the wolves?" Cardinal Leonardo Verdi looked almost gleeful.

Again, it was all the astronomer-priest could do to nod his assent. He started to feel himself breaking out into a cold sweat and his heart-rate started to climb as if he was about to be marched to the scaffold to face a hangman. Leonardo led him back to the door and out of the building and on to the main gate of the Vatican. He muttered some instructions to the Guard and the gate was swung open. Immediately, the camera flashes started up again and it was all Giovanni could do to stop himself from turning around and running away. The Cardinal gripped him by the elbow; he could tell that the priest was nervous. He spoke to the waiting journalists and cameras briefly to introduce Giovanni to them as the man who made the discovery and who would be prepared to answer a few questions.

There was an immediate barrage of voices hurling questions in his direction. At first he couldn't make any of them out, but the journalists nearest him caught his attention and started to fire a couple of simple questions in a loud enough voice for him to hear clearly.

"Father Giovanni," one of the journalists asked, "How did you make this amazing discovery?"

The priest felt on safe ground here and gave a potted version of how he was at the Observatory just drinking in the stars when he noticed it.

Another question flew from the crowd. "Who did you report it to in the first instance?"

Again, Giovanni felt comfortable with this and explained that he contacted the Central Bureau for Astronomical Telegrams in the USA, as was the usual thing to do in such circumstances. He added that he also informed his immediate boss Father Giuseppe Carpentiere, via text message.

The next question came out of the left field and caught Giovanni unawares.

"I understand that your brother and his wife have just had a baby boy. Do you think that there is any connection between this and the star?"

He had almost forgotten about the new addition to his family. At first this seemed a stupid question. Of course there was no connection.

"I doubt it," was all that he could think to say and scowled at the journalist.

However, the questioner was not to be put off and pressed on. "Do you believe that the star marks the Second Coming of Christ?"

The priest now felt like someone was trying to drown him. He turned to look at the Cardinal with an expression that somebody might have if reaching for a lifebelt. Leonardo just nodded as if to say 'answer the question'.

Giovanni swallowed hard and the rabble in front of him seemed to grow quiet. His mind raced, what was he to say to this? He knew what he would like to say and it probably wasn't fit for broadcast. He drew a deep breath and said, "I am a humble priest and astronomer, I do not wish to speculate on such things. The Holy Father has said that the star reminds us to renew our faith and that's as it should be." Giovanni then pulled himself to his full height and steadily turning around ignored the further barrage of questions aimed at him, he asserted his authority and began to walk back through the gate. The Cardinal looked slightly surprised and trying not to be caught off guard, he hurried after him. The priest's mind raced and he immediately asked himself why he hadn't denied that the star marked the Second Coming. He couldn't understand why he didn't just say an emphatic 'NO'.

As the Cardinal drew level with him he said, "Well done Giovanni, you handled that well. The Holy Father was right to put his trust in you."

Giovanni just kept walking at a steady pace back to the door. He wished he had never seen the wretched star.

In the Middle East…

The Syrian government sent a message to the Israeli Prime Minister demanding that the Israelis open their border with Syria with immediate effect and that they would consider any other action to be hostile.

A few extremist Islamist websites were now suggesting that the West were going to be using the appearance of the star as an excuse for a new 'crusade' and suggested that all good Muslims should prepare for 'battle' as they put it.

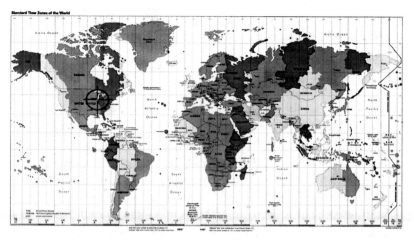

04:30 Central Standard Time 25th December 2012 (UTC 10:30)

The man and woman entered the Chicago General Hospital by the main entrance. The man was quite nondescript other than for his short beard and glasses. The woman next to him was a little over-weight, possibly pregnant, with auburn hair but again nothing that would make her 'stand out' in a crowd. They walked the length of the corridor as if they knew where they were going very well. After a short distance down the main corridor they turned into another, following signs for the maternity wing. Nobody noticed them as they disappeared into a darkened side room, only to emerge a minute or two later, this time the man attired in a white coat with a stethoscope slung casually around his neck in the manner of most doctors. The woman looked very convincing as a nurse in her starched uniform. They continued their march toward the maternity wing, attracting no attention whatsoever.

Salvatore Casparo was now in one of the cradles just down the hall from where his mother was sleeping peacefully. She had fed her new baby and was quite exhausted from this and the labour. The midwife had suggested some hours ago that Marco go home and get some sleep. Marco hadn't needed much persuading as he was quite exhausted himself, and wearily trod down the corridor from the maternity suite towards the main

144

entrance and the car park. His wife was now resting and their baby was fast asleep in the safe hands of the nursing staff.

It wasn't until now that a doctor and nurse opened the door of the nursery. The doctor introduced himself to one of the nurses and chatted to her in a relaxed manner, explaining that he was deputising for the obstetrician who had been called away on an emergency. He then asked to see the Casparo boy, as the obstetrician had asked him to check up on the child. The staff nurse pointed him out and was immediately called away to another infant. The doctor moved towards the baby while his companion hung back, still looking relaxed and as if she meant to be there. The doctor made to examine the baby for a few moments and lifted the child from his cradle which was instantly noticed by the staff nurse who quickly came over to see what was going on. The doctor explained that he thought that the child was slightly jaundiced and should be put under ultra-violet lights for a while as was the normal procedure. The staff nurse looked a little quizzically at the doctor but acquiesced when the doctor insisted. She said that she would take him to the 'light room' herself shortly. The doctor explained that he and his companion were heading that way anyway and would be happy to oblige. At that moment an auxiliary nurse, who was assisting the staff nurse, attracted her attention yet again; she had lost count how many times that evening. The staff nurse thanked the doctor saying that'd be very helpful as she was rather rushed. The doctor said 'don't mention it' and turned and signalled to his companion to come over. The staff nurse hurried away glancing back to the pair as she went. The auxiliary nurse was having difficulty getting another infant to feed from a bottle and the staff nurse turned away from the doctor to give the problem her full attention. When she looked up again the doctor and the nurse were wheeling the baby in its cradle calmly out of the room. She said to the auxiliary she thought there was something odd about the doctor, but another wail from the child in her arms immediately put it out of her mind. The auxiliary nurse seemed disinterested in anything other than trying to get the baby to take her bottle.

04:43 Central Standard Time 25th December 2012 (UTC 10:43)

The hospital CCTV cameras caught a clean shaven man and a slim blonde woman walking out of the main entrance of the hospital. The woman was carrying what was obviously a baby in her arms. They looked unhurried and very much like two happy, new parents. They were seen to wave a 'good bye' to the staff at the reception desk, who happily waved back.

04:52 Central Standard Time 25th December 2012 (UTC 10:52)

The staff nurse had finished instructing the auxiliary how to encourage a new born to take a bottle and decided to go and check on the Casparo child in the 'light room' which was just along the corridor. She opened the door to the room. There were three cradles in there, two with babies asleep under the lights wearing tiny cloth shades over their sensitive eyes. The third cradle was empty. She felt a wave of panic hit her and checked around the room in case she hadn't understood what was going on. The panic she felt turned to cold dread. She turned on her heels and flung the door of the light room open and burst into the corridor once more. She checked the only other room off the corridor and found to her astonishment, a woman's auburn wig, nurses uniform and a doctors white coat and stethoscope. She ran back to the nursery and shouted at the auxiliary to call security. She was now white and shaking. Frantically she checked the nursery again hoping she had made a mistake. The alarm went off and the wing went into 'lock-down'. Two men in brown uniforms ran along the corridor towards the nursery.

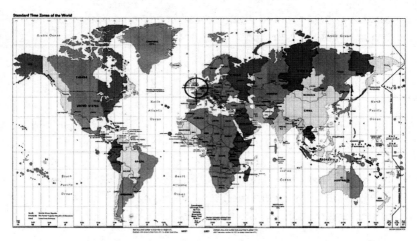

11:05 Greenwich Meantime 25th December 2012 (UTC 11:05)

David Cunningham had arranged for the Prime Minister to give a press briefing at No.10 about the new star. The BBC unit were now on their way to record the interview with him. Sir Donald Lacey, the Government's Chief Scientific Officer had been called in to brief the PM and to help draft a script for the interview. The Prime Minister had been opening a few Christmas presents with his family and seemed a little distracted when Sir Donald arrived, questioning David as to whether he thought a press briefing was in fact necessary at this time.

David assured him it was and suggested that otherwise the Italians and Americans would be seen to be 'on the ball' and the PM would not. The Prime Minister immediately agreed. Sir Donald gave a quick outline to the PM about supernova stars and how this one was somewhat unusual, especially given the timing. The Prime Minister seemed a little slow to grasp this, until David explained that the Internet was alive with speculation about the Second Coming of Christ. The PM merely responded with 'That'll be the day'! The BBC team arrived and began setting up their equipment in a side room. Brian Masterson knocked on the door and entered.

"Prime Minister, I've just heard that both the Syrians and Jordanians have issued formal complaints against the Israeli government about their sealed borders. It seems that the

Egyptians are also getting upset and are discussing taking their complaint to the United Nations."

'That should slow them down then,' retorted the Prime Minister. Brian Masterson allowed himself the merest hint of a smile at the PM's sage wit.

"The Foreign Office is monitoring the situation. I'll let you know should anything further develop."

'Very good; thank you Brian.'

"Prime Minister." Brian gave the slightest bow and left the room.

David and Sir Donald had put the finishing touches to the Prime Minister's script for his interview and showed it to him prior to the recording. The PM seemed happy enough with it and went into the other room and sat in the chair opposite Barbara Daly the reporter who had been assigned to do the interview. The producer asked for quiet and the sound man then asked the Prime Minister to say something so that he could get a 'level'. The interview was due to be broadcast at noon as part of the midday news bulletin and the producer was keen to get on with it, in case it needed re-recording or, much editing. The soundman nodded to the producer who then said 'Okay. Action'.

Barbara Daly thanked the Prime Minister for his time on this Christmas Day, to which the PM mumbled, 'Always a pleasure'.

"And so Prime Minister," Barbara continued, "we have a new star in the sky. It seems to be provoking much speculation and interest all over the world. There has been an overwhelming rush by those who give this a religious significance, to try and get into Israel and we hear that Bethlehem has been swamped with visitors. Israel has closed its borders in response, which has seemingly upset her Arab neighbours. What is the government's take on all of this?"

"Well firstly Barbara, it is not a new star but an old one which has exploded." The Prime Minister was enjoying sounding knowledgeable and authoritative. Sir Donald, who was standing behind the producer, gave a satisfied nod. The Prime Minister continued, "We quite understand that some people may read a religious significance into this..." Barbara immediately interrupted.

"The star was discovered by a Roman Catholic Priest at the Vatican Observatory. That surely gives this a great deal of religious significance." She emphasised the last word.

"Quite so," continued the PM, "but we mustn't get carried away with this. As far as I know, no mainstream church has given any credence to the idea this event heralds the Second Coming or anything like that." Again Barbara interjected.

"But Prime Minister, thousands if not millions of people around the world are now starting to believe just that. Surely it is only a matter of time before the Christian Churches start to proclaim such a thing."

The Prime Minister for the first time began to look uncomfortable. He was slightly annoyed that his interviewer seemed to be going 'off script'. This was not a question they had anticipated. He decided to bring her back on track.

"That will have to remain to be seen," he stated rather coldly. "To answer your other question," he said pointedly, "the situation in the Middle East is being monitored carefully by the Foreign Office and they are urging people not to flock to Israel as they will not be allowed to enter the country. We are however, urging the Israelis to relax their rules somewhat to help ease any tensions that their rather knee jerk reaction might be causing."

"Knee jerk?" Barbara was keen to test the Prime Minister.

"Yes, I think so." The PM was going to stick to his guns. "Although given the sheer weight of number of people attempting to get into their country, perhaps it is understandable. As I said, we are monitoring the situation and we will of course let you know of any significant developments."

This was evidently a signal to his interviewer that he wished to finish. Barbara took the hint and thanked the Prime Minister for his time once again.

"I would like to take this opportunity to wish your viewers a Happy and Peaceful Holiday Season." The PM wished to have the last word. Barbara nodded and the producer said 'cut'.

The Prime Minister immediately glowered at Barbara and said, "Now look here, I'm not very happy with you firing unprepared questions at me like that. This was supposed to be a scripted interview."

Barbara smiled sweetly at him and said coolly, "But Prime Minister, you answered so well. Surely you can't be upset that I'm asking the very questions everyone in the street would be asking you?" She was without doubt an attractive woman and looked slightly coquettish as she smiled at him.

"Oh, I suppose not." The Prime Minister deflated and stood up. "Thank you very much," he added as he headed for the door, swiftly followed by Sir Donald and his Press Secretary.

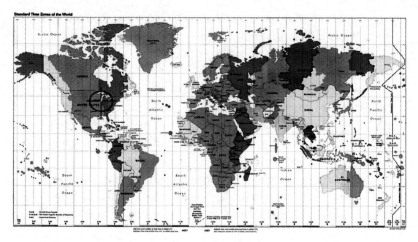

05:12 Central Standard Time 25ᵗʰ December 2012 (UTC 11:12)

The security lock down at the hospital was such that no-one was allowed into or out of the building, barring emergencies. The security guards had performed a thorough search of the maternity wing on all floors and the missing baby could not be found. The duty hospital administrator was now on the ward and the police were on their way. The staff nurse was distraught and constantly blaming herself. Nobody had the courage to wake Mrs. Casparo, yet. The hope was the baby would be found and all would be well. With each passing minute the likelihood of this happening dwindled.

A squad car screeched to a halt outside the main entrance to the hospital and two officers swiftly emerged demanding entrance from the guard at the door who instantly let them in but refused all such requests from the small crowd of people who were gathered there, in spite of their bitter complaints. The officers were directed to the maternity wing and they hurried along the corridor. The first thing they did when arriving on the ward was to interview the nurse, who by now was almost incapable of putting a coherent sentence together. They got a clearer picture from the auxiliary nurse and were particularly interested when told of the discovery of the false beard, wig and nurse's uniform. One of the officers immediately radioed into the station that they needed a 'Crime Scene Investigation' team and a detective, as this was now a serious incident. The senior administrator decided it was time to call Mr. Casparo. He went to the nursing station and reached for the phone.

05:21 Central Standard Time 25th December 2012 (UTC 11:21)

The telephone rang at the Casparo family house. It rang five times before a voice croaked "Pronto."

"Mr. Casparo? This is Damian Kowalski. I'm the acting senior administrator at the Chicago General Hospital."

Marco sat bolt upright in bed. He was immediately alert, as he realised that he would not be receiving a call from this man unless there was something wrong. "Yes, this is Marco Casparo, is there a problem with my wife?" There was an obvious note of trepidation in his voice.

"Er, no, not your wife, sir. I'm calling about your baby."

Before the administrator had a chance to continue, Marco practically shouted down the phone, "What's wrong?"

"There's nothing medically wrong with your child Mr. Casparo, but I do have some bad news." There was a slight pause, which to Marco felt like an eternity. "I'm afraid that your baby has been abducted."

This last word hit Marco like a slap across the face. For a moment he was unable to speak. Damian Kowalski was already wincing in anticipation of Marco's next sentence.

"What the hell do you mean abducted!?" This time Marco was shouting. "I thought that it's impossible for a child to be abducted from a hospital these days. This is a joke? Have you called the police? What do you mean by 'abducted'?"

"The police are here right now sir and I'm quite sure your son has been. We thought it was impossible too, but it's happened. I quite understand that you are upset."

"Upset!? I'll say I'm upset. Have you told my wife?"

"Your wife is still asleep sir; we thought it prudent not to wake her yet."

"I'm coming in." Marco slammed the phone down. His head was reeling. He was trying to make sense of this. How could they let this happen? Who took his baby? Why him? He quickly

152

dragged on some clothes, picked up his car keys from the hall table and ran to the front door.

Damian Kowalski was white and shaking as he put the telephone receiver on its cradle. He instructed the nurse at the station to call the senior administrator and get him out of bed. She quickly complied as he marched toward the two policemen down the hall.

Marco Casparo sped toward the hospital, not caring about the speed at which he was driving. His was a mixture of emotions; anger at the hospital, fear for his new child and dread about having to break this news to his wife. As his car swung up to the main entrance of the hospital he jumped out, not caring whether he was parked illegally or whether his car was locked. A nurse from the maternity wing, who said she would recognise him, had been detailed to wait for Marco by the door. The security guard opened the door on the nurse's instruction and she ushered the bewildered man into the foyer and along the corridor to the maternity wing. Marco now could hardly speak; the primary feeling which was engulfing him in waves, was terror for his new born son. He just ran alongside the nurse towards the waiting police, security guards and the acting administrator.

Damian Kowalski swallowed hard and offered a handshake which was ignored by Marco as he said, "Thank you so much for coming in Mr. Casparo. I'm so terribly sorry about this situation."

Marco didn't speak. He couldn't. He just shook his head in disbelief. The detective, who had arrived a few minutes before Marco, stepped forward and introduced himself.

"Mr. Casparo, I'm Detective Truman from the Chicago Police Department. Might I have a few words?" Detective Truman grasped Marco by the elbow and moved him a short distance from the others. Marco seemed dazed now, almost in a dream-like state. "I'm sorry to have to ask you this sir but do you know of anyone who might want to harm your child?"

"No. Certainly not!" Marco managed to snap back into the reality of the situation.

"Okay, thank you sir. Have you or your wife been in receipt of any personal threats to you or your family, as far as you are aware? Do you have any enemies? I'm sorry to have to ask you these questions at this time Mr. Casparo, I just need to try and establish what has gone on here."

"I'll tell you what's gone on here." Marco's anger was resurfacing. "My child has been stolen and I want to know what you're doing about it. Why aren't you out on the streets searching for him?

The policeman did his best to soothe him. "I assure you we are doing our very best, sir. We have an all points bulletin issued and have called in extra manpower to help in the search for your child."

Marco, now slightly calmer, looked unconvinced. "How did this happen? Who do you think did this to us?"

"It seems that two people, a man and a woman entered the ward disguised as a doctor and a nurse and took your child. It looks like they targeted your son in particular as they asked for him by name. Hence my question to you about whether you had any enemies."

Marco once again looked horror struck. They targeted his child specifically. Why? He couldn't understand why anyone would do such a thing. He didn't have any enemies. Questions rolled around in his head. "I think I'd better go and tell my wife." The thought that he had to now go and wake his darling wife and relay this to her made him feel physically sick.

"I guess you had sir, although I can arrange for a trained police woman to do this for you if you'd prefer sir?"

"No, no thank you I'll do it." The detective stood aside and let Marco move toward the room where his wife slept and her world was about to be shattered.

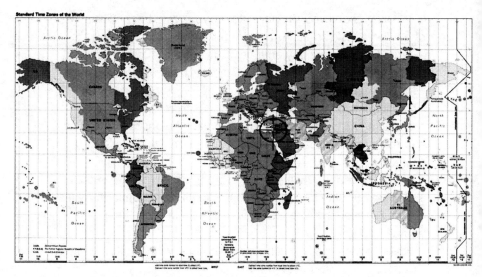

13:45 Israel Standard Time 25th December 2012 (UTC 11:45)

The bomb on the bus in the centre of Bethlehem was completely unexpected. Due to the sheer numbers of people in the town, the security services were stretched to maximum so it was hardly surprising that the bomber slipped through the net.

The scene on the street was appalling. The bus was in pieces and so were many of the occupants. Bodies lay in the road and the sound of sirens was juxtaposed by the wails and cries of the victims of the blast. The walking wounded were being taken away from the centre of the carnage by helpful passersby and were being tended to and given first aid by shop keepers and able and willing members of the public. The paramedics were having difficulty getting through to the scene of devastation and chaos seemed to be the only word that could describe what was happening.

Several news teams who were in the town to cover the events at the Christian shrine, were now hastily running towards the horror unfolding just a street or two away. A couple of reporters were attempting to give a commentary as they ran.

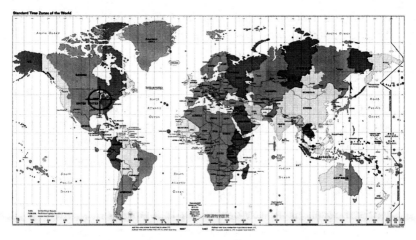

05:53 Central Standard Time 25th December 2012 (UTC 11:53)

Marco Casparo leaned over his wife, tears now running down his face. He kissed her gently on the forehead and she stirred and woke. The smile she gave to her husband quickly turned to a look of anxiety when she saw the expression on Marco's face.

"Marco what's wrong?" Her waking mind suddenly went into overdrive. Before her husband had had time to draw breath to answer her she cried out, "My baby! What's happened to my baby?"

"Lucia, someone has taken him." Marco now began to shake as the tears dropped onto her bed clothes.

Lucy's face was ashen. "What do you mean, taken him?" She felt almost relieved that her husband hadn't told her that her baby was dead or critically ill. Then a wave of blind terror hit her. She screamed at Marco, "Who's taken him?"

"I don't know," Marco wailed back. "The police are here and they are searching everywhere. They say that the kidnappers wanted our baby in particular. I don't understand." Marco shook his head, trying to come to terms with what had happened.

"Kidnappers! There was more than one?" Lucy was now trying to get out of bed and a nurse followed by a doctor moved toward her from the doorway of the room. The nurse gently blocked her movement and ushered her back into the bed. The doctor made soothing noises and held her arm so that she had to stay where she was. She felt completely overwhelmed and now suddenly powerless, began to cry. Her husband looked on, feeling utter despair.

Detective Truman hung back from the door. He didn't want to intrude on the couple's moment of agony but he had a job to do and the sooner he got on with it, the sooner they would have their child back. He walked slowly and deliberately towards the bed containing Mrs. Casparo with her husband slumped in the chair next to her. The doctor had asked the nurse to bring a phial with a mild sedative and the nurse quickly turned on her heels and walked smartly past Victor Truman, barely giving him a glance. Lucy Casparo was now in no position to get out of bed; all she could do was weep with her arms around her knees in a kind of foetal position, rocking gently on the mattress. The doctor looked concerned for her and also shot the occasional worried glance at Marco. The detective stood at the foot of the bed as the nurse returned with the hypodermic. Lucy hardly noticed the doctor insert the needle into her arm.

"Mr. Casparo." Hearing his name brought Marco around a little and he looked expectantly at the policeman. "Mr. Casparo, can you tell me if you have a mobile phone on you sir?"

Marco looked puzzled. Why should he be being asked this? "Yes." He nodded.

"Please leave it switched on at all times sir." Marco looked bewildered. "It's in case the kidnappers call. They may demand a ransom. Please indicate to me if you receive any calls from withheld numbers or numbers that you do not recognise." Marco now looked horror-struck. A ransom! It had never occurred to him that anyone would demand a ransom for his son. Lucy just cried more passionately when she heard this. "When you feel ready sir, I'll need to talk to you and your wife in a little more depth." The detective turned away from the pair and walked deliberately back towards the door, shaking his head slightly and with a grim look.

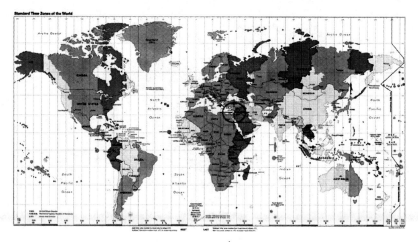

13:54 Israel Standard Time 25th December 2012 (UTC 11:54)

The television crews from several countries were now on the scene of the bomb blast. Smoke still clung to the air and the stench of fuel, explosives and death was almost choking. The noise of sirens had not abated and the reporters were giving account of the unfolding tragedy to their cameras, as professionally as they could. They all stated that no-one knew who was responsible for this terrible act, although the names of the usual organisations were already being uttered. The time for recrimination was coming, but right now, all that people on the scene could think about was to do their best to tend to the wounded. Police swarmed like ants over the wreckage and had started to interview eye witnesses.

The world looked on in horror through their television sets and computer screens as the news flashed live around the globe. Nobody knew the death toll as yet, but it was easily going to be in double figures.

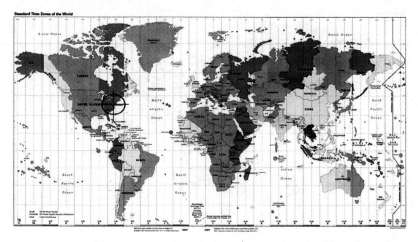

07:05 Eastern Standard Time 25th December 2012 (UTC 12:05)

The President's Chief of Staff, David Orderly knocked on the door of his private suite in the White House. After a few moments the President's wife opened the door and greeted the caller with a smile and a 'Merry Christmas'. She said that her husband would be with him in a moment as he was just opening a present with their children. He thanked the First Lady and said that he would wait. After a minute or two the President appeared at the door and asked what was 'up'.

"There's been a bomb in Bethlehem, sir." The President suddenly looked very grave.

"That's bad, David."

"I'll fill you in on the details we have on our way to the Oval Office, sir." He made a gesture to indicate he felt the President should come with him.

The pair walked down the corridor as the Commander In Chief was briefed about the atrocity that had taken place in one of the most politically sensitive places on Earth. The President shook his head as the details were reported to him.

"What do you think our response should be David?" He questioned his Aide.

"At the moment sir, we are just monitoring the situation. I have woken your press secretary and he is, I believe, working on a short speech for you condemning the violence and a plea for calm and peace."

"Fine, thank you. Have we contacted the Israeli Prime Minister?"

"Yes, we have offered our support at this time of crisis. No doubt they will ask us if they require our help with anything. We've had no intelligence reports suggesting that anything like this was in the pipeline, so we are just as 'in the dark' as they are as to the perpetrators, at the moment."

"Al Qaeda? Hezbollah? The President questioned.

"We don't know, sir. We can't even be sure that it was Muslim extremists."

The President looked puzzled and then shrugged. "Okay. Let me know if anything comes up."

"Of course, sir." David turned and walked out of the office as the President's security advisor walked in.

"You know about the bomb, sir?" The President nodded. Sam Cruikshank was holding some papers in his hand.

"Yes, Sam. David just told me."

"We can't tell at this stage if any Americans were hurt in the blast."

"Ah, yes. I was going to ask you about that. Have we got any idea about casualty numbers?"

"Not yet sir, but it is likely to be well into double figures. I'll put the news report on for you now sir." Sam picked up the remote control to the large TV screen that faced the President's desk across the room. He pressed a button and the screen lit up with the pictures live from the scene in Bethlehem and the CNN reporter describing the devastation. The President looked grim-faced as the horror unfolded in front of him.

"This just adds to the problems in the region, sir." Sam opined. "The Syrians and we hear the Egyptians, are getting irritated with Israel's insistence on keeping its borders shut. The Jordanians are understood to be pretty unhappy about it too."

"I guess that's the least of their concerns now?" The President asked the question that needed no reply.

"Indeed, sir. We have our embassy in Tel Aviv on alert too; just for your information,"

160

"Thank you Sam. That'll be all for now."

The President's chief security advisor nodded and turned towards the door. The leader of the free world continued to watch the report from the small town in Israel that was now the centre of world attention.

The unusual thing about this particular kidnap, thought Detective Truman, was the lack of leads. All he had to go on was the discarded doctor's coat, the woman's wig and uniform and the footage of a couple, probably the captors, leaving the building. He had checked to see if he could identify the car they used to leave in, from some grainy CCTV footage. It was really too dark and the car looked like a dark sedan, but it was difficult to tell and no license plate was properly visible. He hoped the captors would make contact very soon with their demands. There was always a demand for money, in his experience. He'd made sure that for the moment, there was a press blackout on this story. He didn't want spurious calls from cranks and malicious individuals clouding his investigation.

The Internet was buzzing with speculation about the identity of the bombers along with even more opinions about the nature of the 'new star' from the reasonably scientific to the down-right bizarre. People were inevitably trying to connect the two events and several pundits were claiming this was marking the 'end times'. Many more were making helpful suggestions as to the whereabouts of the birth of the new 'Messiah'. Many astrologers were connecting the position of the star in the constellation of Leo with the 'Lion of Judah' and drawing their own conclusions about its meaning or what, in their opinion, would be the likely outcome of these events. Many websites and blogging sites could not handle the stress of the number of visitors and crashed, despite the best efforts of the service providers.

There had been an attempted kidnap of a baby boy from the Holy Family Hospital in Bethlehem the previous night, but this had been thwarted by the vigilance of the staff. The report was almost lost amid the news of the bomb blast. The hospital, for obvious reasons, was not keen for it to become public knowledge and it was thought that the woman, who had made the attempt, had just lost her own baby and was now receiving counselling and psychological care.

No group had as yet claimed responsibility for the bomb blast.

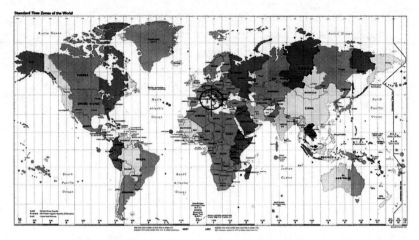

13:05 Central European Time 25th December 2012 (UTC 12:15)

The report of the bomb in Israel was now circulating around the Vatican. His Holiness had sent a message to the people of Israel appealing for calm and saying that his prayers were with them at this difficult time. Cardinal Verdi broke the news to Giovanni Casparo and they sat together in front of a TV set and watched the terrible events unfold.

"You'll need to mention this when you next speak to the press Giovanni," stated the Cardinal calmly.

"I don't know what to say." The priest shook his head to emphasise his feelings.

"You will be asked to comment by the press; all you need to do is reiterate his Holiness's position."

"I suppose so." Giovanni could not help but sound reluctant. He felt as though he was being drawn into a situation which was not of his making and he definitely wanted nothing to do with it. "Do I need to go and speak to them now?" he enquired.

"No, not right away, but in an hour or two you should probably go and talk to them again, if only to show support for the victims of this atrocity."

Giovanni nodded his assent and felt that his world was starting to spiral out of his control.

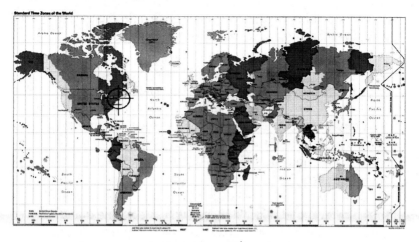

Standard Time Zones of the World

07:23 Eastern Standard Time 25th December 2012 (UTC 12:23)

John Baltar disliked getting up early, especially when he was supposed to be on holiday. However, his wife had pulled herself out of bed just moments before and he could hear his mother-in-law vaguely 'singing' what he took to be a Christmas carol, through the bathroom door. He then remembered the events of the previous evening - especially how warm and passionate Sarah had been. She had not been like that for a while... Then it occurred to him that he should check his email as he now wondered how the Supernova story was panning out. He got out of bed and pulled on his robe and walked into his office. He 'woke' his computer and started scanning through the messages in his 'inbox'. He filtered out the usual 'spam' and read with interest some further updates from the Observatory in Hawaii. He was intrigued by their assessment; they thought that it had not yet reached maximum brightness. The next message had him very excited. It was from a famous TV chat show host who wanted him to come on the programme that very evening, to talk about the 'new star'.

John practically ran out of the room and down the stairs to find his wife in the kitchen to tell her the news. "Honey!" he called out to her as he breezed through the living room, "They want me on TV."

"Whoa, John, who wants you on what and when?" Sarah was now sounding as excited as her husband looked.

"That new chat show host on CBS, you know, Mervyn somebody or other. He asked me on email if I would like to come on his programme as he could give me five minutes to talk about the Supernova. He's given me the phone number of his secretary and said to call her if I'm interested. The only thing is, I'll have to be at the studios in New York by 6pm. It means I'll have to leave here around 2pm. Is there any chance we can have lunch early?"

Sarah suddenly looked worried. She quickly broke into a smile however and said "I'll see what I can do." She threw her arms around her husband and kissed him. Remembering the passion of the previous evening he hugged her closer.

"Uh, uh, no you don't" she said pushing him away, "Especially if you want lunch early," and laughed in that young girlish way that he found so attractive.

"Okay, okay, I'd better go and get dressed and sort out a suit to wear. I hope your mother isn't going to be in the bathroom all morning..."

The words had hardly left his lips when Sarah's mother came into view in the doorway, looking annoyed by her son-in-law's last remark.

"And why shouldn't I stay in the bathroom all morning?" she challenged him in a school teacher kind of voice.

"Oh, Mummy," Sarah interjected, "John's going to be on television." Her mother frowned in disbelief. "Seriously Mummy," Sarah said emphatically, "he's been invited on that new chat show with Mervyn whatever his name is."

"Oh." Her mother looked astonished.

John could hardly believe it. His mother-in-law had been rendered speechless. The grin which he now displayed was as much for that as it was for his sudden launch into the public eye. "Merry Christmas," he said as he kissed Sarah's mother on the cheek and brushed past her chuckling as he went.

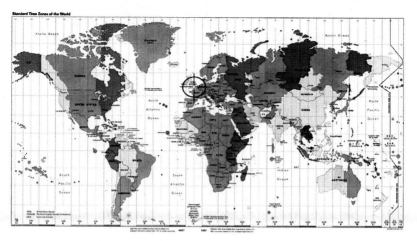

Standard Time Zones of the World

12:45 Greenwich Mean Time 25ᵗʰ December 2012 (UTC 12:45)

The skies had started to clear over Northern Europe. Western Scotland and Northern England were now enjoying cold winter sunshine and the clouds were steadily starting to drift away north-eastward from further south as well.

Many people were now thinking about their Christmas lunch. Conversations in many households varied between the awful events in Israel and the new star which had appeared in the sky. Some people had gone outside to look for the star in the hope that they could see it in the daytime. Unfortunately it had now set in the west. However, people all over the USA could see it clearly in broad daylight, where it wasn't cloudy of course. Pictures and film of the star taken in the Americas were now being used in news bulletins and were showing up all over the World Wide Web.

The Prime Minister was watching the BBC News having been briefed about the bombing in Bethlehem. He looked grave and saddened. He turned to Brian Masterson. "I can't believe anyone would do this, especially on such a day."

"It is probably because of what day it is, that it's happened." Brian sounded even more cynical than usual.

The Prime Minister shook his head and made a noise in his throat of understanding and reluctant agreement. "What has been the reaction of the Israeli government? Do we know?"

"They've given the standard response so far, saying that they will leave no stone unturned in finding the perpetrators and so on."

"Do their intelligence people or ours for that matter, have any ideas?"

"Not at the moment. The usual suspects are being considered of course, but we can't be sure as yet. It may have been a lone bomber with a grievance about something."

The Prime Minister once again made a noise of acknowledgement. "Has anyone made any link to this new star thing?"

"Not at the moment Prime Minister, but the Internet is buzzing with such rumours."

"Ah, the Internet; a blessing and a curse. The problem with it is that it gives any nutter with a half-baked opinion a forum to be heard. But what of this star, has there been any more about it?"

"Yes, Prime Minister, just a little. Apparently it is now so bright it can be seen in daylight."

"In daylight you say? Well, in that case I should go and take a look at it. I'll get the children."

"I wouldn't bother Prime Minister, as it is still quite cloudy out there, although it is clearing."

"Oh, okay then." A look of slight disappointment passed across his face. He went back to watching the news.

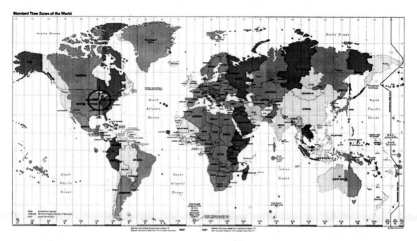

07:25 Central Standard Time 25th December 2012 (UTC 13:25)

Even though the Chicago police department was running with less than a full complement of staff due to the vacation, Detective Truman had managed to get some help with his baby kidnapping case. He now had two other detectives working alongside him which would help reduce his workload and he could detail them to do other, more time consuming tasks.

One of these tasks was to check out Marco Casparo's work background to see if there was anyone who might bear him a grudge. Another was to trawl the Internet for anyone who might have indicated that they were planning such an exploit. It seemed unlikely, but criminals sometimes couldn't help but brag about their plans or their past 'jobs'. So a clerk with knowledge of IT was given the task of checking blogs and websites and some of the darker corners of the Web to see what they could come up with. Detective Truman himself went back to the hospital to re-interview Mr. and Mrs. Casparo in the hope they might be able to shed a little more light on this sad and horrifying event.

When he arrived back on the maternity ward he found Mrs. Casparo considerably calmer, probably from the influence of the sedative. Her husband though, was pacing up and down the ward like a caged animal. As soon as he set eyes on the detective he headed straight for him.

"Have you got any news? Where's my baby? D'you know who did this?"

"No, Mr. Casparo, I haven't any news as yet and I'm afraid I don't know who has taken your baby, but we are working on it."

"Working on it. Working on it!" Marco practically shouted at him. "Why aren't you out there looking for him right now?" He demanded.

"I have a team of people on the case, sir; I promise you, we are doing our best."

Marco looked as if he was just about managing to keep a lid on his rage and literally bit his lip, drawing blood.

"Mr. Casparo, I have a couple of further questions for you."

Marco looked at his inquisitor suspiciously. "Go on," he said, slightly more calmly.

"Has anybody made any threats to you or your wife about your baby before he arrived?"

"No, of course not." Marco looked increasingly irritated.

"Are you aware that the hospital had received a phone call from a journalist asking about baby boys being born around midnight?"

"No, no I didn't know that." Marco now looked slightly puzzled. "What has that got to do with it?"

"It's just a line that we are following. Your son was born at 4pm, is that correct?"

"Yes, well it was probably a few seconds after, but the midwife said that was the time when she looked at the clock in the delivery room. I think it's on his record that he was born at 4pm."

"That's fine, thank you sir. Oh, just one more thing, I take it that you haven't received any calls about this?"

"No I haven't. I would have told you if I had."

"Okay that's fine, thank you. May I speak with your wife?"

"If you must."

The Detective turned and took a few paces towards the bed where Lucy lay looking drawn and almost lifeless. "Mrs. Casparo, I'm sorry to bother you with this right now," Detective Truman's voice had become milder. Lucy looked at him through a haze of drugs and despair, "Can you tell me if anyone seemed

169

particularly interested in your pregnancy, or when you were likely to give birth to your baby before you came into hospital, or even after you had arrived?"

Lucy Casparo just shook her head and began to gently weep once again. Victor looked pained. His heart went out to her. "Okay, I'm sorry I had to ask Mrs. Casparo. I promise you that we will do everything that we can to get your baby back safely for you."

Lucy nodded. Her voice was husky through her tears, "Thank you, I know you will."

The Detective turned and walked out of the room. Marco, still looking puzzled and angry just clenched his fists and returned to his pacing.

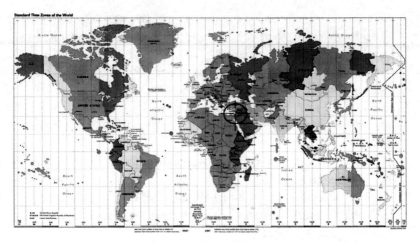

Standard Time Zones of the World

16:37 Israeli Standard Time 25th December 2012 (UTC 14:37)

Things were a little calmer now in the centre of Bethlehem. The paramedics and the ambulances had taken the wounded to hospital and some of the bodies had been moved to a local mortuary. The sound of sirens was less now and a sense of sadness and muted anger was filling the streets. The death toll currently stood at 16 with several more seriously injured. Some were so badly hurt that the casualty figure may have to rise again in the following twenty four hours. The police were beginning to put a timeline together and were surprised by some of their initial findings.

It seemed that a young woman of Palestinian appearance had boarded the bus a few streets further out. Descriptions of her were hazy to say the least, but they all suggested that she was young, although she had no real distinguishing features. It was thought that she had come from out of town, but her exact movements and her origins were still very sketchy. Speculation about the girl from the television and news reporters was growing exponentially. They had decided she was a young radicalised Palestinian who was forced into carrying out this atrocity by ruthless shadowy men from either the West Bank or Gaza. They then went into detail about how youngsters were being indoctrinated and brain washed by these monsters into committing such terrible acts. The name of Al-Qaeda cropped up several times on more than one programme, with nods of agreement from informed pundits. Others were more willing to attribute the crime to a less high profile organisation, which could be considered equally extreme in their views and methods.

Several television reporters had managed to gain access to the hospital that was treating the wounded and were showing fairly graphic images of the injured on the wards.

Strangely enough, none of the organisations mentioned in the reports had as yet claimed responsibility.

Due to the security threat, the Israeli government had decided that for obvious reasons, the borders of their country with their Arab neighbours should remain shut for the time being. There had been talk of lifting the order, but that had now all changed. The police presence in various towns and cities throughout Israel was seen to be increased, with officers walking in pairs around town and city centres. Israeli army troops were also swelling their numbers considerably in the more sensitive areas, including Jerusalem and now of course, Bethlehem.

Israeli Intelligence had been monitoring various websites of known terrorist organisations. None of them had as yet laid claim to the bus bombing, although many of them were openly applauding the perpetrator declaring that she would be hailed as a great martyr for the cause and holding her up as an example to other would be jihadists.

Some slightly more moderate websites were expressing concern about the way the new star was being represented in the media. They felt that either the Jews or more especially the Christians were going to use it as an excuse to oppress their people more. There were a lot of references to the crusades of the Middle Ages and attempts to draw parallels with what was happening today. Some were claiming that it was the intention of certain Christian groups to reclaim the Temple Mount in Jerusalem and even talk of an 'unholy' alliance between Jews and Christians to oust the Muslims from one of their holiest shrines.

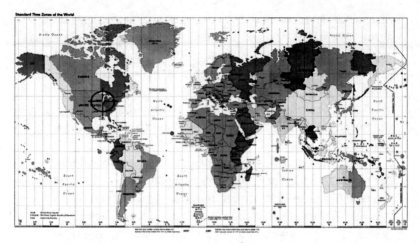

08:55 Central Standard Time 25th December 2012 (UTC 14:55)

The clerk who had been detailed to follow leads connected to the kidnap of baby Casparo had spotted a posting on a local Chicago newspaper's website about the birth of a baby boy at midnight. It went into surprising detail about the child including his name and that he was a healthy 7lbs in weight and how the hospital staff were 'delighted' with being the first to report the birth of the 'Christmas' baby. What did puzzle her was that the name of the baby was not Casparo but Alvarez. She had also picked up a thread on a forum run by an extremist right-wing Christian group about the new star and how it was marking the birth of the new 'Messiah', who had come to take the chosen to paradise. They were encouraging their followers to find this child, to offer him 'protection' from the forces of evil, who would do their best to thwart His mission.

She brought this information to the attention of Victor Truman who thanked her for her diligence. He too was puzzled that the name and birth weight didn't match. It was the other forum she showed to him, which Victor found more interesting. He asked her to keep monitoring this one in particular, for any posting that looked 'odd', as he put it, or in any way appeared boastful about a possible successful mission. Detective Truman asked one of his colleagues to start investigating the 'Church of the Second Coming', whose forum it seemed to be. He wanted to know about their activities, their beliefs and in particular their membership. In the meantime he started to plough his way through videos from traffic and security cameras in the area around the hospital.

The local media had also got to hear about the hospital 'lock down' and were doing their best to find out what prompted it. A television station had sent a reporter and camera man to get some footage of the throng of angry people waiting outside the doors of the main entrance to the hospital. However, when they arrived the angry throng had dispersed, as the hospital had opened its doors and it seemed very much like business as usual. The reporter attempted to get an interview with a receptionist just inside the entrance but was refused, which made the whole thing more mysterious. When they tried to walk down the corridor towards the maternity unit, two large security men appeared and asked them to leave. Janice Gruber, the reporter, was irritated by this and vowed to get to the bottom of what was going on. Both she and her camera man headed back to their office, where she began to make a few phone calls.

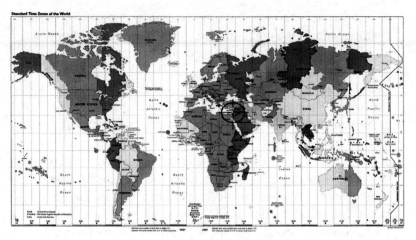

Standard Time Zones of the World

17:05 Israel Standard Time 25th December 2012 (UTC 15:05)

Although it had been quiet for weeks along the border with Southern Lebanon, the lull in the tension between the two countries ended with a rocket attack from somewhere in the mountains, into a small Israeli village a couple of miles behind the lines. Fortunately there were no casualties, but property damage was extensive.

The Israeli government put the country on its highest alert.

It wasn't long before the news teams got to the village in Northern Israel which had been the target of the rockets. The next major news broadcasts around the world had the images of the damage done by the exploding missiles, as well as further updates on the investigation into the Bethlehem atrocity. The new star was still the headline grabber with more reports on its status, including some of the more outlandish views being aired on various parts of the Internet. Many of the more 'fringe' Christian churches were now claiming that it marked the Second Coming and that Christ would be coming to take home the righteous and would punish the wicked and the 'unbelievers'.

Pressure was still mounting on Israel to open its borders. Bethlehem itself was now losing some of the influx of visitors due to fear of further terrorist attacks, with many people trying to catch earlier flights out of the country than they had originally booked.

175

The police department in Bethlehem put in a request to the FBI via Interpol for information on an American national, a girl by the name of Salwa Tahan.

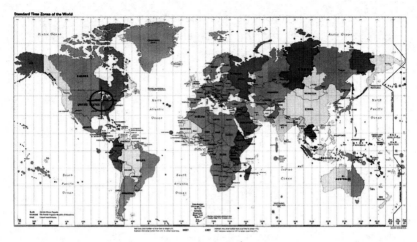

09:45 Central Standard Time 25th December 2012 (UTC 15:45)

Janice Gruber telephoned the Reception at the hospital. A lady answered asking how she may help the caller. Janice didn't let on that she was a journalist; instead all she mentioned was she tried to get into the hospital earlier that morning and couldn't get access and wondered what the problem was. The receptionist apologised and said she probably shouldn't really tell her and asked her not to spread it around, but there had been a child abducted from the hospital in the early hours and hence the security lock down. Janice thanked the lady for confiding in her and when she was asked if there was anything else that she could help her with, Janice merely replied that she would 'come back in later' and once more thanked her for her help. The receptionist put the phone down and thought no more of it.

Detective Truman had looked at several recordings made by CCTV cameras from around the hospital without success. The one that he was currently viewing however did show a vehicle with what appeared to be a driver and front seat passenger who seemed to be holding something in her arms, although it was too dark to be sure of this, travelling away from the direction of the hospital at the time. This certainly interested him. He could just about make out half the license plate number. He froze the video at this frame and called on the technical support people to see if they could extract any further detail from the rather grainy and hazy image.

Tom Schaffer from the technical department came up to Victor Truman's office and took a look at the video. He assured Victor that he would be able to do something with it and that he would give the detective a call as soon as he had anything useful for him.

In the meantime Victor decided to go back and interview the receptionists who said goodbye to the couple who walked out, seemingly quite innocently, from their hospital only three or four hours previously. He was desperate for a better description than they had already been given and this time, he took a police artist with him to see if it would help jog any memories. He and the artist got into his car to drive the short distance to the hospital. The car radio was on, accompanying their conversation with some nondescript music when a voice came over the air waves saying that there would be more on the news at the top of the hour, about the baby stolen from the General Hospital in the early hours. Victor cursed loudly and accelerated to his destination. His passenger looked out of the window and was surprised to see a bright star in the sky. He quickly realised that this must be the new star that he had heard about.

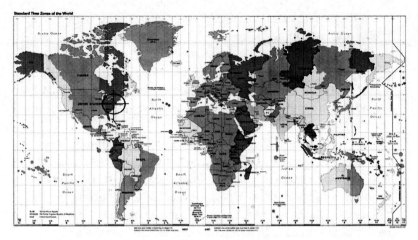

09:48 Eastern Standard Time 25th December 2012 (UTC 14:48)

Sam Cruikshank entered the Oval Office for the second time that morning. He had yet another piece of paper in his hand.

"Excuse me Mr. President."

The President looked up from his desk and invited his Security Advisor further into the room.

"I have an update on the casualty figures from the bomb blast in Bethlehem."

"What have you got Sam?"

"It seems that five Americans were definitely caught in the blast sir, two are dead, three were seriously injured and there are two others unaccounted for. That's all I have so far, sir."

"Okay. Thank you Sam, keep me informed of any further developments."

"There is one other thing, Mr. President."

"What's that?"

"There has been a rocket attack into northern Israel from Southern Lebanon."

"Anyone hurt?"

"No, fortunately not."

"Who fired the rockets? Hezbollah extremists?"

"It looks that way sir."

"Okay. Again keep me updated."

179

"Will do sir." Sam turned and walked smartly out of the room.

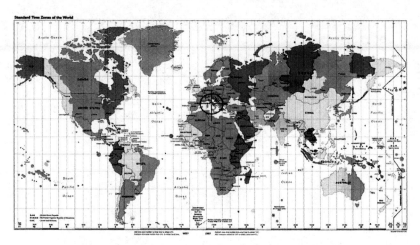

16:55 Central European Time 25th December 2012 (UTC 15:55)

Father Giovanni Casparo had steeled himself to go back and speak to the reporters who still milled around the gates of the Vatican. The Swiss Guard let him pass and opened the gate for him, allowing his approach to the crowd. As soon as the gate opened camera flashes began to fire in his face. Before he had time to speak, questions were also being volleyed at him.

"Father Casparo," one reporter seemed to have a stronger voice than others, "do you think that your star is linked to the atrocity in Bethlehem, which we are hearing about?"

Giovanni knew he was on his own this time. He shook his head. "For a start," he said emphatically, "it is not *my* star. I don't own it, I merely discovered it. Also, I cannot believe that it could have anything to do with the sad events in Israel." He continued, "The Holy Father has asked me to convey to the people of Israel and more importantly the people who have been directly affected by this tragedy, that he is praying for them."

"But Father," someone else shouted, "Surely there must be some link. There are people who believe that your, sorry *this* star marks the birth of the new Messiah. Perhaps it was an attempt to kill such a child?"

Once again Giovanni was rocked. He clenched his teeth and composed himself. "People will believe what they will believe.

All I can say is there is no evidence to back up such an idea, an idea which I may add, I personally think is preposterous."

"But you are a Catholic priest!" another voice in the crowd bellowed, "Surely you believe that Christ will come again?"

"Yes, I believe that but I don't believe that he is coming back right now."

"Why not now?" the voice in the group persisted. "Who's to say when He will return?"

Giovanni realised that he had no good reply to this question at the moment. He chose to ignore it, and with as much dignity as he could gather, turned around and walked steadily back through the gate to the shouts of further questions being fired at him. The Guard closed the gate behind him and Giovanni hunched over in a self protective manner, as if the weight of the world was on his shoulders.

Film of the priest's grilling at the hands of the press was now being edited for show on the next main news bulletin on Italian and world television channels. Giovanni Casparo was quickly becoming an international celebrity.

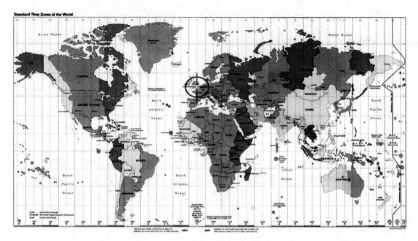

16:10 Greenwich Mean Time 25th December 2012 (UTC 16:10)

The Prime Minister had finished his Christmas lunch with his family and had watched the speech by his Monarch on the television. He was interested to note that the discovery of the new star was mentioned, along with the terrible events in the Middle East. He was just settling down with his second glass of whisky when there was a knock at the door.

"Sorry to disturb you Prime Minister." Brian Masterson was standing in the doorway.

"Come in Brian."

"Thank you Prime Minister. I just thought that you would like to be brought up to speed." There was a slight pause and the PM looked expectantly at his Private Secretary. "I've been given the casualty list for the Bethlehem bombing and it appears that two people involved in the incident were British nationals."

"Dead or injured?"

"Fortunately they were only injured. One was a Methodist minister and the other was from his congregation."

"Oh. Okay, thank you Brian. By the way, are you intending to go home today?"

"I'll be slipping off soon Prime Minister."

"Good. Not that I don't want you here you understand, but it is Christmas and I thought you shouldn't spend all of it working."

"Thank you for your concern, Prime Minister." Brian looked genuinely pleased that his boss should think of this. "I'll wish you a good night and I'll probably look in sometime tomorrow."

"Very good Brian. Good night."

Brian Masterson gave the slightest of bows as he closed the door.

Many telescopes given and received as Christmas presents were being turned skywards, to see if they could see the new star.

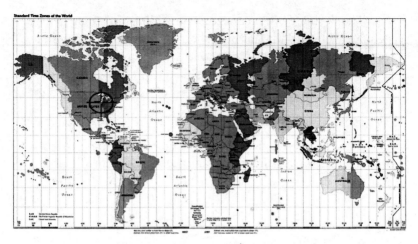

Standard Time Zones of the World

10:17 Central Standard Time 25ᵗʰ December 2012 (UTC 16:17)

Detective Truman had interviewed the receptionists about the events of the morning for a second time. He asked if anyone had mentioned anything at all about the kidnapping. All denied it. Now the artist was working with two of the ladies to try and get a likeness of the couple who walked out of the building at around 04:45. It was slow progress but at last they seemed to be getting somewhere. The man looked to be in his thirties and the woman slightly younger. He was fairly heavily built; the woman blonde, and with an attractive smile. The artist did a good enough job for both the receptionists to agree that his drawing was what the couple looked like.

As soon as he heard this, Victor Truman sent the artist back to the department to get the image out to the officers on the street. He, in the meantime, went to see Mr. and Mrs. Casparo once again.

He arrived in the maternity unit to find them both very much as he had left them earlier. Once again as soon as Marco set eyes on him, he rounded on Victor for information about the man hunt.

"We are following up several leads," stated the detective.

"What leads?"

"Well we have an artist's impression of the likely captors, which we are circulating."

"And what else?"

"That's all I can tell you at the moment sir."

"Huh." Marco seemed unimpressed.

"I presume that you haven't had any phone calls or texts?"

"No, nothing."

Victor looked puzzled. "Okay," he said, "I'll be back later."

"With our baby?" growled Marco.

Detective Truman didn't respond to this. He glanced at Lucy as he walked past her bed. He had seen that look of utter devastation on people's faces too many times in his career. He let out a small sigh and kept walking. Why hadn't the kidnappers made contact? It must be money they want, mustn't it? He felt quite uneasy about this. He tried to think of other motives; replacement of a lost baby? That was a likely scenario, but it was odd that the kidnappers wanted a specific baby. A ransom was still the most likely. After all, the Casparo family was not poor. Marco was quite senior in his bank and it still seemed reasonable that this was what they were after. He then remembered the information about this Church of the Second Coming. Could that possibly have something to do with it? He shook his head as he walked back to his car.

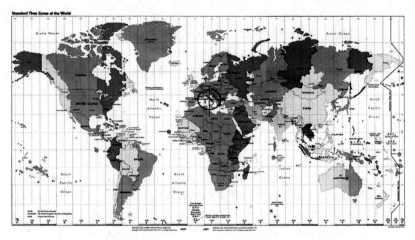

17:45 Central European Time 25ᵗʰ December 2012 (UTC 16:45)

The email arrived at the Vatican addressed to Fr. G. Casparo. It was picked up by an administrator who was about to consign it to the 'junk' file until he became aware of its contents. He attempted to discover who had sent it, but quickly realised that the sender's address had been faked. He forwarded it to Cardinal Verdi with a note letting him know he could discover nothing about the sender and should they take it seriously? When the Cardinal opened it he was very alarmed. It read: *'you're going to die, priest!'*

The Cardinal was unsure what to do about the message but after some thought, decided to ignore it as it was likely from some crank. He certainly wasn't going to mention it to Giovanni. 'The best thing to do with people like this is to ignore them', he said to himself.

The second email arrived just a few minutes later. This one read: *'it's all your doing, now you'll have to pay the price.'* Cardinal Verdi now decided that he would refer the matter to the Vatican Police.

The office of the Vatican Police responded immediately to the Cardinal's request for assistance once he had explained the problem. A young man with considerable IT skills was sent to speak to the administrator who received the emails and he then set to work attempting to discover their source. He had contacts

187

in the Rome police department that would help, should he find the messages were being sent from within the city. He was impressed by the sender's ability to hide himself. He found that the sender was bouncing the messages from servers all over the world. Tracing him would be a nightmare. He needed more to go on; more messages would possibly help. He contacted Cardinal Verdi and explained what he had discovered so far and that they really had to wait and see if the sender was going to post any more. The Cardinal could do nothing but agree and asked that Father Casparo was kept in the dark about the messages.

Giovanni Casparo in the meantime was waiting for the television news to see what they had made of his performance outside the gates of the Vatican.

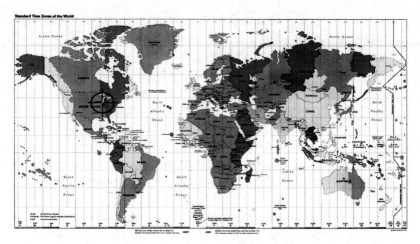

11:10 Central Standard Time 25th December 2012 (UTC 17:10)

Detective Truman was back in his office. A kind of Christmas lunch had been organised for those on duty but Victor didn't feel inclined to participate. Instead he started to plough through information about the Church of the Second Coming, which was passed to him from the clerk who had been researching them.

According to their manifesto, the church believed that Christ would return in their lifetime and it was their duty to find and protect the new Christ child from the clutches of Satan. It was their holy duty to risk their own lives in this endeavour and the breaking of Earthly laws was irrelevant to the pursuit of their sacred mission. This rang alarm bells for the detective. He began to think that his initial theory that this was a kidnapping for ransom was now wide of the mark. He started to realise that he was dealing with a religious group with a serious agenda and who would stop at nothing to achieve their goal. He also understood that the people who conceived and executed this operation, if that is what they had done, would certainly not advertise the fact that they had completed their sacred task.

If the perpetrators of the abduction were, as he now started to believe, members of this church, at least it is unlikely that they would hurt the child. In fact it may be quite the reverse and they were guarding him with their lives. This gave him some hope, as for an hour or two now he had been starting to think

189

they might be looking for an infant corpse. Another possibility that had crossed his mind was that this was a 'revenge' attack, for some perceived wrong doing on the part of Mr. Casparo. He was aware that Marco had claimed he had no enemies, but you could never tell for sure. Even if Marco had considered that he had not wronged anybody, actions are not always perceived in the same way by the other party.

He now had to think through how he was going to move this investigation forward. He considered approaching the senior pastor of the church; however, he thought it unlikely that he would confess to the crime and it would also alert the kidnappers that the authorities were hot on their tail. This would then have the consequence of driving them further underground and making it far harder to find the child. Perhaps he needed a more subtle approach? However, time was not on his side.

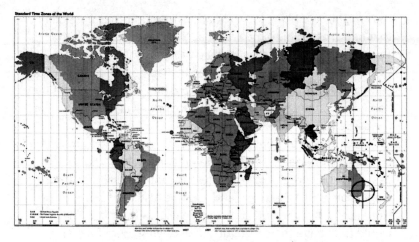

02:55 Australian Eastern Standard Time 26th December 2012
(UTC 16:55)

Observatories in Australia and New Zealand were now monitoring the Supernova. It had increased in brightness up until now, but seemed to be levelling off. It was without doubt the brightest object in the night sky. The Anglo-Australian telescope at Siding Springs had been taking spectra of the star to see what elements were in its make-up. This information was then passed to astronomers and astro-physicists around the world. It was truly a rare and beautiful object and would go down in history. One of the astronomers at the Anglo-Australian Observatory described it as 'The jewel in the Lion's Paw'.

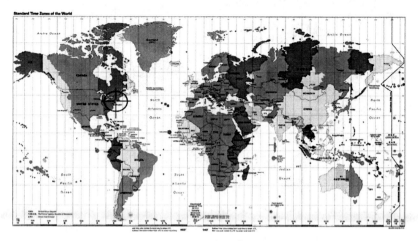

13:55 Eastern Standard Time 25th December 2012 (UTC 18:55)

The FBI had been looking into the details of the girl, as requested by the Israeli police. Salwa Tahan was a 25 year old American national. Her father was a Palestinian who had immigrated to America with his parents in the 1970's, had married an American woman and they had only one child, Salwa. Sadly her father had been killed in the 9/11 terrorist attack on the World Trade Centre in New York when Salwa was only 14 years old. They passed this information on to the Israeli police and they in turn requested clarification from them as to why they wanted this information.

It only took a few minutes for the answer to come back that she was the prime suspect in the bombing incident in Bethlehem, as part of her passport was recovered from the scene and all of the victims had now been accounted for and witness descriptions had suggested that she may have been the perpetrator. The FBI alerted the Department of Homeland Security that there was now a possible terrorist link with the girl.

Dr John Baltar was hurrying for the train to get him to the CBS studios in New York City. He kissed his wife and even his mother-in-law goodbye in his excitement. Sarah's mother had even wished him luck.

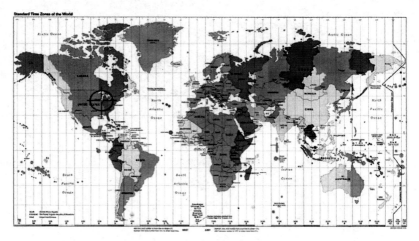

12:55 Central Standard Time 25th December 2012 (UTC 18:55)

Detective Truman, who should have gone off shift a couple of hours ago, was studying a list of the senior members of the Church of the Second Coming. He had noted down two names in particular, judging by their surnames they were either married or brother and sister. He now attempted to find an address for the couple. There were several 'Houstons' in the phone book. He had no idea which one they were likely to be. He guessed that good old fashioned leg work was called for. He stood up, grabbed his coat and car keys and walked down the hall to the stairs.

   The first house he arrived at was rather down market. He rang the bell and heard a noise from inside. He waited and the door was thrown open by a man in his thirties who was tall and slender and had clearly been drinking. Victor Truman showed the man his badge. The man called to his partner, "Hey honey, we've got a policeman at the door. Have you been on the game again?" He laughed on hearing the cackles from the woman within, who sounded even more inebriated than her partner. Victor asked the man if he knew anything about the Church of the Second Coming. The man answered by asking the detective if he had lost his way. He then invited Victor in for a drink. Detective Truman declined and thanked the man for his assistance turned and walked back to his car. He had four more addresses to call at. He hoped that they weren't all going to be like that one.

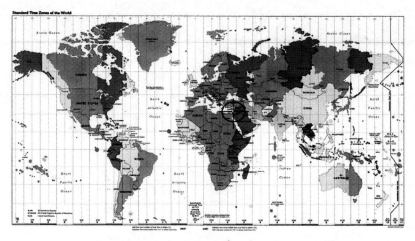

Standard Time Zones of the World

21:35 Israel Standard Time 25th December 2012 (UTC 19:35)

The second salvo of missiles fired from Southern Lebanon was more deadly this time. Two houses were hit in the village, killing five people and injuring another eight. The police and an army bomb disposal team were rushed to the scene. They were quickly followed by camera crews wishing to report the latest outrage.

A group calling itself the 'Brothers of Islam' were claiming responsibility. The Israeli cabinet was called into emergency session. They took the decision to send the military into the region to root out the terrorists.

22:20 Israel Standard Time 25th December 2012 (UTC 20:20)

The Israeli Air Force went into action in Southern Lebanon. Their instructions were to locate and destroy the enemy positions. Several civilians were injured in the ensuing bombing raid.

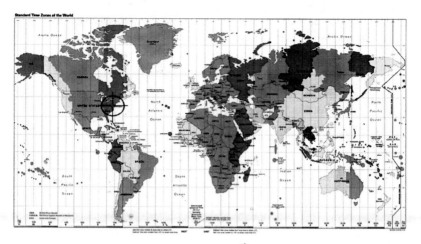

Standard Time Zones of the World

15:45 Eastern Standard Time 25th December 2012 (UTC 20:45)

David Orderly entered the Oval Office. The President ushered him in and asked for news.

"Well sir, there has been another rocket attack on Northern Israel."

"Is that Hezbollah again?"

"They are calling themselves the 'Brothers of Islam'."

"Do we know anything about them?"

"No sir, just another faction that has sprung up in the region, we suspect."

"How are the Israelis responding?"

"They've carried out an air raid."

"I guess you can't blame 'em for that."

"Unfortunately sir, it seems some civilians were injured in the raid."

"Oh." The President looked concerned. "Do you think things are escalating David?"

"It looks that way sir, especially as we have word the Israelis are planning on sending in an armoured division to root them out."

"Do you think I should give the Israeli Prime Minister a call?"

"If you think it will help sir. You might persuade him to relent. More tension in the region is not going to do anyone any good right now. We also have word the Lebanese and the

Syrians are planning to call the UN Security Council to get them to declare Israel is in breach of various 'resolutions'."

"As if that's likely to do any good?" The President snorted. He was quite cynical when it came to the United Nations. "Let's hope things calm down David."

"Let's hope so sir."

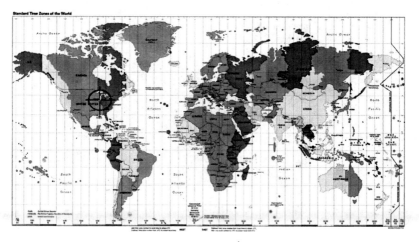

14:47 Central Standard Time 25th December 2012 (UTC 20:47)

The second house that Victor Truman called at was in a quiet neighbourhood. He rang the bell and waited for it to open. After a minute or two, he rang it again. Shortly after, the door opened a little and an old man asked him who he was. Once again the Detective flashed his badge and the old man at the door seemed slightly reassured. He then closed the door for a moment and Victor could hear the sound of a chain being released. The door swung open further. The man seemed to Victor to be in his late seventies with thin grey hair. The Detective asked him if he knew the whereabouts of the Church of the Second Coming.

"Never heard of it." The old man shook his head. He called to an unseen individual inside the property. "Marjory, have you heard of the Church of the Second Coming?" An equally querulous voice returned that she hadn't heard of it either. Victor thanked the old man for his help and apologised for having disturbed him. He turned back to his car, as the man slowly shut the door.

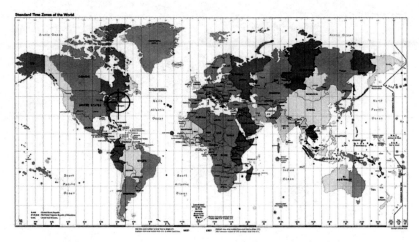

16:50 Eastern Standard Time 25th December 2012 (UTC 21:50)

Special Agent Jefferson of the FBI had been instructed to call at the house of Mrs. Tahan in the Queens District of New York. He went to the address he was given and rang the door bell. After a moment, an attractive lady in her early fifties opened the door.

"Forgive the intrusion ma'am. I'm Special Agent Jefferson with the FBI. Might I have a word with you?" Special Agent Jefferson proffered his ID. Mrs. Tahan looked quite taken aback.

"Why certainly Special Agent Jefferson, please come in."

The dark suited man followed the lady into her house and accepted a glass of water when he was asked if he would like any refreshment.

"So how may I help the Bureau?" Mrs. Tahan had contact with the FBI once before some years ago, after her husband had been lost in the 9/11 attacks. She had started to assume that perhaps there was some follow up information the man wanted. Perhaps he was trying to tie up some loose ends.

"Can you tell me the whereabouts of your daughter ma'am?"

This question immediately struck Mrs. Tahan as strange. "Why yes," she responded innocently, "she's off travelling."

"Can you tell me where she went?"

The lady started to look a little worried. Unformed questions began to build in her mind. "Yes, I believe she went to the Holy Land."

"The Holy Land," Special Agent Jefferson repeated, "you mean Israel?"

"Yes, that's right. But why are you asking me about my daughter. I thought perhaps you were following up on the 9/11 attack? You know I lost my husband there?"

"Yes I do ma'am." Special Agent Jefferson did not answer her question. He pressed her further. "You called it the 'Holy Land' Mrs. Tahan, are you and your daughter Christians? I understand that your husband was a Muslim?"

"Yes, we are Christians. My husband was Muslim only in name really, he wasn't at all devout. I on the other hand am very devout and have given my life to the Lord Jesus Christ as has my daughter. My late husband had no objections to me bringing up our daughter as a Christian. And don't think the Muslims don't consider that land Holy, they do."

Special Agent Jefferson looked slightly uncomfortable at the lady's strong religious protestation. "Your daughter has a Palestinian name?"

"Yes, that was a courtesy to my husband's family. I brought her up a Christian even though she had an Arabic name. I hoped it might help us to stretch our hands across the religious divide. I don't think my husband's family were very happy about their grand-daughter being brought up as a Christian though." Mrs. Tahan looked slightly wistful. "But why this interest in my daughter?" Once again she started to look less than comfortable at the constant questions about her only and beloved daughter. "She is okay isn't she? She's not in any kind of trouble?"

Once again, Special Agent Jefferson avoided answering the questions. "When did she leave on her trip ma'am?"

"Three days ago. She wanted to go to the Church of the Nativity for the Christmas service. She had been saving up for ages. I thought it was a lovely idea. I wished I could have gone with her."

"Why didn't you?"

"I did offer, I even said I could help with her air fare as well, but she was quite insistent she wanted to make the pilgrimage alone."

There was an uncomfortable pause. Then Special Agent Jefferson said, "Mrs. Tahan, do you know if your daughter had any contacts with people who perhaps you thought 'undesirable'? Did she have a boyfriend for example you perhaps disapproved of?"

"No, certainly not! She's not interested in boys. Why do you keep asking me these questions?" Her voice was now becoming shrill as she became agitated by the constant questioning about Salwa.

"Mrs. Tahan," Special Agent Jefferson drew a deep breath, "Have you heard about the bus bombing in Bethlehem earlier today?"

"Oh yes, I think that I caught something about that on Fox News." Mrs. Tahan suddenly turned pale. "My daughter," she shouted, spilling the water from her glass, "My daughter was in Bethlehem, please don't tell me she's been hurt." Tears started to well in her eyes.

"I'm afraid we believe so ma'am."

Mrs. Tahan looked pleadingly at the FBI Special Agent now sitting in her lounge. She didn't even want to ask the next question.

"I'm sorry to have to tell you ma'am we think your daughter has been killed in the explosion." Special Agent Jefferson hoped to get his last question in before the full impact of what he had just told the girl's mother, fully sank in. "May I see her room Mrs. Tahan?"

She pointed to a door just off the hallway. "Thank you ma'am." The Special Agent got up and walked briskly to the door which had been indicated, leaving the poor woman to her grief and in complete shock. He went into the girl's room and took a quick look around. He went to a chest of drawers and began to search them looking for papers, CD's and memory sticks. He lighted upon a few hardback books which looked like they might be diaries. Upon opening them, he found this was exactly what they were. He also found the girl's laptop computer on a table near her bed and gathered this up too. He also picked up what looked to be a recent photograph of Salwa on a vacation in somewhere he didn't recognise. He walked out of the room and approached the girl's mother who was now weeping openly.

"I'm sorry to have to break the news to you in this way Mrs. Tahan. Is there anyone I can call for you who might come and sit with you?" The woman shook her head. Special Agent Jefferson felt very awkward. "May I take these few things with me ma'am? I need them for forensic examination."

Salwa's mother nodded. It didn't occur to her in her state of shock and grief to ask why he should want to take her daughter's things. Special Agent Jefferson then handed her a card which had his name and phone number and other contact details. "Please call me if you need anything ma'am. I may well be back to ask you a few more questions, perhaps tomorrow. I'll let myself out." The FBI Special Agent closed the front door behind himself. He heard her bellow with grief as the tears flooded out. He swallowed hard and walked to his car.

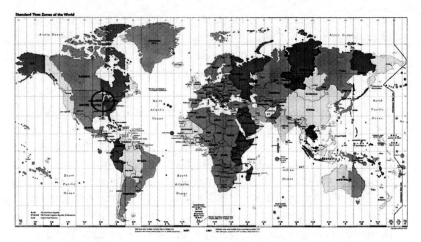

16:05 Central Standard Time 26th December 2012 (UTC 22:05)

Janice Gruber approached a policeman on the street. She didn't have a microphone with her or anything that might give away the fact she was a journalist.

"Excuse me officer."

"Yes ma'am."

"I hear you are looking for a missing baby?"

"That's correct ma'am."

"It's just this morning I met a couple with a new baby, you know it got me wondering. Do you have the baby's name or a picture?"

"Yes, ma'am I do." The policeman reached into his pocket and pulled out his PDA. He tapped something on the screen and said, "The baby's name is Salvatore Casparo." The picture was a little blurred, but good enough for identification if one was needed.

"No, that's not him. Well thank you anyway officer."

"Thank you, ma'am."

Janice went on her way. As soon as she was out of sight of the officer, she pulled out her note book and wrote down the child's name.

The third address Detective Truman tried was quite near the hospital. As he approached the door he could hear the sound of a child crying within. He stopped in his tracks. He reached inside his coat and loosened his gun in its holster. He rang the bell and waited. After a few moments a large African-American woman opened the door. She had a small child, a little girl perched on her hip. The child had obviously been crying.

"Ms. Houston?"

"Who's askin?

"I'm Detective Truman with the Chicago Police Department."

The woman's eyes narrowed. "And what can I help you with, officer?"

"I'm just making some enquiries ma'am." Victor Truman tried to sound nonchalant. "Have you heard of the Church of the Second Coming?"

"No I ain't," said the woman. "Why are you askin?"

"It's just part of an ongoing investigation ma'am. I'm sorry to have troubled you."

"No trouble officer." The child started to cry again. The woman backed out of the doorway and closed the door. Victor shook his head and turned to walk back down the steps to his car. He decided he would call in on the Casparos to see how they were doing and to update them on his investigation.

When he arrived at the hospital he was confronted by a security guard at the entrance to the maternity wing, who he had not seen before. The guard asked him for identification. He waved him through when he saw the ID. When Victor got to the Casparo's room he found Marco asleep on the chair. His wife Lucy was sitting staring into space with the look of a wounded animal on her face. Victor approached Lucy quietly, not wishing to disturb her sleeping husband. He sat by her bed.

"How are you doing Mrs. Casparo?" Victor asked with genuine concern.

Lucy just looked at him as if to say 'how do you think I am doing?' Realising that he probably sounded a bit foolish, Victor immediately said, "I think we have a lead on your son."

Lucy's eyes swung onto Victor's face like a searchlight. "What do you mean a lead?" There was a note of hope in her voice.

204

"We think your son has been abducted by an extreme religious group."

Lucy's face asked the question that her voice did not.

"We think he's therefore being well cared for. You see Mrs. Casparo; I think they believe your son is the new Messiah."

Lucy Casparo looked totally astonished. "How could anyone think that?" She exclaimed. Her outburst woke her husband from his fitful sleep.

"What is it honey?" Marco did his best to drag himself back into consciousness.

"Marco, the Detective thinks Salvatore has been stolen by people who believe he is the new Messiah!"

Marco almost burst out laughing, but realised Victor was being deadly serious. "Why," he roared, "Why should anyone think that?"

"It's because of his birthday Mr. Casparo, he was born at midnight on Christmas Day." It had suddenly all fallen into place for the Detective.

Before Victor had a chance to finish what he was saying, Marco interjected, "But he wasn't born at midnight. He was born at 4pm. There must be thousands of children born at around this time and date all over the world every year?"

Victor suddenly almost shouted, "Yes, it was 4pm here, but it was MIDNIGHT IN BETHLEHEM! And what's more" Victor Truman continued, "this year is important because of the new star in the sky. It's probably connected in some people's mind with the 2012 thing."

Marco looked utterly astonished. His mouth fell open. He seemed to have lost the power of speech. "My God," he said, "My brother. He discovered the star!"

"Exactly!" exclaimed the detective with near triumph in his voice.

"Giovanni. Giovanni; I haven't told my brother about this yet."

"I wouldn't be in a hurry to, sir." Victor shook his head, "He's probably got enough on his plate at the moment."

Lucy nodded in agreement. "No don't tell him yet Marco, he would be so upset, especially as he is so far away. It would break

205

his heart. You know how much he was looking forward to being an uncle."

"You are speaking as if our son is dead." Marco looked imploringly at his wife.

"No, I'm sure he is not," cut in Victor, "I think he is very much alive."

"I still don't understand," said Marco shaking his head.

"I think your baby has been stolen to protect him from the forces of evil, as these people see it."

"That's incredible." Marco once again looked astonished. "We are the best people to take care of our son."

"Yes, absolutely," agreed Victor, "but these people don't see it like that. They think that as the new Messiah, the forces of darkness will try to destroy him. I imagine they think both you and I are part of the conspiracy."

"So where do you think they're holding him?"

"I'm still working on that," stated Victor.

Marco and his wife looked both relieved and confused. Hope was with them, but also deep apprehension. Detective Truman stood up and said, "I promise you I'll do everything in my power to get your child back."

For the first time, Marco thanked the Detective for his efforts. As Victor walked away Marco called after him, "If there is anything I can do?" and then he followed this with, "Please let us know the minute you have any more news."

Detective Truman turned and nodded to the couple and continued to walk purposefully out of the door. He too felt a renewed hope; he just wasn't sure how the next few hours or maybe even days were going to pan out. He was feeling very tired now and wondered if he should go and get some rest. He decided to investigate one more address before he went home.

The next broadcast from the local radio station that told its listeners about the kidnapping of the baby from the hospital now went into more detail, this time giving the baby's name and a brief description. They also put the information on their website.

Victor Truman drove the couple of miles to the next address on his list. This was a sizeable house in a pleasant neighbourhood. He went up to the door and rang the bell. There was no response. He knocked on the door as well. There was still no response. He went around the side of the house and looked in through the window. The place was in darkness. He thought this a little strange, but then he remembered it was Christmas and the likelihood was the people here were away for the holiday. He went back to his car, despondently. He did have one final address to check, but he was now very tired and decided it was going to have to wait until the morning. He felt sure the child was in no imminent danger now, so a few hours would probably not make a great deal of difference to anyone that is, except Mr. and Mrs. Casparo. He knew too, he would think more clearly with a few hours sleep. He turned the key in the ignition and drove back to his apartment.

Day 5

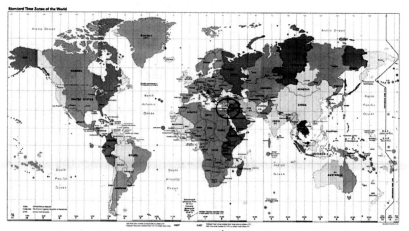

05:00 Israel Standard Time 26th December 2012 (UTC 03:00)

The armoured division crossed the border from Israel into Southern Lebanon. They were on a 'seek and destroy' mission to follow up on the job of the earlier air-raid. Their remit was to find the rocket positions from where they were being fired into Israeli villages. The column were not having any difficulty finding their way as the light from the new star was so bright it was casting shadows. The tanks were rumbling slowly along the road, not concerned at all about stealth. The commander intended to instil fear into any local civilians or enemy combatants alike. He wanted to let them know he was coming for them.

Several websites purporting to be from more extremist Jewish factions were now claiming the new star was marking the birth of their true Messiah, their 'anointed one'. A couple of Hassidic rabbis had told their followers to openly seek the birthplace of this child. Hospitals up and down Israel were being inundated with phone calls enquiring about births of baby boys in the last 24 hours. Most hospitals refused to give any details.

Spy satellites had noticed troop movements in the Golan Heights, the disputed territory between Syria and Israel. This information was being analysed by the military authorities who had placed these satellites in orbit.

Some Israeli troops on patrol in Gaza came under a hail of stones and other missiles and were forced to retreat. This was unexpected, not least by the troops, as early morning patrols were usually quiet. They were not going to allow this kind of violence to last long and so regrouped, this time using the assistance of a tank, and armed themselves with tear gas. The soldiers attempted to disperse the jeering crowd with the tear gas but this had limited effect. The tank rolled forward and strafed the street with machine gun fire above head level. Three people were wounded by ricochets. The riot, for that was now what it was, became uglier. The tank had petrol bombs thrown in its path. The occupants of the vehicle determined the focus of the disorder was a building at the end of the street. The gun turret of the tank tracked around to point at the building. There was a deafening roar as the muzzle of the gun bellowed smoke and the building at the end of the street exploded in a hail of dust and debris. There was moment or two of silence made all the more stark by the concussion just moments before.

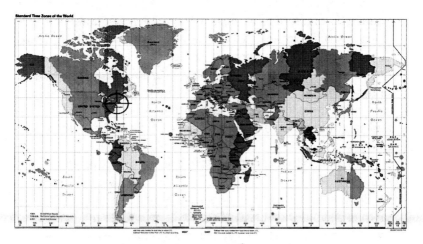

The CBS studios in New York were like nothing John Baltar had seen before. The staff were very kind to him and gave him coffee and a meal and had explained exactly what was going to happen during the show. He had met the host of the show, Mervyn Cosmonagus, who had seemed very friendly and had put him at his ease. He had been 'made up' by a lovely young girl who flirted with him a little and now he was waiting in the 'green room' to be interviewed live by Mervyn in front of an audience of millions. He felt very nervous and his pulse was racing. He heard Mervyn announce he had with him in the studio, the man who confirmed the discovery of the new star and who had brought it to the attention of the entire world. John swallowed hard. The assistant floor manager got him to wait just behind a screen until the music started to play to fanfare his entrance. He remembered his wife was at home watching and determined he would make her proud of him. The music started and the assistant floor manager gave him a small shove. He remembered to smile as he ran down the short flight of steps towards the empty chair next to Mervyn which was facing the studio audience. The audience was applauding him loudly. John felt light headed and deliriously happy.

As the applause died down Mervyn thanked his guest for coming on to the show. John was now smiling broadly and nodded his pleasure to his host. Mervyn then elaborated on his guest's profile explaining to the audience both in the studio and at home, that Dr Baltar work at the Central Bureau for Astronomical Telegrams and made a weak joke about the name of the organisation, suggesting it was out of date and should be renamed the Central Bureau for Astronomical Emails. The audience in the studio found this wonderfully amusing. John smiled on.

"So John, tell us about how you helped to discover this new star?"

John winced slightly at it being called a new star. He went on to explain he didn't really help to discover it, as this was done by a Catholic priest at the Vatican Observatory; he merely did his job in getting the discovery verified by a couple of professional observatories.

"So how long have you been interested in astrology John?"

John looked blank for a moment as he tried to decide how to answer this question and quickly said, "I don't know anything about astrology Mervyn."

"Oh... I'm sorry John, it's astronomy isn't it, not astrology. Astronomy, astronomy." Mervyn repeated this loudly. The audience chuckled. Mervyn then quickly asked "And what star sign were you born under, John?"

This took the astronomer by surprise and he looked confused for a moment and stammered, "Er, well my birthday is in the middle of January, so I guess that makes me a Capricorn, but like I said, I don't know much about astrology."

"You know," continued Mervyn, "A lot of astrologers consider this star to be very important. They are saying because of its position in the Lion, it marks a major event that will or even has taken place in the land of Judea, in other words in Israel. Other people are saying it marks the second coming of Christ. What are your views on this John?"

John Baltar was having to think on his feet. He didn't want to say anything which made him or his host look foolish. He decided that discretion was the better part of valour and said, "I'm not religious Mervyn, so I'd better leave that sort of thing to others."

211

"But surely you must have some opinion on this John. This could be the most important event to happen to the world in two thousand years?"

"Like I said, I'm not a believer, so I'm really not qualified to comment. As far as I'm concerned the position or the timing of this Supernova is purely coincidental. How people wish to interpret it is entirely up to them."

"Ah well then John, I guess this means you are just going to have to burn in Hell." Mervyn had a broad grin on his face and the audience taking their cue, found this tremendously funny.

"So tell me about this star John," Mervyn now tried to look more serious and interested, "what made it explode? That is right, isn't it? It did explode?"

"Yes, that's right Mervyn, it did." John relaxed a little. "This was very unexpected, as this type of star would not normally be expected to develop into a supernova, in spite of the fact it was a hyper giant star. Normally this type of star would shed its outer layers and then collapse into a..." John did not get the chance to finish what he was saying, as Mervyn was now giving a very large and obviously staged yawn.

The studio audience roared with laughter. John did his best to join in the joke and laughed too.

"I'm sorry John; I was just beginning to nod off there." The audience again registered its delight at the humour of the host of the show.

"So tell us about what you think will happen to this star in the future, er... in simple terms if you please John." Again the audience chuckled.

"Well er, in simple terms," he grinned at the audience, "it will shine brightly for a couple of weeks and then slowly fade away."

"So the explosion won't kill us all?" Mervyn smirked and the studio audience chuckled.

"No sir," said John emphatically, "it's much too far away for that."

Mervyn turned to the audience and said "Well folks, you heard it from the man himself, we aren't all going to die a fiery death, so if it turns out that we do, you can blame him." He

212

pointed at John with a broad smile on his face. Again laughter swept through the studio.

"Well John, it's been great having you on the show, that's all we've got time for now, so I give you Dr John Baltar ladies and gentlemen." He shook John firmly by the hand as the audience burst into rapturous applause. John nodded to the crowd and smiled, while inwardly nursing resentment that he had been made to look somewhat foolish and had been brought on to the show as a foil for Mervyn's lame jokes, rather than to be given an opportunity to explain the really interesting stuff about the star. As the show gave way to a commercial break, John stood up and unclipped the microphone from his tie. Mervyn thanked him once again and said that he had been a 'sport'. The astronomer walked back up the steps to the 'green room', feeling rather dejected.

He called his wife from his mobile phone when he got back to the 'hospitality suite'.

"You were great honey," Sarah gushed.

"Thanks. I think the man's an idiot," He added, "He tried to make me look stupid."

"Aw, don't be like that John, you did great. Even my mother was impressed with your performance."

"Hmm," muttered John. "I can't get back tonight honey, so they're going to put me up in a local hotel, I'll get the train in the morning."

"Oh, okay sweetheart. I'm so proud of you," she squeaked. This lifted her husband's spirits a little and he wished her goodnight and blew her a kiss down the phone.

23:12 Eastern Standard Time 25th December 2012 (UTC 04:12)

The President of the United States of America was notified of the developments in the Middle East. He thought there was little he could do to affect the situation at the moment and so decided to retire to bed, asking to be woken should events there become more serious. He was assured the Vice President was also fully aware of the matter. He said goodnight to his staff and went back down the hall towards his private apartment and his wife and children. He hoped the leaders in the Middle East would see sense before things got out of hand.

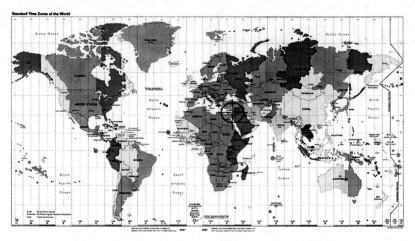

07:45 Israel Standard Time 26th December 2012 (UTC 05:45)

After the demolition of the building in Gaza by the Israeli tank, things were relatively quiet once the ambulances had removed the dead and injured. However groups of people were now gathering around the area, armed with stones, bottles and other missiles and were sporadically hurling them at the Israeli troops, who were now in riot gear. Volleys of stones were answered with tear gas and rubber bullets. News teams attempting to record the unrest were held back to a safe distance by the army. However, some footage had been taken of the devastation left by the demolition of the building and was now being shown on various websites and had already been seen on some 24 hour television news programmes.

The Israeli cabinet was in emergency session to discuss this and also the operation inside of Southern Lebanon. Pressure was being brought to bear by various governments around the world to endeavour to obtain a cessation of hostilities, as yet without success. Feelings on both sides were running high. The cabinet was also made aware of the troop movements being carried out by the Syrians on the Golan Heights. It seemed as if they were moving men and equipment up towards the 'front line'. It was decided this potential threat should be matched and so the order was given for the Israeli army also to move an armoured division into the region.

215

09:30 Israel Standard Time 26th December 2012 (UTC 07:30)

Fighting had broken out between two groups in a side street in Jerusalem, one Christian and the other Jewish. No one seemed too clear as to what it was about or how it started. The police had managed to break it up and injuries were minimal.

Speculation on the Internet was still rife as to the whereabouts of the 'new Messiah'. Extremist religious groups both Christian and Jewish were making claims and counter-claims, with seemingly serious scholars adding their weight to the debate on both sides, quoting the Bible and other religious texts to back up their viewpoints. As yet, nobody, or no group had claimed to have found Him.

Some Islamic websites were starting to suggest true followers of their faith should look out for the 'Mahdi', the Saviour who would be born in Mecca at the 'end times'.

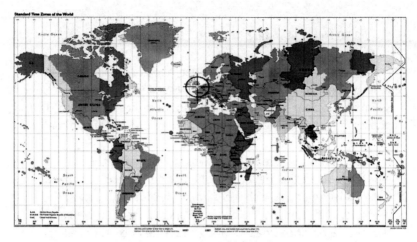

07:35 Greenwich Mean Time 26th December 2012 (UTC 07:35)

The Prime Minister was awoken by a member of his household staff with the message that his Private Secretary Brian Masterson was waiting downstairs to speak with him. He rose, dressed and asked to take breakfast in his office.

He found Brian waiting patiently. He arranged for a cup of tea to be brought for his Private Secretary and asked how things were. Brian brought the Prime Minister up to speed with events in the Middle East.

"We have received intelligence reports saying there appear to be troops gathering on the Golan Heights. Naturally this is concerning given the already heightened tensions in the region, so we also issued instructions for anyone, other than essential staff, to be withdrawn from our embassy in Tel Aviv." Brian said in a matter of fact style.

"Do you think that's really necessary?"

"It's just a precaution, Prime Minister. There has been rioting in several towns there now, and it seems certain factions are blaming the West for their current predicament. So we thought it wise."

"You don't think this is sending the wrong signal to the Israelis at this time?"

"No, not at all Prime Minister."

"Very well. Please keep me informed."

217

"Very good Prime Minister." Brian was about to leave the office when he turned and said, "Oh, by the way, the sky is clear at the moment." There was a brief pause in which Brian was hoping the PM would catch on to what he was referring to. When it was apparent that this wasn't going to happen, he continued, "The star is clearly visible. I was looking at it this morning as I walked into work."

"Oh, I see. Thank you Brian, I'll go and take a look."

Brian Masterson bowed very slightly and swept out of the room.

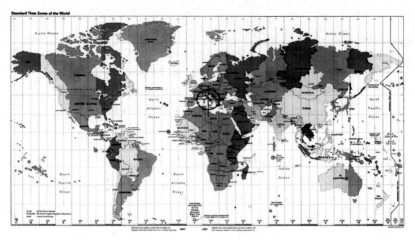

08:55 Central European Time December 26th 2012 (UTC 07:55)

Fortunately, there were very few people in the street when the car bomb exploded in the centre of Rome, only a few hundred metres from the Vatican. The blast rattled windows within the Vatican itself and caused considerable damage to a restaurant and a couple of shops in the street. As these premises were closed for the holiday and it was fairly early in the morning, no one was hurt. The police had blocked both ends of the street and were sifting through debris for clues as to the perpetrators.

Father Giovanni Casparo and Cardinal Verdi were sipping coffee, having just got back from morning Mass, when the thud of the explosion rocked the room in which they were sitting.

"What on Earth was that?" Cardinal Verdi leaped from his seat and hastily put his cup down on the table.

Giovanni looked aghast. He too jumped up and went to the window. They could see a thin pall of smoke rising from somewhere in the middle distance. They went to the door and opened it, only to be greeted by one of the Swiss Guard hastening towards them and ushering them both back inside.

"It looks like there's been a bomb or something a few streets away Your Eminence. I recommend you stay inside for the time being until we can find out more about what's happened."

They both looked amazed such a thing could happen in Rome and, worse still, almost on their doorstep. They took the Guard's advice and retired inside moving their chairs away from the windows. After a few minutes the Swiss Guard knocked on the door and confirmed it had been a car bomb, as there had not been another explosion, they were assuming it was a solitary device. They turned on the television to see a newsflash from the street showing the wreckage left by the blast. The priests sat in silence as the reporter explained that no one as yet knew who had planted the bomb or why.

The Cardinal turned to the priest and said hesitantly, "Giovanni, I'm not sure if I should tell you this, or even if this is a good time to tell you?" he swallowed and paused. Giovanni was immediately intrigued to find out what the Cardinal had been keeping from him and looked at him expectantly. Seeing he could not now go back, Cardinal Verdi continued, "Giovanni, there have been some threats on your life."

The silence at that moment was deafening. Giovanni just looked at the Cardinal incredulously. "What do you mean, 'threats on my life'?"

"We received a couple of emails yesterday, very threatening emails, addressed to you."

"Why didn't you say something?" implored the priest.

"I didn't want to worry you. I thought it was likely just a crank. I'm sorry now. Perhaps I should have mentioned it."

Giovanni sat in silence for a moment. "What did they say?"

"They seemed to suggest that it was all your fault."

"What's all my fault?"

"That wasn't clear, but I suspect they are blaming you for the 'star' and the upset that it has caused in some quarters."

Giovanni looked aghast. Then after a moment said, "You are right; it must be just a crank."

The Cardinal looked reassured that his protégé seemed to take the news so well. "Quite so," he said. "It was just I was concerned there was some link between the threats and the car bomb."

The priest made a motion with his hands and seemed to brush it off. The Cardinal thought he also saw a look of fear

220

cross Giovanni's face, although it was gone almost as quickly as it came.

"I suspect the reporters, who now seem to be camping outside the gate, will expect me to comment on it."

"There's plenty of time for that. You should wait until you get the 'all clear' from the Swiss Guard. They'll let you know if and when it is safe to venture out."

Giovanni nodded. "I'm sure you're right." He continued, "You'll let me know if there are any more threatening emails, won't you?"

Cardinal Verdi nodded a promise. He saw a look of grim determination on Giovanni's countenance. Both men went back to watch the news report.

The news wires were alive with reports of the violence in the Middle East and now the car bombing in Rome.

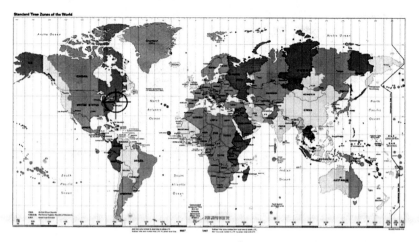

03:30 Eastern Standard Time 26th December 2012 (UTC 08:30)

Special Agent Jefferson had handed Salwa Tahan's diaries to a junior colleague to sift through and her laptop over to an IT specialist to check out, before he went home to bed. They were to see if there was any information within, which would suggest she was the perpetrator of the atrocity in Bethlehem the previous day. The work was laborious and painstaking as the diaries went back several years and there was a lot of reading involved. Likewise, the laptop was not giving away many secrets as the girl had employed software that very effectively erased evidence of which websites she had been visiting. She had also been using encryption software on some documents, which slowed the process right down. This alone seemed odd as the question immediately came to mind as to why a young girl thought it necessary to be so cautious. If there was any evidence to be found here, it wasn't going to show up any time soon.

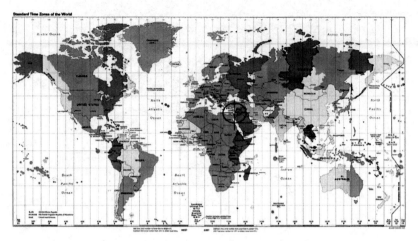

11:10 Israel Standard Time 26th December 2012 (UTC 09:10)

A couple of the tanks in the column which had pushed into Southern Lebanon were firing on positions in the mountains where they suspected the militants, who had fired the rockets into Israel, were based. They too had come under fire, but only so far from stone throwers from some of the nearby villages who were risking being shot at by the troops. Their efforts were of little effect against the armour which was deployed in front of them; however they persisted and managed to slow the column down as the commander's instructions were to avoid civilian casualties. The troops fired above the rioter's heads, which had the effect of dispersing the crowd for a few minutes, only for them to regroup and start the pelting afresh.

Within a short while the protesters were joined by reporters and camera men, much to the irritation of the commander who understood this kind of publicity, did little to endear their actions to the wider world.

Howls of protest were now being received in Tel Aviv from the countries surrounding Israel. The government considered this was only to be expected and ignored them; claiming Israel was within its rights to defend itself from hostile action, from wherever it came.

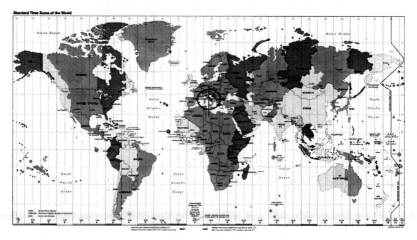

10:35 Central European Time 26th December 2012 (UTC 09:35)

The street in Rome, where the car bomb had exploded, was still cordoned off. Forensic teams were taking samples for analysis and news reporters were milling around just outside the hastily erected police barricade. Some of the reporters who seemed so keen to interview Father Casparo about his views on the repercussions of the star, which in some quarters at least now bore his name, had been redirected to the site of the explosion. They were doing their pieces to camera about how rare and unusual it was to have such a brazen act of terrorism committed in the heart of their city.

Giovanni asked the Vatican Police if they thought it was safe to venture out to the remaining reporters who were still outside the gate. He was strongly advised not to go out there yet, at least until the Rome police had done a sweep of the area to make sure the surrounding streets were safe. It wasn't unknown for terrorists to plant bombs on delayed timers to catch both the police and the public unawares. On hearing this, Giovanni started to fret. He paced up and down and generally seemed quite agitated. The cardinal did his best to soothe him with wise words, but it did little to help. Perhaps he had taken to his role as Vatican spokesman but it was more likely he wanted to show the journalists he was no pushover and was made of sterner stuff than they might think.

The Italian Prime Minister made a television appearance condemning the bombers for their cowardice and declared that 'no stone would be left unturned in the search for the perpetrators of this despicable act'. A journalist asked him if he thought there was any link between the bombing and the events in the Middle East, which the Prime Minister brushed off as 'nonsense'. He replied similarly when the same journalist asked him if he thought that there might be a link between the bombing and the new star. Giovanni likewise tutted at the stupidity of the question as he watched the live report.

Another email arrived at the Vatican addressed to Father Casparo. This one said, *'We have a long reach. You have been warned. The next time will be your last.'* The Cardinal decided to keep his promise and showed it to Giovanni.

"I don't understand," he said. "I can't think what they want me to say or do." Giovanni, the Cardinal and the detective from the Vatican Police went through several possibilities as to who might be sending these messages and why. None of them made any sense. Cardinal Verdi then said, "Well Giovanni, I can only suggest you be very careful. Whoever is sending these messages seems to be serious. We can protect you while you are here in the Vatican, so I suggest that you don't venture outside the gates."

"But the Holy Father wants me to be his spokesman." Giovanni protested, "How can I be if I stay shut up in here? Surely it is safe enough to speak to reporters at the gate? At least I have members of the Vatican Police close by."

The Cardinal then said, "Very well Giovanni but only by the gates and only when there is an important announcement to make."

The priest acquiesced to this, but added "I should go and speak to them soon though, as they will want our reaction to the bombing."

"Okay, but not until the Vatican Police has given the 'all clear'." The Cardinal then rose to go, along with the Vatican Policeman, leaving Giovanni alone to contemplate the events so far.

Websites and blogging sites were now full of rumour and speculation. So far five people had declared themselves as the new Messiah, each more or less saying the world was now in the 'end times' and they had chosen this time to reveal themselves. Three were located in the USA, one was in Brazil and the fifth was purportedly in Canada. The 'Messiahs' were threatening that anyone who did not follow their particular teachings would be damned, therefore those who did would be saved, or they used words in a similar vein. Other extremist religious groups were also predicting the oncoming apocalypse. Some sites suggested that although the deadline for the end of the Mayan calendar has passed without incident at midnight on the 21st December, the world was not out of trouble yet. They suggested the explosion from the Supernova would reach Earth at midnight on the 1st January and would 'wipe the world clean', as one of the more colourful descriptions put it.

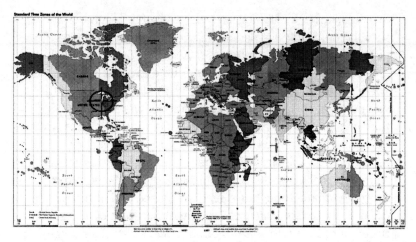

07:32 Central Standard Time 26th December 2012 (UTC 13:32)

Detective Truman arrived in the Department ready to face another day. He was disappointed by a message from the technical guy who had been working on enhancing the license plate number of the dark sedan car which was caught on the CCTV at the hospital. It seemed that he hadn't really managed to get much information from the image. Not enough to be conclusive anyway.

Victor wanted to go and finish visiting the addresses which he had left from his list. Even though he had no response from the last one he called at, he thought he might try it again a little later. He realised that it was still quite early for some people, so he decided to go back through some of the information that he'd based his theory on, in case he'd missed anything which might be important. He kept coming back to the names of the senior members of the Church of the Second Coming. The only couple on the list, namely the Houstons, were in his opinion still the most likely candidates. After all, a couple with a small child would not be considered unusual by anyone and the woman would probably be more able and experienced in coping with an infant than a solitary male.

He also went through the beliefs of this organisation once again. Either the Church as a whole, or certain members of its congregation, seemed to be likely candidates for this crime. He

227

went to get a coffee and a doughnut for breakfast. He kept reminding himself that he'd made a promise to the Casparos and it was a promise that he was determined to keep.

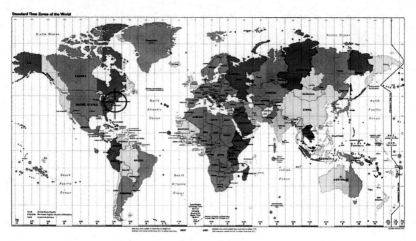

08:35 Eastern Standard Time 26th December 2012 (UTC 13:35)

Special Agent Jefferson arrived at his office to find a message waiting for him to contact the IT people. He hoped this meant that they had uncovered something worthwhile from Salwa Tahan's laptop, so he would be able to say with some certainty either way whether she did or not commit the bombing on the bus in Bethlehem. He noticed another message saying his subordinate had not, as yet, found anything incriminating in the girl's diaries, although he'd not finished going through them all. He went down the hall and took the lift to the IT department floor. He entered the office expectantly.

"I had a message to see you guys about the laptop I left with you yesterday?" he said with a hopeful note in his voice.

The operative looked a little blank at first and then said, "Oh yes, I know, the one Sam was working on."

Special Agent Jefferson nodded patiently.

"We haven't got anything yet I'm afraid." The Special Agent looked crestfallen. "The thing is there are several documents which have been encrypted using a PGP program and strong encryption."

Special Agent Jefferson now looked confused. "Can you say that in plain English?"

"Er yeah, sorry. What it boils down to, is that we need the key. We could probably break the code which was used, but that could take some time. It would be a lot quicker if we had the key."

"So what does this key look like?"

The operative gave a slight laugh, but quickly stifled this on seeing the look of irritation on the Special Agent's face. "It's not an object," he explained, "It's a code."

A look of realization crossed Special Agent Jefferson's face. "So what am I looking for exactly?"

"It's probably a series of letters and numbers, maybe even a word. It might be written on a piece of paper, on a note in a diary, or something like that. Once we have the code we can open the documents in an instant."

"A diary?" The Special Agent repeated. The operative shrugged. "Okay, I'll get it for you." He turned and marched swiftly out of the room. The operative mumbled "And thank you too." He then turned and went back to the large, inviting looking computer screen behind him.

Special Agent Jefferson, on getting back to his office, collected the girl's diaries from his colleague's desk and started to thumb his way through them, looking for anything that stood out to him as appearing like a code. After more than an hour of fruitless searching he slammed the book which he'd been scanning, shut, and made a noise of irritation in his throat. He then decided that he would have to pay another visit to Mrs. Tahan. This was not a prospect that he relished.

The President of the United States of America had been woken to learn of the events which had transpired in the Middle East overnight. He asked for a briefing with his Security Advisor, who was now on the way to give him his assessment of the situation. While he was waiting he went out onto the lawn of the White House to take a look at the star. He expressed his amazement to his body guard and then went back to his office to focus on more mundane issues.

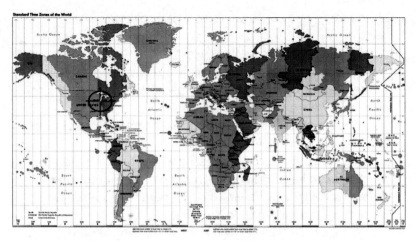

08:55 Central Standard Time 26th December 2012 (UTC 14:55)

Victor Truman headed out of the Police Department building to drive to the final address on his list. He wasn't sure what to expect. This address lay on the outskirts of the city. It took him about twenty minutes to drive to the house. He decided that he would not park right outside the door, but would walk a short distance so as not to alert anyone who might be looking out for 'trouble'. He turned into the street and slowed to a stop. Before getting out of his car he checked up and down the street. He loosened his gun in its holster inside his jacket 'just in case'. When he was satisfied, he got out of his car and walked the few paces to the address he was interested in.

He walked up the steps to the front door and rang the bell. After a few moments he heard a noise inside then a man in his thirties, looking rather dishevelled, pulled the door open.

"Mr. Houston?"

"Who wants to know?"

Victor made to reach for his badge. As he did so he said, "I'm Detective Truman of the Chicago Police Department."

On hearing this, the man banged the door closed in the Detective's face, turned tail and ran down the hall of the house. Victor drew his weapon and shoved hard against the door. It was made of heavy wood and did not budge. He then took a step backwards and kicked hard at the door just below the lock,

231

with the sole of his shoe. The door gave way and he brought his gun up to the firing position. He could see down the corridor that the doors leading to the back of the property were all flung open. He proceeded carefully down the hallway, checking each room to left and right as he went. He moved quickly and confidently. He reached the back of the house to see the foot of Mr. Houston disappearing over the fence at the end of the garden. He gave chase, yelling 'Stop. Police," at the top of his voice. He reached the fence. It was high; at least six feet. He did his best to climb it, but he wasn't a young man anymore and failed to get himself over it.

He realised that his fleeing quarry was probably long gone and so he reached for his radio and called in backup to help search the house and area. He re-entered the property and started checking each room more carefully. The place was not well cared for. He looked for evidence that there was a baby in the house but found nothing in the rooms on the ground floor. He was about to check the basement when a squad car arrived with two officers. He explained what had happened and one of the officers went around the back of the building. The other officer started to help the Detective to search the house. While Victor opened the door to the basement the man in uniform climbed the stairs.

Victor couldn't find the light switch and so had to resort to his torch to find his way into the gloom. It looked as if no one had been down there in years. He found old paint cans, some loose tools and other detritus that people tend to collect over the years. He then heard a call from the officer who ascended the stairs.

"Detective Truman, you'd better take a look at this."

Victor sprang back up the stairs and called to his assistant that he was on his way. "What have you got?"

"Come and see for yourself."

Victor disliked people playing games with him, but he said nothing and ran up the stairs as fast as he could. On arrival on the landing he followed the officer's voice into a room opposite the stairs. He gasped in amazement to see row upon row of plants in pots with powerful lights suspended overhead. He whistled. "So that's why he ran." He looked around as the other policeman approached from the top of the stairs. He too whistled when he saw the sheer quantity of Cannabis plants that met his gaze.

"You'd better get the 'Crime Scene Investigation' people over here," he directed the two uniformed men, "and the drug squad and see if you can't catch that bum." His orders were met with a less than enthusiastic, 'yes sir'.

"I on the other hand have some kidnappers to track down." Detective Truman then turned to go back down the stairs.

"But Detective, aren't you gonna stay and sort things out with the CSI people?" One of the officers enquired.

"Nope, I don't want the paperwork. It's your baby now." The two policemen looked at each other and shrugged. Victor was already in the hallway heading out of the front door.

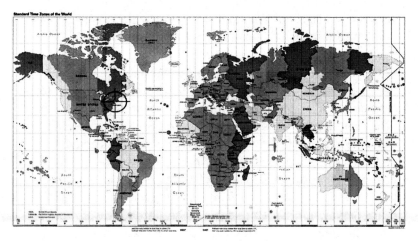

10:17 Eastern Standard Time 26th December 2012 (UTC 15:17)

Special Agent Jefferson pulled up outside the house of Mrs. Tahan. He wasn't sure in what state he would find the lady. He decided he would brazen it out. Even though the evidence was mounting against her daughter, it was not yet overwhelming, so he didn't wish to accuse Salwa to her mother's face. He rang the bell and waited.

Mrs. Tahan opened the door and he almost gasped. She had obviously not been to bed and she looked grey and drawn, almost deathlike. Her face was stained from hours of weeping for her deceased daughter. He swallowed hard and said, "I'm sorry to disturb you again ma'am, I was wondering if I might come in?"

The woman pulled the door open further and without saying a word signalled for her caller to enter. She stood aside as he stepped into the hallway. "Might I take another look in your daughter's room please ma'am?"

At last, Mrs. Elizabeth Tahan spoke. Her voice was dry and tremulous; she sounded quite different to the woman who the previous day spoke to Special Agent Jefferson the first time. "Why do you keep taking my daughter's things?"

Special Agent Jefferson hesitated. He wasn't quite sure how to answer this. Should he come clean and tell the lady that her daughter was a suspect in a mass killing? He decided again on

234

discretion and said, "We need to be able to identify her properly ma'am. I'm sorry if this causes you more distress."

At first, this seemed to satisfy Salwa's mother. She nodded towards the girl's room where the Special Agent had been just a few hours before. He nodded a thank you and walked over to the door and opened it. He immediately proceeded to search the room for any papers that he had missed the previous day. He busied himself opening drawers and cupboards and didn't notice Mrs. Tahan now standing in the doorway, tears once again trickling down her cheeks. "What are you looking for?" The question made him look around suddenly and seemed to take him by surprise. Once again he hesitated. He was more at a loss this time to explain his actions. He made an attempt at a half truth to see if this would placate her. "I'm looking for a notebook or something like that, which might give us an indication of her movements."

Mrs. Tahan's eyes narrowed. She was sure that he was not being completely truthful with her. This made her stop crying and focused her mind on possible reasons why this Federal Special Agent was being less than honest with her. After a few moments silence she suddenly hissed, "My God, you think that she was involved!"

Special Agent Jefferson stood stiffly and waited for the barrage that he knew would follow. "You're mad." Salwa's mother was almost screaming at him now. "My little Salwa would never do anything like that." She moved towards him, fists clenched, she began to rain blows down on this man who stood there silently accusing her beloved daughter of mass murder. He allowed one or two to land on his shoulder and then grabbed her by the wrists to try and calm the woman down. She dissolved into deep sobs and folded herself into him. At first Special Agent Jefferson was unsure how to react. He put a protective arm around her shoulder and moved her toward a chair and sat her down as gently as he could. He was not used to shows of strong emotion such as this. Normally the people he had to deal with were trying to get away from him or worse, pointing guns at him. He let the lady grow calmer and said, "I'm sorry ma'am, I didn't want to have to tell you she was a possible suspect." In an effort to placate her further he added, "She is only a suspect; we don't have any real strong evidence that she was the perpetrator."

Between sobs Mrs. Tahan asked, "So why are you here?"

"I'm looking for a code that your daughter used to secure some documents on her laptop computer. If I can find that, we can take a look to see if they are relevant to the investigation. They may even clear her of suspicion." He did his best to offer the woman a slim ray of hope. His comment made little difference, other than to quieten the howls of protest and declarations of innocence that the revelation first engendered in her. Time was against him, so he took the decision to continue with his search. The girl's mother sat limply in the chair, her entire world laid in ruins around her. The Special Agent did his best to be as quiet and low key as he could. He pulled open the bedside drawer and began sifting with both his hands and eyes, through the contents. He lighted on an old notebook and pulled it towards his face. He flipped through it. There was nothing written in it that looked obviously like a code. However, he put it in his pocket and continued the search. He turned his attention to another drawer only to find that it contained the girl's underwear. He looked a little embarrassed but her mother was not watching him. She was in a place of her own, far away and very dark. Special Agent Jefferson continued to rifle through the contents when his hand touched a book-like object that stood out from the soft material that filled the rest of the drawer. Once again he pulled it towards him and hastily opened it. He quickly scanned the pages, he could not be sure if he could see a code amongst the scrawls and writing. This too he slipped into a pocket in his jacket. He had been through all the obvious places now, short of tearing up the floorboards and ripping open the bed, there was nowhere else he could sensibly search. He turned back to the poor dejected woman sitting on the chair in her late daughter's room. "I think that'll be all I can do for now ma'am."

She looked up at him imploringly. If she had the strength left in her, she probably would have gone down on her knees in front of him to beg. "Please, show my daughter's innocent of this." Once again she started to choke and sob.

"I'll see what I can do ma'am." It was the best that Special Agent Jefferson could say. He couldn't promise because he genuinely didn't know if her daughter was innocent of the crime, or not. He had his suspicions, but at the moment that was all they were. "I'll see myself out." Once again he left the heartbroken, lonely woman to her desperate wailing. He thought that he would rather have faced a gunman.

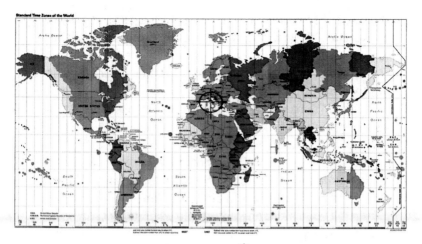

16:45 Central European Time 26th December 2012 (UTC 15:45)

The Vatican Police had finally given the 'all clear' to Father Giovanni Casparo to go out and once again talk to the waiting press at the Vatican gate. It was decided that, in the light of the threat against him, a plain clothed member of the Vatican Police would stay nearby to afford him some protection should the worst happen.

Giovanni marched toward the gate, more confidently than on his previous sojourn. Somehow the threat against his life seemed to instil a new resolve in him which helped him face what he considered to be his duty, with more enthusiasm. It surprised even him. So he found himself holding his head high as the gate swung open. There seemed to be fewer reporters this time. He thought maybe at last they were losing interest in the star. There were now more mundane and so perhaps, more interesting things for newspapers and television news programmes to report. However, the camera flashes still popped and the microphones were still pushed towards him as the priest took his position in the middle of the group.

"Father Casparo," one pressman asked, "What is the Vatican's view of the car bomb, which exploded in the city earlier today?"

Giovanni was happy enough with this question. After all, he had rehearsed an answer to just such a question in his head already, as he walked the few metres to the gate. "His Holiness is, as are all the clergy and staff here, simply appalled at the cowardly bombing in the centre of the City. He is grateful and gives thanks to God that there was no loss of life or injury due to this terrorist act."

"Do you think perhaps the bomb was in fact aimed at the Vatican?"

This was a more uncomfortable question. Giovanni simply had to deny this. "No of course not; why should anyone want to bomb the Vatican?" He hoped that a rhetorical answer might stifle any further questioning along that line.

He felt even more uncomfortable when the journalist who proffered the question responded, "Perhaps it is connected with your star, Father? Maybe some think that because you discovered it, you have effectively 'stolen' it from the rest of us mortals?" There was a note of mocking in the reporter's voice that Giovanni disliked intensely. What was worse, he seemed to be awfully near to one of the possible scenarios which had been discussed with the Cardinal and the Vatican Police only a few hours previously.

Giovanni could only say, "Ridiculous," and hope that another question would hide his obvious discomfort. The next question did anything but.

"Father, would you care to comment on the news of your nephew's kidnapping from the hospital in Chicago?"

The priest had the expression of a man who had been struck dumb. He seemed utterly confused as he tried to make sense of the question. Could this be true? Could this have really happened and his brother not have told him? The babble of noise from the group seemed to grow still, as Giovanni fought to regain his composure. The journalist who asked the question could see the look of horror and confusion on Giovanni's face. He at once understood that the subject of his interrogation knew nothing of this. He felt instantly sorry for the man in front of him but at the same time he was a professional doing his job, so his next question was almost inevitable. He asked without leaving time for Giovanni to recover. "Didn't you know about this?"

This further question acted only to confirm the veracity of the former. Giovanni Casparo once again looked like a drowning man in front of the world's press. He croaked a "No," shaking his head in disbelief. There was once again a moment's uncomfortable silence and then the questions flooded forth from the others, who now stood thrusting microphones towards the panicking priest. Camera flashes went off like fireworks and Giovanni lifted his arm as if to shield himself from physical blows. He instinctively turned and fled back to the gate. His interrogators yells grew dimmer with each step he stumbled away from them. The gate was swiftly closed on them and Giovanni found himself wandering alone back to the relative safety of the rooms which he had been occupying for the last 24 hours or so. His head swam. He felt confused, hurt and angry as he tried to make sense of what he had just been told. His baby nephew had been stolen from his parents - from HIM - and he had just learned about it from a low life journalist. As he stumbled through the door he found himself weeping.

Cardinal Verdi had been watching the live broadcast on the television in the room that the priest now entered. He turned towards the door as he heard Father Casparo rush in. He had a look of horror on his face. "Giovanni," he exclaimed with genuine alarm, "I had no idea."

The astronomer-priest could not speak. He just buried his head in his hands and tried to fathom out why his brother had not told him of this terrible thing. The Cardinal sat there staring at him in bewilderment.

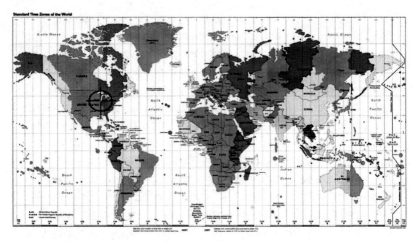

11:55 Central Standard Time 26th December 2012 (UTC 17:55)

Victor Truman had ruled out his entire list of possible kidnappers except one, the people who were not at home when he called the previous day. He decided he needed to go back to that address to see if he could raise a response. He drove once more across town to the quiet outskirts and the prim suburban houses, on the street where he hoped he would find Mr. and Mrs. Houston at home.

He once again approached the front door and rang the bell. Still there was no answer. He rang the bell once more and knocked on the door with his knuckles. He looked up as a neighbour appeared in view.

"They're not at home," he said helpfully.

"Do you know where they've gone?" Detective Truman asked hopefully.

"Nope," the neighbour shrugged, "but they seemed to leave in a bit of a hurry yesterday morning." He continued after the briefest of pauses, "I guessed they were going to visit family or friends, being as it was Christmas Day an' all."

"Do you know much about them?"

"No, not really, they keep themselves to themselves as do most folk around here." His brow furrowed and he then asked, "You seem mighty curious. Who are you?"

241

Victor pulled out his badge. This changed the old man's curiosity to one of surprise. The Detective pressed on with his questions. "Do you know if they had a baby with them?"

"Don't think so. That's to say I didn't see one. I don't think they have a child but like I say, I can't be sure, we don't pry into each other's business round here if you take my meaning?"

Victor looked disappointed and said that he knew what the man meant with a shake of his head. He then said "Okay, thank you sir," and made to go back to his car, feeling deflated. He sat watching through his windscreen as the old man wandered back into his house. He was about to start the engine when he changed his mind and got out of his vehicle again. He looked around the street to see if anyone else was about. Seeing all was quiet, he once again approached the property. This time he walked around the back of the house, peering in windows as he went. From what he could see the house was well kept and tidy. As he got to the back door he noticed a small transom window that was slightly open, which meant that the door lock complete with the key inserted was within reach of a long arm. Once again he looked around. This part of the house was not overlooked, so he reached in and just managed to grasp the key and turn it. Thankfully it moved easily and within seconds he was inside the house.

He moved quickly and quietly through the back of the premises. Out of habit, he loosened his gun. The Detective opened the door into the kitchen and began to search. He looked in cupboards and checked work surfaces. He wasn't quite sure what it was he was looking for, but he would know when he found it. He pulled open a door of a small cupboard and found several tins of baby's formula milk and an infant's feeder bottle. His suspicions were now well and truly aroused. He moved into the hallway treading as quietly as he could. He opened another door, this time into a dining room. Everything seemed tidy and clean and in good order. This was true of the other rooms on the ground floor. He then ascended the stairs. On reaching the main bedroom he spied a packet of baby's diapers. He noted that they were for 'newborn'. He walked across the landing into another room. The contents of this were more chaotic, as if someone had been emptying cupboards out in a hurry. There was also a baby's cot in the room and a few soft toys. This was obviously a nursery, but why was it in such disarray when the rest of the house was so tidy? He went back to the main bedroom and opened the large closet. The first thing he noticed, were a lot of empty clothes hangers. There were a couple of dresses and a few pairs of men's trousers and a two or three sports jackets, but that was all. He then went to the dressing table. He pulled open the drawer and found a few papers. Scanning through these he learned that the owners of the property were indeed Mr. and Mrs. Houston. He also found a leaflet from the Church of The Second Coming giving times of services.

Victor had seen enough and besides, he knew his presence in the house was quite illegal. He went quickly back down the stairs and out the way he had entered. He now felt sure that he was on the trail of the kidnappers, but where to now? Where had they gone? Wherever it was, they seemed to have gone there in a hurry. He needed time to think. He walked quietly back to his car and drove back across town to the Department. On arrival he checked on the national vehicle database for any car registered to the Houstons. He found they owned a light grey Toyota Station Wagon. This was not what he'd hoped for.

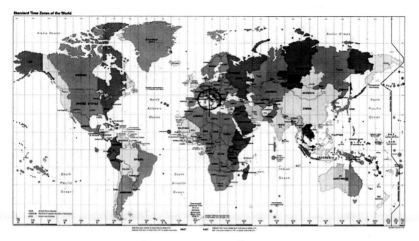

Standard Time Zones of the World

20:30 Central European Time 26th December 2012 (UTC 19:30)

Giovanni Casparo had discussed the situation with the Cardinal who was delighted to see that this young man, who only two days before had been enjoying a quiet life as an astronomer and parish priest, had started to recover his composure. Under the circumstances, he had coped well with the onslaught from the media men at the gate. It was the news his nephew had been abducted that had stopped him in his tracks; no one could blame him for that. Giovanni had decided he had recovered and had thought things through enough to want answers. Why was it that his brother had not told him of the kidnap? Was it that he didn't want to worry him? Perhaps he had phoned and couldn't get through? He pulled out his mobile and started to dial.

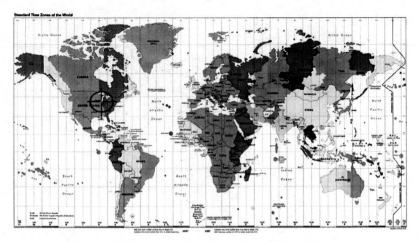

12:30 Central Standard Time 26th December 2012 (UTC 18:30)

Marco Casparo's phone buzzed into life in his jacket pocket. He pulled it from his clothing and examined the display. Giovanni! What should he tell him? The policeman had advised him to say nothing about the kidnap, but could he really keep something so devastatingly important from him? As these thoughts were racing through his mind he pressed the button to talk to his brother.

"Giovanni." Marco did his best to sound light-hearted and pleased to hear from his brother. He knew instantly that something was wrong from the tone of voice that replied to him.

"Marco," Giovanni paused collecting his thoughts, "I've been told about Salvatore. Please tell me it isn't true."

A sense of betrayal swept over Marco. How could he have kept this from his own brother? "Giovanni," he now sounded much more subdued, "How did you hear?"

"A reporter told me."

"A reporter?" Marco was confused. How could a reporter in Italy know of a kidnapping in America? For a moment he was lost for words.

Giovanni filled the silence. "Yes, a reporter. He told me my nephew had been abducted. Is it really true?"

"Si Giovanni, I'm afraid to tell you it is."

245

"But how could it happen? Why didn't you tell me before?"

Marco decided to answer his brother's second question first. "The policeman who's working on the case suggested I shouldn't tell you. He didn't want you to be worried."

Giovanni now sounded exasperated. "Didn't want me to be worried? I was even more worried when I heard it from a journalist!"

"I'm so sorry Giovanni; it was against my better judgment. I did want to tell you, really I did, but I could see the sense in what the policeman was suggesting."

There was a momentary pause, followed by a barrage of questions. How did it happen? Do you know who took him? Do they think he's okay?"

All of his brother's anxiety came pouring out. Marco explained slowly and carefully, the events of the day. He did his best to avoid saying anything that could lead Giovanni to think that there was any connection to his discovery of the star. Giovanni was however not slow in putting things together.

"My God!" exclaimed the priest. "This is because I discovered the Supernova isn't it?"

Marco didn't know what to say. He knew what his brother was saying was likely to be true, but he didn't want Giovanni to feel any guilt. "I don't know Giovanni; it might have nothing to do with it."

"Have the police got a theory?"

Marco really didn't want to tell his brother what Detective Truman had said to them, but he now felt he could no longer lie to him. "The Detective who is working on the case thinks the kidnappers believe our son is the new Messiah." He waited for the outburst that would surely come. There was a moment or two of silence. Marco was puzzled. "Giovanni, are you still there?"

Giovanni's head was reeling once again. How could a star going supernova so far away, cause him so much trouble? And not just him. His brother's baby son had now been kidnapped, he had witnessed a bomb go off in the centre of Rome, which he was sure was somehow connected to his discovery, and he even wondered if the increased tensions in the Middle East weren't somehow also linked. "Yes Marco, I'm still here. Are people really that crazy?"

"Yes Giovanni, I am realising they are? How did the reporter who told you, find out?"

"Maybe it's on the Internet somewhere?"

"Oh, yes. I guess you're right. Giovanni, I am truly sorry I didn't tell you myself, I suppose I must be a coward?"

"No Marco, that's okay. If you were advised not to say anything, then I can't blame you. It was a shock though."

"I'm sure it was."

"I've got to go now, but please let me know of any developments?"

"I promise I will. Goodbye for the time being."

"I will pray for you all."

Marco breathed out heavily and turned to his wife. "Giovanni knows now."

Lucy nodded her head. There was nothing she could say. She understood the pain that it caused her husband and now her brother-in-law too. She wished it would all just go away and that everything could be put back as it was. It was a forlorn wish.

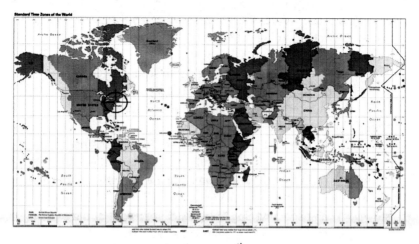

13:45 Eastern Standard Time 26th December 2012 (UTC 18:45)

Special Agent Jefferson had been searching through the notebooks which he found in Salwa Tahan's room, looking for clues as to her movements and motivation and more specifically, a code or key that would unlock the documents on her laptop, which remained tantalisingly out of reach. His mounting sense of frustration grew by the minute, as he realised there was nothing in them he could identify as a 'key', or even an entry in them which might give away her motives for the bombing, a crime that looked increasingly likely she had committed.

He decided to take the notebooks to the IT department. Perhaps a fresh eye could spot something he was overlooking. When Special Agent Jefferson arrived on the floor, he couldn't find Sam. He asked someone else if they had seen him, only to be met with a shrug. After a further search and a short while, another of Sam's colleagues found him in a dark corner glued to a computer screen. He was told him that the Special Agent wanted to see him. Sam stood up and walked the length of the room where his visitor waited patiently. "Special Agent Jefferson, I'm sorry to keep you waiting."

"That's okay." Special Agent Jefferson did his best to hide his irritation. "Do you recall I brought you the laptop of the girl I told you about?"

"Yes, yeah, I remember. Did any of my colleagues tell you I haven't found anything yet?"

"Uhu, they did. They said you might be looking for a key?"

"Yup. She may have written it down somewhere; a notebook or a diary or something like that." Sam suggested.

"I've got a couple of notebooks here. Is there anything in them which looks like it might help?"

Sam took the notebooks and flicked through the pages. He took a couple of minutes to do this and the Special Agent shifted his weight from foot to foot as he waited with anticipation. Sam slowly looked up from the pages shaking his head. "No," he said slowly, "I can't see anything here which leaps out at me as being the key code. Have you got anything else?"

Special Agent Jefferson looked disappointed. "I've only got the diaries, but my colleague downstairs has been through them and found nothing helpful."

"Would you like me to give 'em a go, too?"

"Okay, I'll fetch them for you, thanks."

"Fine. I'll keep the notebooks too and go through them again, in case I've missed something," offered Sam, "but I'm not very hopeful about them."

"Okay. Thanks." Special Agent Jefferson turned and headed for the stairs.

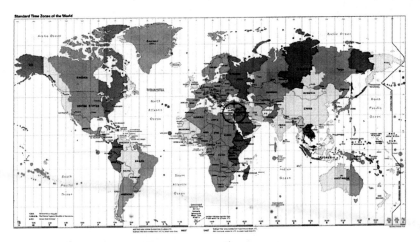

21:00 Israel Standard Time 26th December 2012 (UTC 19:00)

Things seemed quieter on the border between Israel and South Lebanon. The column that was sent across to root out the source of the rocket attacks, had now pulled back a short way. The commander had been trying to assess whether his efforts had been successful. It was difficult to be sure. Had it gone quiet because he had destroyed the terrorist capabilities, or had they merely moved off to regroup elsewhere? He still had the distraction of local youths pelting them with stones and other makeshift missiles now and again, but dealing with this was a much lower priority than stopping the offensive of the rockets. More troublingly, he'd heard word of a military build up on the border with Syria on the Golan Heights. He decided to wait it out and see if there were any more rockets going to be fired into his country. He knew if they tried again at night, it would be easier for him to spot their location and deal with them. He posted guards and lookouts and handed over authority to his second in command. He hoped that he could get some much needed sleep.

Many pundits on the Internet who predicted the end of the world with the end of the Mayan Calendar Cycle on the 21st December were now turning their attention to the end of the year. Suggestions the world would end at midnight on the 31st

December were now being stated as fact. Fringe religious groups were not slow to pick up this idea and were encouraging their followers to prepare for the next life. This included making large donations to their churches so they would be 'free of earthly shackles'. The bright new star was being cited as the messenger from God of this impending apocalypse.

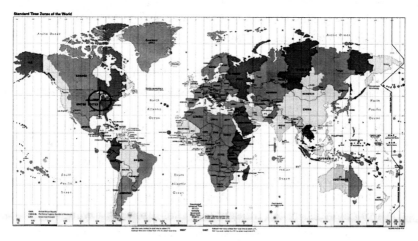

15:32 Central Standard Time 26th December 2012 (UTC 21:32)

Victor Truman wasn't sure how to proceed. His trail had gone cold and he was worried he wouldn't be able to pick it up. The Houstons' could have gone anywhere. They were in a car not registered to them and maybe they had even changed their name. They could have left the city, the State or even the country for all he knew. He tried to put himself in their position. Where would they go? It was while he was thinking about this it occurred to him they may have family elsewhere in the city. His chair shot backwards as he jumped to his feet. He grabbed his coat and car keys for the drive back to the Houstons' house.

He pulled up outside the empty property and got out of his car. This time he didn't feel the need for stealth. He didn't have a warrant to search the place, neither did he care. The street was still quiet, so even though he made no effort to hide the fact that he was there, nobody saw him slip around the back. Once again he broke in through the back door from the garden and walked to the kitchen and on into the body of the house. He headed for the stairs and quickly ascended to the main bedroom. This time the Detective knew what he was looking for. He pulled open a couple of drawers searching for papers. A letter from a family member or an address book would be ideal. Nothing. He couldn't find anything definite enough for him to pin down where they might have gone. He went back down the stairs and turned into the main room. It was a comfortable space with a big sofa and well padded chairs. A large television dominated the room. Then he spotted the computer on a desk in the corner. Victor walked to the chair in front of the screen and sat down. He scanned the device and found the button to switch it on. The screen burst into life as the computer went through its 'boot up' routine. He waited patiently, biting his lip. For what seemed like hours, but was just a couple of minutes, the system whirred and then eventually settled. Victor was now staring at the 'home screen' and wondering where to start. He was not comfortable with computers. He had got used to them through necessity but thought that their usefulness was overrated. He recognised the icon for an email program and grabbed the mouse and clicked on it.

The program opened up to present him with a diary. He quickly scanned through this but found nothing useful other than an entry on the 24th saying 'hospital visit!' Victor then clicked on the 'address book'. This he hoped would prove more fruitful. He dragged his eyes down the list of names. He spotted a couple of names he recognised from the list of members of the Church of the Second Coming. This encouraged him. He came across the 'H's and went carefully though them hoping to see a possible brother or sister or parent. Mr. Houston had an aunt in Maine and a brother in California. Victor took out his note book and wrote these down. Somehow though, he had the feeling that these were not who he was looking for. He was once again, at a loss. He stood up and walked around the room hoping for inspiration. He noticed a photograph on the mantelpiece and went over to inspect it. It was a wedding photograph. The Detective picked up the picture and took a long look at the people who he was now chasing. They looked a pleasant couple, the sort you would be happy to make acquaintance with at a party. The woman in fact was quite attractive. Her blonde hair matched that of the rather grainy image that he had seen on the video taken from the hospital. He didn't see their faces on the video as the CCTV was positioned behind the couple as they left the hospital. They could, plausibly, look like the drawings made by the police artist. There was another blonde woman in the photograph too. Then it dawned on him.

He put the picture down and went back to the computer. If they hadn't gone to shelter with anyone from his family; they had perhaps gone to *her* family. He scanned through the emails once again. He randomly opened an email. It was addressed to 'Gillian'. Now he knew Mrs. Houston's first name. But what was her maiden name? Once again he scanned through the names in the address list. Most names were mentioned only once but there was a small group of names that all had a surname in common. Could these be her relations? He clicked on the first name in the group; Marie Dixon. It gave her address as a town in Virginia. The next one was Greg Dixon; he resided in Tucson, Arizona. He clicked again. Martha Dixon lived in Chicago. It was an address across the other side of town. The Detective wrote this one down as well. Now all he had to do was to confirm the woman's name, before she was married, was Dixon. He shut down the computer and went back up to the bedroom. Once again he began looking for letters addressed to someone other than Houston. He realised that it was likely to be an old letter or envelope; people have a habit of keeping old letters, especially love letters.

The drawer in the dressing table rendered nothing useful. He moved to the large closet and opened it as he had done on his first visit. This time he noticed a small brown box under some of the dresses that still hung there. He lifted it out and opened it. Immediately he saw it was full of trinkets and old documents. Victor knew that this was her box. No man, he thought, would keep treasured possessions in this manner. He placed the box carefully on the table and began to sift through its contents. The first letter he came across had no name on the envelope. It contained a few old pictures, he guessed, of members of her family judging by the blonde hair. He pulled out some more faded jewellery and there underneath was a letter addressed to Gillian Dixon. It was a love letter from her now husband. It was enough to confirm the woman's family name for him. He stuffed the bric-a-brac back into the box and closed

254

the lid and thrust it into the closet. He ran down the stairs and out of the back once more.

As he rounded the side of the house he saw the old man from next door he had spoken with earlier. He approached him confidently hoping to give the impression that he hadn't been inside the house.

The old man looked up. "You again," he uttered in a less than polite fashion.

"Er, yes. I was hoping that you might be able to help me."

"Well, what is it this time?"

"The lady of the house, do you happen to know if she has a sister who lives across town?"

"No idea," said the old man now looking quizzically at Victor. He then suggested, "But I reckon my wife might. Anyway, why you askin' so many questions, what have they gone and done?"

Victor ignored the question. "Could you see if your wife could tell me about the lady's sister?"

The old man shuffled over to the doorway and called, "'Lizabeth, can ya come out here a second?"

There was a moment's pause and then an elderly lady appeared in the doorway. "What is it Seth, what are ya wanting?"

"I've got a man here, a policeman by all accounts, askin' questions about them next door."

"Oh my." The old lady stepped out of the doorway so that she could look Victor in the eye. "How can we help you officer?"

"I'm sorry to trouble you ma'am, I just need to know if the lady next door, Mrs. Houston, has a sister in the city. Your husband said you might know."

"Well yes officer, I believe she does, right across town. I know that she sometimes goes to visit."

"Thank you ma'am; can you also tell me if the lady next door has had a baby recently?"

"Why certainly not officer, I'd have known if she was pregnant. So why are you askin' all these questions? I hope they ain't done nothing wrong?"

"It just an enquiry I'm following up ma'am, nothing to bother you with."

"Okay, officer. Glad I could be of help."

Victor nodded his thanks once again and made for his car. The old man followed him with his eyes, right down the street.

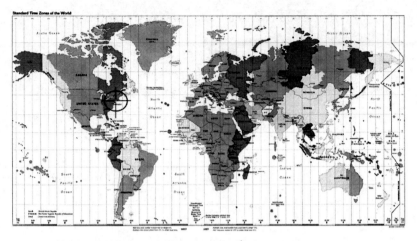

16:45 Eastern Standard Time 26th December 2012 (UTC 21:45)

Special Agent Jefferson was growing increasingly frustrated. He had been through the diaries himself and could find nothing of any significance in them. Now they were in the hands of Sam, the IT man. The Special Agent knew he would just have to wait. He decided he would go home. Tomorrow was another day he told himself, perhaps the IT boys might come up with something then. Just as he was about to get up, the phone on his desk rang. It was Sam.

"Special Agent Jefferson?" Sam asked tentatively.

"Yes, Sam, have you got anything for me?"

"I'm sorry, no I haven't. I've been through the notebooks again, but there's nothing there of any use and nothing that looks like a key code."

"Oh, I see. What about the diaries?" This was Special Agent Jefferson's last hope.

"Well, nothing there yet either. But I'm willing to keep trying. I've got a feeling it could be in there somewhere, I just haven't found it yet."

"Okay. I'm off home in a minute if you are willing to keep trying, please do. Is there any other way of getting into the documents?"

"Well we could try force, but you never know if it will work and it can take some time. It will be better if we can get into them with a key code."

"Okay, thank you Sam. If you come up with anything let me know. Have you got a pencil?" Sam said he did. "Okay, take down my mobile number and text me if you crack it." Special Agent Jefferson then proceeded to give Sam his number.

"Okay, I'll do that." Sam put down the phone and went back to the diaries. He felt there was something in there which he was overlooking. He sat down in front of the last diary, took a deep breath and began to steadily flick through the pages, studying each entry in turn. He stopped at the entry for Salwa's birthday. September 11th. Boy did that day have a lot of connotations. Unlike any of the other entries, which seemed important to the girl, on this one, the date itself was underlined and had a ring drawn around it. Sam had spent most of his working life trying to crack the codes of people who knew what they were doing; criminals, terrorists, governments even. He suddenly realised that this girl was not a cipher expert. He shouted "Of course!" and leapt to his feet.

He grabbed the laptop and opened the lid. It took a few moments to re-access the desktop screen. Once he was there, he opened the program which would ask for the key code that would then allow him to open the documents which were encrypted. The screen appeared and the box which required the code, had the cursor flashing in it, almost beckoning him to try his luck. He carefully entered 09111986 and pressed the 'enter' key. He held his breath and his shoulders fell as a text message stated 'incorrect code'. He shut the lid and went back to studying the diary.

Spy satellites had now observed a military build-up on the borders of Israel and Egypt. Various intelligence agencies had flagged this up and security chiefs were being called in to assess the new images. Rooms in the Pentagon and in Whitehall in London were remarkably busy for a Boxing Day evening.

The President's security advisors, along with his Joint Chiefs of Staff, were heading towards the Oval Office in the White

House. Files containing the latest satellite imagery were tucked into brief cases. The President himself had been relaxing with his family and once he received the phone call, went directly to his office. He was waiting for his guests when there was a knock at the door and the sombre group moved into the body of the room. The President's security advisor spoke first.

"We're sorry to have disturbed you Mr. President, but new information has come to light which you need to see, sir."

"Okay Sam, what have you got?"

The Joint Chiefs of Staff and the President's security advisor sat down around the table. The photographs were spread out in front of the President.

"Can you take me through what we've got here?"

One of the military advisors now chimed in and explained the pictures showed heavy weaponry accumulating on both the Syrian and Israeli side of the Golan Heights. There was also another set of pictures showing troop movement along the border between Egypt and Israel. There didn't seem to be any similar or opposing forces on the Israeli side. This was given some plausible explanations by the military advisors, as the pictures were only around 1 hour old it was possible that the Israelis were as yet unaware of the Egyptian troops, or they didn't take it as a serious threat. It could also be the Israelis had not yet moved their own troops into the area.

"We have some further information sir," Sam said in a matter of fact way. "It seems the Israelis have put their air force on the highest alert."

"Thank you gentlemen," The President looked grave. "Have you any suggestions?"

Sam turned to the leader of the 'free world' and said, "You could call the leaders of Israel, Syria and Egypt sir. Ask them to explain their actions and suggest they might relax, in the interests of peace in the region."

"I'm happy to do that if you think it'll help." The President then asked, "Israel are our allies, do I mention, that in the event of a military conflict, we could not stand idle?"

"It may be a little early for a threat of that nature, sir. It could be it's just a coincidence the Egyptians for example, are carrying out military exercises in the area, but considering the other tensions in the region and the fact it's the dead of night there at the moment, this seems a little unlikely."

"Very well Sam, I'll take it gently; one step at a time eh?"

"Yes sir, one step at a time."

The group of men seemed satisfied that this was all that was necessary so far and rose to take their leave of the President, in the knowledge he was about to make a few important phone calls.

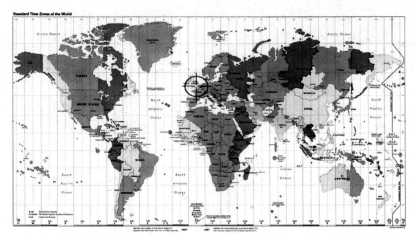

23:30 Greenwich Mean Time 26th December 2012 (UTC 23:30)

The Prime Minister was just about to go to bed when the phone rang. His wife looked concerned as he frowned and said a polite "Thank you, I'm on my way."

"I'm sorry darling," he said to his wife, "duty calls."

He walked to the door, trying to avoid the look of disappointment on his wife's face. When he reached his office he found Brian Masterson and the head of the Joint Intelligence Service waiting for him.

"Do you never go home Brian?" The Prime Minister did his best to lighten the mood.

"I sometimes wonder myself Prime Minister." A wry smile flickered across the face of the Prime Minister's Private Secretary.

"So, it must be important for you to have called me down at this hour."

"Yes, Prime Minister. We've been made aware of a military build up on the borders of Israel and Syria and troop movement on the Egyptian side of their border with Israel too."

"I knew about the incursion by Israeli troops into South Lebanon, but this is a major development. What do you think is happening?"

The head of the Joint Intelligence Services now spoke. "We can't be certain Prime Minister, but these photographs show

261

some very heavy weaponry being moved into position on both sides of the border. It looks as though some troops are also being moved by Israel, to its border with Egypt. The Israeli Air Force is on the highest alert and they are starting to fly sorties around their borders and we are aware that the aircraft are fully armed."

"This doesn't look good gentlemen. How are our American friends reacting?"

Brian Masterson told the Prime Minister about the meeting with the President and his Joint Chiefs of Staff.

"How do you know about that Brian?"

"Let's just say I have a friend in the West Wing, sir." The Prime Minister gave a slight smile. Brian continued, "I gather the President is calling the various heads of government in the countries concerned."

"Do we know what he's said, or the outcome?"

"I am not privy to that information Prime Minister."

"I'm disappointed Brian, I thought you knew everything that went on." The Prime Minister actually grinned this time. Brian raised an eyebrow, unsure whether this was a compliment. "So gentlemen, what do you suggest that we do?"

"We have a few options sir. Do nothing and wait to see how it develops; follow the President's lead and call the parties concerned or you could call the President yourself and ask him what he thinks of the situation."

"Hmm, I think a call to the President is the best move. At least he can tell us what the Americans make of the situation."

"Very good sir." Brian looked satisfied with the PM's decision. He then added, "By the way Prime Minister, it now seems that two or three different factions have claimed responsibility for the Bethlehem bomb." The Prime Minister said nothing but looked quizzical. Brian continued, "A group calling itself 'The Justice of God', obviously an extreme Islamic organisation and another, going by the name of 'Fighters of Allah'. The third, oddly enough, claims to be a right wing Christian organisation named the 'Soldiers of Christ'."

"Do we have anything on any of these groups?" The Prime Minister looked somewhat bewildered.

"No sir." replied Brian. "It could be the Islamic factions are linked to Al Qaeda, although we can't be certain. So many of these groups pop up and disappear again, often just to try and confuse. As for the extremist Christians; this could just be a lone lunatic on the Internet, probably based in the 'Deep South' of America."

The Prime Minister nodded his understanding. "Well, thank you gentlemen. Please keep me informed of any further developments."

The Head of the JIS then said, "Oh, there was just one other thing, sir. We are aware that both the Russians and the Chinese are monitoring the situation in the Middle East carefully too. With such a precarious situation, we need to persuade them as well, that peace in the region is in everyone's interest."

"Quite so." The Prime Minister nodded and the two advisors took their leave. He picked up the telephone and pressed the button to give him a secure line to the White House.

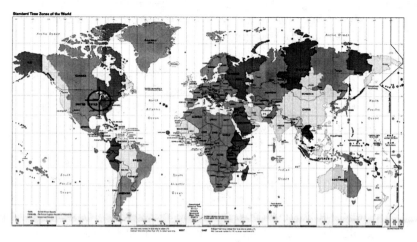

17:50 Central Standard Time 26ᵗʰ December 2012 (UTC 23:50)

Detective Truman had found the address of Martha Dixon quite easily. It seemed she lived alone, although he couldn't be sure of this. The drive across town had been slow. It was raining and windy. Victor found it difficult to pick out the house numbers through the windscreen of his car, as the rain was blurring his view. The houses were small and neat, not as large as the Houstons' place, but pleasant enough. Finally he stopped outside a small house with a trim garden surrounded by a white picket fence. He was sure this was the right address.

He alerted a squad car in the area that he may need back up. They assured him they were less than five minutes away and were heading in his direction. He wasn't expecting trouble but you could never be too sure; experience had taught him well. He still had the scar of a bullet wound to his shoulder from a time he thought he was going to a routine operation...

He took out his gun and checked the clip and the safety catch and settled the weapon back into its holster. The rain seemed to be coming down harder now. He took a deep breath and opened the vehicle's door. The rain beat down on him and he was soaking in an instant. He ran to the front door trying to shelter under the eaves as much as he possibly could and rang the door bell.

After a few moments a woman opened the door and peered at him. She was he thought in her forties, nicely dressed. She had the air of a school teacher about her.

"I'm sorry to disturb you ma'am." Victor proffered his badge as identification. "Are you Martha Dixon?"

"Why yes officer how may I help you?" Before Victor had a chance to reply, she realised that he was standing on her porch getting drenched and suggested that he might like to come in.

"Why, thank you ma'am." This seemed an odd move for someone who had something to hide. That or she was supremely confident in her skills of deception. Once he was in the light, he could see how much she looked like her sister. Her long blonde hair was held up with a clip and she looked relaxed and unflustered. They now stood just inside the front door. The Detective was aware that he was dripping rain water on to the floor.

She asked Victor once again. "So how may I help you?"

"I'm hoping you might be able to help me with an enquiry ma'am. I'm trying to find the whereabouts of your sister and her husband." He let the question hang in the air and studied her face carefully for any sign of fear.

"Why?" Martha exclaimed, "I have no idea where they are Detective. They live right across town, they might be home?"

Victor Truman was impressed. She was good, really good. Not a flicker of emotion did he spot, except one of surprise at the question.

"So why are you asking me this officer? Is everything alright? There hasn't been an accident or anything?"

"No ma'am, there hasn't been an accident."

Still looking puzzled Martha then said, "I can give you their address if you like?"

"No, Ms. Dixon, thank you, I don't need the address; I've just come from there." The look of puzzlement on Martha Dixon's face now changed to bewilderment.

"Tell me Ms. Dixon, does your sister belong to the Church of the Second Coming?"

"Why yes, I believe she does."

"Are you a member yourself?"

"No officer, I'm not. I am a Christian, but Gillian got hooked into that church through her husband. I told her that I didn't like their ideas. Why, is there something wrong at the church?"

Victor ignored the question. "Has Gillian recently had a baby?"

"No, of course not; she would've had to have been pregnant and that isn't going to happen anytime soon. What a strange question, why are you asking me this?"

"I'm sorry to fire all these questions at you ma'am. Like I said, it's to do with a line of enquiry I'm making." There was a slight pause during which it was obvious Martha Dixon was doing her best to work out what was going on. "You said your sister wasn't going to get pregnant anytime soon. Why did you say that?"

"Because she can't have children, officer. She's had tests and she is infertile"

"Would she like to have children?"

"I guess she would. Most women want to have kids, don't they?"

"I wouldn't know ma'am. I've never been married myself."

"Oh, well take it from me, they would."

"Do you have any children Ms. Dixon?"

"No I don't either. And before you ask, yes I was married, but the drunken bum left me for his secretary. I'm afraid that I haven't felt kindly disposed towards men ever since."

Victor nodded with slight embarrassment. All the while, he had been listening intently to sounds in the house, hoping that there might be a giveaway noise, a child's cry or some movement that would suggest that this lady was not alone. All he could hear was the ticking of a large clock. "Well, I'm sorry to have troubled you ma'am."

"No trouble officer."

"Oh, one last thing Ms. Dixon; have you heard from your sister in the last couple of days?"

"The last time we spoke must have been a couple of days ago, that's right, Christmas Eve."

"And what did you talk about if I may ask?"

"Well she said that they might be away for a while, but she seemed a bit vague about that."

"How long is a while?

"I don't know officer. I'm afraid that my sister and I are not close. We see each other from time to time, sometimes she comes over here and sometimes I go over there, but that's about it. We don't spend our Christmas's together if that's what you are angling at. Not since she got married and ended up in that church anyhow."

"Okay, well thanks again. Is it alright if I call back should I need to?"

"Sure officer?"

"Call me Victor, Victor Truman."

"Okay Victor. Nice to meet you, I'm sure."

"Nice to meet you too ma'am." Victor pulled open the door and once again stepped into the rain. He ran back to his car and sat in the driving seat watching the house for several minutes. He was hoping to see signs of activity or maybe Ms. Dixon leaving the house in a hurry, so he could follow her. After ten minutes he decided he was wasting his time. Perhaps she was telling the truth? What he was sure about, was that his trail had once again been brought to an abrupt halt. He hit the steering wheel with the palm of his hand in frustration, started the engine and drove off back to the centre of town and his office.

Day 4

The Supernova was still outshining every other star in the sky and proved to be a source of fascination for millions of people right across the globe. Astronomers and Astro-physicists were gaining a wealth of information about it and were busy figuring out its behaviour and why it went supernova in the first place. Countless numbers of astrologers were also trying to include this celestial event into their systems, as were other practitioners of the more esoteric arts. Religious groups from all faiths were still attempting to interpret the significance of the event. By far the largest number of websites now commentating on the event were peddling 'Doomsday' and other such calamities and were very popular.

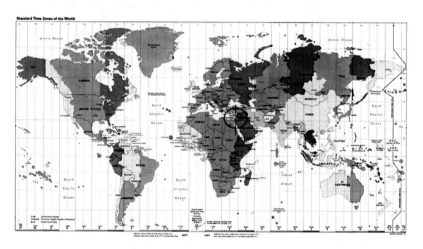

03:17 Israel Standard Time 27th December 2012 (UTC 01:17)

The commander of the armoured column now sited just across the border from Israel in Southern Lebanon was awoken by his guard to be informed that, whereas they had thought all things were now quiet, a salvo of rockets far larger than the last, had just been launched into Israeli territory. He cursed as he tried to drag himself out of sleep. He immediately ordered the tanks forward and gave them instructions to seek and destroy both the rockets and their operators. Explosions were deafening as the tanks started to shell the area they determined as the launch site.

04:25 Israel Standard Time 27th December 2012 (UTC 02:25)

The Israeli Prime Minister was woken by the telephone. He was informed of the missiles that had landed in Northern Israel and more importantly, of some Russian 'Mig' aircraft of the Syrian Air Force which were heading directly for Israeli air space. He immediately called for a meeting with the Chief of General Staff and the Defence Minister.

A squadron of Israeli F-16 fighter jets had been diverted from their route over the West Bank to meet this perceived threat, now approaching from the direction of the Golan Heights. As they flew to meet the aircraft heading towards them, the squadron leader requested instruction as to whether they should engage the 'enemy'. He was told to 'stand by'.

Senior military advisors and Secretaries of Defence were being woken all over the world to inform them of this new potential conflict and the raising of the stakes over the skies of the Middle East. The UN Security Council was called into emergency session.

The squadron leader was informed only to open fire if they were fired upon, but to give chase and make it obvious they 'meant business'. They were also instructed to remain in Israeli airspace. It wasn't long before the F-16 jets picked up the incoming Migs on their radar. As they drew closer, the Squadron leader was alerted that one of the Mig fighters had a weapons lock on his aircraft. He immediately responded by targeting his missiles at the Mig in a high speed variation of a 'Mexican Standoff'." The Mig disengaged its missiles and banked sharply along with the other fighters to head back into the blackness of the night. The F-16's gave chase for a short while, but being aware that they were now in Syrian air-space, the squadron

269

leader ordered that they should break off the pursuit. He stayed circling the area for several minutes in case the Migs decided to return. However, the radars remained clear and fuel was dwindling, so he ordered a return to base.

People were trying to get out of Israel. Visitors who had been desperate to get into the country to visit Bethlehem for the Christmas festivities were now equally desperate to leave. This was only possible by air as the borders remained shut, no longer due to the pressure of people wanting to get in but because of the security situation, which seemed to be worsening hour by hour. All the main airports were still operating but flights were heavily oversubscribed and the airport buildings were a seething mass of people. Fist fights had broken out sporadically and the police and airport security officials were doing their best to maintain order. Tensions were running high, very much like the rest of the country. Many were concerned that, should the security situation deteriorate any further, the airports would be closed too. Everyone seemed to be 'on edge'.

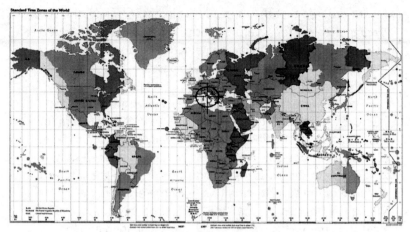

07:35 Central European Time 2th December 2012 (UTC 06:35)

Cardinal Leonardo Verdi was awoken by a member of the Vatican Police. He knocked on the door and entered the room where the Cardinal was sleeping, just down the corridor from Giovanni Casparo.

"I'm sorry to disturb you, Your Eminence."

It took a moment for the Cardinal to fully surface from a heavy sleep. "Yes, yes, what is it?" He said rather crossly, without intending to sound so short.

"I'm afraid we have received another email intended for Father Casparo."

This caused the Cardinal to snap into full wakefulness. "What does it say?"

"All it said was, *'you only have yourself to blame'*."

"Is that it?"

"Yes, Your Eminence."

"Have you got any further with tracing the source of these messages yet?"

"No, Your Eminence, but the IT team is still working on it."

The Cardinal nodded. "Very well, I shall inform Father Casparo of it myself, but for the moment I think we should let him sleep. There is no sense in upsetting him. He had enough upset yesterday to last him a lifetime I'm sure."

"Very good, Your Eminence." The policeman turned and closed the door behind him.

Cardinal Verdi now began to seriously consider a thought that had occurred to him the previous afternoon.

Various heads of State around Europe had been exchanging telephone calls concerning the rapidly destabilising situation in the Middle East. Some had called the heads of government of Israel and Syria in the hope of calming things down, only to be met with denials and protestations of entitlement to defend sovereign territory. The Syrian government was claiming that the Israeli Air Force had violated their airspace, while the Israeli government was making a similar claim against the Syrians. Both sides denied that there were any heavy armaments being deployed on the Golan Heights, other than the usual troop movements, which they claimed went on all the time. The American President had met similar retorts from both sides, as had the British Prime Minister.

The Internet was still awash with speculation as to when the 'end of the world' was coming. The increased tension in the Middle East just continued to add fuel to these particular fires. More alarmingly, some people began to circulate the rumour that the gamma ray burst from the Supernova was hurtling towards our planet at colossal speed and would wipe out all life on Earth within the next few days. This particular idea had gone 'viral' on one or two Internet social networking sites and many people were becoming seriously distressed by it. Efforts by more informed individuals with scientific backgrounds to explain that this could not possibly happen were either ignored or met with deep scepticism. Churches of all persuasions were noticing a great increase in their numbers of parishioners or followers and in particular, their financial income. None of them were displeased with this.

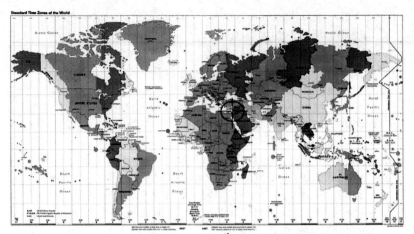

10:43 Israel Standard Time 27th December 2012 (UTC 08:43)

No one was clear how it started, or even who started it, but there was an exchange of small arms fire between patrols across the border between Israel and Syria in the Golan Heights. It ended almost as soon as it began and there were no casualties on either side.

09:48 Central European Time 27th December 2012 (UTC 08:48)

Father Casparo had risen, washed, shaved and breakfasted on his own. He felt ready to face another day. There was a soft knock on his door and Cardinal Verdi then tentatively entered the room.

"Good morning Giovanni and how are you feeling today?"

"Well rested thank you, Your Eminence." He gestured for the Cardinal to take a seat. "So what time do you think I should face the press again today and what would you like me to tell them?"

"Ah." The Cardinal paused and cleared his throat and then continued, "I wanted to talk to you about that, Giovanni. You've had another email I'm afraid." A look of worried enquiry spread over the priest's face.

"So what did it say?"

"It said and I quote, *'you only have yourself to blame'*."

"Is that it?" Giovanni seemed incredulous. If it wasn't so serious he probably would have laughed.

"Yes, that's all." The Cardinal shifted uncomfortably in his seat. "It has got me to thinking that you should withdraw from your duties as Papal spokesman."

"What?" Giovanni sounded almost outraged. "Why, should I do that? I'm quite capable of carrying on with it," the priest protested. "Am I not performing my duties well enough?"

"Yes, yes, my dear Giovanni, that is not the issue. Both the Holy Father and I are quite happy with the way you've handled the press." He dropped his voice a little. "Last evening was obviously a surprise for you."

"Oh, is that it? Because I fell flat on my face so to speak, you want to pull me from the post."

"No, no, Giovanni you misunderstand. I and the Holy Father," a look of surprised suspicion crossed Father Casparo's face, "yes, I have spoken with him about this just this morning; well, we feel that you are possibly in danger. We don't know who is sending these emails to you and how serious the writers are in hurting you. While you are in the public eye, it may just be aggravating them and the situation. It also seems that the press wishes to attack you personally. So we've made the decision that we should withdraw you."

Giovanni felt confused. On the one hand he was rather relieved that he no longer had to face the ordeal of the press who, he had to agree, did seem to be out to get him. On the other hand for some strange reason he had started to take to the role of Papal spokesman and now that somebody wanted to remove him from that post, he felt irritated.

"So are you suggesting that I should go into hiding?"

"That's rather an emotive way of describing a tactical and temporary withdrawal."

"I'm sorry Your Eminence; I shouldn't be so precious about it." Giovanni was now concerned that he had overstepped the mark and had insulted the Cardinal. "I will of course be guided by you and the Holy Father in this situation."

The Cardinal was relieved to see the priest's 'climb down'. He didn't want to have to order him to stop. He disliked using his authority that way. He attempted to soothe Giovanni further and said, "This will only be temporary I'm sure. Besides, you have other concerns at the moment. This will give you a little more time to keep up with the very worrying developments with your brother and sister-in-law and it won't do the press any harm to have someone else to snipe at."

Giovanni could see the sense in this. He was really more worried about his family in the USA than he cared to admit and he never really wanted all this attention. "Okay, hiding it is," he said with a wry smile that prompted a similar display on the countenance of the Cardinal.

Warships of various nations were being diverted to the Mediterranean and the Gulf. These were for 'monitoring' purposes. Fortunately, there had been no more skirmishes for the time being across the Israeli-Syrian border. Insults, claims and counterclaims were still being traded at the political and governmental level. The UN Security Council was scheduled to meet in emergency session at 9:00am New York Time.

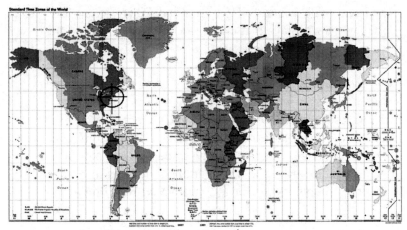

07:32 Eastern Standard Time 27th December 2012 (UTC 12:32)

Special Agent Jefferson had got into work early. He was hoping that the IT people would crack the code for the documents on the girl's laptop today. The whole issue was starting to irritate him. He had other work piling up and he wanted to draw a conclusive line under this. He sat down at his desk and checked for messages on the computer terminal in front of him. He was disappointed to see that there was nothing from Sam or anyone else in the IT department. He decided that he would have to pay them another visit. If they couldn't get into it by cracking the 'code' legitimately, then he would insist that they force entry. He headed for the stairs once more, with a look of grim determination on his face.

When he got to the right floor, he headed directly for the area where he knew his contact Sam, to work. Sam was nowhere to be seen. In fact it all seemed rather quiet. Special Agent Jefferson clicked his tongue in annoyance. He began to circle around the desks and work stations and cables that littered this area of the floor. It was then that he noticed a door in the wall that was unseen from where he had been standing. He moved towards it, knocked and tried the handle. As the door opened before him, Sam looked up from the pile of books that he had been studying.

"Ah, there you are," the Special Agent snapped.

"Oh, good morning." Sam said as cheerily as he could.

"Well, have you had any luck?"

"Not yet, but..."

Special Agent Jefferson did not give him time to finish his sentence. "Well then I suggest that you break into it the hard way." He almost barked this as an instruction.

Sam looked a little surprised. He did not like being 'ordered about' as he would describe it. "If you'll let me finish," he said quite testily and continued as the Special Agent raised an eyebrow, "I think that I'm on to something."

Special Agent Jefferson's eyes narrowed and he now had a look of curiosity crossing his face. "What do you mean, 'you think that you're onto something'?"

"I've been studying the diaries again. Not just to see if I could find a key code, but just reading them."

"Well?"

"Well," Sam repeated, "I was just reading the entry that she wrote on the day of her birthday; you know September 11th, just as you came in."

"Go on."

"She talks about a couple of the presents that she received." The Special Agent was finding Sam's explanation tortuously slow and gritted his teeth. "She also made a rather strange entry, which doesn't seem to be repeated anywhere that I could find on any day around that date, or anywhere else at all for that matter."

"So what does it say?" The Special Agent was now fantasising about picking him up by the collar and shaking him.

"It says, *'I feel all back to front today'.*"

"Is that it?" Special Agent Jefferson now sounded incredulous.

"Yes, that's it, but it occurred to me..."

"What?"

"Well, I was wondering if I perhaps need to put her birth date into the program 'back to front'. So instead of 09111986 I should perhaps put 68911190?"

There was a moments silence as this idea sank into the minds of both the men.

"So what are you waiting for?" The Special Agent now had a note of excited frustration in his voice.

Sam jumped up and ran for the door almost pushing Special Agent Jefferson out of the way, who in turn jostled Sam at the door. Sam dived for his desk and the laptop and threw the screen open. The wait for the computer to wake up and settle, seemed interminable. Eventually, the icon that Sam had been willing to appear popped onto the screen. He clicked it and waited once again for the security program to start up. The box requiring the security key code blinked into view and Sam was now trembling a little as he entered the code 68911190. He looked at the Special Agent, swallowed hard and clicked the mouse. There was a momentary, heart-stopping pause and then the welcome message flashed onto the screen. With a shout of "Yes!" Sam slapped Special Agent Jefferson's upraised hand in a 'high-five' motion.

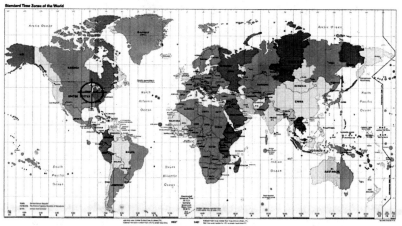

08:05 Central Standard Time 27th December 2012 (UTC 14:05)

Victor Truman crawled into his office. He was tired and very unhappy. He always did his best not to get emotionally involved with his cases, but the abduction of a small child, in this case a baby hardly twenty four hours old, really got to him. Even though he thought that no harm would come intentionally to the child, he knew there was always the risk that, if he could ever find the kidnappers, there was the possibility of violence. This would not necessarily be directed at the child, but nevertheless the child was in 'harm's way.' Another possible scenario that made his blood run cold at the thought was they might kill the child rather than allow him to be taken from them. He knew these painful thoughts were probably born from fatigue; he did feel really tired. He hadn't been sleeping that well. He shambled over to the coffee machine and hoped a hit of caffeine would help get his brain into gear. He needed to think and think quickly.

He sat back down at his desk and reviewed the notes he'd made from the start of the case. He had started to believe Mrs. Houston's sister really didn't know anything of her and her husband's whereabouts. So, he thought if she wasn't actively shielding them, perhaps she could be persuaded to help him find them. He debated with himself about whether he should tell her the truth and see if she was willing to help, or perhaps he should 'modify' the story a little to make it sound less like 'Martha Dixon's sister was a wanted woman who would likely spend a very long time in jail'. He was still debating this with himself as he drove back across town to re-interview the only lead he now had to the whereabouts of his prime suspects and more importantly, the missing child.

He pulled up outside Martha's house and as he got out of his car, he decided to play it by ear. He walked up to the front door of the house and knocked once again. At least this time it wasn't pouring with rain. It took him ages to dry out the previous evening, requiring a hot bath and two glasses of whisky.

It seemed to take a while for Martha Dixon to answer the door. This unsettled the Detective a little and some of his initial suspicions resurfaced in his mind. When she answered the door she was looking a little flustered and had a towel wrapped around her head and it looked as though she had dragged a few clothes on in a hurry.

"Oh, it's you again. Sorry I was a while, I was in the shower."

Detective Truman relaxed as he realised that she was almost certainly telling the truth. "I'm sorry to have disturbed you again ma'am," he said quite contritely.

"That's okay, officer. At least this time I'm damper than you." She gave him a slight smile.

"Oh, er, yes." Victor too tried to smile, but felt a little uncomfortable. He pressed on, "I was wondering if you wouldn't mind answering a few more question Ms. Dixon?"

"Oh, sure, why don't you come on in? Leastways, you won't make the furniture all soggy like you might've, last night."

Victor was starting to enjoy this rather attractive lady's gentle sense of humour. He cleared his throat and tried to snap himself back into his professional mode.

"Thank you." They walked into a modest but comfortable room with a couple of chairs and a sofa. An attractive lamp stood on a table by one of the chairs and a TV set of moderate size nestled in a corner. Martha Dixon was obviously nowhere nearly as well off as her sister. The Detective sat himself in one of the chairs as the lady did the same.

281

"So how may I help Detective?"

"I'm still trying to locate your sister ma'am, because I think she can help us in finding the whereabouts of a missing child."

Martha frowned as she tried to take in what the policeman was telling her.

"So how do you think that she may know where a missing child might be? As I told you last night, she doesn't have any children of her own and so she doesn't frequent places where they might be."

"You misunderstand me ma'am. The child I'm talking about is very young; just a day old baby." Martha's frown deepened. He waited for the implication of what he was saying to sink in. He thought that if she were truly helping to misdirect the police she would come up with a plausible story as to why her sister couldn't possibly be involved. She may even start to look nervous. He studied her carefully.

She shook her head. "I still don't understand what this could possibly have to do with my sis..." Her voice tailed off.

Victor could see the look of shock on Martha's face as she suddenly realised what he was driving at.

"Oh my God," she blurted out, "You think Gillian has taken the baby! The one kidnapped from the hospital." The woman looked both confused and horrified at the same moment.

"I'm not sure at the moment," he lied, "but I need to eliminate her from my enquiries."

"But why? Why should she steal another woman's child?" Martha shook her head vigorously now. "I simply don't believe it."

Victor decided to take a gamble and to tell his prime suspect's sister the truth. "We think ma'am, that there may be a religious motivation to it."

This completely stunned Ms. Dixon. She seemed unable to speak for a moment. She eventually said more quietly and with some hesitation, "W-what do you mean, religious motivation?"

Victor swallowed hard, took a deep breath and started to explain how he thought that Martha's sister and her husband might think that the child could be the new Messiah. Martha Dixon's jaw fell open and her eyes grew wider as Victor Truman spelled out his theory. She tried to form words, but none came. She sat on the chair like a rabbit caught in a car's headlights, unable to move or say anything. Her mind was racing but nothing coherent would come out of her mouth.

Detective Truman began to feel uncomfortable. He wasn't sure if being quite so blunt was such a good idea. She was either in a state of true shock, or she was the best actress he had ever seen. Victor broke the silence. "I'm sorry to have given you such a shock ma'am."

His voice was enough to break the spell that she seemed to be under. "That man," she almost yelled. "That man has made her do this. Him and his crazy notions."

She looked angry. Victor realised that she was referring to her brother-in-law.

"Do you think he led her astray?"

"I'll say," Martha spat. "She would never have done such a thing if it wasn't for him."

"What do you know about the church they belong to?" While she was still a little dazed, Victor hoped that she may tell him more than perhaps she would like to.

"I don't know much about it at all, except they've got some crazy idea that the Lord will be coming back real soon and that they intend to be among his 'chosen few'." Martha's head was still reeling. She was doing her best to come to terms with the idea that her sister was now a wanted criminal. "It's that star isn't it? They think that the star has got something to do with the birth of the new Messiah." She then looked imploringly at Victor. "Please Detective," she sounded like she was begging; "please understand that this is completely out of character for my sister. She would never hurt anyone, not least a tiny child. She's been led astray by that man and his stupid ideas."

"I understand ma'am." Victor did his best to sound soothing. "However, I still need to find her and her husband. Have you any idea where they might've gone?"

Martha shook her head. She couldn't think clearly now, even if she had wanted to. She really couldn't imagine where her sister would have gone. She was white and trembling. "I, I can't think officer," she said weakly. "I really can't understand

283

why she would do this." Then after a few moments her mind seemed to clear a little. "Have you asked the Church? They might tell you where she has gone." Martha saw the folly in this idea almost as soon as she uttered it.

"I'm afraid Ms. Dixon that they wouldn't be very helpful, especially if they were 'in on it'. In fact they would most likely be very misleading!" Martha nodded her appreciation of this. "Look Ms. Dixon, Martha," Victor hesitated at his own familiarity, "I'll give you my card. If you think of anything that might help me find them in the next few hours or days, please, please let me know. To tell you the truth, you're my only hope at the moment." Victor got up from the chair and made for the front door. He was quickly followed by a much shaken woman who suddenly seemed to have aged. She looked rather vulnerable to him and none the less attractive for it.

"I'm sorry to have had to land this on you." Detective Truman sounded genuinely concerned for the lady. "But please think hard. I really do need to find that child. His parents are worried to distraction." This last statement made Martha seem even weaker as a look of pain swept across her face.

"I will," she promised as he walked out of the door. Victor felt quite sorry for her and at the same time strangely hopeful. He couldn't work out if this was because he thought she might really be able to give him the lead he so desperately sought, or for another reason that somehow played with the thoughts at the back of his mind.

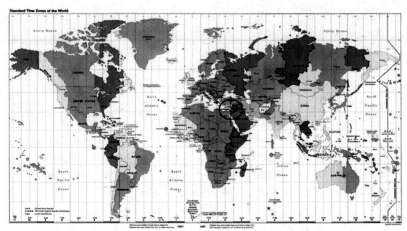

17:05 Israel Standard Time 27th December 2012 (UTC 15:05)

The next skirmish to take place was across the border between Israel and Egypt. This too consisted an exchange of small arms fire and was a little more drawn out than the previous outbreak of hostilities on the Syrian border. However, it did die down after an hour or so. The world's press was there to report it, with anchormen wearing helmets and bulletproof vests giving a moment by moment breakdown of the conflict.

During the United Nations Security Council's emergency meeting, insults were exchanged between the parties in conflict. The other nations did their best to broker a peace deal. This was hampered by disagreements between Russia and China on the one hand, showing support for Syria and Egypt and the United States, the UK and other member nations of the European Union showing some sympathy for the position of Israel. A few non-permanent members did their best to remain unbiased. Initial attempts to draw up a resolution were unsuccessful.

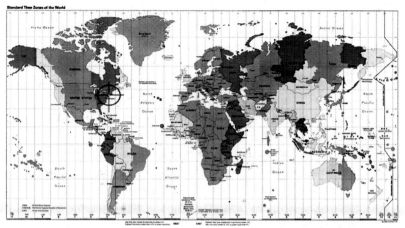

09:05 Eastern Standard Time 27th December 2012 (UTC 14:05)

Special Agent Jefferson now had access to the documents on Salwa Tahan's laptop computer. He hurriedly asked Sam to open them.

"Okay, here you go," said Sam.

"Thanks." There was an awkward silence. Sam then realised that the Special Agent expected him to leave him to it. He wasn't sure if it was because there were 'State secrets' on there, or what. After all his work, he felt slightly irritated by this. He thought he had a right to know what it was that had taken him so long to break into.

"I'll leave you to it then?" Special Agent Jefferson nodded a thank you. Sam with a scowl, did an 'about face', and marched back to the room he had been sitting in.

Special Agent Jefferson opened the first document to see what it contained. As he began to read he realised that it was an extension of the girl's diary, but this contained much more personal information, thoughts and feelings, than the handwritten books had. This had all her hopes, dreams, fantasies and wishes. It made uncomfortable reading. It gave an insight into a young woman, who in spite of her strict religious upbringing seemed quite normal in most other respects. She mentioned her likes and dislikes of other people; the boys who she found attractive and who obviously found her the same. It even gave fairly lurid descriptions of some sexual fantasies that she'd been having, which made Special Agent Jefferson even more uncomfortable. Above all else, what came through several times was how much she missed her father. Every birthday was a mixture of happiness and almost inconsolable sadness that her father wasn't there to celebrate the day with her. She also mentioned how she found her mother 'repressive' and although she obviously loved her dearly, she felt her religion was a source of contention. The Special Agent realised that Salwa wasn't as fervent in her beliefs as her mother had led him to understand. As he continued to read, his mobile phone vibrated in his pocket, on checking, he was made aware that someone back on his floor wanted him. He picked up the laptop and carried it with him towards the stairs.

When he arrived back at his desk there was a message from his Assistant Director asking to see him. He knocked on the door of Assistant Director Martin's office and entered.

"Ah, come in and sit down George." Assistant Director Martin liked to use his staff's first names. Special Agent Jefferson thought this was much too familiar. "How's the Israeli bus bombing investigation going?"

"I'm working on it right now, sir." Special Agent Jefferson was now feeling irritated as he could be doing just that, rather than answering dumb questions about it from his boss.

"Good." Assistant Director Martin had failed to see the annoyance on his subordinates face. "And how's it going?"

"We've just cracked the code to get into the girl's computer this very morning, sir."

"Have you learned anything yet?"

"No sir, as I said, we've only just got into it."

"Very good." The Assistant Director now looked awkward. "Just let me know the minute you've got anything conclusive. I've got all sorts of people on my neck pushing for answers, not least Mossad."

"I understand, sir. I'll let you know as soon as I have anything concrete." The fact that the Israeli Secret Service had been pressuring his boss was of little consequence to him.

287

There was another uncomfortable silence. "Very good, George," Special Agent Jefferson winced, "Carry on then." The Special Agent stood up and turned towards the door, the muscles in his jaw alternately flexing and relaxing as he ground his teeth together. He walked back to his desk and opened up the laptop once more. He had a lot of reading left to do.

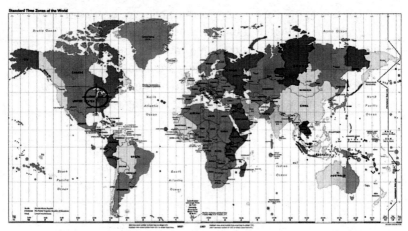

12:00 Central Standard Time 27th December 2012 (UTC 18:00)

Detective Truman decided that he should go and give an update to the Casparo family. He felt unhappy that he had so little to tell them. Still, he thought that it was the right thing to do. He drew up at the hospital and made his way to the maternity ward. He was surprised to be told that Mr. and Mrs. Casparo were no longer there. They had left only twenty minutes earlier. The ward sister explained that there was nothing physically wrong with Mrs. Casparo and after due discussion it was felt that she would be more comfortable at home. Victor Truman thanked the nurse and headed back to his office.

He sat at his desk and wondered. The 'all points bulletin' that had been issued on the Houstons' car, had turned up nothing. Had there been anything in what Martha Dixon had told him that could give him the slightest clue where her sister had taken the baby? He shook his head; he couldn't think of anything. Maybe there was something he missed at the house? He made for the coffee machine and decided to grab some lunch on the way to visiting the Casparos at home.

Astro-physicists from around the world were still analysing the supernova. There was enough information being gathered now and theories a plenty to fill the pages of many learned papers for years to come.

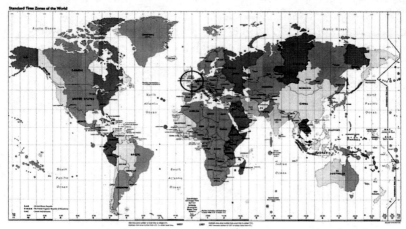

20:34 Greenwich Mean Time 27th December 2012 (UTC 20:34)

The telephone rang at the house of Professor Andrew McVeigh. It was the BBC inviting him to contribute to a programme that they were putting together about the Supernova. He was requested to arrive at the studios in Edinburgh the following morning at 9:30am. He would be interviewed and he was told that his obvious knowledge of the subject would be 'invaluable' to the content of the programme which was due to be aired on the evening of 31st on BBC 2.

"Well," Mary his wife said, after he had put down the receiver and told her about the invitation, "you're becoming quite the celebrity now." She gave her husband an affectionate kiss. Andrew gave her a satisfied smile.

In the Middle East...

Although it had been fairly quiet again in Israel, the news reports were grim, giving endless details of the build up of the current tensions and of the casualties suffered in both Israel and Southern Lebanon. Talks at the United Nations were still ongoing, but it looked increasingly unlikely that any decisions would be made one way or the other regarding the conflict, at least not until the next day.

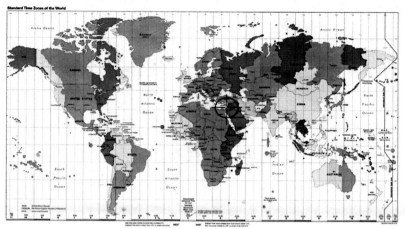

22:00 Israel Standard Time 27th December 2012 (UTC 20:00)

The commander of the force that crossed the border with Southern Lebanon decided that they should pull back. No rockets had been fired into Northern Israel for many hours and from intelligence he had been getting, he believed that they had managed to carry out their mission successfully and destroy the missile launchers and probably their operatives also. As they turned to head back to the Israeli border they were once again pelted with small stones and other missiles from an angry crowd of Lebanese.

The commander hoped that he would be reassigned to the Syrian border. He felt that this was where his men and his personal military skills would be put to better use. He happened to look up into the starlit sky and saw the bright beacon of the new star in the constellation of the Lion. He felt sure that this was a good omen.

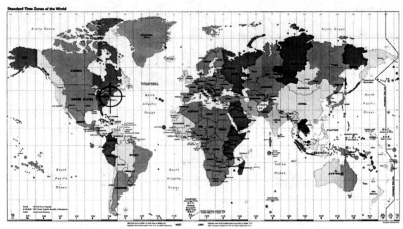

15:30 Eastern Standard Time 27th December 2012 (UTC 20:30)

Special Agent Jefferson had been reading right through the document that Sam the IT specialist had opened for him. He was beginning to develop a picture of the young woman who was a prime suspect in the murder of at least 16 people. She didn't seem like the kind of person to perpetrate an action of that kind.

He opened up the next document. This alarmed him much more. It was information about how to make a simple bomb.

The third document was an address book. Most of the people listed were Palestinians living in the West Bank and East Jerusalem. He wondered if they were relatives of her father. This list he would have to show to his opposite number in the Israeli police department. He then attempted to open the fourth and final document, which had also been encrypted. As soon as he typed the number into the box in the security program, he got a message saying *'incorrect password'*. He slammed the desk with his fist. He couldn't believe that this had happened again. He picked up the laptop and marched back to the stairs. "Sam better sort this out," he muttered darkly, as he made his way towards the IT department.

Sam was still in the room when he got back to the IT floor. He didn't bother knocking. Sam looked surprised to see the Special Agent again so soon.

"Hello Special Agent Jefferson. How can I help you now?"

"There's another document." The Special Agent practically barked at Sam.

"And the problem is...?"

"It's locked. It's damn well locked." Special Agent Jefferson was not hiding his frustration.

"Okay, Ah! So the code didn't work on that one."

"Obviously." The Special Agent snapped and glared at him.

Sam started to think that Special Agent Jefferson should get some anger management counselling. "Okay, leave it with me."

"Can't you look at it now?"

"No, not right this minute. I've got other things to do."

"What other things?"

"Other *important* things." Sam stressed the second word. He was really beginning to feel that he didn't like this Special Agent. He also suspected that this was mutual.

Special Agent Jefferson clenched his fists, which alarmed Sam a little. He turned to leave the room. "Call me as soon as you have something." He snapped.

"I will." Sam did his best not to sound dismissive. He shook his head as Special Agent Jefferson walked smartly out of the room.

The Special Agent decided that he should inform the Assistant Director of what he had found so far and when he had calmed down a little he knocked on the door of his boss's office. He opened the door and put his head into the gap to gain sight of Assistant Director Martin.

"May I have a moment sir?"

"Yes, come in, come in George."

As Special Agent Jefferson opened the door wider and walked into the room he realised that the Assistant Director was not alone. "If I'm disturbing you sir, I can come back later?"

"No, that's okay George. Come and meet Special Agent Smith. He's from our colleagues at the CIA. He's been here discussing the case you are working on."

Special Agent Jefferson looked hesitant. "A pleasure to meet you sir."

"And you likewise George. May I call you George?" Special Agent Jefferson nodded coldly.

"So what have you got, George?" Assistant Director Martin cut in impatiently.

"I've now looked at most of the documents that were encrypted, sir."

"And?" Both Assistant Director Martin and Special Agent Smith were now staring expectantly at him.

"Well sir. I've developed a picture of the girl and her motivations." Special Agent Smith sucked air through his teeth. Special Agent Jefferson shot nervous glances between the two men and continued, "I also found a document about how to make a bomb sir."

"Well that's it then," burst in Assistant Director Martin almost triumphantly, "She definitely did it." Special Agent Smith too, gave a satisfied nod. "Good work George."

"There's just one thing sir." Special Agent Jefferson looked uncomfortable.

"And that is?"

"There's another document that I as yet, haven't been able to open. It looks as though it has been encrypted using a different code sir." Assistant Director Martin's eyes narrowed. "We can't say for sure that she carried out the bombing until I can access the other document. Just having a description of how to make a bomb does not necessarily mean that she did." Both the Assistant Director and Special Agent Smith now looked displeased.

"It's pretty damning circumstantial evidence though." Special Agent Smith attempted to rescue the situation as he saw It. Assistant Director Martin nodded his agreement.

"I agree it doesn't look good for the girl, sir, but perhaps we should wait until we can open the other document."

"And how do you propose to do that?"

"The computer is back with the IT people, sir. I have every faith in them."

Assistant Director Martin sat back in his chair. "Very well, but keep the pressure on them to crack it. We need to have something conclusive very soon. I've got all sorts of people breathing down my neck on this one." He paused and looked at Special Agent Smith. "Begging your pardon, Special Agent Smith." The man sitting opposite the Assistant Director nodded magnanimously back at him. "Very well, Special Agent Jefferson, you can go."

George Jefferson stood up, slightly concerned that his boss had gone back to using his title. "Thank you, sir." He also nodded towards Special Agent Smith who returned the gesture. As he walked out of the door, he was aware that the two men began to talk quietly between themselves. He couldn't hear what they said.

He went back to his desk and composed an email to his counterparts in the Israeli police, including the name and address list recently opened containing what he thought were friends and family of Salwa, in the West Bank. He hoped they could identify these people. If they turned out to be known terrorists, it did not look good for Salwa.

The United Nations Security Council agreed on a Resolution that required all parties in the conflict to retreat to their respective borders. A statement was also issued calling for an immediate cease-fire. Various spokesmen went on television declaring this a first for peace and good sense.

Astrologers and other pundits were still having lots of airtime on radio and television discussing the portents and implications of the bright star still outshining all others. Many viewed it as apocalyptic.

Sales of privately owned firearms increased dramatically in the United States and Canada. People still continued to flood into churches and join religious groups. Individuals continued to declare themselves as the new Messiah and attempted to attract a following.

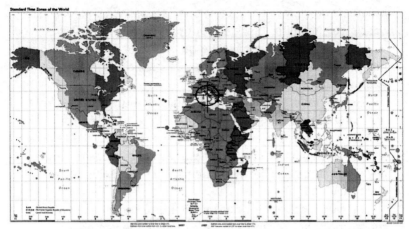

22:35 Central European Time 27th December 2012 (UTC 21:35)

Another email arrived at the Vatican addressed to Father Casparo. This one read, *'don't think you can walk away from this. You are going to die.'*

Cardinal Verdi requested that the Vatican Police supply an armed bodyguard for Father Casparo. The request was approved. He didn't inform Giovanni of this, or the email.

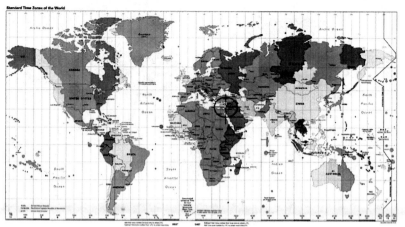

23:55 Israel Standard Time 27th December 2012 (UTC 21:55)

Things had been reasonably quiet on the borders of Israel. A group of Palestinian youths hurled stones at a handful of Israeli army soldiers who entered East Jerusalem on a 'routine' patrol, but they were dispersed with tear gas and a volley of shots over their heads.

The uncertainty and instability in the Middle East was forcing up the price of oil on the world markets. This sent the cost of fuel soaring. This in turn had effects on the cost of everything else, including food and clothing and necessarily, the shipping of goods around the world.

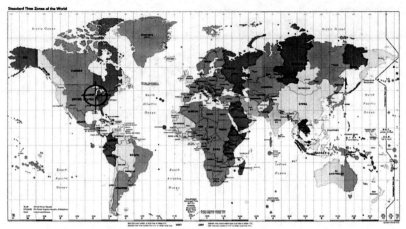

16:15 Central Standard Time 27th December 2012 (UTC 22:15)

Detective Truman had applied for a warrant to thoroughly search the house of Mr. and Mrs. Houston. He felt sure that he was missing something and he felt sure it was in that house. He was disgusted to hear that he may not get the warrant until late the following day, if at all, due to the holiday season. He felt thwarted, so he decided to call in on the Casparos on his way home, to see how they were doing.

On reaching their house, he rang the bell and Marco came to the door.

"Oh, Detective! Come in, please come in." The unspoken question was written on Marco's face.

Victor thanked Marco and as he walked into the hall, he explained that he didn't have much to tell them, but he was willing to share what he could. Victor entered the main room to find Lucy sitting stiffly in a large chair. She had obviously been crying and looked grey and drawn. He sat down opposite her.

"How are you Mrs. Casparo?"

"I'm okay," she lied. "Please," she looked imploringly at him, "do you have any news about my baby?" Marco quickly joined his wife, sitting on the arm of the chair and placing a comforting arm around her shoulder.

"I don't have much ma'am, but I can tell you that I'm following up another lead." He didn't know why he lied. He genuinely wanted to offer some comfort to the wretched woman sat in front of him. To try and make this sound more convincing he said, "I've applied for a warrant to search a house here in the city."

Lucy immediately caught on to this. "Does that mean that you think my baby is still here in Chicago?"

"Yes ma'am, I do." A ray of hope crossed Mrs. Casparo's face.

Marco seemed less convinced. "Can you tell us where?"

"No, I'm not at liberty to say at the moment."

Lucy cut in, "Do you think my baby's there?"

Victor now felt a little guilty that he had perhaps raised this woman's hopes, only to dash them with his next words. "No ma'am, in truth I don't."

"Then why are you looking there?" Marco spluttered in outrage at this apparent waste of time.

"I think there may be some information there that might lead me to your child, sir."

Marco looked despairingly at him. His wife shrank into his body.

"I hope to have some news for you tomorrow." Once again Victor felt obliged to 'stick his neck out'. He so wanted to give some thread of comfort to the pair whose pain was obvious.

The room went quiet and Detective Truman used this as his cue to leave. "I'll look in or call again tomorrow if I get the chance or if I have any news for you."

Marco nodded his thanks, stood up and made to show Victor out.

"Please, please find my baby," Lucy Casparo said beseechingly as Victor walked out of the room. He turned and nodded.

"Goodnight Mrs. Casparo." Victor walked out of the front door without another word being spoken.

Day 3

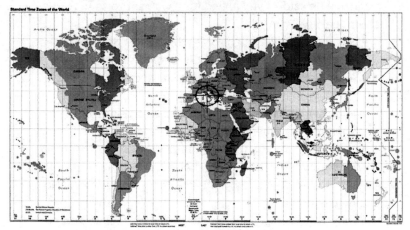

07:45 Central European Time 28th December 2012 (UTC 06:45)

Giovanni Casparo had woken, washed and dressed and was about to have breakfast when he felt the desire for a breath of fresh air. He opened the door to his apartment to be greeted by a man in uniform carrying a side arm. He stopped in his tracks. After his initial surprise, questions immediately started to form in his head. He thought it was only polite to greet the officer.

"Good morning."

"Good morning Father."

"What are you doing here?" He questioned hesitantly.

"I've been assigned to guard you Father."

"By whose orders?"

"On the authority of Cardinal Verdi, Father."

"Oh! I see. Thank you." Any thought of a quiet stroll evaporated in Giovanni's mind. He closed the door, went to the telephone and called the Cardinal.

"Pronto."

"Your Eminence, it's Giovanni."

"Giovanni," the Cardinal bellowed in greeting, "I hope you slept well?"

"Quite well, thank you, Your Eminence." There was a slight pause and then Giovanni asked, "Leonardo, why is there an armed guard outside my door?"

There was another slight pause as the Cardinal tried to think of the best way to answer this. "I'll come and explain face to face, Giovanni. It'll be easier." The phone went down and Giovanni frowned.

Within a few minutes, there was a soft knock at the door. This time the Cardinal did not let himself in, but waited for the priest to answer. Giovanni opened the door and motioned for the Cardinal to enter.

"I'm sorry my boy," the Cardinal said in a very paternal tone, "I should've told you yesterday, but you seemed very preoccupied."

"Told me what, Your Eminence?"

"I'm sorry to say, you received another nasty email. I thought it a wise precaution to ask for a guard on your rooms."

"What did it say?"

"Oh, just the usual vitriol."

Giovanni pressed the Cardinal. "Which was what exactly?"

There was another slight pause during which Cardinal Verdi looked searchingly at the priest's face, trying to decide if he was ready for this information.

"It said, 'don't think you can walk away from this, priest. You're going to die anyway'."

Giovanni swallowed hard and went a little pale.

"You see why I posted the guard now, Giovanni?"

"Surely you can't believe that it would be anyone in the Vatican?"

"We just don't know for sure. It is safer to take these precautions." Father Casparo fell quiet. For the first time, he began to realise that his life may well be genuinely in danger. The Cardinal continued, "Please don't take this the wrong way, but I think that you should keep out of sight for a while. At least until we've got to the bottom of this."

Giovanni's shoulders fell. He sat down heavily in a chair. "Does this mean I'm confined to my quarters?"

"You make it sound like you're a prisoner Giovanni. No, not at all, but you should only walk in the gardens with the guard at your side."

"I'm starting to feel like I am a prisoner."

"Nonsense." The Cardinal tried to sound cheerful to lift Giovanni's spirits. "As I say, I'm sure the Police will find the culprit and then everything can go back to normal."

"Normal? I don't know what that is anymore." Cardinal Verdi raised an eyebrow, remembering the trauma that his charge went through discovering that his new nephew had been kidnapped.

"I'll have some books sent to you Giovanni; or you could work on your paper that you were telling me about?"

His paper; Giovanni had completely forgotten about his paper. This made him remember, it was going to retrieve this document that seemingly started this whole chain of appalling events. He thought his paper would now never get written.

The Cardinal stepped forward and clasped the seated priest on the shoulder encouragingly. "I have to go now Giovanni. I'll call in later, or phone you if I have any news." Giovanni nodded and Leonardo Verdi turned and walked towards the door.

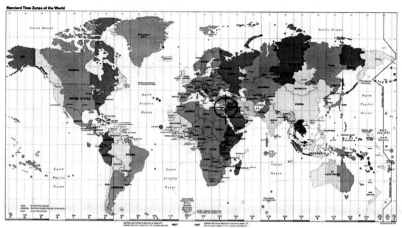

11:37 Israel Standard Time 28th December 2012 (UTC 09:37)

The dogfight started when the Israeli jets locked on to the Syrian Migs on their radar. The group leader decided to engage the fighters and the shooting started in the skies over the Golan Heights. There was a lot of argument afterwards about who had entered whose airspace first, but the result was that one of the Syrian fighters was shot down and one of the Israeli jets was damaged. More Israeli aircraft joined the fray and the Syrian fighter jets broke off and headed back, deep into Syrian airspace. The battle was filmed by various television news channels on the ground and was flashed all around the world.

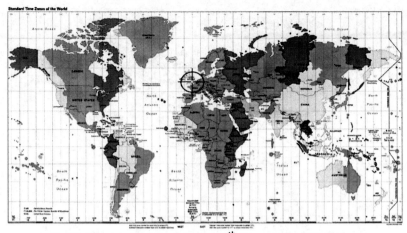

11:12 Greenwich Meantime 28th December 2012 (UTC 11:12)

The Prime Minister had been watching developments on the BBC News. He was dismayed to see a breach of the UN Resolution so soon. He made calls to many of his European counterparts in an effort to see if the European Union could bring pressure to bear on both parties to cease fire. In spite of spending over an hour on the telephone the result was, he felt, disappointing. Many European leaders agreed that something should be done, but they seemed unable to agree on exactly what.

Professor McVeigh was enjoying his time in the BBC studios in Edinburgh. He had been made to feel very welcome and his first interview with the presenter of the programme had gone well, he thought. He had been explaining the nature of stars that go 'supernova' and why they were so energetic. He hadn't yet discussed R Leonis, the star that had triggered the making of the programme in the first place.

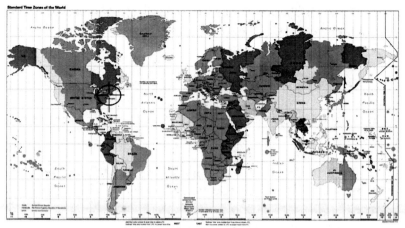

08:15 Eastern Standard Time 28th December 2012 (UTC 13:15)

Special Agent Jefferson arrived at his office not sure what the day would bring. He hoped Sam and his colleagues had managed to break into the last document on Salwa Tahan's laptop computer. He opened his email almost forgetting he had asked for verification of the list of names and addresses, which he had sent to the Israeli police. Among several emails waiting in his 'inbox' was just such a message. As he read, he began to frown. Most of the names on the list were known to the Israeli police as suspected terrorists, or at least having a connection to suspected terrorist organisations.

He could see now the evidence was strengthening against Salwa. What he couldn't figure out was why? Why should a bright young girl with a great future ahead of her, commit mass murder? He hoped that the answer to this might be found in the, as yet, unopened document. He realised that he was going to have to report his findings to the Assistant Director. George Jefferson walked over to his Assistant Director's office and knocked on the door. As he stepped into the room Assistant Director Martin greeted him with a hopeful look in his eyes.

"Excuse me, sir." Special Agent Jefferson was slightly hesitant.

"Come and sit down George. What have you got?"

"I've heard back from the Israeli police after I sent a list of names and addresses that I emailed to them, which were on the girl's computer."

"And?"

"Well sir," he paused, "it seems that most of the names on the list are known to the Israeli police and counter terrorist units. I'm thinking that the girl went to visit some or all of these people when she went over there and perhaps obtained the bomb from them.

"Well, that's it then," Assistant Director Martin said triumphantly, "there's no two ways about it now, she's as guilty as hell."

"The thing is sir, I can't understand why?"

"Well, no need to worry about that now. I'll contact Mossad and let them know what we've discovered." Special Agent Jefferson's mouth drooped at the corners. He for one was not satisfied with this. Assistant Director Martin added, "Oh and good work George."

George Jefferson raised an eyebrow. "Thank you, sir. If I find out anything else, I'll let you know."

"Okay George, but don't worry about digging too much further. I think we've got all we need on this case now."

Special Agent Jefferson got up and walked to the door. As he went to go through it, he turned to the Assistant Director and said, "I'll tell Mrs. Tahan myself sir, if you don't mind, before she gets to hear about it from the press." His boss nodded in a non-committal way. As he paced back to his desk he felt decidedly unhappy. He still couldn't understand why Salwa Tahan would want to take her life and those of others. He took his jacket off the back of his chair and headed to the car park by way of the IT department. He thought he should tell them that the pressure was off. However, he didn't want them to think the pressure was completely off. He still wanted to know what was in that document, even if the Assistant Director didn't.

Spy satellites had picked up the fact that two Russian aircraft carriers had sailed into the Arabian Gulf. This added to the contingent of warships amassing in the region. The

President, when he was informed, looked alarmed. His chiefs of Defence Staff advised him that they were 'no match' for the American and Allied forces already in those waters. He was keen to make sure, for the time being, no challenge should be made to the Russians either militarily or politically. In darkened rooms in the Pentagon, war games scenarios and strategies were already being run on powerful computers.

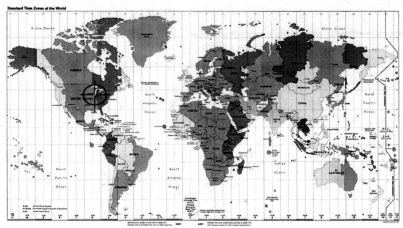

11:35 Central Standard Time 28th December 2012 (UTC 17:35)

Detective Truman was delighted when he finally got his warrant to search the house of Mr. and Mrs. Houston. He wasted no time in organising a search team and headed over to their property in a posse. They were very thorough. Closets were emptied, floor boards were taken up and bins were sifted through. Victor Truman was dismayed when they turned up little of any help. He himself had been going through various papers in a desk and he had taken another look at the computer in the main room. He felt sure there was something in one of those documents which would lead him to the Houstons and the kidnapped child, but he could not find what he thought he was looking for. He packed the team off and decided that he would confront the leader of the Church of the Second Coming. After all, now the whole street had seen the police turn up and ransack the Houstons' house, he thought it wouldn't be long before the church hierarchy got to hear about it.

He drove to the church in the hope of finding the 'pastor' at home. He walked up to the door of the church, which was a modern clean and very twenty first century looking building, and pushed it. To his surprise it gave in to his pressure and swung open. Inside it was light and airy. No one seemed to be in the body of the building, so he walked towards the back of the church where he could see a door standing ajar. As he pushed this door open, he saw a man sitting at a desk in front of a computer screen. He jumped up in surprise to see Victor.

"Who are you?" he demanded.

Victor reached for his badge. The man looked surprised and then said, "And how may I help the Chicago Police Department?"

"The first thing you can tell me," Victor sounded stern and businesslike, "Is who you are and what are you doing here?"

The man gave his name as Paul Richardson the pastor of the Church of the Second Coming. Without hesitation Detective Truman said, "You have a Mr. and Mrs. Houston in your congregation. Is that correct?" He watched the man's face carefully.

Pastor Paul nodded, seemingly unfazed by the question. "Why do you ask?" He quietly went to sit back at his desk and reached for the computer mouse. Before Victor could react, he clicked something on the screen.

"Don't touch that!" Victor barked at him.

"Oh, I'm sorry, I didn't know that I couldn't continue my work as we speak." His hand left the mouse.

There was something about Pastor Paul that Victor instantly disliked. He couldn't see the computer screen from where he was standing and so he walked around the desk to get nearer to the focus of his questions. The screen showed a 'desktop' picture of a highly stylized image of Christ riding on some clouds, light radiating from his head. Victor's eyes narrowed. He continued to press his questions.

"I'm looking for the Houstons, because I believe they may be involved in a serious crime."

The man still looked quite calm. "And what crime might that be?" he countered.

"Kidnap and impersonating medical professionals for a start." He thought that he saw a flicker of a smile crossing the man's face.

"I'm sure that you must be mistaken, officer. All the members of our congregation are good Christians. I can't believe that they would become embroiled in such criminal acts."

310

Victor ignored the protestation from the Pastor.

"You believe that Christ is due to come back and take His chosen ones to heaven. Is that correct?"

Pastor Paul nodded. "That is correct officer."

"And when do you think this is going to happen?"

"We believe that the Second Coming is imminent"

"How imminent?"

"How will these questions help you find the Houstons?" Pastor Paul had an unpleasant smile of satisfaction now showing on his face.

"I believe that I'm asking the questions at the moment."

"And so you are."

"Where can I find the Houstons?"

"Have you tried their house?" The sarcasm in his voice was obvious.

"Don't be smart with me, Pastor."

"I apologise if I have given any offence."

"Do you know the current whereabouts of the Houstons?" Victor pressed once again.

"No, I don't. Who are they supposed to have abducted anyway?"

"A small child; a boy child." Detective Truman waited for a reaction.

"I'm sorry to hear it." Pastor Paul was cool, very cool.

"I believe they think that this child is in fact the re-born Christ child."

The Pastor looked amazed. "I can't understand why they should think that."

"I wondered if they were operating under instruction?"

The Pastor's look of amazement now changed to one of innocence. "Are you implying that I ordered this kidnapping?"

"The thought had occurred to me."

"Be careful officer. You need to have evidence before you go making accusations like that."

Victor frowned at the Pastor's impertinence. "If I discover that you are involved in this in any way, be sure that I will be making more than accusations." With this, Detective Truman turned and walked out of the room. He really wanted to know what the Pastor had been doing on his computer as he arrived, but he wasn't going to find out without a warrant and by the time he got that, the Pastor would surely have deleted any files that were incriminating. He had a feeling in his gut that this man knew a lot more than he was letting on. In fact he felt sure that he was involved. He was also now sure that the Houstons would be alerted to the police interest. He didn't know if this would drive them out of hiding or whether it would drive them further underground. He had made his play and he would have to live with the consequences.

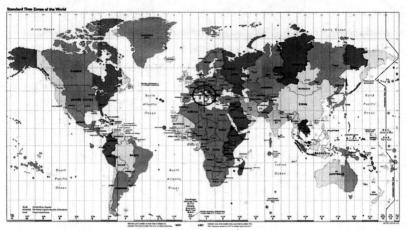

19:55 Central European Time 28th December 2012 (UTC 18:55)

Giovanni Casparo was pacing in his room. He couldn't settle to reading, studying, or even watching television. He had finished a phone call earlier with his brother in Chicago which had left him feeling depressed and worried. There was no news of his nephew. All he could do now was pray and he did that, fervently. He felt like a prisoner even though he was assured that he wasn't. Someone was, it seemed, trying to kill him and he was the one who was denied his freedom. His head was reeling. This had been an insane few days for a quiet astronomer-priest. There was no word from the Vatican Police, so he had to assume that they were unable to trace the person or persons who had threatened his life. There was no word from his brother to say his nephew had been found. All he wanted to do was to go home and pretend that he had never discovered the Supernova and that he had not been thrown into the limelight because of it.

The Cardinal had visited him and made suitably sympathetic noises, but Giovanni felt that even he was beginning to lose interest. The media seemed to have moved on from the excitement of a new star to the threats and rumours of war and predictions of the end of the world. He went to hear Mass in St Martha's Chapel. As this was closed to the outside world, his bodyguard was happy enough for him to do this. During the

313

Mass he started to fantasise about escaping. It was dark; perhaps he could slip away unseen; and then what? What would he do? Where would he go? At the end of the Mass he returned to his quarters and watched the news about the brewing trouble in the Middle East. He went to bed feeling very wretched.

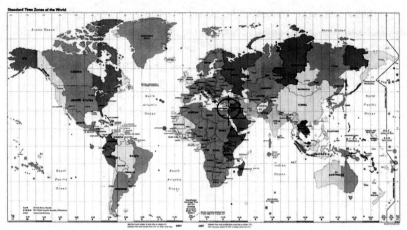

21:00 Israel Standard Time 28th December 2012 (UTC 19:00)

A couple more skirmishes along the border of Syria and Israel had been reported. Casualties were minimal. Tensions were however, running extremely high. More troops were being moved into the area on both sides. Emissaries from the United Nations were holding high level talks with the leaders of all the factions involved in the conflict, but with little effect.

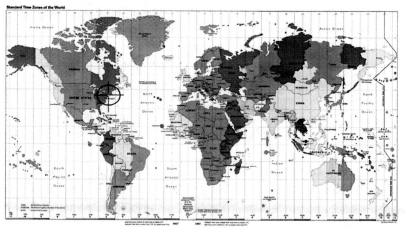

14:30 Eastern Standard Time 28th December 2012 (UTC 19:30)

Special Agent Jefferson's car pulled up outside the house of Mrs. Tahan. He had been hoping to arrive earlier, but was diverted by various other issues that needed his attention. He rang the bell by the front door and waited. After a minute or so, he rang the bell again; still no reply. He thought this strange and tried the door. It swung open with moderate pressure. This immediately put him on his guard. He drew his gun and pushed the door open further. He silently entered the hallway and began scanning the rooms leading from it, his gun raised and ready to fire at the slightest provocation.

As he neared the main room of the house, he thought he heard a noise. He called out, "Mrs. Tahan? This is Special Agent Jefferson. Is everything okay?"

There was still no response. He followed the muzzle of his gun carefully into the room. The sight that greeted him made him catch his breath. The lifeless body of Mrs. Tahan was swinging from a cord wrapped around her neck and attached to the light fitting in the centre of the room. A small step ladder, which she had obviously stood on, had been kicked away from beneath her. Quickly holstering his gun he ran towards the body. She was still warm. He grabbed her legs in an effort to take her weight. It only took a moment for him to realise that she was past help. He let go of her and stepped back. A wave of pity swept over him. In the corner of the room the television was on. The sound level had been turned down to be almost inaudible. It was a rolling news channel that was on view. As he looked he saw the name of Salwa Tahan scrolling past on the 'ticker tape' at the bottom of the screen. He spotted the remote control on the arm of a chair and picked it up and turned up the sound. The reporter was relaying how the police in Bethlehem had now ascertained that it was a young woman who exploded the bomb on the bus...

Special Agent Jefferson swallowed hard. He pulled the mobile phone from his pocket and called in to the Department. As he sat and waited for the police and ambulance to arrive, he suddenly felt a wave of anger hit him. The anger was directed at himself. If only he had got to Mrs. Tahan earlier, perhaps he could have saved her or even persuaded her not to consider taking her own life. He felt pain for the despair she must have felt which prompted her to take such drastic action. He was now more determined than ever to discover why her daughter became a suicide bomber.

Day 2

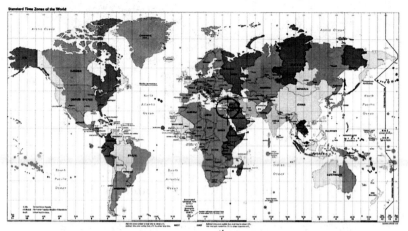

06:30 Israel Standard Time 29th December 2012 (UTC 04:30)

Five jet fighters of the Egyptian Air Force crossed the border between Israel and Egypt. They flew low and fast. Israeli anti aircraft defences were quick to pick them up and track them. It took very little time for the automatic ground to air missile systems to lock onto the aircraft. As soon as the targeting radar had locked onto them, the jets turned and headed back to the Egyptian border. No shots were fired.

The Israeli government protested in the strongest terms to the United Nations. The Egyptian government denied that the aircraft had entered Israeli airspace.

Further skirmishes were taking place along the Israeli border with Syria, on the Golan Heights. Once again shots were exchanged. Two Israeli army soldiers and five Syrian soldiers were killed and three were wounded.

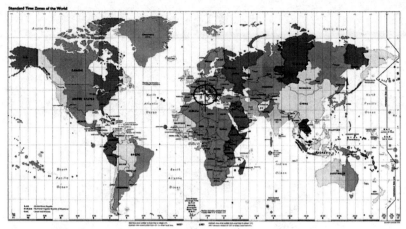

08:25 Central European Time 29th December 2012 (UTC 07:25)

A package arrived at the Vatican, addressed to Father Giovanni Casparo. It was a plain brown padded bag bearing an Italian postmark. It was intercepted by the Vatican Police and x-rayed. The package was opened very carefully. It contained a bullet. There was a hand written scrawled note with it. The note read *'The next one will come a lot faster.'*

This sent a great deal of alarm through the normally quiet walls of Vatican City. Cardinal Verdi was informed immediately. He decided to call Giovanni into the offices of the Vatican Police in order that he may see it for himself. He hoped that this would persuade the priest that he was doing the right thing by keeping a low profile.

Giovanni entered the room and Cardinal Verdi turned and thanked him for coming, then asked the officer to show Father Casparo the contents of the package. Giovanni went pale when he saw it.

"You see now Giovanni, we must keep you safe. Whoever this madman is, he seems quite serious." The priest just nodded.

"The good news is the Police think the perpetrator may have made a mistake by sending you something material. So far, it has been near impossible to trace the source of the emails, but a package such as this..."

319

"Do you really think we can discover who sent this?" Giovanni was looking for any sign of hope in this regard.

"The Vatican Police have requested the help of the Rome police. They have some forensic experts coming over straight away to look at it."

"Good, good." Giovanni looked very shaken. "I'll go back to my rooms now if you don't need me anymore?"

"That's fine Giovanni; you should go and get some rest. Be assured that we will discover who is running this campaign against you and they will be stopped."

Giovanni Casparo swallowed hard, turned around and left the room, escorted by his bodyguard.

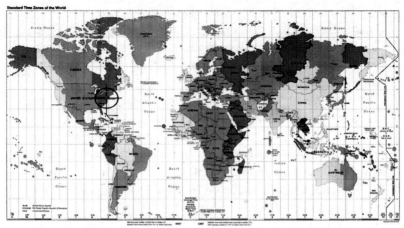

09:15 Eastern Standard Time 29th December 2012 (UTC 14:15)

A request had been received at the White House from the Israeli Government, for military support from the American Government. A meeting was now taking place between the President and his Chiefs of Defence Staff and his Security Advisor.

"So what do you think gentlemen?" The President was looking for guidance on the military perspective of the request.

"It's doable, sir. We could send them anti aircraft missile systems right up to air launched cruise missiles themselves, if you think it is the right thing to do. However there are a lot of political implications."

The President frowned. "That's *my* problem. It's knowing how much to get involved, or even whether to get involved at all. American intervention may only fuel more anti-American feeling in the region. Then again it may keep the lid on it, with us waving the big stick."

"There are also the Russians and the Chinese to consider, sir." Sam Cruikshank chimed in.

"Would you care to expand on that Dan?"

"Well Mr. President, the Russians have moved two aircraft carriers into the area in the last couple of days. The Chinese are also sending similar hardware, if our satellite tracking is anything to go by."

321

"Should that bother us?"

"I just wanted you to know the facts, sir."

"Okay Dan. Thanks for that."

The President paused for a moment and then said, "Let's take it one step at a time. The Israelis have asked for help. They didn't specify exactly what kind of help, so let's offer them a couple of the latest anti-missile missile systems and some technical backup in the form of operators to go with it. We'll be a little more reticent about heavier weaponry for the time being. We also need to be seen to be pressing all sides for a peaceful settlement."

"Very good, sir."

"Oh, let me know what the Russians and Chinese are up to. We don't want them supplying the Syrians or any of the others with anything that could give us a problem."

"Yes, sir."

"Very well gentlemen; that will be all for now."

The meeting broke up and the men dispersed. The President went back to his desk and started studying a map of the Middle East.

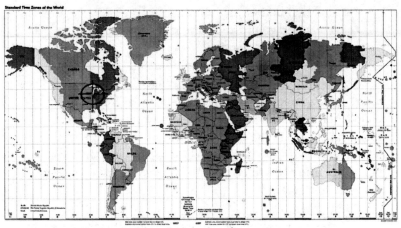

11:30 Central Standard Time 29th December 2012 (UTC 17:30)

Victor Truman drummed his fingers on the desk. He was feeling like he had hit the buffers. He'd had nothing to go on, for a day now. As time went past, he became more and more concerned that he would never find the Casparo child. He did his best to put himself in the position of the Houstons, asking himself what he would do in their position. The Detective really wanted to put more pressure on that slimy Pastor. He didn't like him and he was sure that he was hiding something. That's it! He almost cried out. Hiding something; he wondered if the Houstons were hiding at the Pastor's house. He decided he would raid Pastor Paul Richardson's house. The only thing he had to do was justify it to the Captain and after the seemingly pointless search of the Houstons' house, that might not be easy.

Victor knocked on the door of the Captain's office and entered the room. The Captain looked at Detective Truman quizzically. "Yes, Detective, what can I do for you?"

"I need some men for a raid, sir."

"In connection with which case?"

"The Casparo case, sir. I believe that the Houstons might be sheltering in the house of their Pastor."

"Believe. Might. They're not words that give me confidence Detective."

"I understand Captain, but I'm sure that the Pastor is hiding something."

"Hiding what? The child?"

"The only way to find out is to go in and take a look."

There was a long pause. Victor knew when he had said enough. The Captain pursed his lips. "How many men do you need?"

Victor knew this meant his boss was softening to the idea. "Four at the most, sir."

"Make it two and you can go."

Victor knew it was senseless to argue with the Captain and agreed to take two uniformed men with him. Besides, he thought that this would be enough anyway. He always found that by overstating his requirements, he usually got what he needed in the way of resources. "Very good. Thank you, sir."

Detective Truman walked out of the office with a slight smile. He wanted to see the look on the Pastor's face when he turned up with a search warrant and two uniforms to turn his house upside down. He would have to wait though; he knew it would take a few hours for the Captain to obtain the warrant from the judge for him. He headed for the coffee machine, still smiling.

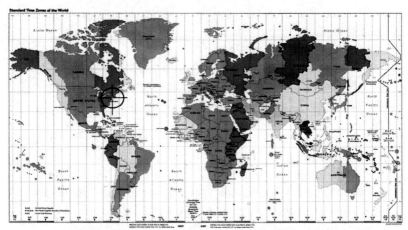

15:20 Eastern Standard Time 29th December 2012 (UTC 20:20)

Special Agent Jefferson decided that he needed to call on the IT department to see how they were getting on with Salwa Tahan's laptop computer. Even though her name was now linked with the bus bombing in Bethlehem, he still wanted to know why she had done it. He ran up the stairs and into the office where he found Sam just the previous day.

Sure enough, Sam was there working in front of a computer screen. Special Agent Jefferson walked up to him.

"Hello Sam."

"Oh, hello Special Agent Jefferson, how can I help you?"

"How are you getting on with that girl's laptop?"

"Er, yes, to be honest I haven't had much chance to look at it."

A look of deep disappointment swept across Special Agent George Jefferson's face.

"I'm hoping that I might get some time with it a little later."

"Uh huh. I really do still need to know what's in that last document."

"Okay, yes. I promise I'll get on to it as soon as possible."

Special Agent Jefferson looked steadily at Sam for a few moments, which made the IT man feel quite uncomfortable. He then turned and walked away and out of the office, much to Sam's relief.

325

Sam immediately recovered the laptop from under a pile of papers, on his desk. He opened the lid and booted it up. He waited for a few minutes while it settled down and then looked at the document files once again, hoping for inspiration. None came. He picked up the diaries that were also on his desk and started to look through them once more. He was beginning to think he had missed something, but he wasn't sure quite what it was.

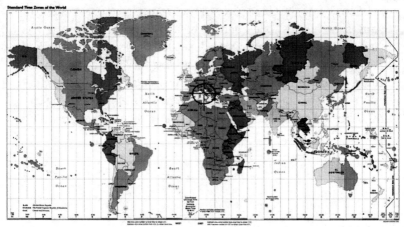

22:12 Central European Time 29th December 2012 (UTC 21:12)

The forensic team from the Rome police had taken the bullet and the package which it came in, away for further tests. At last they had come up with something. There were traces of DNA on the bullet and the post mark on the package had led them to narrow down the area in which the sender lived. They didn't think he would be stupid enough to use his local post office, but it gave them a region to home in on.

It had taken several hours to process the DNA data but at last they had a result and they had a match. The DNA belonged to a man who was known to the police and last known to be living in Turin. This was backed up by the Turin postmark on the package. The Turin police were informed.

Day 1

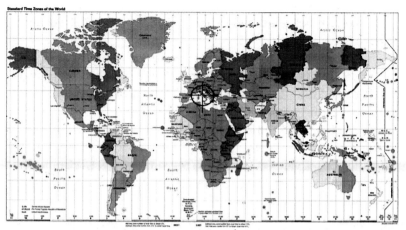

04:32 Central European Time 30th December 2012 (UTC 03:32)

The Turin Police raid team were poised outside the building where lived one Luigi Gagliano. He was known to the police for a history of violent crime, intimidation and theft. Several of the police who knew him personally thought that he was crazy, 'mad and bad' is how they often described him. The policeman with the ram burst the lock on the door without too much difficulty and they quickly rushed into the building, shouting warnings as they went. They found Luigi in bed asleep. They pulled him out of his bed and handcuffed him. He protested his innocence for whatever crime he was supposed to have committed.

The Detective, who organised the raid, spotted the computer in the corner of the room and went to switch it on, amid threats protests and warnings from their prisoner. Once the computer had booted up the detective opened the email program and started to scroll through the list of sent items. Sure enough he found the emails which Luigi had sent to Father Casparo. He stood up and turned to the growling man.

"So why the priest, Luigi?"

"It's all his fault."

"What's all his fault?"

"The star. It was the star that turned me bad."

"The star?"

"Yes, if that priest hadn't told everybody about it, I wouldn't have been bad."

The policeman looking puzzled, read him his rights and the charge against him, all the while the man in handcuffs struggled and cursed the star and the priest and the policemen who were now arresting him.

The Detective shook his head. "Take him away." The other policemen jostled their captive to the door and then into the waiting police van. On the way to the station Luigi Gagliano told the policemen that God told him that if he killed the priest he wouldn't be bad any more...

06:40 Central European Time 30th December 2012 (UTC 05:40)

Father Giovanni Casparo was woken by a soft knock at the door of his rooms. He got up and went to it. Standing facing him was a smiling Cardinal Leonardo Verdi.

"Giovanni, I have some good news for you."

The priest was still trying to bring himself around from his fitful sleep. "What's that Father?"

"The man who was threatening your life has been captured."

"Captured?" Giovanni was now very wide awake.

"Yes, captured. He was tracked to his house in Turin and the police there, arrested him. He had copies of the emails he had been sending you on his computer. You're safe now, Giovanni." The Cardinal clapped his hands together in delight.

"Who was he and why did he want to kill me?"

"Apparently the police tell us that he is quite probably insane. He is also a known criminal. He was quite incoherent when they arrested him. He kept trying to say that it was connected with the star."

"The star? I don't understand."

329

"Yes, he told the police it was the star that made him 'bad' and God had spoken to him and told him to kill you and in that way it would absolve him of his 'badness'."

"I still don't understand." Giovanni looked very confused. He was doing his best to make sense of what he had just heard. "Why should threatening and then killing me make him less 'bad'?"

"I don't know Giovanni. The man is, as they said, insane. We must pray for him and for forgiveness for him."

"Er, oh, yes." Father Casparo sat down in a chair, his head still spinning.

"I've called off your bodyguard. You can move about freely again. Would you like to go back to your role as Papal spokesman? I've spoke to his Holiness and he would be delighted if you would."

Still sounding bewildered, Giovanni nodded and said "Yes."

"Excellent. Excellent. I will make arrangements."

"What arrangements?"

The Cardinal ignored this question and breezed out of the door. Giovanni now felt relieved, certainly, and also still quite confused.

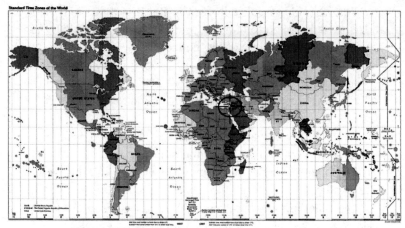

07:45 Israel Standard Time 30th December 2012 (UTC 05:45)

The Israeli Air Force F-16's flew very fast and very low over the Syrian border. The five aircraft headed with deadly accuracy towards their target. They overflew the desert towards the city of Adra to a known missile base on the outskirts of the town. Their task was to destroy it. By the time the Syrian Air Force had scrambled their fighters the Israeli F-16's had completed their mission and were on their way home. When the base was blown up, seven Syrian military personnel had been killed. Two Syrian Migs attempted to engage the F-16's before they reached the Israeli border. It became clear to them quite quickly they were outnumbered and out-gunned and broke off their attack.

A quantity of armaments bearing a Russian insignia was now on its way overland to a base deep inside Syria. Spy satellites had not recorded it.

Howls of protest erupted from Syria after the Israeli attack on their missile installation, which they claimed was for defensive purposes only. The Syrian government asked for an emergency recall of the United Nations Security Council. Their request was being considered.

331

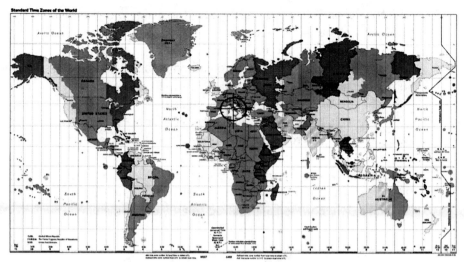

09:37 Central European Time 30th December 2012 (UTC 08:37)

Giovanni Casparo had washed and breakfasted and was now sitting at a desk with a laptop computer, for the first time in several days. He was monitoring the reports on a couple of astronomical web sites about the progress of the supernova.

He was feeling a lot better now that his life was no longer under threat. He was also delighted to see how much information was being gleaned from the star, which was now inexorably attached to his name. Quite a few astro-physicists had to do a rethink about the nature of this type of star. He also noted that it was now beginning to fade slightly from its peak brightness. Nevertheless it was still the brightest object in the night sky and continued to be clearly visible during the day. He was interrupted by a knock at the door. He opened it to find the Cardinal with a beaming smile on his face.

"Giovanni, I have good news. The Holy Father would like you to hold a press conference."

Giovanni's eyebrows nearly jumped off his forehead. "A press conference!" he repeated.

"Yes, you must explain to the media what happened to you; the threat to your life and how the Vatican Police in conjunction with the Italian Police managed to stop the dangerous madman from carrying out his threat."

"Do you really think that's wise?"

"The Holy Father has instructed me to organise it for you. Surely you do not want to go against his wishes?"

"Oh! Er, no, not at all." Giovanni gulped.

"Very well, I will set it up for early this afternoon. Oh, and he would also like you to refute the nonsense that is filling the Internet about the end of the world."

Giovanni was much more willing to agree to this. He gave the Cardinal a smile of resignation, to which his Eminence said, "Splendid;" then turned and walked smartly out of the door.

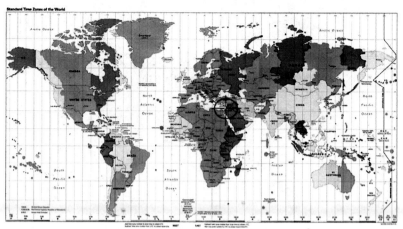

12:41 Israel Standard Time 30th December 2012 (UTC 10:41)

A Scud missile landed just outside a small Israeli town near the Sea of Galilee. It was thought to have originated from somewhere in Syria. American made anti-missile systems were now being deployed in the Golan Heights and along the border with Egypt.

Intelligence reports cited that a shipment of missile launchers had arrived at the Syrian port of Latakia, probably from Russia. However, this report could not be verified.

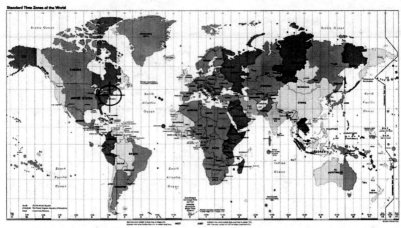

08:30 Eastern Standard Time 30th December 2012 (UTC 13:30)

Sam had come into work puzzling over the last document still to be decoded on Salwa Tahan's laptop computer. It had now captured his imagination. He didn't like codes he couldn't break, no matter how simple or difficult. He could of course plug in the heavy code cracking software and break it that way, but there was no way of telling yet what kind of encryption she had used and there was his intellectual pride to consider. He liked to think that he could easily break into any key code that a twenty something year old girl could come up with.

He sat down and started to look through the diaries again. He felt sure the answer was in there, as it had been last time. He had started leafing through the end few pages of the final diary when his phone rang. It was an urgent job and he had to leave the diaries and the laptop on his desk; the diary was left open at the last page.

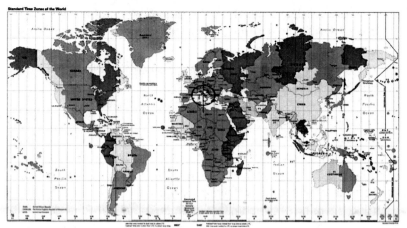

15:45 Central European Time 30th December 2012 (UTC 14:45)

Cardinal Verdi led Father Casparo to the room with the waiting journalists. There were a couple of microphones sitting on a desk with two chairs behind, two television cameras and a sea of faces.

A wave of trepidation rushed over Giovanni, relieved slightly when he realised that the Cardinal was going to take his place in the chair next to him. As they walked towards the desk, camera flashes exploded in a strobe of white flickers. As soon as they sat down the Cardinal who had, until now, shied away from the media, spoke up.

"Ladies and gentlemen, as you can see I have with me Father Giovanni Casparo, who I am pleased to say is hale and hearty and unscathed from his ordeal of threats of death visited on him from the ravings of a madman." Giovanni thought that this was accurate, if not a little uncharitable and definitely overstated. The Cardinal continued, "He is willing to answer your questions." With this he made a gesture to Giovanni to take the stage and a wall of voices surged towards him. The Cardinal once again took control and pointed to one of the journalists near the front.

She introduced herself, "Francesca Comberti, RAI News. Father, would you mind telling us if you know the motive of this man who threatened your life?"

Giovanni cleared his throat. "I cannot be sure Miss Comberti. All I know is this poor man is probably mentally ill and definitely delusional."

"Yes, thank you Father, I think we know this, but why should he threaten you, specifically?"

"I am given to understand that he was suggesting it was because of the Supernova."

"The Supernova?"

"Yes, he seemed to think that somehow I had brought it into being and it represented all that was evil in him. I believe he has a long criminal record and mental health issues. I cannot get inside the mind of a madman you understand, but I suppose that if I had brought it into being, I too must be evil. He then felt sure that God had instructed him to kill me and that way, he could redeem himself."

There was another clamour of voices and the Cardinal once again pointed at a journalist. This time a man introduced himself. "Edward Thornley BBC News, Father Casparo. Why do you think he threatened you with the emails and then sent you the bullet? Surely if he was to 'redeem himself' as you put it, it would have been better if he just got on and did it?" He looked a little uncomfortable as soon as he asked this question, as he realised that it must have sounded rather heartless.

Giovanni gave a wry smile at this and said, "Yes, he could have just tried to kill me and I would have known nothing about it until it was too late! As I said before, I cannot understand his twisted mind, but perhaps somewhere, somehow, he was attempting to give me the opportunity to save myself?"

Once again the voices welled up. The Cardinal this time indicated a man in the middle of the crowd. He neglected to introduce himself.

"Father, do you think your star is sending people mad?"

"It isn't my star." There was some muffled laughter in the room.

"That's as maybe Father, but there is no doubt it is having an effect, seemingly on the whole world at the moment. Is there some special radiation that it is giving off?"

337

"No!" Father Casparo said emphatically, "It is not giving off any 'special' radiation."

"Can you be sure of that?"

"Yes, quite sure. It is an ordinary supernova, it just happened to have gone off near us."

The journalist persisted in his questions. "You say it like it is just a coincidence. Considering the date it went off, don't you think it marks the end of the world, as so many people are now believing will happen at midnight tomorrow?"

"Of course not." Giovanni was becoming a little irritated. "Some stars explode at the end of their lives. We've known this for some time. This one just happens to be quite near us, astronomically speaking."

Another voice piped up, "But don't you think that God has caused this to happen now? Surely this can't be a coincidence?"

Giovanni sensed the Cardinal stiffen beside him. He paused for a slight moment. "We cannot know the mind of God. It says in the Scriptures, no one will know the day or the hour. If people believe that this star marks the end of the world or the Second Coming or whatever, it is up to them. The explosion of the star is just pure coincidence. How we as human beings interpret this is up to us."

The questioner persisted, "What is the Church's view on all this? After all, the Church and science haven't always been easy bed fellows. You didn't forgive Galileo until 1992! And now you are sounding almost like an atheist Father."

Once again Giovanni was aware of the tension emanating from the Cardinal. "I am obviously not an atheist," Giovanni gave a slight grin as he pointed to his white collar. "His Holiness has already said that we should treat the event as a sign from God to renew our faith." He felt the Cardinal relax a little. Giovanni felt compelled to continue, "Even if there are members of the Church, perhaps the Cardinal here, or even his Holiness himself, who individually think that this celestial event marks something more significant down here on Earth, then that is not the teaching of Mother Church." Cardinal Verdi gave a sharp intake of breath.

Giovanni swallowed hard. Perhaps he had overstepped the mark? He was almost relieved when another questioner from the back of the room suddenly indicated that he wanted to ask a question. "Is there any news of your nephew Father Casparo?" The room went a little quiet at this.

Giovanni replied in a much more subdued voice and shook his head, "No, no news yet."

Cardinal Verdi grabbed the opportunity to end the conference. He thanked the journalists for coming and ushered Giovanni out of the room. As the two walked away, Giovanni felt slightly uncomfortable that the Cardinal did not say a word. He said, "I hope that I didn't say anything wrong back there?"

The Cardinal raised an eyebrow but gave little else in the way of expression and continued walking.

08:45 Central Standard Time 30ᵗʰ December 2012 (UTC 14:45)

Detective Truman was standing outside the house of Pastor Paul Richardson, with two uniformed officers. They had their weapons drawn. Victor knocked loudly on the door and rang the bell, while shouting a demand for entry. After a few moments a rather bleary eyed woman in a dressing gown opened the door. The Detective held up his badge and explained that he wished to come into her house. The woman looked confused as Victor pushed past her. As he entered the hallway, Pastor Paul came down the stairs also in his dressing gown.

"What is the meaning of this?" He demanded with some anger in his voice.

"We have a warrant to search these premises Mr. Richardson."

"What? What the hell for?"

"We believe that you may be harbouring fugitives."

"Fugitives?"

"Yes sir, one Mr. and Mrs. Houston."

"You are insane Detective. They're not here."

"Well if you don't mind sir, we'll satisfy ourselves of that."
While the two men were talking, the police officers moved through the house checking each room.

The lady who had now identified herself as Mrs. Richardson stood in her hallway, still looking bewildered.

340

The officers returned to the hallway and reported that all the rooms were 'clear'. Victor's eyes narrowed.

"You see," yelled Pastor Richardson, "like I said, they're not here."

"Where are they Mr. Richardson?"

"I don't know." Pastor Paul said deliberately slowly as if talking to a dim child. "Now get the hell out of my house."

"Do you have a cellar?"

"Yes."

Victor nodded to one of the officers to go and check it.

"I tell you, they are not here. This is police harassment. I have friends at City Hall; I'll have your badge for this Detective Truman."

Victor looked unruffled by this. He repeated his question, "Where are they Mr. Richardson?"

The Pastor looked really angry. The policeman came back from his search of the cellar shaking his head. Victor clenched his teeth.

"Get out of my house and leave us alone!"

Detective Truman gave the Pastor a very cold hard stare. "If I find that you've had anything to do with this Mr. Richardson, I'll make sure that you go down for it." He indicated to the uniformed men to leave. As they walked through the front door he turned and followed them.

"And I'll make sure that you never work in this city, ever again." Pastor Paul shouted after the Detective.

Victor walked back to his car with as much dignity as he could muster. He apologised to the uniformed officers and ordered them back to base. He sat in his car and banged the steering wheel with the palms of both hands. "Shit!" He was going to have a lot of explaining to do to his Captain and he was still no nearer finding the child.

341

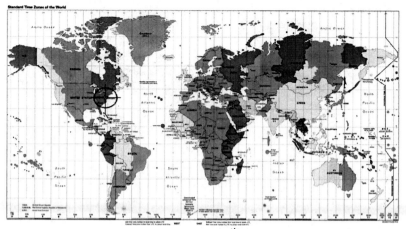

09:47 Eastern Standard Time 30th December 2012 (UTC 14:47)

A strongly worded message had been sent to the Russian government from the White House, suggesting that they desist from supplying arms to the Syrians. The Russians replied that the Americans should likewise cease supplying the Israelis.

Right across the United States of America and some other parts of the world, groups of more 'fringe' Christians were starting to organise themselves for the 'Rapture'. General stores and food stores were being practically emptied of supplies in some parts, as many were preparing for the 'end times'. The Internet was still buzzing with apocalyptic predictions. Many people were now convinced that they were about to spend their last 24 hours on Earth.

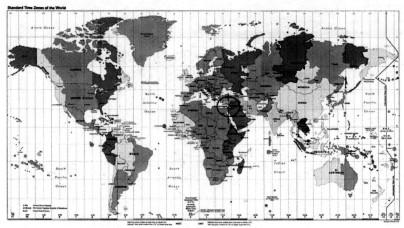

17:12 Israel Standard Time 30th December 2012 (UTC 15:12)

Two Russian jet fighters from one of the aircraft carriers in the Gulf overflew an American warship twenty miles due east of the Russian carrier's position. The American ship's targeting radar locked on to them and several sea-to-air missile launchers were poised ready to unleash their deadly cargo, should the aircraft carry out any manoeuvre that seemed remotely threatening. The aircraft circled once and then headed off back to their ship. It seemed that they were testing the American's radar defences.

An extended exchange of fire was taking place between Israeli and Syrian troops, on the Golan Heights. Israeli Air Force jets were circling overhead and the noise of high powered aircraft engines was mingled with heavy machine gun fire.

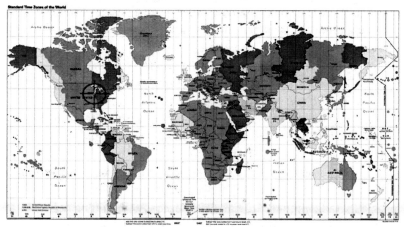

11:35 Central Standard Time 30th December 2012 (UTC 17:35)

Victor Truman had just received the biggest dressing down of his life, from his Captain. He had been lectured about wasting police resources, harassing innocent members of the public and making the department look foolish. He was given a warning that he was on a very short leash and if he did anything like that again he would be asked for his badge. He stood there and took it. He could do nothing else.

When he was dismissed from the Captain's office he headed for the coffee machine and then sat down at his desk. Had he allowed his judgment and professionalism to be clouded? He didn't like Pastor Paul one bit, but he had come up against many people, most of them criminals, that he didn't like, but that didn't stop him being professional. Maybe he was getting too personally involved? He finished his coffee and tried to decide what to do next. He felt uncomfortable in the office and so made up his mind to go out. It then struck him that he could go and talk to Martha Dixon, Mrs. Houston's sister, once again. She may still be able to throw some light on the situation. As he got in his car he began to think that she was his last hope.

He drove the few miles across town to her house. It wasn't until he turned into her street that he realised he had come unannounced. Perhaps she wasn't at home? He pulled to a stop outside her property and walked to the front door. He rang the bell and was relieved when he heard a noise inside. The door swung open and Martha smiled at him. It was the first nice thing that had happened to him all day.

"Why Detective Truman, would you like to come in?"

"Thank you ma'am," he said, "I'm sorry to disturb you."

"That's okay, I wasn't doing much."

Victor followed the lady into her house. She offered him coffee which he gladly accepted. "So how may I help you Detective, or is this just a social call?"

Victor flushed ever so slightly. "Er, no ma'am and please call me Victor." Martha smiled and gave a slight nod of acknowledgement. "I've had little success with finding the missing child and your sister and her husband. I was hoping that you might have thought of something, anything which might help me further."

Martha sat opposite him now. The cold winter sunlight coming through the window caught her hair. He thought she looked beautiful. She looked thoughtful for a moment or two, and then she leaned forward with a look on her face as if she had just remembered something.

"You know, I seem to remember Gillian telling me Craig's family had a house somewhere out past Elgin on the Belvidere Road, I think. A small farm house, a little isolated. I think that's where Craig grew up. I believe the farm was called 'The Stables'. I don't have an address though. I guess it's just possible that they might have gone there?"

Victor's face lit up. He jumped up, so did Martha in surprise at his sudden movement. "Ms Dixon, thank you. I think you might have just given me the information I needed." In sheer delight he leaned forward and kissed the lady on the cheek. She looked a little shocked and Victor's face fell, he thought that perhaps he had overstepped the mark, and not for the first time today. He felt a rush of relief when he got a smile back.

"Oh and call me Martha," she said as Detective Truman rushed out of the door. He smiled back at her and to himself.

Victor accelerated away. He realised that he had to go back to the Houstons' house across town; because that was the only place he could think of where he might find the address of Craig

Houstons family house. There was a glimmer of light at the end of this particular tunnel and he was now feeling a whole lot better. The icing on the cake was that Martha genuinely seemed to like him.

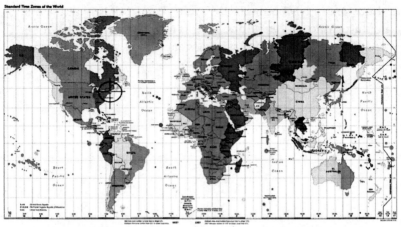

14:25 Eastern Standard Time 30th December 2012 (UTC 19:25)

The telephone rang at the house of Dr John Baltar. He picked it up and said 'Hello'.

"Dr Baltar?"

"Yes?"

"Ah, good. Dr Baltar, my name's Amy Rice I'm calling from the Discovery Channel."

John Baltar started to take more notice. "How may I help?"

"Dr Baltar, we are planning a 10 part series on astronomy and we'd very much like you to be involved."

"Oh, um yes! I'd be delighted."

"That's great, sir. Would it be possible for you to come and see us, perhaps tomorrow?"

"Sure, I'd be happy to. Where are you?"

"We are in Springfield, Maryland."

"Oh."

"Don't worry Dr Baltar; I can book you on a flight for the morning if that would be alright?"

"Can I take your number and call you back? I just need to make sure I'm free."

Amy Rice gave John the number and he put the phone down. He took a deep breath and ran down the stairs. "Sarah," he called, "you'll never guess who just phoned..."

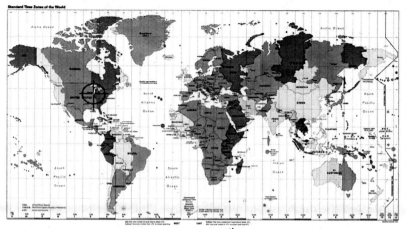

14:55 Central Standard Time 30th December 2012 (UTC 20:55)

The traffic in Chicago had been particularly bad. Victor Truman was getting increasingly frustrated at the long delays. However, he finally arrived at the house of Mr. and Mrs. Houston. The only evidence that the police had been there before, was some blue and white tape stretched across the front door.

He wasted no time in once again letting himself into the house. He went upstairs and into the master bedroom. He began to open drawers looking for envelopes, records or note paper that might have the vital address that he now sought so very fervently. Nowhere could he find any document that looked even remotely helpful. He sat on the bed feeling deflated. It was then he remembered the box in the closet, which belonged to Gillian Houston.

He pulled open the door and grabbed at the box tucked into the shadows of the clothing, as if it were a lifebelt and he a drowning man. He threw open the lid and started to sift through the papers. Near the bottom he found an envelope addressed to Gillian and with a postmark date of 1995. He flipped open the envelope and pulled out the folded paper from within. A small faded photograph fell onto the floor. He picked it up. It showed a younger Craig Houston standing in front of an old farm house. He turned it over and in pencil scrawled on the back of the

picture was the name, 'The Stables'. He looked at the letter. It was a love letter to Gillian from Craig. More importantly it had the 'from' address written on it:
The Stables
Old Farm Track
Belvidere Road
Jane Addams Memorial Tollway
Marengo
Illinois

He wrote it out carefully in his notebook. At last, he had the address. Next he needed to know where this place was. He stuffed the photograph into his coat pocket. He began to wish that he'd kept up with technology, as he would probably be able to look the place up on the Internet. There was nothing else for it. He would have to head out towards Belvidere and see if he could find it. Maybe he could ask the locals if he got lost.

As he drove out of the city, he wondered if he should call in to the Department to let them know what he was doing. He thought better of it. If he needed backup, he would call the Belvidere Police. He was probably out of his jurisdiction, but 'needs must when the devil drives.' He now had so many hopes that he was finally on the right track. If the Houstons and baby Casparo weren't there he began to consider the possibility that he would never find them. He shook himself out of that. Failure was not an option. It was starting to get dark. He wasn't sure if it was a help or a hindrance. At least darkness would prevent them from seeing him coming.

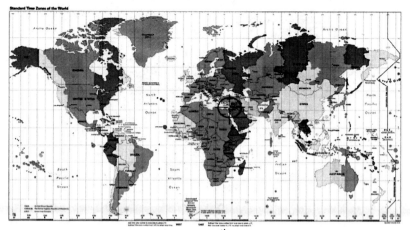

23:52 Israel Standard Time 30th December 2012 (UTC 21:52)

Two jet fighters from the American fleet in the Gulf now took their turn to overfly the Russian aircraft carrier. The aircraft were greeted by a missile lock from the anti-aircraft equipment onboard the ship and then the launch of two TOR-M1 missiles. The American jets deployed countermeasures just in time and the missiles exploded harmlessly behind them. This was enough however, to persuade the American pilots to return to their own vessel.

Fighting was occurring sporadically on the Golan Heights. A Syrian Scud missile had been shot down by American made anti-missile systems. Air-raid sirens had been heard in several towns in the north of Israel. There was still the occasional exchange of gun fire on the border between Israel and Egypt, although this was not as intense as on the Syrian border.

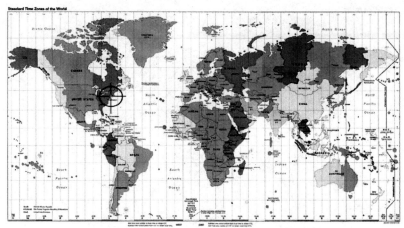

16:55 Eastern Standard Time 30th December 2012 (UTC 21:55)

Sam finally returned to his desk, the laptop and open diary. It had been a difficult afternoon. He was almost glad of the chance just to sit quietly and think. He turned to the very last entry in Salwa Tahan's diary and then it hit him. Salwa described how she was looking forward to her trip to Israel. The last sentence read *'I am hoping to find solace at the Shrine of the Nativity in Bethlehem.'*

Sam lifted the laptop to place it in front of him. He clicked on the document and the encryption software immediately opened asking for the key code. Nervously now, Sam typed in one word, 'Bethlehem' and clicked the button to execute the command. The document opened and he began to read. His mouth fell open in shock as he skimmed through the words. He lifted the phone and put a call in to Special Agent Jefferson.

The Special Agent happened to be at his desk and lifted the receiver.

"Special Agent Jefferson," he intoned.

"Special Agent Jefferson," Sam repeated, "you better get up here. I've opened that document on the girl's laptop."

No sooner were the words out of Sam's mouth then George Jefferson crashed the handset down and bolted for the stairs. When he got to the right floor he practically ran to Sam's office and threw open the door. Sam looked up with a start; he seemed shocked and upset. "You'd better read this."

Special Agent Jefferson spun the laptop towards him and started to read. The document was basically, a suicide note. In it, Salwa described how much she missed her father and how the pain of that seemed to increase every year, rather than diminish. She blamed the Muslims for the attack on 9/11 and laid out her plan to blow herself up on the steps of the Dome of the Rock in Jerusalem. She said first, she would make a pilgrimage to the Church of the Nativity in Bethlehem to ask God for forgiveness for what she was about to do. She described how she would wait to make sure that there was nobody near her before she exploded the bomb as, unlike the people who perpetrated the attack on the World Trade Centre, she did not want to harm any innocent passersby, she just wanted the world to see what such an act can lead people to do. She asked her mother to forgive her and then signed off.

George Jefferson sat down heavily on a chair opposite Sam. There was silence between the two men for several moments. At last Special Agent Jefferson began to speak, while shaking his head in disbelief and sorrow.

"So now I know." He paused again. "The poor girl was desperate. She must have realised that her father's family would procure her a suicide belt, believing that she was going to become a martyr to their cause. Instead all she wanted to do was make a final and irrevocable protest about the horror of terrorism by using a terrorist weapon on herself."

Sam looked slightly puzzled. "You mean you don't think she intended to kill the people on the bus?"

"No, quite the reverse, I think it went off accidently. The bus she was on was heading for Jerusalem. That's where she meant to detonate it; standing on the steps of the Mosque away from anyone that she thought might get injured. It wasn't a very big bomb, but in the confined space of the bus it did a lot of damage."

Sam gave a nod of understanding. Special Agent Jefferson continued, "I think she hoped that her suicide might bring others to their senses. After all, she could have detonated it in a crowd and killed countless others. Her father's family would have considered her a martyr, but all she wanted to do was to make a point. Sadly, the bomb went off before she wanted it to and did what her suppliers had hoped. Maybe they even set it up to do this, unbeknownst to her. We will never be able to tell for sure. She must have been in such torment."

There was silence again between the two men. After a few more moments George Jefferson stood up, picked up the laptop and turned and thanked Sam for his efforts. Sam just nodded, still shocked by what he had read and the explanation from George. "I'll need to show this to the Assistant Director." With that, Special Agent Jefferson turned and walked out of the door. Sam put his head in his hands and breathed out heavily.

Day 0

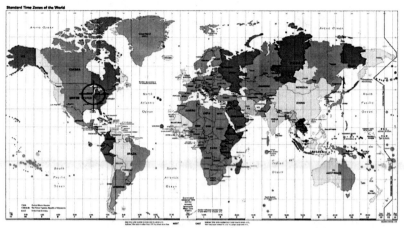

18:45 Central Standard Time 30th December 2012 (UTC 00:45)

Victor Truman pulled into a 'diner' not far from where he thought 'The Stables' might be. He was hungry, really hungry and he hoped that he might ask some 'locals' if they knew the whereabouts of 'The Stables'.

He sat down and ordered his meal from the waitress and tacked on the question about the house. He was met with a, 'never heard of it'. This happened when he later asked the girl at the counter. He was starting to feel like he was on a wild goose chase. He went to the bathroom and on coming back into the dining area he saw an older man with a bucket and a mop. He walked over to him and said, "Excuse me. Do you know of a place called' The Stables' anywhere around here?"

The man thought for a moment and then said, "Ah, I know, you mean that old farm house off the Belvidere Road." Victor nodded encouragingly. "I don't think there's been anyone living there for some time. It's probably derelict. Why d'ya want to know?"

Detective Truman made some excuse about being an old friend of the family, who knew them from years ago. He explained that he'd forgotten just where the place was.

"The Houstons - that was it. The Houstons - that was their name." The man nodded with satisfaction at his own memory.

Victor now knew he was onto them. He did his best to hide his growing excitement. "Can you tell me how to get there? I'd just like to look the place over once more as I'm in the area."

The man gave the Detective some directions which Victor carefully committed to memory and thanked the man for his help. He walked back to his car and took a deep breath as he sat back in the driving seat. Hopefully at last he was about to find the missing child. He knew though, he would have to be careful and he decided to proceed with great caution. He checked his gun, re-holstered it, started the engine and pulled away steadily, turning out onto the road that should lead him to his quarry.

A couple of miles down the road he saw the signpost the old man had mentioned. Just after the sign was a road, not more than a dirt track that could easily be missed in the daylight let alone in the dark. He turned on to it and dimmed his headlights. He drove carefully for about a mile and could just make out by the dim light of his car's side lights another track turning off to the left. Again he remembered the man mentioning this and that the house was about three of four hundred yards down this track. He killed the engine and the lights. He reached into the glove box for his torch which he was relieved to find, was working. He quietly closed the door of his vehicle and began walking cautiously down the track.

The Moon came out from behind a cloud and briefly illuminated the landscape. He could just make out the shape of the house in the Moonlight. He became even more cautious, straining his ears and eyes for the slightest sound or the dimmest light. He switched off his torch in case it gave away his approach. The house seemed dark and still, nothing to suggest any habitation. Just as he was beginning to think that he'd come a long way for nothing, a light went on in a window. He crept a little nearer. He could make out a shadowy figure by the dim light, who then disappeared back into the room. The Detective moved closer still. As he was edging closer to the property, he put his foot in a fox hole and tumbled over, with what seemed to be a deafening thump. He just managed to stifle a yell from

355

the pain in his ankle and knee. The porch light came on and a man opened the front door. Victor lay motionless on the ground not daring to move. The silhouette of the man walked up and down the veranda looking out into the yard where Victor Truman now lay, watching his every move. He noticed that the figure seemed to be carrying something. He realised as it caught the Moonlight, that it was a shotgun. Then he heard a voice say to someone inside the house, "I guess it was nothing, just an animal."

The man went back inside the property, but the porch light stayed on. Victor rubbed the pain out of his ankle and crouching low moved steadily around the side of the building. As he rounded the corner of the property he saw a car parked in the shadows. It was a dark sedan. He couldn't make out the colour, but he thought it was brown. As he turned, he could see another light shining from a window. He was now quite close and peeked into the room. There was a woman cradling something in her arms. Judging by the way she held it, he guessed that it was a baby. She was talking softly. He couldn't quite make out what she was saying, or who she was saying it to, so he moved a little nearer to the window. Now he could hear the woman's voice. "We can't stay here forever. We could take the child down to Mexico. He said that they were looking for us. It won't take them long to figure out where we are."

A man's voice, sharper than the woman's replied with a note of annoyance, "No, we can't do that. If we move around, we are more exposed to the forces of darkness. We're safer here for the time being. We have to protect the child. They'll try and kill him."

Victor now knew that he had found what he was looking for. He had noticed a door at the side of the building, as he'd moved around the property. As stealthily as he could, he inched back towards it. He quietly turned the handle and to his amazement and relief found that the door swung open. The Detective pulled out his gun and removed the 'safety' from it. His heart was beating fast. He slipped into the darkened corridor and edged forward towards where he reckoned the couple would be. As he sidled along the wall, he put his foot on a floorboard, which

356

gave a loud creak. He froze. Less than a second later, which seemed like an eternity, there was a huge explosion that ripped through the hush of the house. The man had fired the shotgun through the door, the pellets drilling holes through the thin wood allowing the light to pour through them. The pellets narrowly missed Victor who was pressed up against the wall. The child and the woman started screaming. The wreck of the door flew open and the man brandishing his firearm was silhouetted against the light. Victor raised his weapon and fired at the figure before the gun, which was now pointing directly at him, was discharged for a second time. The .38 calibre bullet struck the man in the shoulder and from such a short range, knocked him over backwards. As he fell the shotgun erupted again, this time peppering the ceiling and the lintel of the door, with pellets. Victor moved forward, his heart now racing, his gun aimed and ready to fire the final and fatal shot directly at the man's heart.

Craig Houston lay on the ground groaning in pain and clutching his shoulder. The screaming woman had curled up in the chair around the baby in a gesture of protection. Victor entered the room fully now, still pointing the gun towards Craig but keeping an eye on the woman. His training and experience had taught him that she too could be carrying a weapon. He kicked the shotgun away out of reach and yelled at the woman to stand up. Still clutching the child she raised herself out of the chair and made to move towards her husband in a gesture of protection of him, and of defiance. Victor saw that she looked quite like her sister, but slightly heavier built. Victor noticed a child's cot in the room. He then ordered her, "Put the baby down."

She resisted his demand. "Please don't kill him," she sobbed.

"Kill him?" Victor couldn't believe that she thought he was there to assassinate the child. "I have no intention of killing him. I just want to take him back to his parents."

Gillian Houston looked puzzled. "Don't believe him," Craig spat, between groans of agony. Satan wants the child dead."

"Gillian, I won't hurt the child, just put him in the cot."

"Don't do it Gillian. He's our hope of salvation."

The woman looked torn. Her instincts were telling her to believe the man pointing a gun at her husband. After all, if he wanted them dead, then he would have killed them all by now. Tears streaked down her face. The child was still crying but she now started to edge towards the cot.

"No, Gillian, no." Craig gasped. He tried to move but winced in pain. He was losing blood quite quickly.

"That's the idea, "said Victor. She leaned into the cot and placed the bundle on the mattress. "Now, go back to your husband and put some pressure on that wound, it'll help stop his blood loss." As she moved back towards her husband, Victor took out his mobile phone and called 911. He identified himself to the person who received the call and requested an ambulance and police back up.

Craig Houston was gasping and panting and was now starting to slip out of consciousness. "I'm so sorry," Gillian kept saying to him and then turned her head and repeated it to the Detective.

Victor looked pityingly at her. "Do you really think he is the new Messiah?"

"Craig said he was. He was adamant. He and Pastor Paul told me it was the right thing to do. We had to protect the child from the forces of evil."

"I think his parents are probably the best to do that."

Gillian now looked like her world had collapsed on her. Her husband lay on the floor in danger of dying. The child, who she believed to be the salvation of the human race, was just a small baby and now realised that she was likely to go to prison for a very long time. In the distance the sound of sirens could be heard. Victor breathed out. At least there was a chance that Craig would survive. Victor really didn't want his death on his conscience. He wasn't really a criminal, just incredibly deluded. The blue and red flashing lights were now outside the door and Victor went to show the paramedics and police officers in. As the paramedics set to work on Craig, Gillian was moved away. Victor said, "Go and comfort the baby for a minute." Gillian nodded and went to pick up the still crying child. She began to rock it in her arms and he began to quieten down. The uniformed police questioned Victor for a minute and then moved to take Gillian and the baby outside. As she walked past Victor, he said, "Gillian. If you'll testify against Pastor Paul, it may help your case. You may get off with a lighter sentence."

Gillian paused for a moment and without saying anything, but nodding, she allowed herself to be led away. Victor stood in the dim light of the room and breathed out heavily, shaking his head. As Gillian Houston was then led to the ambulance, Victor called in for a check on the license plate of the car parked a few yards away. It was registered to one Mrs. Richardson, Pastor Paul's wife.

The paramedics wanted to check the baby and Gillian Houston out, at the hospital. The ambulance sped down the road followed by the two police cars and Victor. They were met at the hospital by another police vehicle containing a woman police officer, who was to take charge of the baby once the medics were satisfied he was unharmed.

22:55 Central Standard Time 30th December 2012 (UTC 04:55)

At the hospital, the doctors told Victor and Gillian that Craig would live. He had lost a lot of blood but fortunately the bullet had missed any vital organs. Gillian too was pronounced fit, as was baby Casparo, who had been fed and changed by the nursing staff and was now sleeping in the nursery. Gillian was led back to one of the waiting police cars in handcuffs. The woman police officer asked Detective Truman what he wanted to do. Victor suddenly felt very tired. It had been a very long day, but there was one last duty that he wanted to perform.

The woman police officer, now cradling the baby asleep in her arms, placed him gently in the car seat, which had been supplied by the hospital, and then put the seat complete with sleeping child in Victor's car. In an hour or so, he should be able to present baby Casparo to his parents. For the first time in several days Victor Truman felt good.

Right around the world, people were gathering and preparing for the impending 'Rapture', which they believed, was going to happen just before the end of the world. God was going to take the righteous to Heaven, or so they hoped.

The Supernova was starting to slowly grow dimmer. Even though it was visible in the daylight, it just wasn't as bright as it had been at first. Astronomers and astrophysicists were still gathering information from it. All in all, it had been an unprecedented celestial light show. In a week or two it would fade to invisibility and no doubt people would get back on with their lives, as it would all but be forgotten.

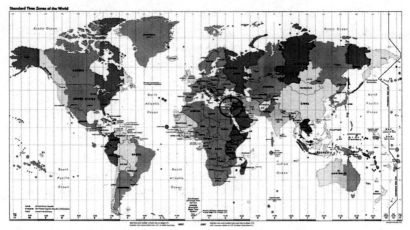

08:00 Israel Standard Time 32st December 2012 (UTC 06:00)

The shooting had intensified on the Golan Heights. Casualties were increasing on both sides. Rioting was breaking out sporadically in the West Bank and the Gaza Strip.

Two warships, one British and one French, had now joined the flotilla in the Gulf, as had two more Russian battleships. Some Israeli warships were attempting a blockade of Syrian ports on the Mediterranean coast. Various envoys from the United Nations were engaged in 'shuttle diplomacy', doing their best to ease tensions between the protagonists in this deadly scenario. No one wanted an all out Middle East conflagration, but it seemed that no one really knew how to stop it.

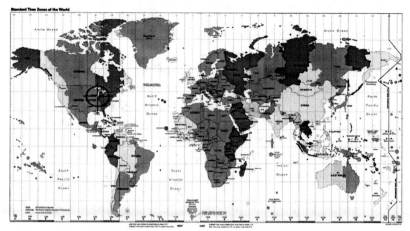

00:15 Central Standard Time 31st December 2012 (UTC 06:15)

Victor pulled up outside the Casparo house. He got out of the car and took the baby from the woman police officer. He walked to the front door and rang the bell. A light came on in the hallway and Marco opened the door. Victor beamed at him. Marco stood for a moment, trying to take in what he saw. His wife's voice called, "Who is it darling?"

"It's Salvatore. He's come home!"

Lucy Casparo rushed to the door. Her mouth gaped wide in disbelief and astonishment. The moment that she had hoped, dreamed and prayed for, had come to be. Tears were streaming down her face and she was unable to speak as she took the child, proffered to her by Victor Truman. The two could say nothing now other than "Thank you. Thank you," over and over again. Marco eventually said, "Victor, please come in."

The Detective shook his head. He didn't want to intrude on this moment. "I'll call back in a day or two, to see how you're doing," he said.

Marco understood and nodded again mouthing countless times, "thank you." He didn't think to ask where the Detective found his son, or even how. He was just so overwhelmed with relief and gratitude. No doubt the questions would come in the days to follow. Victor turned away and sighed as the door closed behind him. All he wanted to do was go to bed.

Crowds of people were gathering at ancient and mystical sites all over the world, waiting out what they thought would be their last hours. Police were having trouble keeping control at Stonehenge in England and many other prehistoric structures. Even the Pyramids in Egypt were experiencing larger than usual crowds for the time of year. Throughout the United States of America and also in parts of Europe and Australia, Christian churches were holding vigils for those who believed that the world was living through its last day.

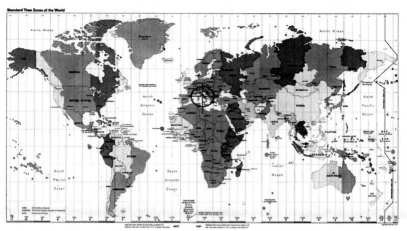

Standard Time Zones of the World

08:03 Central European Time 31ˢᵗ December 2012 (UTC 07:03)

Giovanni's mobile phone rang. He struggled to remove it from his pocket as it seemed caught in the material. He answered it just before it diverted the call to his voice mail.

"Si, Pronto."

"Giovanni, it's me Marco."

"Marco, come stai; how are you?"

"I have wonderful news Giovanni; Salvatore has been found, safe!"

"He's been found?" Giovanni almost shouted with delight.

"Yes, brother and he's here with us, alive and well."

"Thank God. Marco, you must be so happy?"

"I still can't believe it; I thought that we would never see him again. Lucy won't let go of him, it's like she's stuck to him."

"I'm not surprised." Giovanni started to laugh, which in a moment turned into tears of relief.

"Giovanni our prayers have been answered."

"Yes, Marco. I'm so happy, I can't tell you. I've been so worried."

"Giovanni, you must tell your Cardinal that you need some time off to come and meet your new nephew."

"Yes. Yes, I'll do that once all this is over."

"All what's over?"

"I'm still officially the Pope's spokesman on all things to do with the star. Mind you, attention seems to be being drawn away from this now, due to events in the Middle East. It's all looking so grim and dangerous."

"Yes. Let's hope people see sense."

"I hope so too, Marco."

"I must go now, brother. Come and see us soon."

"I will."

With that Marco put the receiver down, leaving Giovanni the best he had felt for almost a week.

09:25 Israel Standard Time 31ˢᵗ December 2012 (UTC 07:25)

Further skirmishes were taking place on the border between Israel and Egypt. To the north, the Golan Heights were a battlefield. F-16's from the Israeli Air Force were bombing and shooting at Syrian positions and having the occasional 'dog fight' with Syrian Mig fighter aircraft. While most of the warships now in the Gulf and the Mediterranean seemed content to monitor each other closely, all factions were on the highest state of alert. Any act that could be considered hostile by one side or another would likely trigger an exchange of fire that would be devastating both militarily and politically. Threats and even insults were being exchanged at diplomatic levels. Tensions were at an all time high. Diplomats and peace-makers continued their efforts with ever increasing determination, in an attempt to head off a conflict of unimaginable proportions.

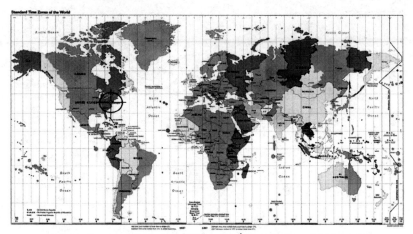

06:12 Eastern Standard Time 31st December 2012 (UTC 11:12)

A message had been received at the White House from the Russian President warning the Americans to withdraw their troops, which they had been moving up to the Syrian border with Iraq for several hours, or face the direst of consequences. The President had not slept all night and was now in conference with his military advisers and the Joint Chiefs of Staff. They were suggesting to him, the nuclear option should be considered. The threat of a 'first strike' from the Russians was tangible and even if the Russians didn't intend to use inter-continental nuclear missiles against American soil, they might well be considering the use of tactical nuclear weapons in the Middle East Theatre, possibly against the American troops now on the borders of Syria and Iraq. The President could order their ships in the Gulf to rearm their Cruise Missiles with nuclear warheads. The President seemed reluctant to give such an order. He ended the meeting saying that he wished to have some time to consider the options. Some of the more hawkish members of the military hierarchy obviously considered this 'weak', although they would not say this directly to the President's face.

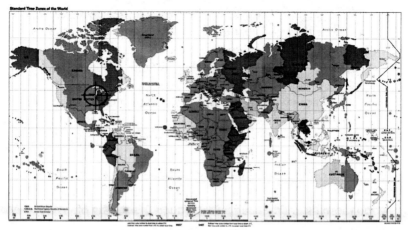

07:35 Central Standard Time 31ˢᵗ December 2012 (UTC 13:35)

A small group of journalists had now encamped on the door step of Mr. and Mrs. Casparo. Marco and Lucy weren't quite ready to talk to the press, yet. Besides, they knew little of the circumstances of the rescue mission of their child. A car pulled up outside the house and the waiting journalists turned to see who had arrived. They were delighted to find it was Detective Truman, the 'Hero of the Hour' as some headlines were already displaying.

Victor gave a brief interview, modestly telling them how he rescued the child from his captors. He then knocked on the door. After a few moments Marco who had checked through the curtains to see who it was this time, flung the door open and greeted Victor like an old friend.

"So how's the baby?"

"He's only just woken up, unlike his parents who haven't slept a moment!" Victor thought that Marco didn't look too bad for his lack of sleep.

"Come in and speak to my wife, Detective."

Victor walked in to find Lucy Casparo hugging the child while feeding him a bottle of milk, like she was never going to let him go. He sat down and started to fill them in on the details of the previous night. Both Marco and Lucy were amazed by the story and congratulated Victor on his bravery.

"The thing is," Victor said, "the child was being well cared for. I'm sure they had no intention of harming him. After all, they believed him to be the new Messiah."

"We know he's special," chuckled Marco, "but not THAT special."

"Well, there you have it. I'm glad it all turned out okay."

"So what now, Detective?"

"I'm off to make an arrest that I've wanted to do for the last couple of days. Some very interesting information has turned up about the car the kidnapper's used." Detective Truman had a wry smile on his face. With that, he stood up, wished them a good morning and headed back through the throng of journalists.

08:45 Central Standard Time 31st December 2012 (UTC 14:45)

Detective Truman arrived at the house of Pastor Paul Richardson. He had a squad car with him as 'back up'. He rang the bell on the house and received no reply. He rang again; still no reply. He checked the back of the house and it was obvious that no one was at home. It occurred to him to go to the Church of the Second Coming, which was just a couple of blocks away.

He arrived at the church to find it full of people. He instructed the uniformed officers to wait outside. As he went in, he was greeted by a lot of singing. He looked towards the front of the church and there was Pastor Paul holding the service. Victor walked down the centre aisle. As soon as the Pastor saw the Detective he turned pale and made to run for an exit. The congregation was confused. Victor sprang after him. Pastor Paul had dived into a back corridor and was attempting to wrestle with a locked rear door, when Victor caught up with him. The Pastor reached into his robe and immediately Victor drew his gun and ducked for cover. The Pastor however only withdrew a set of keys and was fumbling them in the lock. Victor stood up and approached the Pastor, still pointing his gun at him. The Pastor realised that it was useless to try to escape.

"You're under arrest, Pastor."

"I haven't done anything."

"Well if you are so innocent, why did you run?"

"You scared me, marching into the church like that."

"Is that so?" Victor now reached for his handcuffs and started reciting the man's rights to him.

"I haven't done anything I tell you."

"There's an email on Craig Houston's phone that says otherwise."

"You can't pin it on me, it was their idea."

"Oh, I think we can; how about incitement to kidnap, obstructing the police and resisting arrest for a start? Oh, and they were using your wife's car!" As he said this, he closed the cuffs around the Pastor's wrists. Victor found the sound of the click of the cuffs very satisfying. He holstered his gun and grabbed the man's arm and began to walk him back through the body of the church. The congregation fell silent.

At first the Pastor said nothing; then he began to shout, "It makes no difference; we're all going to die later anyway, except the chosen few." The congregation still remained quiet until someone shouted "Hallelujah." As Victor pushed the man out of the door at the back of the church, a chorus of 'Hallelujahs' and 'We shall be saved,' broke out. Victor handed his captive over to the uniformed officers and told them to take him back to the department and process him. At which point Pastor Paul started to threaten them with dire consequences, as he once again stated that he had friends in 'high places'. The policemen ignored him and pushed him into the squad car and drove away.

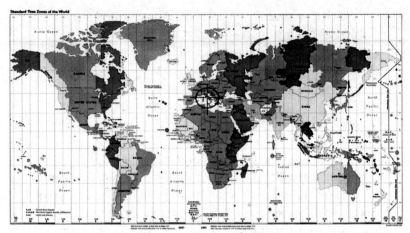

15:47 Central European Time 31ˢᵗ December 2012 (UTC 14:47)

Father Giovanni Casparo received a message from Cardinal Verdi. It said that his Holiness no longer required his services as 'official spokesman' and he was now to return to the Vatican Observatory and his parish, as soon as 'convenient'. There was an additional note from the Cardinal instructing the priest that if he ever made any other 'important' discovery, he was to clear it with him personally, before he made contact with any other authority.

Giovanni began to pack his suitcase, with mixed feelings. It was strange, he thought, that the Cardinal did not deliver the message personally.

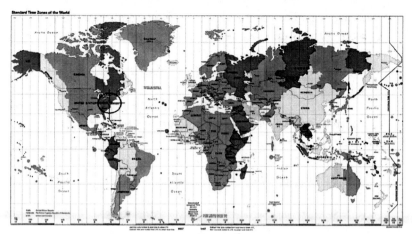

10:06 Eastern Standard Time 31st December 2012 (UTC 15:06)

The President decided to call the Russian Premier. He hoped that a conversation may help halt a global catastrophe. The Russian demands were simple; they wanted the Americans to withdraw their troops from the Syrian border with Iraq and to persuade the Israelis to cease their blockade of Syrian ports in the Mediterranean. The President in his turn demanded that the Russians stop sending heavy weapons to Syria. There seemed to be a standoff. The Russians said that if the Americans continued their build up of troops on the Iraqi border, they would consider this a hostile act against their allies the Syrians and would be forced to take 'drastic' action.

The President paused and said that he would consider removing some of the troops from the border, providing the Russians were willing to concede something also, such as persuading their Syrian allies to stop shelling Israeli positions on the Golan Heights. Both parties said they would consider the proposals and get back. The President was quite pleased, as he felt this bought some time for consideration, although he knew that he didn't have long to make up his mind about what to do next.

The hoards of people, who had gathered at venues in New Zealand and Australia holding vigils for the last hour of the

372

world, were feeling confused and let down; that was until someone suggested that the end of the world would not happen until midnight Greenwich Meantime. This helped to alleviate the disquiet felt in some quarters. Still, no one quite knew what to expect.

The United Nations Middle East Peace Envoy was redoubling his efforts to call a halt to the headlong rush to disaster, as he saw it. He was now holding a meeting with the heads of government of the Israelis, Syrians and Egyptians. Everybody realised that the stakes were very high.

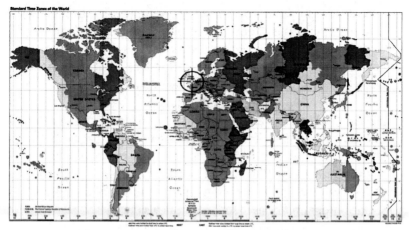

20:00 Greenwich Meantime 31ˢᵗ December 2012 (UTC 20:00)

The television programme on the Supernova, made by the BBC Science department, including Professor Andrew McVeigh was just going on the air. It started with an interview with the Professor, about the notable effect that the 'new star' seemed to be having on the world. The Professor agreed that it did indeed seem to be causing 'quite a stir', as he put it. Then the interviewer asked him the crucial question: "In your opinion, did the star mark, or could it contribute to, the end of the world?"

The Professor looked at the interviewer steadily for a moment and then said, "No, of course it couldn't. When you think of the vastness of the universe, an event so far away could not possibly have any effect on our planet, other than to intrigue the inhabitants of said planet." He then paused again briefly and continued, "You must realise that the time that we use every day, 'clock time' if you like has no meaning in the rest of the universe. The Supernova, due to its distance, must have exploded at least 370 years ago, because that's how long the light has been travelling towards us. Just because somebody happened to notice this at any given time, is pure coincidence. The mind of man is very complex and we seem to be willing to believe all sorts of things because it suits us, or because someone else has convinced us that something is true." He paused again as the camera slowly zoomed into his face.

374

"People look for 'salvation' in all sorts of things on the 'outside', whereas salvation is almost certainly to be found deep within. I would appeal to anyone who thinks that the world is going to end at midnight, whatever that is, just to look up at the star and enjoy it, as it is nature at its most powerful and glorious."

The interviewer said in a near whisper, "Thank you Professor." The programme continued with a clear explanation of the life cycle of a star such as the one that had just exploded and why in this case it was unexpected and how it would cause scientists to rethink their models. As soon as it was over it was hailed by various pundits on the Internet, as one of the best science programmes ever made for television.

New Year's Eve parties were in full swing, although in many areas this was subdued due to the thousands of people who still thought the end of the world was approaching. Many believed that it would end as a fireball or that radiation from the Supernova was going to wipe out all life on Earth. Others were concerned that a global conflagration was about to be unleashed in the Middle East, which would herald the Second Coming of Christ and the battle of Armageddon. Some people actually hoped this was true, as they believed that they were among the 'chosen few'.

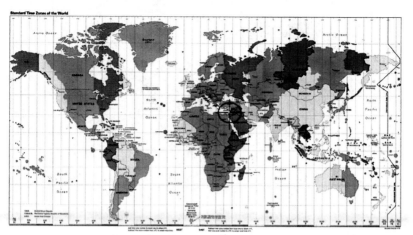

22:53 Israel Standard Time 31st December 2012 (UTC 20:53)

The United Nations Peace Envoy to the Middle East finally got an 'eleventh-hour' cease fire deal between the Israelis, the Syrian and the Egyptians. The leaders shook hands across the table. The Envoy had no idea if it was going to hold, but it was a start.

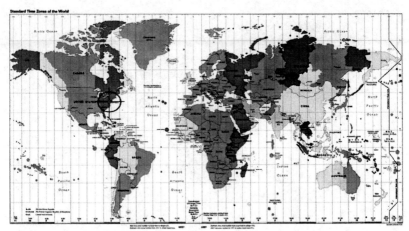

18:12 Eastern Standard Time 31st December 2012 (UTC 23:12)

The President called his Joint Chiefs of Staff and ordered them to begin removing their soldiers from the border between Iraq and Syria 'with immediate effect'.

18:49 Eastern Standard Time 31st December 2012 (UTC 23:49)

The President received a message that a cargo ship containing missiles, which was escorted by a Russian warship and heading towards the Syrian port of Jabla, had just altered course and was heading back out into the Mediterranean.

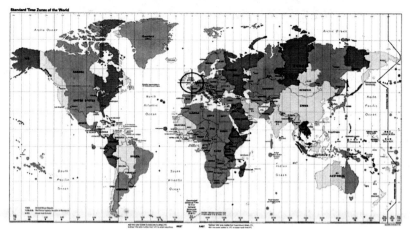

23:55 Greenwich Meantime 31st December 2012 (UTC 23:55)

The large groups of people that were gathered at Stonehenge and other ancient sites around the British Isles were singing and chanting. Some were crying and hugging each other and others were in alcohol or drug induced stupors. Similarly, there were thousands of people packed into churches singing hymns and praying.

23:59 Greenwich Meantime 31st December 2012 (UTC 23:59)

Revellers were dancing and singing on the Thames Embankment in London, waiting for the clock on the Palace of Westminster to reach midnight.

As the seconds ticked away and the countdown began, millions of people all over the world held their breath...

00:00:01 Greenwich Meantime 1st January 2013 (UTC 00:00:01)

Millions of people breathed out.

Acknowledgements

I would like to thank a variety of people for their help and support in the creation of this book: My son Benedict for reading the first draft and giving me his frank assessment, also my son Joseph, for his sage understanding of punctuation. Thanks also to my friends Pat and Graham for their excellent proof reading skills and consideration alongside Pete for giving it the 'once over'. Tom Evans, for his knowledge of how to help a first time novelist get published and his creative suggestions and finally, my wife Sue for always believing in me even when I didn't believe in myself.

Ninian G Boyle

Emsworth

18th October 2011